the PLAY

BETH BOLDEN

Chapter 1

Thirteen years ago

Everyone on campus knew who Deacon Harris was.

In one of those '80s Brat Pack movies, he'd have been called "The Big Man on Campus."

Grant wouldn't have counted himself as one of the crowd in basically anything else. He had no freaking clue on just about anything else of universal importance: like what coffee shop didn't track how many espresso shots you'd consumed during an all-nighter, or which writing professor would take it easy(*ier*) on non-arts majors, or what must-attend party was happening this weekend.

Grant went to class, went to the library, worked long into the night in his tiny shithole of an apartment on the code for the new security system his mentor kept saying could revolutionize everything—if he could just get it to freaking *work*—but, even he, despite his head-down attitude, knew who Deacon Harris was.

"Hey. You must be Grant," Deacon said, flinging himself into a chair in the tiny study room Grant had reserved for his tutoring, three afternoons a week. The chair creaked ominously under his big frame.

"Hi," Grant said cautiously. He nearly said, *And you must be Deacon*, but clearly the guy was used to being identified without introduction.

"You can do this?" Deacon asked, pulling a wrinkled paper from his back pocket.

Grant reached over and took it, unfolding it, realizing it was actually two pages: a syllabus for one of the introductory statistics classes, and a quiz, with a big F circled in red pen.

He'd triple checked his email when the first message had come in from someone claiming they were Deacon Harris.

At first, he'd been convinced it was a friend playing a prank on him. Surely Deacon Harris—*Deacon Harris!*—did not want Grant to tutor him in statistics. Surely Deacon Harris did not even know Grant Green existed.

But after a few email exchanges, it had become clear this was no prank. Deacon needed tutoring help to pass his statistics class, and Grant had come highly recommended.

The recommendation had come as less of a surprise than Deacon's email, as Grant had spent the last three years of college supplementing his meager income and scholarships with tutoring.

Grant tapped the paper. "Yeah, shouldn't be a problem," he said. He'd learned early on that it pissed all the other students off to learn that he'd been taking the classes they were struggling in when he'd been a teenager. A *young* teenager.

Deacon pushed his hair back. He wore it thick and long, just touching his collar, and his eyes were equally dark. Intense, like he could see right to your soul *and* right down into your underwear, Grant had heard one girl sigh happily as Deacon had walked by.

Grant—who was as far from a football fan as you could possibly get and didn't even *have* crushes—had nearly run into a tree the first time he'd passed the guy on the quad.

He'd given himself a pep talk this morning, but now, faced with the guy, nerves bloomed. His palms and under his arms were both uncomfortably damp. He resisted the urge to tuck a finger under his collar and yank it away from his sweaty neck.

"So how does this work?" Deacon asked, leaning forward, setting his big beefy arms on the table. It wobbled, and Grant's breath quickened. The guy's muscles had muscles—a situation not helping his nerves.

Grant, who couldn't remember the last time he'd watched a sports event of any kind, had taken to tuning into games, just because he'd discovered the guy in front of him liked to wear his jerseys cropped, better to display the absolutely mouth-watering abs currently covered by his T-shirt.

"How does it work?" Grant hated how his voice shook a little.

"Yeah." Deacon quirked up an eyebrow.

Possibly the most frustrating facet of Deacon Harris was he didn't seem to comprehend the complete distraction and utter destruction he left in his wake.

He probably didn't even know how Grant's heart stuttered at that look he was giving him.

"Did you bring your text?" Grant asked.

"I got a text?"

Normally this cluelessness would've made Grant internally crazy. Externally, he tried to brush it off. *Just another student who doesn't give a shit about learning. Only partying. And in this case, tackling other big, muscley dudes on a muddy field.*

But today, Grant rolled his eyes. "Yes, your *textbook*," Grant said.

Maybe Deacon Harris in the flesh had short-circuited his brain.

Or maybe he was just fundamentally disappointed that Deacon Harris had turned out to just be a pretty face and a drool-worthy set of abs.

"We get textbooks?" Deacon seemed even more clueless than he'd been a minute ago, and Grant told himself that was not making him a little crazy.

Except it was.

"This is a *school*, you're supposed to *learn*. From *textbooks*. You know. Those overpriced books you buy that you need to study so you can pass your classes."

Deacon burst out laughing. "Oh my God," he said, chuckling so hard and for so long one of those big calloused hands—hands that had starred in way too many of Grant's fantasies—gravitated to his pectoral muscle, gripping it as he lost it. "Your *face*. You actually thought . . .I didn't know . . .what a *textbook* was."

Normally, Grant's back might've gone up at Deacon's words. He might've believed Deacon was laughing *at* him. But then Deacon flashed him a conspiratorial smile, and instead, Deacon was laughing *with* him.

'Cause yeah, Grant couldn't deny he was laughing, too.

"Well, you looked at me like I was crazy," Grant said.

"Well, *you* looked at *me* like I was crazy," Deacon said. "Maybe I'm failing statistics, but I'm not some big dumb football player."

Grant wouldn't admit, even under torture, that *yes*, he'd thought exactly that.

"Yeah, I got the textbook, it's back at my place," Deacon said. He crossed his arms over his chest, and damn him, if that didn't make him look even more impressive.

"Is this you inviting me back to your place?" Grant didn't know what gave him the courage. He wasn't that kind of guy—even if Deacon Harris did have that kind of reputation; everyone said he didn't care what sex you were, as long as you were hot and funny and charming, he'd be happy to grace your bed for a short, but memorable time—but Deacon made him *wish*, even for a few seconds, that he was.

Deacon stared at him, like he was finally really looking at Grant.

Grant nearly squirmed under that intense gaze. He didn't want his soul analyzed, though he wouldn't be averse to having his underwear invaded. Still, he knew the score. He just wanted to take Deacon's money and use it to buy himself coffee and egg and cheese sandwiches for the rest of the semester.

That's not all you want from him.

But those late-night fantasies, they were just that: fantasies. Because Grant knew he was not the kind of guy Deacon gravitated towards. He'd seen enough of them, assertive, confident girls and laughing, charming guys, tucked under his big arm, as they strolled through the quad.

"You are not what I expected," Deacon finally said.

"What, you expected some kind of mousy guy afraid of his own shadow? A guy drowning in pocket protectors? Unable to make even basic conversation?" Grant retorted.

Okay, he was sort-of that guy. Minus the pocket protectors, anyway.

"Kinda like you expected a big dumb football player who relies on brute force but doesn't have a hope in hell of passing statistics," Deacon said, the corner of his mouth quirking up.

Grant didn't know what was loosening his tongue. Perhaps it was a temporary insanity brought on by the tantalizing and yet ultimately hopeless possibility of Deacon's nearness.

"Fair," Grant acknowledged.

"Why don't we do this?" Deacon suggested, waving in the space between them. "We'll leave our expectations at the door. Both of us."

"Works for me." Grant told himself he was also leaving any pipe dreams of Deacon being interested in his underwear behind, too.

"Good. I'll bring the textbook next time."

Grant's fingers were trembling as he pulled out his tablet, glanced at his calendar. "I usually do Mondays, Wednesdays, Fridays," he said, "but I don't think—"

"I can't do Fridays," Deacon agreed. "We're often traveling on Fridays, for games."

"Right," Grant said. Normally, he never made exceptions. He tutored Mondays, Wednesdays, Fridays, *period*. But he already knew he was going to break his rules for Deacon. "I could do Thursday, instead, if you wanted."

"Yeah?" Deacon's face lit up. "Oh, man, that would be a lifesaver, if you could."

"Sounds good. We can do Mondays, Wednesdays, Thursdays for the rest of the semester."

Somehow that sounded like way too much one-on-one time with Deacon, and also not nearly enough.

"You sure?"

Deacon had the nerve to look grateful, with none of the easy, ready smug acceptance of a man who believed people rearranging their schedule to suit him was only what he deserved.

Ugh. There was a part of Grant who wished that Deacon Harris really had been that big dumb football player with an ego the size of the field he played on.

"I'm sure," Grant said. He outlined how much each week would cost, hoping even though he knew it was stupid to worry that the explicit topic of money wouldn't derail the easy friendliness they'd found in the last ten minutes.

But it didn't. Deacon just nodded. "I'll bring you a check tomorrow," he said. As easy as that. He didn't even try to negotiate the rate, which was something Grant was sadly used to by now.

"Let's talk about this," Grant said, changing the subject as smoothly as he could, pointing to the test paper in front of him, with the big circled F at the top.

"Ugh, do we have to?" Even looking like he was being marched to the gallows, Deacon's eyes still twinkled, unexpectedly bright despite their depths.

"Yes."

As much as Grant liked looking at him, he was here for a purpose. If Deacon did fail to pass statistics, it would jeopardize his future on the football field. Not just his collegiate career, but the future NFL career everyone kept talking about in big capital letters, punctuated with too many exclamation points.

"Gonna be tough on me, huh?" Deacon teased. "I like that."

Grant certainly intended to be—though Deacon flirting with him wasn't going to make anything easy. "Yes."

"Alright, then. Where did I go wrong?"

So many of Grant's tutoring clients needed their hands held, but even more than that, they needed their egos stroked. They might need help, but they never wanted their faces rubbed in that particular fact. But Deacon didn't seem to be needing the gentle treatment, if his blunt, straightforward words were to be believed.

Grant glanced down, scanning the quiz. The problems were readily apparent even though he barely took a minute to identify them.

"We're gonna work on some of your basics," he said, pulling out a blank sheet of paper from the stack next to his elbow.

"That sounds . . ." Deacon winced. "Not very interesting?"

"It's not, but it's gonna mean these go away," Grant said, pointing to the big red F.

"Then basic away," Deacon said, waving at him.

Deacon hadn't had very many expectations of his statistics tutor. *Lie*, his brain supplied: *you had zero expectations of your statistics tutor.*

The frustration that he'd *needed* a statistics tutor at all had sucked up most of his brain power whenever he'd considered the situation.

But he hadn't expected Grant Green.

The cliche Grant had dished back at him—*What, you expected some kind of mousy guy afraid of his own shadow? A guy drowning in pocket protectors? Unable to make even basic conversation?*—had been *exactly* what he'd predicted when booking his first tutor.

But Grant wasn't really like that.

He might be quieter, and more apt to blush than to flirt back whenever Deacon couldn't help himself, but he could also be unexpectedly and slyly funny and was such an excellent tutor that Deacon kept going to his tutoring appointments, even though each one became progressively more and more difficult.

Not because he didn't understand statistics.

Nope.

The problem was not statistics.

It was the crush Deacon didn't want to have on his tutor.

Would he have ever looked at this guy normally?

He could at least be honest with himself and say *no*, probably not. Grant had shaggy brown hair, desperately in need of a trim, always falling into his eyes, hiding a pair of shockingly clear green eyes. He was at least five inches shorter than Deacon, maybe an unassuming five foot ten, and looked like he'd never been to a weight room, though his trim build had begun to star in every single one of Deacon's dreams.

He'd claim he didn't know why, but that would be a lie.

Maybe he wouldn't have looked twice at the guy if he walked by him, but he'd gotten to know him. And he was so smart. Funny and clever and charming, in a completely understated way that had won Deacon over.

Even more, he really gave a shit about Deacon's grade in statistics, and not just because of the money Deacon had given him.

Deacon didn't think he'd ever met Grant's awkward-ly-earnest-but-undeniably-charming equal.

"Look at that!" Grant crowed with obvious pleasure as Deacon set his latest test on the desk. "A B+! That's awesome, Deac."

Deacon was used to people using his nickname. People who didn't even know him called him *Deac*. Being on the football team and relatively well-known around campus meant that lots of students believed they could claim him as a friend.

But it felt like nobody ever called him *Deac* in that intimate, proud way that Grant did. Like he not only felt entitled to use the nickname, but also that he intended to earn that privilege one day at a time.

He's not your friend. He's your freaking tutor. Get it together, Harris.

But getting it together wasn't going to be happening any time soon. Deacon's heart rate accelerated just from taking a seat opposite the guy.

If Grant had been like any other guy—or girl—around campus, he'd have made his move ages ago, not worrying about acceptance or rejection. But Grant wasn't like anyone else. He was fucking *brilliant*. He was so ridiculously smart Deacon might normally be intimidated by the size of the brain across from him, but Grant never let him feel that way. Never rubbed it in that even though Deacon was struggling to pass statistics, Grant had aced the class *years* ago.

What had stopped him from asking him out? Partly that, for sure. Because even though he was not the big dumb football player he knew Grant had assumed up front, he was nowhere near Grant's league.

Even though they spent most of their time focused on Deacon's tutoring, Grant had opened up a little about his graduate work and his internet security project, and from the excited, impassioned way Grant had discussed it, it was readily obvious that the guy was going places. Major places.

It's not like you aren't either, Deacon reminded himself. *Think of how many NFL scouts were at the last game.*

Yes, he would undoubtedly get drafted, high in the first or second rounds. He'd head to the NFL and Grant would go on to reinvent the whole concept of online security. Their orbits were going to collide, briefly, now, and then that would be the end of it.

That was that, and Deacon just had to accept it.

But two months into their tutoring arrangement, with two to go, Deacon didn't *want* to accept it, the way he once had.

"Let's go to chapter thirteen. That's what the syllabus says you're starting this week. Standard deviations."

"Did you know you're even more brutal a taskmaster than some of my football coaches?" Deacon teased him.

"Maybe next time we'll meet at the practice field and I'll make you . . ." Grant hesitated. Like he wasn't sure what kind of physical task would prove to be difficult enough.

Deacon chuckled. "You'd make me run stairs? Do sprints? A hundred pull-ups?"

It wasn't easy to make Grant flush. He had a quiet composure that Deacon really admired. But of course that made Deacon even more determined to mess him up, just a little.

"A hundred?" Grant asked, with wide eyes. "You can do a hundred pull-ups?"

"Two hundred, baby," Deacon said, flexing with a grin.

Yep, there it was. That faint reddish glow on Grant's cheeks. And he kept looking everywhere except at Deacon. Specifically anywhere that wasn't Deacon's arms.

Okay, yes, he was showing off a little.

Could anyone blame him when faced with this guy?

"Ah, well, uh, there's some good studies relating physical exertion to mental capacity," Grant stammered out.

Deacon leaned forward. Caught Grant's eye. Maybe nothing would ever come of this. He'd told himself a hundred times—maybe even a thousand—that was true. And most of the time, he was okay with that. Alright, not okay, but *resigned* to it. He wasn't even sure Grant was interested, though any one of his friends would have told him he was being stupid. He was *Deacon Harris*. He didn't usually have to work to get anyone, which was probably why he didn't really find any of those relationships worth continuing past a few nights.

"Maybe worth testing out some of them?" Deacon suggested.

"With your pull-ups?" Grant dished right back, all stammer gone, and a knowing gleam in his green eyes.

"Sure," Deacon said. "We'll do it after the season. I'll bring the pull-ups, you bring the brains, okay?"

"It's a date," Grant said and then clammed right up, like he'd realized what he'd just said. "Chapter thirteen," he said, clearing his throat, flipping the textbook open.

They were halfway through the first lesson when Deacon remembered what had happened this weekend—not that they'd had a game, and *won*, thank you very much—but that Grant had had a big meeting with an investor who knew one of his grad school professors. He'd tried to downplay it last Thursday, but it had been clear to Deacon he'd been nervous.

Here he'd forgotten about it completely, too caught up in his excitement over his quiz grade and his almost-certainly-pointless flirting.

What kind of friend would he be if he didn't even bother to ask?

"How was your meeting, by the way?" Deacon tried to be casual about it, but the eagerness in his voice probably gave him away.

"Oh, uh, it went great. Really great, in fact." Grant paused. "He wants to invest."

"Yeah? That's great."

"And perfect timing, I'm finally getting the tests to run the way I want them to, so . . .yeah, I think . . ." He trailed off. Like he didn't want to even voice his conclusion out loud.

"You think?" Deacon prompted.

"It might actually happen?" Grant phrased it as a question not as a statement.

"You mean, in a few years I might be telling people I knew Grant Green when he was just a lowly tutor in grad school?"

Grant rolled his eyes. "I doubt it. If anyone's gonna be famous—"

Deacon didn't let him finish his sentence. "Don't," he warned.

He hated it when people assumed he'd end up not only being drafted high in the NFL but that his NFL career—yet to actually begin—would be hugely successful.

So many great college players never made the transition.

While Deacon certainly didn't intend to be one of them and actually was working hard at making sure he was ready for NFL-caliber competition, there were no guarantees.

"I know you're paranoid," Grant said affectionately. Like he found Deacon's superstition charming.

"I'm a realist," Deacon said. "Still, I'm fucking thrilled for you, man. That's great. Seems like everything's falling into place for you."

"Yeah," Grant said, not sounding as enthused as Deacon had expected.

"You're not happy about it?"

Grant hesitated. Deacon had learned some of his expressions over the last few months and he saw so many emotions cross over his face. Some he could identify. Some he couldn't.

"Yeah, of course, it's great," Grant said. "Just . . .change, you know?"

Deacon couldn't say exactly what change he didn't like, but it was clear there was something he wasn't thrilled with.

"Maybe it'll be a good change," Deacon said, trying for optimism.

"Guess we'll see," Grant said. "Okay, standard deviation. Does it make sense? Do we need to go through a few more examples? Practical work? I can set you a few problems. Would that help?"

Deacon shook his head. "Nope, makes sense. I think I've got it."

"Okay, let's move on to a slightly more complicated version."

Grant usually kept them moving, though he was conscientious about making sure Deacon understood exactly what they were talking about. Sometimes Deacon could get him to relax and flirt a little more, but today was apparently not one of those days. Instead, Grant seemed to be on a mission.

Ten minutes later, Deacon tried again.

"So what about the change don't you like?"

Grant stared at him in confusion.

"You said—well, you *implied*—it wasn't going to be a good change."

"You don't give up, do you?" Grant huffed out. Frustrated, yet clearly affectionate. "I just thought I'd finish my degree, you know? Get my doctorate. Slave away for a few years in complete obscurity, first."

"And you're not going to?" Deacon didn't like the frisson of unease that skittered through him. Or the way Grant's eyes wouldn't meet his right now.

"The investor wants me to leave school. Focus on the project. Get it off the ground now, while the market's ripe."

"Ah." Deacon didn't know what to say. *You can't leave, not now. Not like this.* But he couldn't say that. Even with Grant talking around it, it was clear this was a once-in-a-lifetime opportunity.

"The terms of the deal are very favorable. If things go well, I'd get to buy him out in a few years. Own the company outright."

"And you can't wait to do this?"

"Technology changes too fast."

Deacon didn't understand that at all. Only that every few years he got a new phone and it seemed to do more than it did before. Maybe he was just that big dumb football player.

"I haven't decided yet," Grant added hurriedly.

"But you'd be insane not to do it?" Deacon questioned.

And I'm insane for thinking about asking you to stay. To freaking tutor me in statistics. A class I'm now passing. Just because I want another lesson. Even another minute.

"Yeah," Grant said, nodding.

"Then you should do it." It was hard to get the words out of his mouth even as his brain yelled at him that this was always going to happen. He just hadn't expected it would happen *yet*.

"Next year, you'll be in the NFL, and I'll own a company." Grant smiled, but it looked forced.

It felt like a reminder to Deacon—maybe even a reminder to both of them—that this wasn't going to happen.

He hadn't needed one. He'd known the score. And yet, it still stung, deep down, in a place it didn't feel like any other person had ever touched.

"Look at us, killing it," Deacon said, attempting lightness. But failing.

Grant bowed his head towards the textbook, and Deacon nearly said something, something insane, like *we can still be friends*.

But were they even friends?

No. Grant was his statistics tutor, whom he paid to teach him. They weren't friends.

"Guess we're gonna have to do that experiment some other time," Deacon said when Grant still didn't say anything.

"Yeah," Grant mumbled, and then he was flipping the page of the textbook, dragging them back to the reason they were here.

The only reason he's here. And you're here.

Deacon got the message.

And he got the message, three days later, when Grant emailed him, the date stamp saying two thirty-four in the morning, to tell him that he'd made his decision. He was leaving school and starting his company. A refund for the remainder of the semester would be in the mail to his address.

Deacon stared at the email for ages. Looking for something else. Hoping that he could read between the lines. But Grant had kept the email scrupulously polite and professional. Like they'd never flirted together. Like they'd never made that date.

When the check came in the mail a few days later, he tore open the envelope with trembling fingers, even though after that impersonal email, he'd only expected to see the check.

The check was in there, blue ink on a white background. And a Post-it note, bright yellow, stuck to it.

Good luck in the NFL, it read.

Grant hadn't signed it, but the man who'd written it felt like the *real* Grant. Not the stranger who'd tried to distance himself in that email.

He shouldn't have, but he saved the note anyway, carefully folded in his wallet.

Every time he was afraid—the night before the Combine, at the Draft, when he first went to Charleston, and for so many moments in the years after that—he'd pull it out, brush those bold blue letters with his fingertips.

Remember that Grant had believed in him, even though he'd had no reason to.

CHAPTER 2

Twelve years later

There were just over three thousand billionaires in the world—and in Grant's humble opinion, despite being one of them, that was just way too many. Nevermind how none of them actually had that kind of money in their accounts. Most of them were billionaires on paper, only.

Grant certainly was, these days.

He'd been broke before. Not that long ago, in fact, he'd scrounged for pennies in his couch, bought the small coffee and not the large, and tutored for extra cash.

Now his accounts, twelve years of hard-won and accumulated wealth, were essentially cleaned out. Yet, on paper, he was not only very, *very* rich, he was the owner of the Charleston Condors football team.

The *conditional* owner of the Charleston Condors football team.

He was here at the annual meeting, outside Miami, at the Piranhas' owner's enormous compound, on his own *private island*, waiting for the rest of the NFL owners to pass the final vote.

In the last twelve years, Grant had faced a number of hostile board members, gone toe-to-toe with titans of his industry, and yet he'd never been as nervous as he was now.

It wasn't even the thirty-one other team owners that terrified him.

It had started yesterday, with the NFL commissioner pulling him to the side, into one of the small empty meeting rooms, to say some of the other owners had made a request of him.

With the way the last owners of the Condors had destroyed the team from the inside out, there was a . . . *reluctance*, the commissioner had said, to allow the team to be purchased by someone the team didn't approve of.

And, he'd continued, there was one player, who had become the de facto representative of his teammates.

The commissioner hadn't even had to say who it was.

Grant had known.

He'd expected to have to see him sometime, of course. He was going to be the owner and general manager of Deacon's football team, and probably perform half a dozen other jobs too, because they couldn't exactly afford to pay people right now. Avoiding Deacon Harris wasn't going to be possible.

He didn't even *want* to avoid Deacon Harris.

So why was he so terrified right now?

It might be the vehement argument his body—his brain, his heart, his whole fucking self—was making to *stop* avoiding Deacon Harris.

They hadn't parted well. Grant knew that. He'd written and rewritten the email he'd sent Deacon probably a thousand times. There'd been so much he wanted to say. So much he *shouldn't* say.

So in the end, he'd said nothing at all. That had seemed like the only safe choice.

It was entirely possible Deacon might not be happy to see him. It was entirely possible Deacon had forgotten him completely.

But Grant didn't think so.

He took a short breath, centering himself the way his business coach had taught him, way back at the beginning, when he'd first started facing down hostile boardrooms, and he approached the big broad back sitting in front of the shiny mahogany bar.

Deacon had been big back then, when they'd hunched over those spindly library tables, Grant helping him to pass statistics. But Deacon was even bigger now, his shoulders impossibly broader.

But on cue, like he could sense Grant's presence behind him, he turned, and it was like being back there, in that library on campus, with its old-book smell and the scent of undergraduate desperation.

Deacon's eyes were just as dark. His hair pushed back from his face, even though he was wearing it shorter than he had, back then. There were a few days of scruff across his perennially tan cheeks, the remnants of a goatee and a mustache buried in them.

He looked good.

Scratch that.

He looked freaking *phenomenal.*

Like every fantasy Grant shouldn't have been indulging in, over these last ten years, but had anyway.

"You must be Grant." Deacon's eyes were just as deeply brown as they'd been before, filled with amusement.

Not anger.

There'd been a time when only Deacon had been recognizable. That was no longer the case.

But it was cute how Deacon kept playing along.

Deacon held out his hand and Grant hesitated. Marley, his old business coach, was screeching in his ear to be the professional she knew he was, and to take it.

It was just a handshake.

But he and Deacon had never touched.

He'd have remembered it. Probably obsessed over it, along with every single thing about Deacon Harris, for the last ten years. And he didn't want it to be like this, an impersonal handshake.

But he still knew that was all it could be.

He's one of your players now. He belongs to you. Not like you always hoped, but this is better.

Grant took his hand, and they shook briskly, impersonally, for a second. He got the brief impression of a big, strong hand, calloused and capable. And then it was gone.

Deacon gave a cute little shrug—when he was practically the opposite of *cute* or *little*. "I practiced that line, you know? I didn't know what to say to you, so might as well say what I did, back then."

"Is that what you said?" Grant said, taking a seat. Doing a good job, he told himself, pretending that he didn't remember every single word they'd said to each other.

Deacon nodded. Like he didn't feel an ounce of shame about remembering, even though it had been over ten years.

Ugh.

The bartender approached. "Can I get you anything, sir?" he asked.

Grant looked over at the glass in front of Deacon, filled with some golden brown liquid. Probably whiskey. Or bourbon.

"I'll have a gin and tonic," Grant said. Here, at Martinez's compound, there was no need to specify a brand of gin.

Grant remembered very clearly when he'd begun going to different kinds of bars, high-end places, for business meetings and a few dates that hadn't ever gone anywhere, and he'd learned there was no longer a need to specify he didn't want to drink well gin.

You're practically back there, he reminded himself.

He watched as the bartender went through the act of making the drink. Watched as Deacon took a sip of his own.

"I'll say," Deacon said quietly, after the bartender deposited a glass in front of Grant and then disappeared, "I was very surprised to hear it was you, buying the team."

Grant had been both shocked at his own insistence, and not very much, at all.

Probably because he alone knew how much he'd thought about Deacon Harris in the last ten plus years. While of course, Deacon had no clue how thoroughly and how long he'd occupied Grant's thoughts.

So yes, probably a huge surprise to him.

"It's a good investment," Grant said with a light shrug.

It was not even a particularly good lie.

Deacon's eyebrows rose.

"Eventually, it will be," Grant corrected.

"Is that how you're approaching it? As an investment?" Deacon wondered. He didn't sound particularly pleased about the idea. And Grant understood. The last owners, they'd siphoned every bit of money off the team, along with half a dozen other absolutely shitty actions.

Not limited to awarding the only huge contract on the team to a known abuser.

Grant had followed Deacon's entry into the NFL and his subsequent rise to prominence with eagerness. He'd followed the unfolding story of the Condors' garbage fire the last year with a hollow pit in his stomach.

Even at twenty-one, Deacon had been brimming with honor and loyalty. He and Grant hadn't been *friends*, exactly, but those were two things Grant hadn't ever doubted about him.

Grant knew the question he was really asking: *are you gonna put profits above everything else? Even your own players? Even above what's right?*

"I'm considering it the right move for me, at this time. Diversification and all." Grant waved a hand, absently, like he bought football teams all the time. His investment bankers had not felt so sure about it, but Grant had overridden all their protests.

Yes, it was semi-insane, him buying a football team.

It only made sense if you knew it was *Deacon's* football team.

But he certainly wasn't going to tell Deacon that.

"Ah." Deacon didn't sound any more convinced than he had before Grant's bullshit answer. Not surprisingly.

You need to convince him it's good. That you're good. Your past isn't going to be enough.

Grant had hoped it would be.

But clearly that was not the case.

Deacon Harris had become a much tougher nut to crack.

You're not supposed to think about nuts. Or cracking them.

"I know things weren't good last year. The last few years, probably. But that's partly why I'm doing this. I want to fix this. I *can* fix this." Grant told himself to treat Deacon as one of his shareholders, one of the board members he didn't necessarily like, and *persuade* him. "My company has one of the best employee satisfaction rates not just in the IT sector, but in *any* sector. Because I don't believe a job should be just a job. And I don't believe a job should ever make you feel out of control or unsafe."

Deacon glanced over at him. "You can save the hard sell for the other owners."

"It's not a hard sell if that's what I believe," Grant said.

Let me make this team safe for you.

Deacon's forearms clenched, and Grant's stomach clenched right along with them. In arousal. And fear.

"I never expected that this was how we'd meet up again," Deacon finally said.

Grant had certainly fantasized about it, though.

"It's only weird if we make it weird," Grant said.

Deacon shot him a look. "Seriously?"

Grant shrugged. Aware of how badly he was fucking this up. It should've been easy. But then nothing about Deacon had ever been easy.

Walking away from him had been one of the hardest things he'd ever done.

Would the owners really not approve the sale if Deacon told them not to?

Grant wasn't sure. Of course, they'd *prefer* Deacon and the other players to be on board, in this extraordinary circumstance, but then they also wanted to transfer ownership as quickly and painlessly as possible. Minimize the bad press.

Let Grant get on with trying to save the Condors from total destruction.

"I'm here only as a favor to the rest of the guys on my team," Deacon finally said. His voice quiet but filled with determination. "I don't intend to play next year. I don't care what you do with the team, as long as you don't fuck it up more, for them."

"What?" Grant could barely croak out. That couldn't be right. Deacon couldn't be calling it quits, finally retiring, just when he'd arrived, hoping to save him.

"I've had enough," Deacon said with finality. He finished his drink, his strong tanned throat working as he swallowed.

He stood and Grant nearly reached out, helplessly, to grab him. To drag him back.

"Wait," Grant croaked, but Deacon was already gone.

He'd let him go once. Okay, correction, he'd been the one to leave, but he wasn't going to do that again. In a move lacking any kind of coordination and any of the dignity of one of only three thousand billionaires on the planet, Grant scrambled off the barstool and followed him.

Deacon's back was still visible as he marched out towards the veranda that ran the entire length of the enormous guest section of the compound.

"*Wait*, will you," Grant called out between gritted teeth.

Deacon only turned when he'd made it outside.

The sun had set and the stars were beginning to come out. It was very warm, for March, and the tropical breeze that caressed Grant's cheek ruffled both their hair.

It was an unbearably romantic moment, Deacon outlined in the moonlight, and if he was sane at all, Grant would say, *okay, retire, then, and now I can do this,* and then he'd kiss him.

It was saying something that was the *sane* choice.

Grant knew that. He did.

And yet he was still committed to the *insane* side of the coin.

"You can't retire. Not like this." Grant tried to get his breathing under control.

Deacon looked at him, and it was like every single tutoring session, when the guy had always looked *at* him, not just through him, like everyone else. "Why not?"

Because I came here to save you, and if you don't let me, you're gonna ruin everything.

"Don't let the last year be your final season," Grant said.

Deacon hesitated, and Grant saw it. It had been so long since they'd seen each other in person, but he'd embarrassingly spent his few precious moments of free time over the last twelve years following Deacon's career. Watching every interview he'd probably ever given.

So when Deacon hesitated now, Grant saw it and knew it—and he didn't intend to let him get away now.

He leaned against the veranda wall, trying to look casual. Like Deacon retiring just when he'd shown up to save him wasn't terrible and horrible and actually acutely embarrassing.

"You've got some juice in the tank, still. I can see it," Grant continued.

Deacon shot him a questioning look. It sent a frisson of *something* skittering through Grant, but he ignored that. If he gave in to his attraction, in to his *lust*—because that was what it was, right?—then he couldn't do this. Not the way he needed to.

"Isn't that a tired metaphor?" Deacon asked in a darkly amused voice.

"Maybe," Grant conceded. "Doesn't change that it's accurate. I know you've got it, you're just tired of the bullshit. Anyone would be. But I'm here to fix it. I *intend* to fix it all, every bit of it. Let that be the last piece of your legacy. This team's reputation, resurrected, and you a part of it. Keep playing, Deacon."

Play for me, Deacon.

It was the most persuasive argument he could deploy.

Deacon braced his hands on the railing, glancing over at Grant.

His muscles, impressive in college, were on a whole other level now. Grant could see them tensing and flexing under his long-sleeved shirt.

"It was bad," he said quietly.

Grant knew. He'd read everything he could get his hands on. Every report. He'd insisted, over and over again to the NFL, that he needed full disclosure of the existing situation before he agreed to rescue their current PR disaster. He'd interviewed countless staff, past and present. Even a handful of players. Deacon had been at the top of every list of players available to talk to him.

But he hadn't reached out to Deacon yet.

Grant had entertained some semi-insane idea that he didn't want to see him, to talk to him, until the deal was done. Until he knew he could face Deacon and make all the promises he was making now.

The irony—that he couldn't make them true, not until Deacon gave his approval.

"But then," Deacon continued, before Grant could figure out what to say to that—which vow he could make that would convince Deacon it would never be like that, not ever again—"you knew that, didn't you?"

"It's why I'm here," Grant said with a confidence he hoped wouldn't be completely misplaced.

He'd never run a football team before. He only knew anything about the sport because Deacon had caught him and ensnared him and he hadn't been able to free himself in the last twelve years.

But he still believed he could do this.

Of course, it would be a hell of a lot easier if he had not only Deacon's approval but his cooperation.

If they became a team of two—two people who cared about the Condors so much they were willing to risk everything to exorcise the rot from the inside out.

"I don't know how to do this, not really. I can run a company. I run a *damn* good company," Grant confessed. "But I've never run a football team."

"Hey, me neither," Deacon said.

"But you've been playing in the NFL long enough that you *do* know. You've been a team captain for the last five years. You *were—you are*—this team, Deacon."

Deacon didn't know why he'd expected Grant Green to play fair, not after all these years.

Sure, they hadn't been *close* back in college—only spending a handful of hours together every week for part of a semester, but it had been enough. He'd seen how good Grant was. How smart. How insightful.

It shouldn't surprise Deacon that he was even better now.

Or that after over a decade in corporate America—fucking *running* corporate America, in fact—he'd be exceptional at reading people and then using what he'd learned for his own purposes.

"But you've been playing in the NFL long enough that you *do* know. You've been a team captain for the last five years. You *were—you are*—this team, Deacon."

He'd known, coming in, that Grant would try to persuade him to stay. To give it one more year, at least. He'd steeled himself against the inevitable request. Reminded himself of all the terrible things he was desperate to escape and put behind him forever.

But he hadn't counted on Grant Green in the flesh.

How he'd grown. The easy confidence he wore like a cape making him even more deliciously attractive. He hadn't counted on his own crush, resurrected, just that easily.

Could a grown man of thirty-five even *have* a crush? Deacon supposed it had to be true, because if this wasn't a crush, he didn't know what else it was.

If it wasn't a crush, he didn't even want to put a name to it.

He hadn't counted on Grant using the one argument that could possibly win him over.

Help me.

But Grant didn't leave it there. No, he was formidable now. He'd been impressive then, in an entirely unassuming way.

But that was gone, now. He was most definitely *assuming*.

"When you think of your career in ten years, in fifteen, in *twenty*, help me make that a memory you *want* to have. A memory you can look back on fondly, with affection. Not with dread or embarrassment."

It was so annoying Grant knew exactly which buttons to push.

If Deacon hadn't known him, he'd have guessed that the guy had done his research.

Maybe he had, still. After all, it had been twelve years.

"How do you know I'm embarrassed?" Deacon asked as a stalling tactic.

Grant shot him a look. "Of course you are," he said bluntly.

Deacon sighed.

Grant clearly took that as an indication his armor was cracking. *If only he knew.*

"If it doesn't work out, if you don't like what I'm doing, if it's not enough, if you want to retire, then do it. But give me a chance, first. Give *us* a chance."

Deacon wanted to laugh, even though none of this was particularly funny. *Give us a chance.*

"I'll think about it," Deacon hedged.

But Grant frowned, clearly unhappy Deacon hadn't just crumbled in the face of his most persuasive arguments. "You do realize why you're here, right?" Grant asked.

"Still not stupid," Deacon said testily.

The tropical breeze wrapped around them, the blanket of stars overhead making this seem like every date Deacon hadn't taken Grant on.

He'd left school before he'd ever had a chance to do it.

"I know you're not," Grant reassured him.

But just before Deacon wanted to say, *stop, stop, quit pushing me*, Grant went quiet. Like he *knew* he'd pushed Deacon as far as he could before Deacon held up a hand in protest.

Deacon gazed out at the darkening ocean and considered what Grant was asking of him.

Before he'd come downstairs, he'd sat on the edge of his bed and stared at the worn note in his wallet.

Good luck in the NFL.

Over the years, he'd imagined so many second sentences to that simple phrase.

Even if you don't need it.

I know you can do it.

Call me sometime.

Look me up after you've made it.

But those had all been Deacon's imagination, not usually so overactive, but in this particular case, he'd gotten downright fanciful.

But, still, the sticky note had been something personal, in the midst of such an impersonal goodbye. Proof that Grant, much as he might deny it, had given a shit.

What else was this, right now, other than more proof?

He put his money where his mouth is.

Of course, Grant buying the Condors probably was everything he said. A good investment. Good diversification. Certainly he'd made enough money over the years. Deacon knew enough about financial planning from his own advisors to know that money just sitting in a bank account didn't do anything.

Deacon turned to Grant. "Why are you really doing this?" he asked. "And yeah, sure, it's a good investment. A football team isn't ever going to devalue, unless of course, you run it into the ground, but I'm assuming you don't want to do that."

"I don't," Grant said. Shoved his hands in his pockets. Kept his eyes trained on the horizon, not meeting Deacon's. "I like to fix things. And this is a team that needs fixed. Saved. Rehabilitated. There's a streak of rot in it, and I want, more than anything, to root it out, not for morality's sake alone, but because . . ." Grant took a deep breath. "Because I've been watching what the Piranhas are doing, and it's something special, isn't it? Something worth replicating, if we can."

There was that *we* again.

"And because it just seemed like a goddamn awful waste," Grant continued. "All that potential to do more than just play a game against twelve other guys, and it was just wasted."

Deacon nodded. He felt the same. It had just about killed him when they'd played the Piranhas—he'd understood then what was really possible—and when he'd read about the Los Angeles Riptide and seen what they'd done with his own eyes.

Grant was not wrong. There was more to this, if only they could reach out and take it. If only they could *build* it.

There's something there, something he's not telling you, Deacon's brain whispered.

But what Grant *did* say had to be just as good as what he *wasn't* saying.

"I tried to save us, last year," Deacon said quietly.

It was hard, still, to admit it.

To admit that he'd completely fucking failed when it had mattered most.

"But you were alone, you were doing it alone. Without help. This year, it's gonna be different," Grant promised. There was an undeniable empathy in his gaze as it moved from the ocean to Deacon's face. An empathy Deacon hadn't even realized he wanted. That he'd have hated from anyone else.

But not from this man.

He wanted to go to him and rest his head on one of those slim but clearly strong shoulders, under his navy blue coat, until he felt ready to fight again.

Yes felt like an unbearable temptation.

Deacon found himself wanting to just say it, way more than he'd ever anticipated.

Was that why it was so unexpectedly difficult?

Or was that because Grant was so much more potent now than in his faded memories?

"You'd have to get rid of anyone I say," Deacon said, realizing how he was weakening. "*Anyone.*"

"Anyone," Grant agreed. "Though I've done my own research too. Lots of interviews. Came to a lot of conclusions, probably same as you."

"Maybe," Deacon said. He wasn't convinced.

But would anyone be able to convince him any better?

He wasn't sure.

Nobody else could've made him rethink his retirement decision, that was for sure.

What would it be like, if he could actually look back on his last year playing the game he loved with pride?

Deacon could imagine it now, and it *did* feel good.

But what felt even better was the shadowy figure next to him, in his imagination. A man with beautiful green eyes and a spine of steel.

He turned to the same man, now.

"Last time, we weren't partners," Deacon said.

Grant nodded in agreement. "I taught you. And you'll have to teach me, some, this time around. But I'm sure I can give you something, too. We'll be partners, instead." He held out his hand towards Deacon, this time. "How about it?"

Deacon looked at his hand. Slim and capable, but undeniably strong.

They'd touched, briefly, during their handshake only fifteen or so minutes ago.

But it felt so different from this touch when Deacon reached back and clasped that hand in his own.

Maybe it was the way Deacon gripped his hand and never wanted to let it go.

Didn't let it go.

He watched as Grant inhaled, his eyes dilating further in the dusk, and it was so tempting to take a step closer and then another.

See if it was only he who'd thought about this, during the last twelve years.

But you can't. Not anymore. He might've said you're partners, but he's really your boss now. And even worse, with all the bullshit from last year's Condors, the last thing either of them needed to do was give the media or the team or even the NFL any reason to believe anything inappropriate was going on.

Including a team owner fucking a player.

Disappointment flashed through Deacon, even as he felt a surprisingly strong surge of hope.

"Partners," Grant said with a sharp nod and removed his hand, stepping away.

Right back to safety.

Maybe it had just been him, but Deacon didn't think so.

Doesn't matter. This is how it is, now.

CHAPTER 3

July

Once Deacon had made the decision to come back, he'd done two things.

One, he'd convinced his favorite partner-in-crime and fellow defensive end, Jem Knight, to join him for one last year.

Jem hadn't really been ready to retire, anyway. He'd said he was, but considering how easy it had been to convince him to play one more year now that the team was under new ownership and management, Deacon had known the truth.

He'd wanted this, just as much as Deacon realized *he* had.

Two, he'd decided to spend the summer back at home, with his younger sister and her family, down at the lake. His parents, whom he'd grown apart from over the years, had even come down for a few weeks.

It wasn't that he didn't want to be hands-on while Grant gutted the team. He *did*, but there was a part of him that wasn't entirely convinced.

He'd known the Grant Green of twelve years ago.

He didn't know *this* Grant Green. The self-assured man who'd made a billion dollars since they'd last seen each other. The technology he'd revolutionized had been part of it, but every article and interview Deacon had ever read about Grant had made it clear that it wasn't just the software he'd developed. It was the way it was deployed. It was the way Grant navigated the business end of it.

Less than a year after starting the company, he'd bought out his initial investor and proceeded to run the company the way he wanted to run it. Deacon, preparing for his first year in the NFL, had followed along, because he hadn't been able to help himself.

A lot of people had predicted that Grant would fail. That he wouldn't have the business acumen to handle himself.

He'd proven them all wrong.

But that didn't mean Grant could fix the Condors.

He'd built InTech from the ground up; he'd never had to excise rotten tissue, carefully saving the good while getting rid of the bad.

Deacon wasn't even sure *he* could've done it, and he was far more familiar with the situation.

For a few weeks, almost a month, after Deacon had agreed to come back, there'd been silence.

But then Deacon had begun to get emails. Stiff and impersonal at first, but as he'd gotten more, and texts, then phone calls, they'd gotten downright friendly.

They'd begun to talk daily, Grant keeping him apprised of the changes he was making. Deacon sat in on the interviews Grant conducted for the new head coach, the assistant coaches. Grant regularly asked him what he could change, if he could have free rein, and Deacon found himself being more honest than he'd imagined himself being.

Bring back free food, he'd texted one morning. **It made us feel like crap to have to buy dinner. Nickel and diming the shit out of us**.

God forbid you millionaires feel nickel and dimed, Grant had texted back. Like he wasn't a freaking billionaire! But then, a day later, there'd been an email in his inbox, outlining the new dining options at the practice facility. All free.

There'd been a hundred other suggestions, some minor and some huge. Grant didn't take all of them, but he had an undeniable skill for picking out the things that really mattered.

In the end, they'd become friends.

The friends that Deacon had always kind of wanted to be, back in college, but they hadn't ever been, because he hadn't known how to bridge the gap between them. The football star and the tech genius weren't supposed to be close. They had nothing in common.

But they had *this* in common now.

Not just the Condors, but their mutual desire to save the team.

But all through the spring and summer, they'd done it all over text. Some phone calls, too, and when Deacon had participated in the coaching interviews, he'd been on video, but the camera had faced the interviewee, not Grant—and it had seemed completely ridiculous to make a request that Grant be more than just a disembodied voice, coming over the computer.

Now, though, Deacon was back in Charleston and it was the first day of camp, and there was no way to avoid seeing Grant again.

Maybe it won't be the same. Maybe you'll just feel friendly towards him, 'cause you do now. Undeniably.

Deacon finished tying his shoes and exited the locker room in the practice facility, heading out onto the field. It had a vaulted roof, with fans blowing air around, but the upper walls were all open.

Some NFL teams held their camps at separate facilities, but not the Condors, though Deacon wouldn't have minded avoiding the muggy, hot Charleston summer that kept blowing into the building.

His temples were already damp, and he'd risked the new coach's wrath by his regular method of chopping his practice jersey in half, trying to give himself some much-needed additional air circulation.

"Hey."

He turned, and Grant was standing there.

He'd thought he was ready. He'd thought it would be no big deal to see him again, now that they were friends.

It was a huge fucking deal, if the way his heart rate accelerated was any indication.

Grant was in khaki shorts and a polo shirt, buttons open at the neck, likely in deference to the heat, and while back in college the guy looked like he hadn't known what the inside of a weight room looked like, he clearly did now.

He wasn't big, nothing like Deacon. But there was no avoiding the way his polo shirt clung damply to his pecs and his chest and his stomach. Or the muscular curves of his legs, dusted with light brown hair.

You are not supposed to lust after your team's owner.

Deacon knew it was true, but he'd left *should do* behind ages ago and was now smack-dab in the middle of *worst-case scenario.*

"Hey," Deacon said.

Grant smiled at him, walked over, stopped by Deacon, but not close enough.

Stop it. He's plenty close enough. Professional distance is a thing.

"First day of practice," Grant said. "You ready?"

"It's gonna be a hot one. I don't think any of us are really *ready*," Deacon said, shrugging.

Grant's gaze trailed down his body.

Why had he cut off his practice jersey? Oh yeah, it had seemed like such a good idea at the time. His abs tightened almost instinctively as Grant stared at them.

"You look . . .uh . . .well-ventilated," Grant said. And he was flushing red, not just because it was July in Charleston. Deacon was sure of it.

He'd been so positive in college that his crush was one-sided.

But Deacon knew enough now not to believe the flash of heat he felt was just him.

It was mutual, and they couldn't do anything about it.

The Condors were going to be under a microscope this year—and probably for years to come. The NFL was tired of them making the whole league look bad. Tired of the bad publicity.

Grant couldn't take a step out of line.

Even if he wanted to.

Even if Deacon wanted him to.

He'd just need to swallow it. Redirect all of this onto the field.

He could do that.

Right?

"You think Coach Kelley is gonna do right by us?" Deacon asked.

Grant shot him a look. Coach Kelley had been Deacon's first choice, but Grant's second.

Ironically, Grant's one complaint about Coach Kelley was that he'd been too young.

"I do, actually," Grant said. "You still standing by your first choice?"

"Absolutely," Deacon said. He really liked Coach Kelley. He was young, sure, but he was hungry. Innovative. Willing to do what it took to not only win games but to rebuild the team.

He reminded Deacon of Asa Dawson, just fifteen years younger, and frankly after the way the Piranhas had turned their team culture around in only one season, that could only be a good comparison.

"I talked to Landry a bit yesterday, when he got in," Grant said. "You were right there, too."

Landry Banks had been at the top of the list of players Deacon had sent to Grant during the offseason. Players that the team could afford, who would make a real impact on the team *now*. Players, also, that Deacon *knew* would positively affect team culture.

"Of course I was," Deacon said, grinning.

Probably more pleased than he should've been at Grant's approval.

"You're good at this," Grant said.

"So are you, but then I think you've made that kind of a career hallmark—doing things nobody thinks you can do," Deacon teased. Somehow they'd ended up closer together. Who'd moved? Had it been him? Had it been Grant? Or both of them?

Grant smiled, and it felt sweetly intimate. A smile meant just for Deacon. "I can't say it was easy, but you made it easier."

"It was honestly my pleasure," Deacon said. *Let me do more. Let me take you up on all those looks you keep trying to pretend you're not giving me.*

But that would be insanity. He knew it. And still he thought about it.

He didn't say it, though.

"Well, go kick some ass, okay?" Grant said, and there was that smile again.

"You got it," Deacon said.

Grant watched as Deacon jogged towards the practice field.

The artificial breeze from the huge fans above them ruffled his dark hair, and Grant wasn't proud, but his gaze was drawn to those big broad shoulders, to the narrow waist, the slope of Deacon's tanned back muscles leading into his shorts. The way those shorts clung to his ass and thighs.

Jesus, the man was a walking fantasy.

Grant's walking fantasy.

"Did I catch you at a bad time?"

Grant glanced over, fully aware he'd just been caught by his assistant. Not just his assistant. His best friend. The person who kept him *and* all the shit he had to do relatively straight and him relatively sane.

Darcy Walker.

She'd been one of his very first hires at InTech, and while she was capable of doing so much more—and he'd *pushed* her to do more, to become a program manager or even a CEO in her own right—she'd insisted she liked the challenge of working directly for him.

Darcy was the first person he'd told he wanted to buy the Condors. She'd looked at him like he was absolutely nuts, and then because she was Darcy, she'd pulled out her tablet and her stylus and had begun to make a list.

Darcy loved a list—and Grant loved her for it.

"I'm just . . .uh . . .checking in with the team, before the first practice," Grant said.

Darcy shot him a knowing look. "You're the owner of this team, not dead," she reminded him quietly.

"If you say again that even a dead person would find Deacon Harris attractive, I will fire you," Grant joked weakly.

She looked unimpressed. Though frankly, that was Darcy's normal expression, too. Nothing scared her, which was one of most reassuring parts of having Darcy at his side. He might be tough, but she was even tougher.

"Empty threats," Darcy said calmly.

They both knew it. He couldn't live without her. If she ever did decide to leave him and do something easier than keeping Grant organized, like running a small to medium-sized country, he'd be lost.

He'd probably have to hire a whole platoon to replace her.

"I was just checking in with Deacon. That's allowed."

Darcy rolled her eyes. "Checking *out* Deacon, maybe."

Grant huffed under his breath. "Come on. I'm sure we've got paperwork to do."

"Enough to keep a billion-dollar company *and* a football team running," Darcy said cheerfully.

"All I'm saying," Darcy said, when they got in the elevator to take it to the top floor, where Grant's office was, "is that he's a *very* good-looking man, and nobody would blame you for looking."

The only problem with Darcy was that she was just way too smart. Way too observant.

She'd picked up on Grant's crush—could you even call it a crush at thirty-three?—in approximately one-point-four seconds. He hadn't even had to be in the same room as Deacon. He'd gotten an email response, and only his *face* as he'd read words that Deacon had personally typed to him had been enough.

He was officially pathetic.

"No," Grant said, though he wasn't sure that was actually true, "but they'd sure as hell blame me for touching him."

Darcy glanced over at him. Her dark hair was pulled back from her face and her glasses had bright blue rims today. "It's not really any of their business."

"It is when the last owners ran this team into the ground and made the NFL look bad," Grant argued. "You think I *enjoy* those status meetings I have with the commissioner's office every week?"

Darcy knew he hated them. Hated that every move the Condors made had to be done under the observation of the commissioner and his minions. He didn't really blame them for keeping a close eye, because NFL franchises were worth too much money to destroy, the way the prior owners had tried to do, but it still annoyed him that he had to answer for every little thing.

"You hate them," Darcy said frankly. "They make you crazy. *Crazier,* actually."

"Cute," Grant said as the elevator doors opened at the top floor.

He'd had two choices when he'd bought the Condors—he could take over the prior owner's suite, which was completely removed from the coaches' offices and almost impossible for any players to access, or he could make the general manager's office his own.

In the end, that had been the easiest choice he'd made since buying the team.

He'd taken over the general manager's office, and symbolically, he'd removed the door.

His office, he told the staff and the coaches and the players, was *always* open to them.

"I'm just saying," Darcy said, "how would they ever know if you didn't tell them?"

It wasn't like he hadn't considered this once or twice or a thousand times.

Grant sat down at his desk. He knew there was an unreal amount of work to get through today—not just the running of this team, but InTech, too. He didn't have time to argue with Darcy about Deacon.

"Even if it was mutual, which there's no guarantee it is, I'm not going to disrespect Deacon that way by making him creep around." He made his tone as final as he could. The same tone that convinced everyone else he was dead serious.

Darcy still shot him a skeptical glance as she took her favorite chair across from his. Tucked her knees under her.

"You clearly do not see the way he looks at you," Darcy muttered under her breath.

Grant set his elbows on the desk. "What's first on the agenda?"

Message received, Darcy clicked on her tablet, bringing up one of her many lists.

"We need to approve the season ticket design and some of the early marketing pieces for the season that the in-house graphic designer's put together. There's an email." Darcy paused. "Scratch that. There's three emails."

Grant did not roll his eyes, but he opened his laptop, and after typing in his password, he barely noted the little green checkmark that popped up in the bottom right corner of the screen. The indication that InTech was working—monitoring every keystroke, using the unique way he typed and used the built-in mouse pad to verify that he was in fact Grant Green, owner of this laptop.

It was the technology he'd pioneered. Everyone typed slightly differently. Used their mouse in their own unique way. Sometimes the differences were so miniscule they couldn't be detected by a human mind, but the system Grant had designed wasn't human. It could generate hundreds of thousands of calculations in a second. It knew exactly how each person typed and used their computer and the second it detected an anomaly, it would shut down immediately.

"Is the designer someone we hired or was this someone who already worked for the Condors?"

Darcy clicked something on her tablet. "He was here last year. And um . . .the year before." She glanced up at him. "I think the three emails speaks for itself."

"It does." One of their early programs at InTech had been implementing efficiency training. An employee at InTech would know to never send three emails when one would do.

"Who'd we put on the season ticket?" Grant asked while he searched for the right folder. Another program he'd designed, three years in at InTech, automatically sorted email using subject line and content to determine which folder it belonged to. Grant had designed it to learn and adapt with time and additional data, until the longer it was used, the more foolproof it became.

After they'd introduced this program to the market, Grant had gone from pretty rich to very, *very* rich.

"You told the designer to make a 'reasoned choice'," Darcy said.

Grant wasn't surprised by that. He wasn't a micro-manager, believing instead in hiring smart people and letting them prove their worth by making good choices. It was also one of his favorite ways to test his employees.

In this case, he knew who he'd probably have picked to be on the season ticket, and the test was if the designer agreed with him. If he didn't, Grant would listen to the reasoning, and was willing to be wrong—but also willing to cut bait when it became clear through a number of these tests that an employee was the wrong fit for Grant's vision.

He finally found the folder and pulled up the first email. There was the draft of the design, and right in the middle, blond hair to his shoulders and holding one of the Condors' signature red and silver helmets, was Landry Banks.

"It's got flair," Darcy said. "And even though you wouldn't tell him your choice, I knew you wanted to put Landry on the tickets. He's the perfect pick. New to the team, your big signing in the offseason, and let's face it, he's got the looks too."

When she'd first started working for him, she'd held back voicing her opinion until Grant had said his own. But he'd trained her out of that quickly. He wanted to know what the exceptionally talented people around him thought.

Grant sat back in the chair, rested his hands behind his head. Took in the overall feel of the design.

Darcy was right; it had flair.

And yep, she was right again, his first inclination *had* been to put Landry on the tickets.

"All true," Grant said.

"Any changes?"

Grant considered the design for another thirty seconds. Didn't let himself think about the alternate timeline in which Deacon had been the choice. Darcy *was* right, Landry was an attractive man. Grant could acknowledge that. But it was hard to see Landry when Deacon was *right there.*

"No changes," Grant said. "And please tell him he knocked it out of the park." He never wanted to be stingy on praise.

"Sure thing," Darcy acknowledged, fingers racing along the keyboard. "Next thing."

Deacon was tired as hell.

It had been such a long day—two practices, one in the morning and another in the steamy heat of the afternoon, and even though he made sure to keep in shape during the offseason, it was never the same as stepping onto the practice field again.

But to get in game shape, all this was necessary, because that was another level entirely.

He climbed the last stair to the roof, huffed out a breath, shook his hair, and walked across the deck towards his favorite seat in the whole facility—the platform right above the highest set of suites. He'd taken to coming here in the last few years, to gain perspective when it had felt like there was none. When the negativity enveloping the organization had threatened to overwhelm him.

But he wasn't going to be alone, because in his regular spot, where he always liked to sit, right by the last of the upright metal supports, was a back Deacon would've recognized anywhere.

What was Grant doing up here?

He stopped in his tracks, but the noise before he did must've tipped Grant off, because he turned his head, his gaze meeting Deacon's.

Deacon was unpleasantly aware that he hadn't showered after afternoon practice. That he'd tugged his practice jersey off the rest of the way and that his back still felt uncomfortably damp, a line of sweat leading right down his spine into his shorts.

Grant froze, too, like a deer in the headlights.

Was it because he was half-naked?

Or because he was probably the last person Grant had expected to see up here?

"Don't tell me you've been coming up here," Deacon said in the friendliest voice he could muster. He wasn't *unhappy* Grant was here. Not exactly.

In fact, there was a part of him that was *very* happy he was here.

Down, boy.

"Yeah," Grant said, rubbing his neck, looking as awkward and uncomfortable as Deacon felt. Like he'd been caught out.

He looked more like the statistics tutor right now than the in-control CEO he'd become, the confident, suave businessman Deacon had met this year.

"Do you mind sharing?" Deacon asked, even as he regretted the words that came out of his mouth.

There was no denying it. He'd come up here partly because the whole day, during both practices, his neck had prickled so many times, far too aware of how Grant's office overlooked the practice field.

Had he been watching?

Deacon couldn't say for sure, but just the thought aroused him, heating his blood, until he hadn't been able to stand it.

So he'd come here, to the one place he knew Grant wouldn't be.

And here he was.

"No, no, not at all." Grant gazed up at him as Deacon walked over, taking a seat a good distance away from him.

It was self-preservation as much as the fact that he hadn't showered that kept him apart.

The last thing he wanted to do was disgust Grant, of all people.

For a long moment, neither of them said anything. Deacon gazed out onto the field, feeling the breeze from the industrial-sized fans so much closer to them than they'd been when he'd been down below.

"I found this spot my second day," Grant offered, finally.

Deacon looked over at him.

He looked just as put-together as he had this morning, but there were stress lines next to his eyes.

It occurred to Deacon that maybe he wasn't the only one who was completely exhausted.

"I've been coming up here for at least two years," Deacon said.

Grant nodded, and Deacon realized he didn't even need to explain. Grant had probably already correctly guessed why.

"Some days, it feels like I can't fix problems fast enough," Grant said with a little sigh.

"But you have," Deacon said. Hating that Grant felt, even for a second, that what he'd done wasn't good enough. This year was already a hundred times better than last year. Just beginning the season, walking onto the practice field, without that human garbage can Tom Taylor was an improvement.

If that had been all Grant fixed, it would still be huge.

But Grant had done so much more than that. He'd listened to every one of Deacon's suggestions, and as far as he could tell, he'd genuinely attempted to implement most of them.

"Appreciate you feel that way." Grant's expression twisted into a wry smile. "Doesn't mean *I* feel that way."

"What would Darcy say?" Deacon teased, because he'd quickly learned that while it was typically easy for *him* to grab Grant's attention, Darcy was an excellent substitute.

Without being told, with only observation over the last few months, Deacon had figured out that the person who kept Grant together and organized and *sane* was Darcy.

And he also knew, without being told, that Darcy didn't let Grant beat himself up, either. Even when he deserved it.

"Darcy would say I'm being overdramatic. In fact, I believe those were her exact words, ten minutes ago." The corner of Grant's lips quirked upwards.

"It's Darcy, so you should probably listen to her," Deacon said.

Grant was quiet for another long moment. For so long Deacon was afraid he'd lost him in thought. But then he spoke up again. "You're still not that dumb football player, you know."

"Yeah, I know," Deacon said, grinning. "You want to talk about it? I promise not to tattle to Darcy that you're being overly dramatic."

"Just wait til she hears whose side you're really on," Grant said.

"I'm gonna assume you won't tell her," Deacon said. "But the offer still stands."

Grant hooked his chin over the safety bar. "Season ticket sales are down. I didn't even realize. And not because I have fifty million things, a hundred details, to look at every day, but because the marketing and sales department deliberately didn't tell me."

"Ouch," Deacon said.

"The numbers aren't so much a surprise. I assumed they'd be down. The commissioner's office told me to expect the same. They aren't even down as much as I worried they might be." Grant's sigh was much heavier this time. "It's that they chose not to tell me."

Deacon didn't know what to say. He knew Grant realized why that was. The old owners wouldn't have wanted to hear the bad news, and they wouldn't have reacted well even if they did.

But Grant was cut from a different kind of cloth entirely. He never wanted to be shielded from the worst of a situation. He wanted to know the whole truth, no matter how painful it was.

It was one of the many reasons Deacon liked *and* respected him.

And wanted to pull those ridiculous khaki shorts down by his freaking teeth.

"I just don't know how else to convince them that I mean it. That I *want* to know. The good, the bad, even the ugly. I can't get them to trust me. It's been months, and half the staff still creeps around like Taylor's gonna pop out of the nearest doorway."

"You gotta give them time. They're . . ." Deacon took a deep breath. "You know what they're used to. You also know how long trust can take to build, especially after it's been not only damaged, but trampled all over."

"You trust me, right?"

Grant's eyes were wide and very green—the light leaf green of spring. Deacon understood exactly why the sales and marketing department hadn't wanted to tell him the truth, because disappointing him wasn't easy.

For a split second, Deacon did consider lying.

But they'd agreed to be partners. To be truthful with each other.

Well. About everything else, anyway.

It would be pointless to tell Grant how many times Deacon had fantasized about him, and Deacon tried hard not to be a masochist.

"I do trust you. *Now.*"

Grant's eyes widened even further, and Deacon plowed ahead.

"Not at first, though. I wouldn't have trusted anyone. Not after what we'd been through. Not after the old owners told me they were gonna give me a good contract and then they turned around and gave it to Taylor, instead. All that guaranteed money."

"That we're still paying," Grant grumbled.

"That's what I'm saying. I wasn't going to trust *anyone* after that. But it became pretty clear, pretty quick, that you were different. Then there's the fact that you and me . . .we've got a shared past. An experience together that didn't have anything to do with this football team. And we're uh . . .*closer* than you are to the sales and marketing department. It was easier for me to trust you, because of that. So, just give them some more time. They'll come around. You're doing all the right things. If you weren't—"

"You'd tell me," Grant finished for him, his tone dry. "And I'd sure as hell expect you to."

"Exactly. This is *why* I trust you."

"I did talk to them. Explained my point of view. Didn't lose my temper, even."

"That's why you came up here."

Deacon wouldn't have needed to become friends with Grant Green to know he wouldn't ever lose his temper on his employees just because he could.

Grant nodded. "Some days, just . . .*ugh*."

"I felt that way, every single day, before. Every time you don't think you're making a difference . . .think about that, okay?"

"Okay."

Grant was quiet for a long time before he turned to Deacon. "So, if we're sharing, why are you up here?"

"Not 'cause of frustration or anger or anything like that. Just . . .getting my head on straight. Gettin' ready for the season. First day of practice is always overwhelming."

"I can imagine. I caught some . . .uh . . .moments. From my office."

So those prickles on the back of his neck hadn't been Deacon's imagination, after all. He hadn't thought so, since he wasn't a particularly fanciful guy.

Except in one case.

"It's just the first day, but I feel good about it," Deacon said. "Don't want you to think I don't."

"How about this." Grant paused. "Based on what I saw today, and what I've felt since he showed up here, two months back, I think you were one hundred percent right about Jonathan Kelley."

Deacon grinned. "Where's Darcy with her little recorder thing when you need her? I want to record that for posterity. Press play every time you're contrary and don't listen to me."

Grant rolled his eyes. "Hilarious."

"Listen, I might not be that big dumb football player, but you're still brilliant, so much smarter than I could ever imagine being. So you sayin' I was right about Coach K? Feels damn good."

Felt more than good. Felt warm—no, it felt *hot*, burning almost, a flame lodged in the base of his stomach. He'd been fighting the sensation for ages, and it seemed, by now, that it wasn't going anywhere.

"Obviously, we'll still see what happens with the season. Don't worry, you could still be wrong." Grant's eyes scrunched up at the corners as he shared a conspiratorial smile with Deacon. God, he was so fucking cute.

Cute and hot and utterly delectable.

Deacon dug his fingers into his thighs. Felt the muscles protest. But the pain was a good reminder that he was supposed to be keeping his hands—and his *thoughts*—off the gorgeous owner of his team.

A buzz interrupted the silence that had fallen between them.

Grant pulled his phone out of his pocket, stared at it for a second and then groaned a little under his breath.

Deacon very deliberately ignored the pulse of heat that licked up his spine, spreading from that place at the base of his stomach, at the noise.

At what he might do to make Grant groan like that again.

"I gotta go," Grant said and reached over, casually putting his hand on Deacon's shoulder to push himself upright.

Deacon froze.

Then Grant froze. Like he'd just realized what he'd done.

"Uh," Grant stammered.

He was not the stammering kind.

Deacon had suspected he might not be alone in his crush, though of course, that didn't change a thing, but this kind of confirmed it.

He didn't know if that made it all better—or far, far worse.

Grant's fingertips grazed his skin. Each touch felt like a firework going off underneath it.

Deacon took a deep breath and then another.

Grant finally moved, standing up, and removed his hand.

"Uh, sorry," Grant said.

"Whatever you need," Deacon said, shrugging, deliberately trying to brush both their reactions off as casual, even though he knew better. "Whether it's a hand up or to bitch to me about the sales team or to get the locker room in order—you just tell me, okay?"

Grant stared at him. This couldn't come as a surprise.

The Condors meant everything to Deacon. But it wasn't just that—and it was like Grant was just now realizing that, too.

That Deacon's dedication and willingness to do *anything* wasn't just because the Condors were his team.

"I'd ask if you really mean that, but it's clear you do," Grant said slowly.

"I do," Deacon said.

I'll even keep my hands off you, even if it's killing me, because it's the right thing for this team and for us.

"Thanks, Deac," Grant said and after offering him a smile, turned and walked away.

But Deacon didn't move for a long time. Instead, he stared out at the field, but somehow didn't see a single thing.

CHAPTER 4

November

"That turkey is terrifying," Deacon confided to Grant, his head dipping close.

Closer than he might, normally.

Grant knew why they scrupulously preserved the line between them. Knew why it had to stay bold and uncrossed.

But it was harder to remember why on nights like tonight, right after such a great team win, when the Condors were riding high—not only on their way to a playoff berth, but nearly done resurrecting a reputation the prior owners had thrown away with both hands.

It was also harder to remember when Deacon was like this, standing close, even larger than life, dark hair still a little damp from his post-game shower, scruff dusting his jaw, eyes glued to Grant's face, hypnotically appealing in their singular focus.

"I don't know, I think it's kind of festive," Grant argued. He'd put Darcy in charge of decorations for the team Thanksgiving party, held right after the game against the Cowboys, and she might've gotten a little carried away.

Grant tore his gaze away from Deacon for just a moment to look over at the gigantic papier-mâché turkey, and okay, she'd gotten a *lot* carried away.

Grant had gone into their partnership turning this team around hoping for the best.

He'd never imagined that every day would be better than the last—or harder, too.

Or that his crush would reach such an unmanageable size.

Or that his crush was almost certainly mind-bogglingly mutual.

If he'd known then, back in March, what he knew now, would he still have pushed Deacon so hard to join him?

The answer was instant and undeniable: *yes*.

What they'd done here, together, was special.

"Are you gonna let Darcy decorate for Christmas, too?" Deacon asked, finally, after taking a long drink of beer.

Grant could barely tear his eyes away from Deacon's throat as he swallowed. It was strong and tanned a deep olive, from a long summer and fall spent outside.

The thing was, a crush at twenty-one was one thing. A crush at thirty-three was a different thing entirely.

"Spoiler alert: me being the boss and her being the assistant is just a ruse. Really, she's in charge. So, the answer is almost definitely yes, because I think she secretly enjoyed decorating."

"If that turkey is any indication, yeah she did," Deacon agreed.

"Honestly, I can't believe we're actually second in the division and if the playoffs started today, we'd make it as a wild card team," Grant said, laughing incredulously. That fact had been bubbling inside him since the last quarter of the game, and it was inevitable that the bubble would burst and it would just explode out of him at some point.

Probably inevitable that it would choose *this* moment and *this* person to explode in front of.

The commissioner's office had been *very* blunt. At best, they could probably expect to win a handful of games. Until they got out from underneath that ridiculous contract the prior owners had awarded to Taylor, there was no money to pay players, and without players, wins were going to be hard to come by.

But from the beginning, the Condors had fought. So much harder than Grant had ever predicted. Then, he'd taken that risk on Riley Flynn, which had paid off in spades.

Deacon nudged his shoulder. "Maybe it's 'cause you're really fucking good at this," he said, sounding unbearably proud.

Like this idiot didn't have anything to do with their record.

"I don't know, maybe *you're* really fucking good at this," Grant retorted.

Deacon grinned.

"That's the rumor," Deacon said.

He *was* really good. The best, probably. Nobody else could have gathered together the tattered remnants of their defense after the Rex scandal had rocked the team and then Jem's injury had left them reeling.

But they'd played well today, and Nate, Jem's backup, was coming along. Grant wasn't as good at evaluating talent as he wanted to be, but even he could tell.

Probably half of Nate's improvement could be placed squarely on the shoulders of the man next to him. Without making any kind of deal about it, Deacon had taken Nate under his wing and coached him personally, spending time before and after practice with him.

From his favorite bird's-eye view of the practice field, Grant had watched just the two of them out there, Deacon patiently teaching Nate every one of Jem's moves.

"I've seen you, you know," Grant said, a little recklessly. His tongue was so much looser than it normally was. Probably that was because of the gin and tonics he'd drunk during the game and then the handful of beers he'd already shared with Deacon at this party.

Or maybe he felt drunk because Deacon was standing half a step too close, and he was letting him.

Deacon raised an eyebrow. "You've seen me, huh?"

Oh, fuck it. "I've watched you."

"Have you?" Deacon's gaze grew impossibly darker.

Grant nodded, because he was clearly a little drunk and a lot insane. "You've been teaching Nate. Out on the field. Before practice. After practice."

"So, what you're really saying is you've been keeping an eye on me." Deacon's voice dropped and suddenly he was another half-step closer and his shoulder was resting right against Grant's. It felt so warm and solid. He'd feel that way *everywhere*. Grant swallowed hard, the knowledge resting rigid and hot right under his breastbone, making it tough to even take a breath.

Seriously, what even was a crush at thirty-three?

So much more than just a crush, that was for goddamn sure.

"Both eyes, actually," Grant confessed.

"I can feel it, you know, when you watch me," Deacon said.

Grant's throat was so dry it made perfect sense to drain the rest of his beer. Somehow, that didn't help.

"Want another one?" Deacon asked conscientiously. Like he was Grant's date and they were here at this party together. Which they weren't, of course. It was just . . .coincidence that they'd gravitated to this corner together. Total coincidence.

"Sure, why not." Grant felt something rush through him that was a lot nervier, so much hotter, than mere recklessness.

What were they doing?

Probably nothing still. They hadn't crossed any lines. But their toes were currently resting on the edge, so solid and black in his mind.

That was okay, though.

This was all okay.

It might be the beer talking, or maybe it was his crush.

A moment later, Deacon was back, handing Grant a bottle, his own fingers lingering on it even as Grant took it. Their pinkies brushed, and it felt as explicit as a kiss.

"You feel it?" Grant asked. Definitely tipsy. There was no denying it. And he couldn't even blame the booze.

"When you watch me? Yeah, it's like this . . .I don't know . . .prickling at the back of my neck."

"That could be anyone watching you," Grant said.

Except they both knew that wasn't true.

"Yeah, no," Deacon said wryly. "It's just you."

That was the clearest Deacon had ever been about it.

At first, when they'd met last spring, Grant had been sure it was just him feeling this way. But the more time they spent together, the clearer it became that whatever this was, it was mutual.

Friends didn't look at other friends that way. Or call their bosses *Grant* in that tender-rough way of his, not when the rest of the players and staff all scrupulously called him Mr. G.

Grant was most definitely not stupid, and whatever he was stuck in the middle of, Deacon was right there with him.

But just like Grant, Deacon hadn't done anything about it. Hadn't once stepped out of line. Surely because he also understood that crossing the line would be risking everything they'd spent the last six months building.

"It's alright," Deacon continued, "'cause I watch you, too, you know?"

Grant nearly choked on his beer.

Deacon patted him on the back as he tried to clear his throat, his big, warm hand stroking him for at least twenty seconds longer than strictly necessary.

"You okay?" he asked.

Nodding wordlessly, Grant searched for the brakes. They needed to find them, or else who knew what was going to happen tonight.

What had gotten into Deacon?

What's gotten into you?

Because Deacon hadn't been the only one pushing. He'd done it too, and he couldn't even blame the alcohol he'd drunk.

"I told Jem about me retiring," Deacon said. Clearly he also agreed it was a good idea to change the subject.

"Yeah, how he'd take it?"

"Well, you know. He knew. He didn't like it, but then I think he's sort of . . ." Deacon took a deep breath. "Lost. But he'll find himself. He's got a solid head on his shoulders and a lot of people who care about him."

"Yourself included," Grant said.

At first, when he'd bought the team, he'd been a little embarrassingly jealous of Deacon's best friend.

Jem Knight was carelessly handsome, very charming, and undeniably close to Deacon. *And* queer.

How many of those stories have you heard? Two best friends, discovering more than friendship, after so many years of keeping it platonic?

But as Grant had gotten to know Jem, he'd realized there truly was nothing there. Nothing to be jealous of. Though frankly, even if there was, it wouldn't have changed anything.

Deacon Harris was Off Limits.

Even though he knew Deacon wasn't going to be playing next year and there were no contracts to negotiate, Grant still signed his game checks. Grant was still the owner of this team, and his boss. With the scrutiny of the commissioner's office, Grant couldn't risk it.

Couldn't risk damaging Deacon's reputation. Now. Or in the future.

No matter how much he wanted to.

"Yeah, it's weird not having him here, but Nate's a good backup. You're right, I've been putting in the work with him. And it's showing."

"Have you thought about what you'll do next year?"

He and Deacon had discussed it a handful of times. Always like this, in situations when they weren't quite as careful as they could be.

And always, Grant wondered, if Deacon might say, *I don't know what I'm doing but it's nothing to do with the Condors, so I can finally do something about this.* In his imagination—his clearly overactive imagination—Deacon would lean forward and kiss him then. The way he'd dreamt of for too many years.

But of course, Deacon didn't say that. Or do that.

"Not sure yet, but something here. Whatever you want me to do. Whatever you need."

Grant pursed his lips together. His unkissed lips. He shouldn't be unhappy about this proclamation. Deacon had only made it at least a dozen times, and clearly, from his behavior over the last six months, meant it.

What about me? What if I'm the thing that you need to do? Before I explode from all this sexual tension?

"You'd be a good scout. And a good coach."

"Just don't put me in the sales department, okay?" Deacon wasn't as suavely charming as his best friend, Jem, but every once in awhile, he apparently enjoyed carelessly hammering away at Grant's good intentions.

Tonight he was making free with them.

"I don't know, you could sell quite a few season tickets, I'm sure." *You could sell anything to me, and I'd buy it.*

"I think you might be biased," Deacon said.

Oh, if he only knew.

"Maybe a little." Grant finished his beer and noticed that most of the room had cleared out. The families had taken their kids home. Carter and Ian were just leaving, some of the other linemen trailing behind them.

Grant thought he heard Carter mention something about the Pirate's Booty. Hoped that wouldn't result in a frantic phone call in the early morning hours. But then, with Ian around and Carter happier and more settled than Grant had ever seen him, he no longer worried as much as he had.

"Looks like the party's winding down," Deacon noted. He must've noticed Grant's gaze as it took in the mostly empty room. The caterers were breaking down the demolished buffet table. Darcy was nowhere to be seen, but he already knew she and her minions would pop back in late tonight or early in the morning to clean up the decorations.

Including that ridiculous turkey.

Anytime now Deacon would give a reluctant sigh and say he was heading home. Alone. Grant would keep his mouth shut and not ask to come with him.

It didn't matter how many times they did it, Grant disliked it each and every goddamn time.

"I could use some air," Deacon said and glanced over at Grant. "How about you?"

Grant opened his mouth, too ready to give his rote reply, then snapped it shut again, because he realized Deacon hadn't followed their normal script.

"Uh, um," Grant hesitated. *Danger, danger, danger*, his brain cried, complete with red flashing lights. But air wasn't dangerous, was it? No, it was just air. How could air be dangerous? You needed it to breathe.

"Just up to our spot," Deacon said, shrugging like it was no big deal if Grant said no. But Grant could see the tense line of his shoulders, the earnestness in his gaze.

Grant's mother had always told him he was too curious for his own good.

Our spot.

Not just *his,* anymore, but *ours.*

What was Deacon up to? There was only one way for Grant to find out.

"Sure," Grant said and followed Deacon out the door.

The elevator they took to the top floor of the practice facility was bright, but after they exited it, the hallways of the office level were dark, hushed, intimate.

Grant pressed his hands together behind him and gave himself a very firm lecture, even as his heartbeat accelerated.

They'd gone up there lots of times. Usually separately, running into each other by accident. He couldn't remember every going up deliberately, *together,* but that didn't have to mean anything. They were friends, right? What did it matter if they went up there together?

Grant took a deep breath of air as soon as they hit the platform, and even though it was late November, the Charleston night was still plenty balmy.

Unfortunately, Grant thought they could have used a nice dose of frigid air to bring both of them to their senses.

"Better?" Grant asked as he leaned against the railing, keeping a scrupulous two-foot distance between his arm and Deacon's.

They'd been too close downstairs. In the best kind of way.

"Yeah," Deacon said. Shot Grant a surprisingly lopsided grin. "Not that it was bad before."

But now we're alone.

Deacon didn't have to finish the sentence for Grant to know what he meant.

"You really think I'd be a good coach?" Deacon asked before Grant could unscramble his brain and come up with something innocuous to say.

"Of course you would. What do you think you're doing with Nate, now?"

"I didn't really think about it," Deacon admitted with a shrug.

"That's because you just do what needs done. Just step in and do it. That's . . ." Grant was suddenly very aware that the two feet of distance had somehow shrunk to less than one. Mere inches. That was how far his hand was from Deacon's.

That's why I'm absolutely crazy about you.

If he turned, he'd practically be on top of the man.

It would be fucking glorious.

Grant cleared his throat. "That's what makes you such a great player and what would make you such a good coach."

"So you've never regretted convincing me to un-retire?" Deacon's white teeth flashed in the gloom as he grinned.

I'm regretting it right now.

"Uh, um, well . . ." Grant hesitated. *Just say no, you've never regretted it, even if it would be a lie.*

"Come on, Grant, we've never lied to each other," Deacon said.

No, and he didn't want to start now.

"I've never really regretted it, but sometimes . . .I . . .uh . . .wish things could be different," Grant said carefully trying to pick his words—even though that was hard, because not much of his blood was currently in his brain.

Back in college, he'd dreamed a thousand times what it would feel like if Deacon Harris ever gazed at him like that. Dark and intent.

Nothing like I ever imagined.

Because he was staring at him like that now.

"But they're not," Grant finished belatedly, breathlessly. "Different, that is."

Take a step back, his brain screamed at him, but it was shockingly easy to just ignore that voice. So easy to instead move even closer. His hand landed on Deacon's broad chest, felt the shudder that went through Deacon at his touch.

"I wish they were too," Deacon said, his voice low and rough.

The line, so solid in Grant's mind, wavered for a second.

What would it hurt, if they crossed it? If nobody but them knew? What could the commissioner's office really do? Insist the team be sold again? They couldn't do that. The bad publicity would only hurt the league more.

Sure, his personal life would get dragged through God only knew how many meetings and emails and memos, but he could tolerate that, couldn't he?

Normally, the answer would be emphatically no and he wouldn't have even considered it, but this was *Deacon.*

He'd never wanted anyone the way he wanted him—and Grant *needed* that to mean something. To mean it was okay to not just cross the line, but to forget that it existed entirely.

But Deacon flinched, suddenly, and took a step back.

It took Grant what felt like an eternity but what was in reality only a moment to realize why.

That noise he'd heard only a moment before, that he'd been sure was the ringing in his ears or the rushing of his blood somewhere other than his brain, was actually a voice.

Specifically Darcy's voice.

Darcy saying, "Grant? Are you up here? You're not answering your phone. Oh, there you are."

He looked over as she stopped in her tracks, his hand still on Deacon's chest. He hadn't moved *that* far back. Grant was still partially shielded by Deacon's much bigger body.

But not enough, because Darcy had clearly seen him.

Seen *them*.

Grant braced himself for weeks of knowing looks and persuasive arguments—the same arguments he'd just been trying to justify to himself, now reduced to ashes in his mind.

They couldn't do this.

He hadn't come here to destroy Deacon's—and the Condors'—reputation even further.

He stepped around Deacon, pulling his hand away. Pretending the whole time that it wasn't the hardest thing he'd ever done.

"Darcy," he said, stopping short of where she stood.

"There's a problem in Singapore," she said briskly, like she hadn't just caught them practically kissing—*practically kissing, but not ac-*

tually kissing, his brain yelped, not sure whether to be thrilled or devastated about this.

"You could've—"

"You weren't answering your phone," she said, tilting her head.

"Yes, I guess I wasn't." Grant didn't pull it out of his pocket. Check for missed calls. Because he knew he'd see them.

He'd let Deacon distract from not just his responsibilities to the Condors but to InTech, too.

"What kind of problem?" Grant asked, trying to get himself back under control. Thinking about work—that usually helped.

He didn't glance back at Deacon. Wasn't sure what he'd see if he did.

Couldn't be held responsible for what he'd do if Deacon looked as disappointed as he felt.

"Small to medium-ish," Darcy said. She was the one who looked back at Deacon as they headed for the exit. "Do you need to . . ."

"No," Grant said resolutely. If he looked back, if he talked to Deacon, his good intentions would crumble, and he couldn't afford for that to happen.

Thousands of people depended on him to make good, reasoned decisions. And Grant already knew Deacon wasn't a good *or* a reasoned decision.

"Alright," she said, shooting Deacon one more glance.

Deacon went home.

Took a cold shower.

Lay in bed, stared at the shadowed ceiling, and tried to tell himself that he hadn't fucked up everything beyond belief.

Part of him wanted to call Jem.

Beg his best friend to tell him what he should do.

Nothing. You should do absolutely fucking nothing.

But that had been what Deacon had been doing. No matter how he'd felt, he'd pushed it all down. Focused on what mattered: the *team*.

Doing the right thing for the Condors.

Tonight, he'd lost sight of that. Tonight, he'd let his desire off the chain, and look what had happened.

Almost happened.

Deacon clearly wasn't a good person, because he was more disappointed at the *almost* than angry at himself that they'd ended up in that situation to begin with.

But no matter how much self-flagellation he was currently enduring, Deacon didn't want to call Jem. He was with his family, in Christmas Falls, and if Deacon called him, he knew he'd come back, immediately.

You should be able to figure this shit out, without needing your hand held.

He couldn't even blame Grant for walking away without even looking at him. That had been the right call. They'd been right on the precipice of breaking all their unspoken rules, and if Deacon had leaned down and kissed Grant . . .

Deacon groaned out loud.

What he needed was another cold shower, not to think about what could've happened if they'd both lost their collective minds.

His phone dinged, and for a split second, Deacon hoped it was Grant.

He imagined what Grant might say. *I'm coming over.* Nevermind that Grant had never been to his townhouse before. *I want to see you. I need you. I don't care that you're off-limits, I can't stop looking at you. Or thinking about you.*

Grant's words merged with his own thoughts until they were one and the same.

But when he rolled over with a pained grunt, trying to ignore his rock hard cock, and glanced at his phone, he was inevitably disappointed.

The text wasn't from Grant. Wasn't from Jem, either.

It was from Carter. **Official victory party tomorrow night at the Pirate's Booty**, the text read. And then right under it, another message. **You want to invite Mr. G or should I?**

Deacon groaned again.

He didn't want to go to a Pirate's Booty party. And he especially didn't want to go if Grant was there.

The problem with Carter was now he'd found personal happiness, he wanted everyone to have it, even if it wasn't in the cards.

Of course, it didn't matter how many times he told himself that Grant wasn't the man for him, the more his dick seemed to cling to the idea and refuse to let it go.

And not just his dick.

Deacon wasn't stupid enough to think it was only his body that wanted the guy.

He typed back. **I'll be there. Don't invite Mr. G. Don't make it weird, Carter.**

Carter responded almost immediately. **Shouldn't we be saying that to you? I saw you two gettin' real cozy tonight before we left.**

Deacon tossed his phone back on the table, deciding that it wasn't a good idea to even get into that circular argument with Carter.

Better that, though, than the circular argument you're having with yourself.

He rolled back and grabbed his phone. But didn't text Carter. Pulled up another conversation. The last message was from earlier today, when Grant had wished him luck before kickoff. **Not that you'll need it,** he'd added.

For a long time, he fought himself. He knew what he wanted to say. *I don't regret it. I only regret that Darcy interrupted us.* But Deacon didn't know if that was true. If he kissed Grant, he wouldn't want to stop there. He'd want all of him, all of the time. And Deacon wasn't stupid enough to think that was even possible. Grant successfully ran the Condors *and* a Fortune 500 company. Even with his skills at delegating, he was still one of the busiest people Deacon knew.

Instead, he ended up sending something else.

Hope you got your small to medium-sized Singapore problem worked out.

He was sure that Grant wouldn't answer right away. After all, he was no doubt busy untangling the small to medium-sized Singapore problem.

But to Deacon's surprise, his answer came through right away.

All fixed, Grant replied. **Happy Thanksgiving.**

Deacon told himself, as his gaze reverted back to the ceiling and he tried to fall asleep, that Grant's text hadn't been a brush-off.

And, additionally, that even if it had been, that might be a good thing.

A safe thing.

But Deacon couldn't convince himself of either.

CHAPTER 5

Deacon had forgotten entirely that Fridays were 90s Night at the Pirate's Booty until the moment he walked in.

Boyz II Men was playing loudly, and it felt like half the bar was in ripped jeans and Doc Martens and flannel. *So much flannel.*

Even Kieran behind the bar was in a flannel shirt, open at the neck, blond hair pushed back, as he poured drinks and chatted with the various patrons lined up to grab some of his magic for themselves.

He was grinning when Deacon finally made his way to the bar.

"The other guys are all over at the dance floor," Kieran said. "Your usual?"

"Whatever you think I should have." Deacon wasn't stupid enough to flout Kieran's famous superhero skill—which was that he knew exactly what you *should* be drinking, not what you thought you wanted to be drinking.

Kieran nodded absently, and then to Deacon's surprise, he didn't reach for the small fridge underneath to grab a bottle of his favorite beer. Instead, he filled a glass with ice and began to make a drink.

He was *pretty* sure Carter wouldn't ignore him and invite Grant anyway and even more sure Grant wouldn't actually come. But there was Kieran making him a mixed drink, so maybe stranger things had happened. Deacon shoved his hands into his jeans and tried to ask as casually as he could, "Anyone else here besides the usual suspects?"

Kieran shot him a look. "Who are you expecting?"

"Hopefully nobody," Deacon said and meant it. He and Grant had almost made a monumental mistake last night, and yet even though he knew some space would be a good thing, he felt disappointed when Kieran gave a little shake of his head.

"Nobody I wouldn't expect," he said, setting a glass full of fizzy clear liquid in front of Deacon.

"What's this?" he asked, curious as he lifted it to his mouth to take a sip.

"Gin and tonic," Kieran said.

"It's good." All Kieran's drinks were good, but Deacon didn't think he'd ever even *thought* of ordering a gin and tonic. Why had Kieran decided he needed one of these tonight?

"Don't ask," Kieran offered with a lopsided smile. "That's not how the superpower works."

"Ugh," Deacon said. But he kept sipping it as he moved away from the bar, across the room, and down the hallway that led to the dance floor.

"Hey," Riley said, tilting his head in greeting as Deacon approached. "You're not drinking beer?" He glanced down at Deacon's glass.

"Guilty as charged. Thank Kieran for that."

"What is it?" Riley asked.

"Gin and tonic." Deacon glanced around the dance floor. Underneath the flashing lights, he could see Carter and Ian, Beck and Micah, and even Nate was there.

Of course, Deacon had texted him and told him to come, because he deserved to celebrate, too.

"Your new protege is here. You invite him?" Riley gestured to where Nate was dancing with Beck and Micah.

Deacon nodded.

The guy was grinning widely, his teeth white in the darkened room.

He reminded Deacon a little—or a lot, actually—of Jem. Played like him, or would when Deacon got done with him, and even looked a little like him, with his dark hair and hazel eyes.

But he wasn't Jem. He wasn't Deacon's best friend.

Jem's absence shouldn't hurt, but it still did. Deacon knew he was making his peace with the hand fate had dealt him, and Deacon should be too, but it turned out it wasn't all that easy.

"Where's Landry?" Deacon asked, changing the subject.

"Grabbing us drinks. Surprised you didn't see him."

It was hard to miss Landry Banks—the guy was built like a small mountain.

"Me too," Deacon said. Didn't mention that he'd only been looking for one person when he'd stepped into the Pirate's Booty.

"Oh, good, you came," Landry said, walking up to them. He gave Riley one of the drinks in his hands and a kiss on his cheek, his lips lingering there. He whispered into Riley's ear and then, drink in hand, took off towards the dance floor.

Deacon took a long gulp of his drink, glancing away from the private moment.

He wasn't jealous of either Riley or Landry—but together? The happiness they'd found? He was at least man enough to admit he was envious of that.

Same with Micah and Beck. He could see flashes of them on the dance floor, smiling at each other, the lights glinting off their matching platinum wedding bands.

God, even Carter had found someone, his head ducked down low, his expression tender and his smile undeniable as Ian whispered something in his ear.

"It's okay to feel that way," Riley said, putting a hand on his forearm, squeezing reassuringly.

Deacon jolted a little. Surprised. Had his melancholy been written all over his face? God, he hoped not.

Maybe Grant had only come outside with him yesterday because he felt *sorry* for him. That would be even worse than the fact that it had happened at all.

"I don't feel—"

"Bullshit." Riley's voice was still kind as he interrupted him. "There's nothing wrong with feeling lonely. Especially with Jem gone."

"I'm not . . . I'm not *lonely*," Deacon said. "I have more friends on this goddamn team than I know what to do with. Y'all are giving me gray hair, too."

"You know, that Nate kid is nice," Riley said, his smile dimpling his cheeks. He looked like he was up to something.

At least he and Carter were painfully straightforward in their attempts to set him up.

"Yeah, you were right there. He's a *kid*," Deacon said.

"I think he's got a crush on you," Riley pointed out, still sounding kind, but there was an echo of steel in his tone now.

Just in case anyone had forgotten that Riley had been forced to fight like hell for everything he'd gotten, every opportunity he'd made the most of, there was the evidence. Riley didn't fuck around.

Which made this . . .*worse*, Deacon decided.

"It's just a bit of hero worship, 'cause I'm helping him out," Deacon argued. He didn't want anyone to have a crush on him. Even if he had the time for romance, he knew he was essentially unavailable.

Lie. You want one man and one man only to have a crush on you.

And that was the problem.

He was already taken.

Metaphorically.

Fuck.

"If you say so," Riley said, sounding entirely unconvinced.

"I do say so," Deacon said forcefully.

Riley crossed his arms over his chest. "Deac, don't be like this. I know Carter's been trying to convince you to make a move on Mr. G. And you won't."

"I *can't*," Deacon pointed out.

"Yeah, yeah." Riley waved a hand. "So you say."

"So the *NFL* says, Riley," Deacon said, grinding his teeth together. It was bad enough having this conversation with Carter, who had newly discovered love and had decided that everyone should experience it with the same heart-stopping intensity that he currently was. But Riley was even worse, because Riley was the most stubborn person that Deacon had ever met.

More stubborn than even himself.

Riley wouldn't let it go. Deacon could see it now, in the hard line of his jaw.

"But there's nothing stopping you from going over there and dancing with Nate," Riley said. Neatly maneuvering him into a position Deacon didn't want to be in.

Namely, the position where Nate might assume that some of his hero worship might be returned.

"Except common sense," Deacon hissed.

Riley shot him a look. "You're dancing with him, not proposing marriage. You might try to hide it but I just saw you, Deac. You're lonely. You want what the rest of us have found, and if you're not going to find it with Mr. G—"

"I just made it clear that's not going to happen," Deacon said in a tight, hard voice.

It was fucking hard enough to keep resisting his feelings when it was just him and his painfully circular thoughts. Other people trying to convince him to give in? Made it even worse.

"Then do something else," Riley said. "Go dance with Nate. Poor guy's third wheeling it with Micah and Beck and you of all people should know what that feels like."

Yeah, he did.

"You could always go rescue him," Deacon suggested. He *did* dance, because you couldn't come to the Pirate's Booty with Carter and Riley and the sappiest husbands of all time and not dance at all. But he didn't make it a normal habit.

"I'm gonna go dance with my boyfriend," Riley pointed out reasonably as he finished his drink. Set the glass on one of the empty tables ringing the dance floor. "Don't think that's gonna help his third wheel situation."

Deacon groaned. He'd almost have guessed that *Riley* invited Nate to the Pirate's Booty tonight but no, Riley had only taken advantage of the situation. The situation that Deacon himself had created in the first place.

"Fine, fine," Deacon grumbled. He set his half-drunk gin and tonic down next to Riley's drink and followed him onto the dance floor.

"Heeeeey, look who's decided to join," Carter teased in a loud voice, one arm wrapped around Ian's shoulders.

"Hey, Carter," Deacon said. "Ian."

He turned to Nate, and yeah, there it was shining somewhat undeniably in his light brown eyes. Hero worship. *A crush*, Riley whispered in his ear.

"Hey, man, glad you came," Deacon said, turning to Nate. He extended a hand and tugged the guy into a quick hug.

It felt just like hugging Jem. No fireworks whatsoever.

Nothing like last night, when Grant had moved close to him and it had felt like his whole body lit up.

But Riley *was* right about one thing: it wasn't right to leave him with Beck and Micah.

He loved those two, but they were a *lot*. It was tough to witness such an epic love and not want a little bit of that for yourself.

"Glad you invited me," Nate said shyly.

"You wanna dance?" Deacon said, hoping that he wouldn't regret it and this wouldn't make anything awkward.

"With you?" Nate squawked.

Deacon nodded. "Don't tell me you wanna keep dancing with the husbands over there." Beck had his hands all over Micah, Micah's head bent down low as he murmured something in his ear.

Yeah. Nobody wanted to interfere with *that*.

Nate followed his gaze and grinned. "Nope, no sir, I do not."

"There you go. You got me, now."

"Do I?" Nate gazed over at him like he was a cross between Superman and JJ Watt.

"Well, *yeah*. Us third wheels have to stick together," Deacon said, nudging him with an elbow. They melted deeper into the crowd, currently writhing to one of Biggie's hits.

They'd just found a groove, Deacon making sure he kept a decent amount of distance between them—after all, he didn't want to lead the guy on. He *liked* Nate, and he wanted to keep him as a friend—when they were joined by Landry and Riley.

Nate took the opportunity to slide a little closer. Had he been bumped? Had he done it on purpose? But then they were hip-to-hip, and Nate was gazing at him shyly, like he *was* the greatest thing in the whole freaking world.

Deacon wasn't always a good man. A good man wouldn't take advantage of such a nice young kid like this. But it felt undeniably sweet after the cold shoulder Grant had given him last night, after they'd almost kissed.

He hadn't blamed Grant for leaving the way he did, after. He'd been smarter and more restrained than Deacon himself. He'd made the hard choice that Deacon hadn't been able to.

But Deacon could acknowledge now that yes, it had stung.

Maybe that sting went both ways, and it had frozen Grant too.

Then Carter arrived.

"Oh my God," he exclaimed, even more loudly than before. "He's *here*. He *came*."

Deacon felt his stomach drop out, right to his feet.

There was only one person he could be talking about.

Maybe he's here to apologize . . .

But Deacon cut that thought off hard and fast. An apology wouldn't change a thing.

Deacon tucked a hand around Nate's waist. Leaned in.

"Did you hear that?" Nate's eyes were shining. "Mr. G is here!"

Like he'd needed any more bucketfuls of cold water dumped on his head.

"Yeah, I heard."

"He's such a good owner," Nate said. "Wasn't sure I'd be happy I was picked up by the Condors, but man, it's been great. He's great. And you? God, Deac, you are the *best*."

Okay, even Deacon could acknowledge that glow in Nate's eyes was not just hero worship. He really should extricate himself.

"I *worshipped* you as a kid," Nate said.

Ouch. Deacon hid his wince. He wasn't that old, was he?

But Nate continued, because apparently Deacon was better at hiding the alarm in his expression than he'd assumed. "Then it turns out you're even cooler than I ever imagined. Helpin' me with my reps, getting me trained up. And now, here . . ." Nate's expression morphed and suddenly it was no longer quite as shy. He was gaining confidence. "You're here with me."

Jesus.

Deacon needed to get out of here *now*.

Even if getting out of here meant coming face-to-face with Grant before he was quite ready to deal with him again.

"I gotta—"

"Yeah, let's get a drink." Nate flashed him a knowing grin. "I feel you."

Yeah, he was. There was Nate's hand drifting down his back, heading right towards his ass.

Deacon cursed Riley a hundred ways to Sunday. This hadn't just been a bad idea to encourage Nate; it was a catastrophic one.

They got through the crowd, Nate's hand settling in the small of his back. Not exactly friendly, but not crossing the platonic line either.

Deacon considered shaking his hand off. He didn't want to encourage the kid. But then, did he want to discourage him?

Before last night, he'd have said, yes, absolutely, without a question. But there was that cold shoulder Grant had given him last night. Even though he'd just said, *I wish things were different.*

Deacon sure fucking wished they were.

Maybe he was a little bit of what Riley had just said. Lonely, wasn't it?

"Didn't know you guys relaxed like this," Nate said, and his glance over at Deacon made it clear that *you guys* actually meant one person and one person only.

Deacon.

"Uh, yeah, sometimes," Deacon said.

He could see Grant, holding court with a few Condors players surrounding him, and the last thing he wanted was to join them. He nearly said, *let's not go over there, let's go to the bar instead,* but before he could, Carter looked over and gestured at them.

Like a good little puppy, Nate changed directions, and Deacon had no choice but to follow him.

Could this get any worse? Deacon decided that no, it could not.

And then it did.

Because right when they approached, Nate slung an arm around Deacon, like they were together. "What can I get you?" he asked. "Another one of those . . . what was it?"

Riley spoke up. "Think it was a gin and tonic, right, Deac?"

Grant's eyebrow skidded up. Darker than usual in the dim light of the room, a slash against his pale skin.

"You drink gin and tonics?" Grant asked, because that was surely the most innocent question he could ask.

Because he couldn't ask: *what the hell are you doing with Nate? After yesterday, when I almost . . . when we . . .*

Deacon cleared his throat. "Uh, yeah, I guess. Tonight, I do."

"It's the bartender's superpower," Carter confided. "He always knows what you want to drink better than you do. And trust me, you don't want to question it."

Grant lifted his own drink. Clear and fizzy.

Oh, God.

"You've got good taste, I guess," Grant said wryly.

Deacon was very proud of himself for not running away. But he did gently disentangle himself from Nate.

"I gotta . . . uh . . . bathroom." Deacon said.

He was nearly down the hallway to safety—AKA the bath-room—when he heard footsteps behind him.

A voice telling him to slow down.

Okay maybe he'd been running a little.

But when he glanced back, it wasn't Nate he spied but the *last* person he should be talking to. Especially alone. Especially after last night.

"What's going on?" Grant asked as Deacon pushed the bathroom door open. Annoyingly, it was also empty, a whole empty line of urinals against one wall and two clearly empty stalls, their doors swinging open.

Shit.

Deacon crossed his arms over his chest. Even if he'd needed to pee, he was not going to whip his dick out with Grant right here.

Nope, that way lay disaster.

Not that this wasn't already a semi-fucking disaster.

"What do you mean?" Deacon asked. More belligerently than he'd ever talked to the owner of his football team—*or* his old statistics tutor.

Grant frowned, but didn't call him out for it. "You just took off so fast with that look on your face, I wasn't sure if you were okay. If it was okay that *I* was here."

"I can't deny I'm surprised you showed," Deacon said. That much was true.

"I wasn't going to," Grant admitted. "Seemed like crossing some lines that shouldn't be crossed, but then Carter told me I deserved to be here, too, to celebrate with you guys. And you know what? He was right. I should be here, letting you know just how much it means that we're kicking ass this year."

"Right." Deacon hated how right he was. Couldn't quite believe *Carter* had known to vocalize it just that way to Grant.

But then Carter wasn't stupid, when he wasn't thinking with his overabundance of hormones.

"We are, and you should share in that."

Grant cleared his throat awkwardly. "I didn't know you and uh . . .Nate were so close."

Was that the best they could do, then? Dance around what had happened the night before by talking about *Nate*? Who, surely Grant knew by now, he wasn't really interested in. Not like that.

Grant had to know what Deacon was like when he wanted someone—because he'd made it so painfully clear who he wanted was Grant.

"We're just friends," Deacon said.

A crease had appeared between Grant's brows. "Oh. Right. Of course."

"Last night—" Deacon got out only two words, before Grant interrupted him.

It was both a blessing and a curse, because Deacon hadn't been entirely sure what he was going to say.

But still, Grant didn't let him say it.

"We're not going to discuss last night," Grant said. "But I just want to make it clear. It was . . .it was a mistake. A mistake that's not going to happen again."

"We didn't do anything wrong." Not technically, anyway. Even Deacon knew that fantasies were just that—*fantasies*. But what would have happened if Darcy hadn't interrupted them?

They'd never know.

"But you wanted to." Grant paused, hesitating. "*I* wanted to."

Of course, he'd realized his feelings weren't just his own. Especially after last night. But it still felt sweet to hear the truth.

Not that sweet, though.

Especially not when Grant was telling him it couldn't happen again, in that emphatic, declarative tone.

Like he was both saying it *and* meaning it.

Ugh.

"I don't want you to ever have to choose, though, between football and uh . . ." Grant hesitated again. "Whatever this is." He waved in the air between them. "So this is me saying this isn't happening."

"Because you own this team?" Deacon repeated it and tried not to sound incredulous, but that happened anyway.

Grant gave a sharp nod.

"Then why do we keep doing *this?*" And *that* sounded actually wrenched out of him, as he took a step closer and then two steps and then three until he was practically right on top of Grant.

Watched as his eyes dilated in the fluorescent light of the bathroom.

He was in a dark blue button-up shirt, which made his eyes look like an ocean, fathoms deep.

Why did they keep doing this?

Because they couldn't stop themselves.

Because *he* couldn't stop *himself.*

When Carter had sent that text, inviting him to the victory party at the Pirate's Booty the night after Thanksgiving, Grant had argued with himself a hundred times and come up with a hundred different conclusions.

He shouldn't go. It was inappropriate.

But then Carter had texted him again, convincing him that it was actually *more* inappropriate to skip the gathering.

So he'd come, thinking that if he had a chance he'd tell Deacon that last night had been a mistake. No doubt Deacon would already be on the same page but saying it clearly would reemphasize the line that they never should've crossed.

Except that it backfired.

Because Deacon was right there, in his space, smelling so good and looking so good, and suddenly it was so much harder to remember why they were such a catastrophically bad idea.

"Then why do we keep doing *this*?" Deacon asked, and he sounded just about as wretched and desperate as Grant felt.

"I don't know," Grant said. No closer to answers than he'd been last night. Why *did* this keep happening? Why did it feel like fate, so inevitable that they were powerless to fight the surge of it?

Maybe he should've been more jealous of Nate, cuddled up next to Deacon like he was more than just his friend, but it was hard to be jealous when Deacon was literally drinking his preferred beverage. All because that bartender with the crazy ability had said he should.

"Yes, you do," Deacon argued. "It's why I let that kid flirt with me. It's why I try not to look directly at the husbands. It's why you came here tonight, no matter what persuasive logic Carter used."

Grant sighed.

"What do you want me to say?" he asked, resigned. "I told you last night, yeah, I wish things were different. But they're not. I'm still having these fucking calls each week with the commissioner's office. They didn't come out and say it, but they *weren't* happy about all those pictures and stories that came out of Vegas, when Beck and Micah got married. It looked *bad*, according to Cheryl."

He hadn't wanted to tell Deacon this.

Sure, they were partners, but Deacon was a player, while Grant *owned* this team. Had bet his entire financial future on it, no matter how sunny a prospect it looked now. And would continue to pin everything on it next year and next year and the year after, long after Deacon retired.

Everything he'd put on the line for Deacon's reputation. For his own reputation and for the Condors' reputation. If they did something about this, Deacon wouldn't be the only one who paid the price.

It would be both of them, over and over again.

And everyone he was responsible for, the people whose salaries he paid, the money that made it possible for them to put roofs over their heads and food on the table for their families.

Only once had he been forced to make layoffs at InTech, because he'd recklessly, in his fourth year, authorized an aggressive expansion that had backfired. They'd grown, but not that fast. He hadn't slept for a week. Had thrown up in his office bathroom after being forced to announce the ten percent workforce reduction.

After that, he'd vowed never to ever, *ever* compromise any of his businesses—but more importantly, his employees—like that ever again.

Buying the Condors had been a risk, but he'd made one hundred percent sure that if the team failed, it wouldn't ever come back to InTech.

"What?" Deacon's eyes went wide, and he looked downright shocked. "They said that? Who's Cheryl?"

"Cheryl Smith. She's my liaison with the commissioner's office." Grant tried to keep his voice steady.

"She didn't like that Micah and Beck got married—"

Grant interrupted him, before Deacon could get a full head of steam going on his angry rant. "No," he corrected. "No, she didn't mind that. She minded *how* they did it."

"Oh."

Deacon's fists unclenched and then clenched again, slowly.

It was easier to look at them than to look at Deacon's face. Especially as he let both of their hopes down as softly as he could. "That's why we can't do this. They've got us under a microscope. Do we want to be the Riptide? The Piranhas, someday? Yeah, we do. But they've got established ownership. They didn't drag the NFL through the mud, first."

"You shouldn't be paying for that." Deacon still sounded outraged.

"No," Grant agreed.

But he was. He'd known it was part of the deal when he'd bought the Condors.

At the time, he'd believed it was a fair-ish trade-off.

He wasn't so sure, anymore, but it was too late to turn back now.

He chanced a look upwards. Deacon was still too close, his dark eyes intent on Grant's. "You knew all this when you bought the team. When you convinced me to come back," Deacon said. They might've sounded a little like questions, but Grant knew the truth.

He nodded.

"God," Deacon said, and his voice was rough, wrenched from his throat. "I . . .I . . ."

Grant didn't know what he was trying to say. Knew what he *wanted* Deacon to be trying to say, even though he didn't think he could stand here and hear it.

That he'd hoped that maybe once this season was over, and Deacon was an ex-player, they could do something about this. But it could never happen.

Maybe it was that Grant was always beating his head against the *shoulds* or the *can'ts*. Maybe it was the finality of it that broke his brain. Or maybe it was actually the sanest thing he'd done since March. Depending on his point of view.

He kissed Deacon.

Reached up and just *took*. Pressed their lips together, curled his fingers around Deacon's neck, and for a brief, entirely delirious, moment kissed him.

He'd just got done saying all the reasons why they couldn't do this, and then he'd gone and done it anyway.

Grant wanted to laugh hysterically, even as the heat of the kiss blasted through him.

He'd always wanted to know what Deacon tasted like. And now he knew. Like coffee and sugar and evergreen.

Like a gin and tonic.

But before either of them could do more than just *feel* it, for a moment and then another, Grant broke away.

He was breathing hard, but it wasn't just him, Grant far too aware of how hard Deacon's chest was rising and falling, like he'd just finished running sprints.

Grant met his eyes. He'd kissed him, after all, so he could take responsibility for it.

"I . . ." But *what* to say? *Sorry, I just needed to know what that felt like, once?*

"I get it," Deacon said, and he sounded just as resigned as Grant felt. He tipped his forehead against Grant's. "Maybe it'll be better now."

If the kiss had been *bad*, maybe it would've been.

But somehow, a taste had only whetted Grant's appetite.

He needed to get out of here before the slippery slope led him to do it again. And again. And *again*.

Grant laughed, short and unamused. "Not likely," he said.

Deacon smiled, too. "No," he said.

But there was an acceptance in his eyes now. Like he knew, just like Grant did, that this kiss, in this mostly clean bar bathroom, was the only time they'd ever get what they really wanted.

Only a fraction, but it was going to have to be enough.

Part of Grant wanted to scream in protest, but before he could say anything else, the door opened behind them and Riley walked in.

He stopped short in his tracks.

"Everything okay?" he asked.

Everything was not okay, but Grant nodded anyway.

"Sure," Deacon said. But Riley must've seen the truth in his eyes, because he put a hand on Deacon's shoulder, just a brief touch, but it meant so much more than that, Grant was sure, as Deacon walked by him to get out.

When the door swung shut behind him, Grant felt awkward. Exposed.

Sure, Riley hadn't caught them kissing, but he had to know they had been, only a moment earlier.

"I appreciate you signing me and then extending me," Riley said conversationally, heading to the row of urinals, apparently feeling no qualms whatsoever about whipping his dick out in front of the owner of his football team. "But if you break his heart, I'll kill you."

Grant's jaw dropped.

"I don't—it's not—*no*," he said emphatically. Awkwardly. God, why would the earth not rise up and swallow him whole?

Riley shot him a look as he finished and zipped up. Meandered over to the sink to wash his hands, like this was a routine, everyday conversation.

"You could, you know," Riley said softly. But the look in his eyes as he glanced over at Grant was full of heat and steel.

A reminder that Riley was not as sweet and kind as he initially seemed. That he was a Flynn, too. That he'd been forced to work twice as hard as his brother, a fact that before this moment, Grant had actually *liked* him for, because it made him such a damn good quarterback.

"I—"

But Riley didn't let him get the rest of the sentence out, even if Grant had a fucking clue what he was trying to say.

"You could, and you won't," Riley said, patted him on the shoulder, just as he had Deacon, and exited the bathroom.

Grant stared at the utilitarian tile wall, unseeing, as he tried to process what the fuck had just happened.

He knew Riley meant well. But here was the thing Riley didn't understand at all: if, somehow, he broke Deacon's heart, he was surely going to break his own, too.

CHAPTER 6

Grant lay back on the couch in his penthouse apartment, barely glancing up at the enormous television in front of him as the broadcast switched from the Piranhas game to a preview of the halftime show.

He had a ton of work to get through today. Normally on a Sunday, he was either in his suite at the Condors' stadium or he was on the road, in another team's stadium, watching his team play. But this week, they'd already played early, on Thursday, so he'd decided to stay home, not take off his sweatpants, curl up on the couch, and get some work done.

Darcy would be over in a few, and she'd said she was bringing beer and wings. They'd make a long afternoon of it, working through Darcy's latest To Do list.

For right now, though, Grant was glancing through his various email folders at the new messages that had come in overnight, and trying, desperately, not to think about the kiss.

The kiss he shouldn't have shared with Deacon.

Okay, it hadn't just been *a* kiss; it had been so much more than that. It had been *the kiss*.

The Kiss.

There was a part of him that desperately wished it had been bigger and better and more intense. Less a simple brushing of their lips and more an eager meeting of mouths. That he'd gotten to touch Deacon. That Deacon had touched him.

He couldn't even say it had been ultimately dissatisfying. It had been really, *really* nice, in fact. Just . . .not everything he wanted.

Not even close.

How had he ever thought one single kiss would be?

Grant scrubbed a hand over his face and tried to refocus on either his email—not working—or the game in front of him—not holding his interest either, even though the Toronto Thunder were playing the Piranhas hard, only down three points heading into halftime.

Aidan Flynn, Riley's older brother, was playing lights out, and they seemed to be one of the only teams in the NFL that could match the Piranhas this year.

And us, we can match them and we're gonna beat them the next time, Grant thought.

At least *that* was a better—and more productive—thought than kissing Deacon.

Grant glanced down at his phone. He'd been contemplating texting Deacon all day. And yesterday, too.

But he hadn't.

What could he even say?

They'd said everything, already.

Which was why, Grant assumed, he'd not heard a word. And why he hadn't texted Deacon either.

He groaned and forced himself to look from his phone to the TV, just in time to see Dylan Leonard, the Piranhas kicker, send the ball through the uprights, a forty-eight-yard field goal attempt to put the Piranhas up six going into halftime.

A moment later Darcy bustled in carrying a big takeout bag of food in one hand and a six-pack of hard cider in the other, her big shoulder bag slung over one arm. He could see her tablet and her laptop peeping out of the corner of it.

"You look terrible," she said, assessing him with one single penetrating look.

Like he had *Shit, I kissed Deacon Harris* written on his forehead in bright red marker.

"I haven't slept well the last two nights," Grant admitted, pushing himself up from the couch and helping Darcy arrange the food on the coffee table. She shot him a look.

"Why not?" she asked.

He probably didn't need to tell her about the kiss. She'd seen the *almost*-kiss, hadn't she? It was probably obvious, but clearly, she wanted him to tell her.

But he could be just as stubborn as Darcy.

"There's not much going on right now at InTech. Stock's up, and you solved the Singapore issue," Darcy said, ticking off items on her fingers. "As for the Condors . . .well, you won this week. You're second in the division, only to the Piranhas, who look like they're gonna take it all this year. But if you make the playoffs, which is looking pretty good, you're going to massively exceed every pre-season expectation. So why on earth aren't you sleeping?"

Grant flopped back against the couch. She definitely knew.

It wasn't even like he didn't *want* to tell her. Darcy was not just his assistant, she was also his best, closest friend.

"You know why," Grant grumped to her.

She popped the top on a bottle of hard cider and handed it to him. He took a small sip, staring unseeing at the commercials playing on the TV.

"If you end up dating Deacon, can I watch when you tell Cheryl Smith where she can stick all her 'concerns and worries'?" Darcy asked, sounding far more eager than Grant was entirely comfortable with.

"I'm not going to date Deacon, and I'm not going to tell Cheryl Smith to fuck off." But oh, he *wanted* to. On both counts.

If he had to see her perky, smug face one more week, overreacting about things that weren't really any of her concern, he was going to lose it.

She would absolutely believe the crush he couldn't help having on Deacon Harris was her *and* the NFL's business.

Of course, was it even a crush anymore? Grant was beginning to think it had to be love.

Because that was what happened when you had a crush at thirty-three. It wasn't a crush at all. It was head-over-heels, wildly-in-love.

Maybe that was why he'd thrown all caution to the wind and after detailing exactly why he couldn't be with Deacon, now or *ever*, had kissed him anyway.

And then couldn't stop thinking about it.

"Except I know how much you want to tell her to fuck off." Darcy grinned, opening her own hard cider, clinking her bottle against his. "Cheers to another week down."

"Thanks."

"You know," Darcy said, curling her feet underneath her, "I really thought this whole NFL thing was going to be a drag, but I'm feeling it. It's *fun*."

"Don't say it's because you can ogle lots of hot, nearly naked men at the height of their physical prowess," Grant said.

He didn't need any more reminders of what a prime specimen Deacon was.

"Oh, but it is. There's that, of course, but it's more than that, too. It's fun to watch us win. Terrible to lose, of course."

"Of course," Grant replied dryly. That was what he'd told her they were in for, all season. What the NFL had promised him. *Losing.*

"I know you said we'd lose, a lot, but isn't it fun to be wrong?" Darcy sounded absolutely delighted.

When it came down to it, Grant was equally delighted. It was fun to destroy everyone's expectations. He'd been doing it his whole career and yet it never got old.

"So," Darcy continued, "are you going to tell me what happened with Deacon?"

Ugh. Just when he'd been sure he'd distracted her enough.

He should know better. This was *Darcy.*

"No," Grant said testily.

"Something, or else you wouldn't be so grumpy." Darcy took a long sip of her cider. Tilted her head. "But not sex, or else you wouldn't feel about to vibrate off the couch with all this tension. So he kissed you. *Finally.*"

"Actually, I kissed him," Grant admitted.

Darcy looked even more pleased. "Did you really? Well, I didn't think you had the balls, but kudos. Was it awesome? Did the stars light up? Did you hear wedding bells clanging? Did you promise to love and cherish each other forever?"

Grant shot her a look. "I need to give you more work to do if you have the time for your imagination to be this active."

"Oh come on, this is exciting. You pining after Deacon has been one of the most entertaining parts of this whole Condors experiment. I thought you were asexual or aromantic, you dated so infrequently. But apparently, you were just waiting for the right man. For *him*. God, it's so romantic." Darcy fell back in a dramatic swoon.

"Are you done?" Grant asked, really hoping she was.

"Yes, yes, sorry. Tell me about it. What happened?" Darcy looked at him expectantly. Like whatever he said was going to be a swoon-worthy, sweet story. A sexy story, even. A story to tell his children later. A story to recite at their theoretical wedding.

"Uh, well, you know I went to the Pirate's Booty 'cause Carter invited me. I wasn't going to go, but it made *sense*, so I went."

"And because you wanted to see Deacon," Darcy interrupted.

"Okay, okay, yes, maybe a little," Grant conceded. "So, I was there, and Deacon was there, of course, and he was dancing with Nate."

Darcy looked surprised. "He was dancing *dancing* with Nate?"

Had he been? Well, kind of. Deacon hadn't seemed nearly as into it as Nate was—which made sense.

"Sort of," Grant said.

"So you got jealous. Confronted him. Oh, this is *hot*," Darcy said. He hated to burst her bubble.

"Actually," Grant said, hesitating. "It wasn't like that. He sort of . . .ran off. To the bathroom. When he saw me. And I followed him, to make sure he was okay. I didn't really want to talk about um . . .the other night, but *he* did, so I reminded him of all the reasons why we couldn't do anything about it, and then I kissed him."

"You told him why you couldn't kiss him and then you . . . kissed him?" Darcy's jaw fell open.

Grant nodded, reluctantly.

Stated like that, it sounded even less romantic than it had been in Grant's head. God, why had he done that?

Because he hadn't believed he'd have another chance.

Because he'd intended to make sure he didn't have another chance.

But now, he was left feeling . . . glad, but also disappointed. Happy, but also filled with regret.

It wasn't great.

It wasn't the epic star-crossed kind of love story Grant had hoped, for all those years, that he and Deacon might find someday.

"God, no wonder you can't sleep," Darcy said.

"Thanks," he retorted.

She leaned over the takeout containers, rooting around for a wing, chewing away on it happily. "You could always fix it."

"I don't think so," Grant said. "I was supposed to be doing the opposite of kissing him. So kissing him again sounds like . . ."

Sounds like the best idea you've ever freaking had.

"Sounds like a plan," Darcy finished for him triumphantly.

"It would be a huge mistake," Grant said firmly. Hoping he'd manage to convince both her *and* himself.

His phone rang before Darcy could continue trying to convince him, thank God. Glancing down at the screen, he realized it was Nicole, the head of PR for the Condors, calling.

He picked up. "Hey, Nic, everything alright?" Usually they spent Sundays together, but on a non-game Sunday, there would be no real reason for her to be calling him. Except for bad reasons.

His stomach sank, and he set his cider down on the coffee table.

"I just got a head's-up that there's about to be a breaking story," Nicole said, and she sounded about as concerned as Grant suddenly felt. "I can't get much out of my contact, but the rumor is, it's Rex."

"What?" That wasn't what he'd expected her to say. He'd expected that someone had seen him at the Pirate's Booty. Not seen him in the bathroom with Deacon—because he'd known the bathroom was empty when they'd kissed. But maybe someone had seen . . .*something*.

But that wasn't it at all. No, this was going to be a different kind of pain in his ass.

"Yes. I'm sorry to have to say this thing with Rex is probably going to blow up. It seems he has an axe to grind with the Condors." Nicole sighed.

Rex James had been a corner on the Condors. He'd made it through both Deacon *and* Grant's stringent vetting process for keeping players and staff. Grant had been a little hesitant—a few times he'd believed Rex was only telling him what he wanted to hear, not the truth, but he'd also needed to field a complete team of players, and Rex was a decent enough corner.

But then Rex had gotten injured, and right on the heels of that, under the influence of pain meds in the hospital, he'd inadvertently revealed that he'd been betting on NFL games.

His *own* games.

The NFL hated players who broke the rules. But there was nothing they hated more than players who broke any of the many rules about gambling.

Though really, only one mattered: that you couldn't do it, not at all, not ever.

And Rex had.

Grant had done what he could to mitigate the damage. He'd covered Rex's medical expenses but kicked him off the team. Convinced the NFL that he'd already taken care of it—though he'd been this close to telling Cheryl to fuck off, for real this time.

But they'd gotten through it. They'd traded for Micah Rose, from the Piranhas, reuniting him with his college teammate, Beckett West, and not only had their on-field relationship flourished, solidifying the Condors' secondary, but they'd finally sorted out all their personal issues. Culminating, of course, in something else Cheryl hadn't liked: their impromptu Vegas marriage.

"I'm assuming," Grant said, "that anything he has to say ranges from likely suspect to completely fabricated."

"I'm sure of it. You did more for Rex and his family than you were certainly required to do. He couldn't have any complaint about that, not when he was breaking the rules. But we'll know more when his interview comes out."

Darcy made a strange noise next to him, half-shock, half-panic, and he glanced up at the TV. There was Rex, his handsome face creased in concerned lines, as he no doubt unloaded a whole bunch of lies about the Condors organization.

Just what he fucking needed, now that things had *finally* evened out, and they were not only winning, but contending for a playoff berth.

"He's on now," Grant said with resignation as he glanced up at the TV.

Darcy unmuted the sound, and Grant put Nicole on speakerphone.

They listened to Rex rant and rave about how he'd been shoved under the bus to hide all of Grant's "indiscretions."

Darcy sighed, heavily, as the interview went to a commercial break. It was all lies, of course, and even the other announcers hadn't seemed particularly convinced by Rex's assertions, but the point was that they were out there now.

This was all anyone was going to be talking about.

"Find out more," Grant told Nicole. "I want to know what else he's going to say. Whatever it is, we need to get ahead of it."

"Got it," Nicole said.

"And I'm sure I'm going to be fielding a call from Cheryl, any time now."

Darcy lifted her phone, buzzing in her hand, and yep, there was Cheryl's name on the screen.

"Scratch that. She's calling now," Grant said, shifting automatically into disaster-control mode. "Do you have any objections to me taking drastic measures to control this with the commissioner's office?"

Nicole hesitated for a moment. "What kind of drastic measures?"

"Like sending them all hard drives from the admin side of the team. My drives. Darcy's drives. Everyone who's involved business-wise. Let them dig around, if they want. I don't have anything to hide, and I'm tired of having to defend ourselves every month. Let's just get everything out in the open. Let them read every single damn thing, if they want."

"If you've got nothing to hide, then I don't see the harm," Nicole said. "I'll put it out, too, that you're taking that step. It'll go a long way to proving that there's no more skeletons in the Condors' closet. A guilty man wouldn't give someone the noose to hang him."

"Exactly," Grant said, glad they were on the same page.

"Be in touch," Nicole said and hung up.

Grant picked up the remote to mute the TV, but then changed his mind. Listening to Rex lie made him sick to his stomach, but he hadn't gotten to where he was by ignoring what he didn't want to hear.

"You'd really do that?" Darcy asked as they listened to the interviewer question Rex about his gambling addiction.

Addiction, my ass, Grant thought with heat. Rex hadn't been addicted to gambling, and it was insulting to everyone who was to spout that as an excuse.

"I would," Grant said, nodding.

The interview wrapped up, but clearly Rex was holding a few things back because he insinuated there was more *and* a tell-all book coming later this year.

"I know you've got nothing to worry about, but do you really think opening up all our files is going to stop the commissioner from opening a full-blown investigation?" Darcy sounded concerned.

"I don't know," Grant admitted. "But I'm going to call Cheryl back."

"Don't tell her to fuck off," Darcy warned.

Grant shot her a look. "Did you really think I would?"

"No, but I know she works your last nerve. God knows, she works *mine*."

"I got this," Grant reassured her as he dialed Cheryl's number.

His conversation with her was short and sweet and to the point.

She'd have the hard drives by tomorrow morning—but Grant was only offering it if they could make their copies and get the drives back by Tuesday morning, because they'd need them to prepare for next week's game against the Steelers.

Cheryl reassured him that it would be done, and Grant hung up, feeling like he'd done everything he could to get ahead of the ugliness of this story.

Sure, the media would probably drag them through the mud—though Nic was right, and if his offer of the Condors' hard drives just happened to leak to a few select reporters, it *would* go a long way to exonerating him and the rest of the team, too—but the NFL wouldn't cause them any more problems, and that was Grant's main concern.

They'd just have to block out the remaining media speculation. Not easy, but doable.

"You don't think this could possibly come back and bite you in the ass?" Darcy asked, tucking a strand of hair behind her ear after Grant set his phone down.

"If it does, then it bites us in the ass. I don't see another way to make sure everyone who matters knows we're innocent of whatever bullshit Rex is accusing us of."

"Accusing *you* of," Darcy reminded him.

Oh yeah. That had really been the topper on the whole mess.

Rex had insinuated that he'd been gambling and cheating because Grant had asked him to.

"The good news is that's easy to disprove," Grant said. "Especially if we're transparent."

"If you're sure," Darcy said, sounding unusually unsure.

It suddenly occurred to him what Darcy was nervous about. "You think they're gonna find out about Deacon," he said.

Darcy nodded. "I know we haven't exactly been exchanging gossipy notes about it in the office, but what if someone said something?"

"Then someone said something," Grant said inexorably. Though he doubted anyone would. They had a football team to run; they shouldn't have time to gossip. Besides, what did they even have to say that the NFL didn't already know?

That the rest of the players called him Mr. G, and only Deacon referred to him as Grant? The NFL *knew* they'd been friendly in college, and it was easy enough to use as an excuse. Grant had disclosed that fact when he'd first made overtures about buying the team. The rest of it was mere gossip and rumor, and easy to disprove.

After all, that bathroom at the Pirate's Booty had been empty.

But more important, more important than *anything else*, Grant needed the NFL to know that whatever shit Rex was spouting was just that: total bullshit.

"Alright," Darcy said. "Do we need to do any more damage control or we set for now?"

"We'll need to go over to the offices. Get the drives together. Overnight them to the commissioner's office."

"Even better, I'll fly them there on the jet. Wait for them to copy them and then come back with them," Darcy said. "Let me just clear my schedule."

"Good." It was a typical Darcy suggestion—cutting out the difficulties of other people and going directly to the source.

One of many reasons she was such a valuable employee.

And a valuable friend.

"Finish your wings," Darcy ordered him. "God knows without me here to harass you, you'll forget to eat."

Grant obeyed because eating the wings killed two birds with one stone: *one*, he ate something, because just like Darcy said, when he was caught up in something he often forgot to do that, and *two*, because his fingers were messy, so for at least fifteen minutes, he couldn't look at his phone and see if Deacon had texted.

About this mess.

Or about the kiss.

But of course, when he finally finished eating and washed his hands in the bathroom, his phone was full of messages, emails, and missed calls. He'd need to put out a statement to the team, immediately. He could draft that after he'd helped Darcy gather the hard drives.

But after sorting through the avalanche of notifications, Grant realized Deacon was still silent.

Shit.

Deacon was pretty sure he was going out of his mind.

"Don't do it, he's got his hands full with this Rex bullshit," Beck said very reasonably as Deacon paced across their patio.

"Yeah," Micah echoed.

"What if someone had told you that you couldn't do a goddamn thing to help *him*," Deacon said, pointing right at Beck's husband. Micah held up his hands in mock surrender.

"But I don't need Beck's help," Micah pointed out.

"Yeah, not his *help*, maybe," Deacon grumbled.

Grant had just sent out a statement to the whole team and staff on the Rex situation. They'd all seen the interview, of course. It was impossible to be on any fucking channel even tangentially related to sports and *not* see it, flashing across the bottom of the screen.

It made Deacon fucking sick.

He knew Rex was a liar. And it was bad enough he was lying about the Condors. But lying about Grant?

It made Deacon want to demolish his face.

Grant had made it clear he had this taken care of, and he'd gone into brief detail about what steps he was taking to remedy the situation. All the admin personnel would be having their hard drives copied, minus any sensitive personal information, and sent to the NFL offices so they could exonerate themselves, once and for all.

Beck might be right; Grant *might* have everything under control.

But Deacon couldn't just stand by and do nothing, either.

Especially not after . . .Deacon clenched his fists.

Especially not after Grant kissed him.

Especially not after Grant's kiss had brought him so much clarity on his own feelings.

This wasn't a crush.

This was so much more than that.

This was *I'd do anything for him.*

"I'm just saying," Beck said, "sit down. Hang out. We're gonna grill out later. You don't need to go down there and create more problems for him."

"How is me making sure he's okay—that the *team* is okay—creating more problems for Grant?"

Beck and Micah exchanged knowing glances.

"What?" he barked.

"I'm just saying . . .you charging in there like his knight in shining armor—"

"Like you *love* him," Micah added and Deacon made a face.

"—is only gonna look like . . .like maybe there's another story, there, too," Beck finished.

He hadn't told them about the kiss. He hadn't told *anyone* about the kiss. Even Jem.

How could he? He didn't have a fucking clue what it meant when someone detailed all the reasons why they shouldn't kiss you—why they *wouldn't* be kissing you—and then kissed you, anyway.

"I don't . . ." Deacon took a deep breath. He couldn't say he didn't love Grant. It might be a lie. The truth was somewhere nearer to: *I don't know what the fuck I do feel.*

No, that wasn't right either.

It was more like, *I'm terrified of what I might feel.*

"It's okay," Beck said, dislodging Micah from his side and stepping over to where Deacon was pacing. He put a hand on Deacon's arm. "It's really okay. We get it."

Deacon could see the wildness—the utter panic—in his expression reflected in the concern in Beck's eyes. "Do you?" he retorted.

"Well, yeah," Beck said. "What did you tell me about Micah?"

Deacon laughed shortly. "I don't remember what the hell I said to you. Whatever you needed to hear."

"It's okay to care about him," Beck said carefully.

"Is it though?" Deacon heard how bitter he sounded. "It's not like it's going anywhere, no matter how I do feel."

"How do you know that? Because *I* thought that," Micah said.

Deacon didn't roll his eyes but it was a close thing. "Just because you told yourself Beck wouldn't forgive you. And because you didn't think you could actually date a guy."

"He might not have forgiven me," Micah said bluntly. "And no, I didn't think I could—though by the time I came here to Charleston, I was as ready as I'd ever be. But I thought it was too late. Too late for me. Too late for us."

Beck glanced over at him, and Deacon ached at the look the two of them exchanged.

He wasn't jealous of them.

It was something more than mere envy, something hard and painful lodged in his stomach.

"But you know what I didn't do? I didn't fucking give up," Micah continued.

"It's true," Beck said. "He wouldn't quit. He kept trying to talk to me. To hang out with me. To make it up to me."

"And it worked," Micah said.

"Yeah, yeah, we all know. You're the most fucking married couple of all time," Deacon grumbled.

"What we're trying to say is that we *weren't*, not at first. Not for a long time. And you *know* that."

"What *are* you trying to say?" Deacon asked. "Like real concrete fucking advice."

"You want him?" Micah's face made it clear that the question was only hypothetical. Everyone knew he wanted him. Everyone knew they wanted *each other*.

Deacon pressed his lips together. Nodded. It was pointless continuing to deny it.

"Then go get him."

"But—" Deacon argued.

"No," Beck interrupted him. "Is he a genius or isn't he?"

"You know he is." Deacon wished that big brain of Grant's made him less attractive, but it was actually the opposite. He was so goddamned attracted not to just the parts of him, but to the whole package.

He'd thought his crush in college had been consuming enough, but it was nothing compared to how much he just straight up *liked* Grant now, now that he knew him. Now that they were friends.

Now that they were partners.

"And you're hardly a slouch," Micah said. "Figure it out, but do it together. That's my advice. *Talk* to each other."

"I thought you told me *not* to go there," Deacon complained. "Beck was just telling me not go charging in there."

"Yeah, and I meant it. Don't go charging in there, blustering around about fucking saving him. He can save himself, can't he?"

"Maybe," Deacon said grudgingly. Though that was not entirely true, either. Grant could absolutely save himself.

"So *help* him. Don't just show up and expect to solve everything. That's all I was saying." Beck sounded so fucking reasonable; Deacon *hated* it.

"Alright," Deacon said, though he didn't know what that looked like.

The one thing about the last few years, the crucible the entire Condors organization had suffered through, was that it had honed all his instincts to take charge and to fix everything.

Why else had he been sure he wanted to leave?

Because he'd known he'd never be able to really fix what was broken.

He'd turned himself inside out trying, and when Grant had come on the scene, he'd finally given up.

But Grant had convinced him not to give up. To trust him. To become his partner.

They'd done it with football—but could they do it with . . .everything else?

CHAPTER 7

Deacon knew where he'd find him, when he showed up at the facility, early the next day.

It was still dark outside, but he'd waited long enough to give Grant the chance to resolve some of the mess on his own. Now it was time for him to step up.

To make his *own* feelings clear.

When he walked into the office Grant had claimed as his own, he wasn't surprised to see Grant already sitting here.

But he wasn't sitting upright. His head was on the desk, his dark hair mussed, and he was snoring away.

Deacon stopped in his tracks.

Had he been here all night? How often did he sleep like this at his desk? Deacon felt a pulse of serious concern. He could ask Darcy, but suddenly, he wasn't sure if she would tell him the truth, or if she'd cover for Grant, who was clearly working way too hard.

But before he could turn back around and come back later, maybe much later tonight, when all the coaches and players had finally cleared out of the building—nobody else needed to be here for this conversation; that was the *only* thing Deacon knew for sure—Grant raised his head, opening his eyes.

He jolted a little when he saw Deacon standing there.

"Oh, uh, hi," Grant said, pulling himself upright, running a hand through his hair.

"Hi," Deacon said.

This was the first time they'd been in the same room since the bathroom.

Deacon felt the jolt of knowledge that *he'd kissed him* jump-start his pulse.

He took a step closer and then another.

Close enough that he could see Grant was still in a pair of gray sweatpants.

"Sorry, uh, did we have a meeting this morning?" Grant asked, scrubbing a hand over his face.

"No," Deacon said. He set his hip on the corner of the big wooden desk. "I came by to talk to you."

"About . . ." Grant trailed off, and then Deacon watched as his brain finished waking up and he remembered what had happened yesterday.

Rex and all his bullshit "revelations."

"Right," Grant said. "God, that happened, didn't it?"

"Yeah, it happened. And I thought I'd come by and say, whatever you need, however you need me, I'm here."

For you.

Deacon didn't say it, but hoped that Grant would hear it, anyway.

Maybe Beck and Micah were right, and he needed to fight for Grant. Fight his certainty that they couldn't get involved. Convince him that they had something strong enough, something with enough potential, that it was wrong to continue pretending it wasn't anything at all.

But he couldn't just come out swinging.

Grant would shut down before he got half a dozen words out.

"I don't know what you'd do to help," Grant said wryly, leaning back in his chair.

There was a faint imprint of the wood grain of the desk on his cheek. His hair was messier than Deacon had ever seen it—except in his imagination. Deacon's heart clenched. He *did* want Grant. More than anything else. Like nobody else.

"*Anything,*" Deacon said. "You need me to talk to the media, make a statement—"

"You hate doing that," Grant interrupted, the corner of his mouth tilting into a smile.

You kissed that mouth. Only two days ago.

It hadn't been anything like the kisses he'd dreamed they'd share, in that faraway future when it wasn't a distraction or against the spoken and unspoken rules. But it had *still* been a kiss.

"I do, but I'd do it, if you needed me to," Deacon said. He *vowed.* He could hear it in his voice. *I'm trying to tell you something, and you're not understanding it. You've got this huge ass brain, but you still don't get it.*

"I'd do more," Deacon continued, because he *needed* Grant to understand. "I'd . . .I don't know . . .I'd stand by you, at your side, if that's what you needed. I'd . . .I'd be more than just your captain, your partner. I'd be your *everything,* if you needed me to be that. I'd . . ." It sounded crazy. *He* sounded crazy. Wild. All the things that Beck had warned him not to do.

The problem was he'd shown up and Grant had been sleeping at his desk, and it had unwound something in him that he'd always kept so tightly chained.

For a fucking reason.

Grant's expression was already shutting down.

"You don't need me," Deacon said, the realization hitting him like a ton of bricks. Suddenly, he was so empty. All that fight, all that need, just drained right out of him.

No—that wasn't true.

The fight was gone, but the need was still there, pulsing deep inside him. Inexorably alive, because nothing seemed to kill it.

Not impersonal emails.

Not twelve years of silence.

Not even too-brief kisses in bar bathrooms.

"I don't know if that's true," Grant said carefully, but it was clear he was getting ready to brush him off.

He'd done it in the bathroom too—ironically, *right* before he'd made it impossible for Deacon to ever get over this—but Deacon could only remember one piece of advice now.

Blaring loudly in his brain.

Fight for him.

He didn't think any more.

He'd done way too much thinking. *Both* of them had.

He was off the desk in a second, and in the next, his arms were around Grant. He was more solid than Deacon had imagined. Not just unbreakable in mind, but unbreakable in body, too. And after winding his fingers around his shoulders, around his waist, he leaned down and kissed him, the way he should've kissed him in the bathroom.

Grant melted into him like he was a fire, and immediately, instantaneously, this kiss was different.

The kiss in the bathroom had been hesitant and regretful—but not this one.

Deacon poured all his need into it, all the want he'd never been able to forget, and one of them—Deacon thought it might be him—groaned as he pressed them into the desk. Grant's hands dug into his hair, into his scalp, tilting his mouth at a better angle as his tongue slipped into it.

Grant's clear and obvious desire was all it took for him to be hard as a rock.

It was one thing to know Grant wanted him, and another entirely to feel Grant's fingertips digging into his shoulders, his tongue brushing eagerly into Deacon's mouth, the way his body plastered against Deacon's own.

He hadn't thought past, *fight for Grant* and *you need to kiss him now, like you mean it this time*, and now he couldn't think at all.

Deacon's hands slid down his back, reveling in the feel of him. He didn't even hesitate, he gripped Grant's hip with one hand and his surprisingly curvy ass with the other and pressed him even closer against the desk. In this moment, Grant wasn't his team's owner. He wasn't even his statistics tutor. He was just a man, same as Deacon.

Grant mumbled against his mouth. Deacon wasn't sure what he said. Hoped it was, *more, now, please.* He could do more. He could do it now. And Grant didn't even have to ask—though begging could be fun.

"I'm going to need to start coming in here with a bullhorn, aren't I?"

Deacon sprang back at the sound of the amused voice.

Grant was panting hard, eyes dilated and hair even messier than it had been a moment ago.

Shit.

There was nothing Deacon wanted more than to dive back in.

Without interruptions.

He glanced up at Darcy, who didn't look offended or perturbed, only amused.

"Yes, definitely a bullhorn," she repeated, tilting her head as she looked at them.

"I . . .ah . . ." Words were never Deacon's strong suit. Exactly why he'd just relied on *action*.

But Darcy just laughed. "Are you two done?"

Grant cleared his throat. Gave Deacon a look that said, *we need to talk about this, but not now, definitely not now.* "Yes," he said firmly. "I'm going to get dressed and . . ." He waved in Deacon's direction. "I'm sure you have . . .uh . . .somewhere you need to be."

He did have somewhere he *needed* to be. In a bed, with Grant wrapped around him. *Naked.*

"Um, yeah, sure. Yes."

"Do I need to give you two a moment?" Darcy was still laughing.

"No," Grant said, and Deacon watched as he pulled himself together the rest of the way, managing to look dignified even with hair messed up from Deacon's hands, lips red and wet from kissing, and an obvious hard-on in his sweatpants.

"Alright," Darcy said. "I'll just be in my office. Call me when you're ready for the day, Grant."

"Do you have—" Grant asked Darcy even though he was still staring intently at Deacon.

"Yes," she finished. Then Darcy turned and walked out.

Leaving them alone again.

"I was going to tell you that there wasn't anything for you to do, because I already did it. I sent all our hard drives to the commissioner's office. They copied them overnight, and Darcy brought them back. As proof, for them, that we didn't do anything Rex said we did."

"You sent all the hard drives? Like the Condors' computers?" Deacon asked.

Grant nodded. "From the admin side, yeah. They would've wanted them eventually. But this way, by volunteering them, hopefully we can get some good PR in the press, nip the stories in the bud before they become an avalanche."

"You're not worried—"

Grant's expression morphed into shock. "You think I've got something to hide?"

Deacon remembered how he'd asked, only a few months back, if he trusted him. Realized that for Grant, his trust was a precious, important thing.

"No, no, of course you don't. But you don't think anyone else does?" Deacon wanted to touch him again, to reassure him, or else that was the lie he told himself, but he knew if he did, he wouldn't stop at a single touch.

No matter how much he wanted to fight for Grant and wanted to love him the way he deserved, he knew it was wrong to do this here.

In his office. In this building.

"No," Grant said. "And I'm betting my ownership of this team on it."

Deacon nodded. "Alright. We need to talk—"

Grant raised an eyebrow and he lost his train of thought.

"We *do*," he repeated. "Just talk. I mean not that I would mind . . ." He was unsure if he should even *say* what he wouldn't mind here, in this office.

You were ready to do *it in this office, before Darcy walked in.*

"Yes," Grant said. "But this week is crazy busy. I don't know when I'll have a free second."

Deacon could tell he was pushing him away. Cold-shouldering him. Even after that kiss. When it was absolutely fucking clear just how much Grant wanted him.

"No," Deacon said.

Grant eyed him steadily. This was CEO Grant. Grant who faced down a whole boardroom out for his throat.

It wasn't like Deacon couldn't hold his own—he *could*—but Grant had never looked at *him* like this. Like he was something he needed to fight against. Like he was the enemy.

"I'm sure *both* of us are busy this week." Grant's voice was still conversational, and yet Deacon wanted to put his fist through the wall, anyway.

That's not fighting for him. That's just fighting him. Beck's voice echoed in his head and kept him from losing his temper entirely.

"Not too busy to discuss this," Deacon ground out.

"There isn't anything to discuss," Grant said. He looked like butter wouldn't melt in his mouth, but he was lying.

Deacon knew it. Grant knew it. Even Darcy probably knew it.

"That's bullshit. We have something. We *are* something," Deacon argued.

But Grant was implacable. "I told you the other night, this *can't* happen. The commissioner's got a freaking microscope on us. I'm not going to burn this all down because I have a . . .a . . ." He hesitated.

"A hard-on? Because you did. So did I." Deacon knew how bitter he sounded. "Of course, if that's all it is for you." That wasn't all it was for him. Didn't think it was for Grant, either, but what did he know anymore?

There had to be a reason Grant kept pushing him away like this.

Maybe it was the commissioner's office, but maybe it was something else.

Deacon looked away because it hurt too much to look at him like this. At Grant rejecting him like this.

When Beck had told him to fight for Grant, he hadn't imagined how hard it might be.

"You know it isn't," Grant said, and when Deacon glanced up, the sternness in his eyes had melted away, but not to love. To regret. "I'm sorry, I know I keep giving you mixed signals, but it's true. We *can't*. I can't, specifically. But I do hope we can stay friends."

He was trying to be nice. Deacon knew it, and his temper flared anyway.

"We've never been friends," he said and meant it.

Hated it, as pain flashed across Grant's face, right before he turned and walked away.

Chapter 8

It was a terrible week.

Exhausting and busy and full not only of the self-recriminations Grant couldn't seem to stop, but a hundred—maybe even a thousand—reminders of Deacon.

Every time he looked at his desk, he remembered how the edge of it had dug into his thighs, just as Deacon's fingers had dug into his hips, his ass.

Remembered just the way Deacon had tasted.

How good it had felt, for the single moment when he'd actually let himself enjoy it.

But then he always forced himself to look at his laptop, at the placard at the front of his desk. Reminders that he was responsible for more than just himself.

That he couldn't make selfish decisions.

He'd had half a dozen conference calls with the commissioner's office, as they'd waded through all the hard drive data Grant had sent them.

Each day seemed to be worse than the previous one.

He hadn't even had time to look outside the windows. Knew if he did, he'd see Deacon looking equally pissed off, destroying anything and everyone in his path.

Every time he entered a room, he heard the whispers of how single-focused Deacon was on the field, these days. How hard he kept pushing himself—and everyone else on the defense.

And every time he felt sick with guilt, because he knew it was his fault.

If he hadn't kissed Deacon first, Deacon never would've kissed him back, and maybe Grant could have avoided saying those things to him.

No, it was always coming, from the very beginning. You were stupid as shit to think you could avoid it forever.

Maybe. Maybe that was true.

But in moments like this one, it was a little bit of a cold comfort.

"Cheryl, we'll have to consider that," Darcy spoke up, and Grant was vaguely aware that she'd probably just asked him a question that he'd ignored because it was better to do that than to tell her to fuck off.

"The commissioner is just tired of having to continually vet your organization," Cheryl said. "It always seems to be in the news. The understanding when you bought the team, Mr. Green, was that it would stay *out* of the news."

"Except that ticket sales are up, probably because we can't stay out of the news," Darcy said, and normally Grant might be amused at the way she bared her teeth at the speaker in the center of the conference room table.

But he couldn't dredge up even a molecule of amusement.

Not this week.

"Everyone's just curious, right now," Cheryl said. "Nobody is sure if you're going to host a carnival or a football game."

Grant had been letting Darcy handle Cheryl for the first ten minutes of this conversation, but he was done letting her cover for him. Done playing nice. "Cheryl," he said, leaning forward, elbows resting on the hard surface of the table, "now that's just not true, and you know it."

She spluttered across the line, but Grant didn't let her retrench.

"We're selling tickets because we're seven and four, and we're playing for a playoff spot. That's why," he continued.

"It might be why," Cheryl said guardedly.

"It's why," Grant retorted in a steel-edged voice.

"So, the constant stories about the happenings on your team don't have anything to do with it? Signing *Riley Flynn* and making him your starting quarterback? Landry Banks running onto the field in the middle of a game to make sure he's not hurt and then practically kissing him on the sideline? Your secondary getting *married* in Las Vegas? Your star receiver becoming a one-man party or a one-man wrecking ball, depending on his mood?"

Grant grimaced. It wasn't like other teams didn't have unusual occurrences. They did. But it did sure feel like the Condors had more than their fair share of them. It felt like he couldn't go a single fucking week without having to put out a fire.

And those were only the fires the NFL knew about.

He could only imagine how Cheryl could've finished her list, if she'd heard about the kiss in the Pirate's Booty bathroom—or the kiss he and Deacon had shared only a few dozen feet away, in his office.

Grant dragged his attention back to Cheryl.

Where it didn't want to stay.

"And yet, Cheryl, we're still winning. Isn't that what the NFL prizes above all else? *Winning*?"

Cheryl sniffed, wordlessly.

"And we're going to keep winning," Darcy added, looking like she wanted to reach through the speaker in front of them and strangle Cheryl herself.

"We'll see about that," Cheryl said.

"What about the hard drives?" Grant pushed.

"It's been less than a week since we got them, *and* you made it clear they're only copies—"

"And yet," Grant interrupted, "I didn't expect you to need so much time to go through them. I've only owned this team for six months, Cheryl."

"And I thought I'd just made it clear *what* a six months it's been," Cheryl reminded him, her smug tone obnoxious.

Deacon had looked at him incredulously when he'd told him he hoped they could be friends.

Maybe if he'd been listening in to his meetings with Cheryl since buying the Condors, he wouldn't be so surprised at Grant's insistence they keep things *only* platonic.

"You did," Grant said steadily. Trying to keep his temper.

You gave up a chance for happiness for this. For Cheryl and her patronizing attitude and her admonitions and her restrictions.

But he'd given it up for more than this, too. He'd given it up for the way Riley and Landry looked at each other when they thought nobody else was looking. For how Beck and Micah played like one person on the field. For the happy, calm glow in Carter's eyes. The giddiness in every single player's face when the Condors won, against all the odds.

He'd done it for all those things, too.

When Grant figured those things in, it *did* feel worth it. Just barely.

"We're almost done with your files. We're just making one more pass," Cheryl said.

"Why?" Darcy asked, because she clearly couldn't help herself. "You haven't found anything. We're clean, and you know it. And I think it kinda kills you that we are."

Grant looked over at her swiftly. She mouthed *I'm sorry*, but she didn't exactly look sorry.

"Ms. Jackson, I'm not sure what you're trying to insinuate," Cheryl said.

"We're just ready to have all our files back under our own roof," Grant added smoothly.

"And they will be soon," Cheryl promised.

But as far as Grant was concerned, her promises didn't carry much weight. She kept saying, over and over again, that these pleasant chats might occur less frequently, but then something always happened to change her mind.

Grant hadn't held it against his players, because their happiness and safety was the most important, but he would be really fucking glad when he didn't have to talk to the commissioner's office multiple times a week.

"We need to leave for Pittsburgh," Darcy said tightly. "Mr. Green's plane is waiting for him."

"Of course. Good luck this weekend, against the Steelers." Cheryl's sniff at the end of her sentence made it clear what she thought of their chances.

Grant thought their chances were pretty damn good, as long as Deacon continued to play like a man possessed.

"God, she's the worst," Darcy said, after she'd disconnected the call. "I'm sorry I lost my temper, but she was being so . . .goddamned pretentious. Like *she's* the freaking commissioner. Like we asked for this. Like we aren't the victims here, it's *Rex.*"

"I know," Grant said. He put a hand on Darcy's shoulder. "It's alright. You just said what I was already thinking."

"Yes, but pushing back on her doesn't seem to fix anything." Darcy sounded as frustrated as he felt.

"No, it doesn't." *It doesn't fix my broken heart, either. Or the fact that I had to break it myself.*

Because that was what this had to be, right?

Only a broken heart could feel this wretched.

Grant had felt *horrible* twelve years ago, when he'd left school and stopped tutoring Deacon—but this was so much worse.

Like all he wanted to do was huddle in the corner with his hands over his head, blocking out the world, so he'd just stop *feeling* all the imaginary rocks thrown at his head.

He'd be feeling very sorry for himself, except for the fact that he knew who was throwing the rocks.

Himself.

"Are you ready to go?" Darcy asked, changing the subject.

At first, she'd tried to talk to him about Deacon. But he'd refused to engage with her about it. Refused to discuss it, in any way or form. Changed the subject whenever she brought it up.

The worst of it was that she hadn't even looked angry when he'd shut her down, only sympathetic, and the sad look in her eyes had burned him, deep down.

"Yes," Grant said, nodding.

"Good."

Less than five minutes later, they were in the car heading to the airport, where Grant's jet was indeed waiting.

The rest of the team had headed to Pittsburgh yesterday, on the team plane. But he'd had too much to do to travel with them, so he'd made the executive decision to stay in Charleston and get another twelve or so hours of work done.

And, that annoying inner voice teased him with, *because you were afraid if you went to Pittsburgh yesterday, you'd find a reason to be alone with Deacon. It would be so easy, and then you'd*

. . .

Not kiss him again, that was for damn sure.

But he'd have *wanted* to.

Darcy settled on the seat opposite him. In her normal spot when they traveled together. "Are we going to talk about it?" she asked after the flight attendant, Benjamin, brought them their normal flight beverages—gin and tonic for Grant and a limoncello spritz for Darcy.

"Talk about what?" He might pretend he didn't know what Darcy was asking about it, but he knew better. "How you lost your shit with Cheryl, earlier?"

"No, how you've been in the worst mood I've seen since you hired me," Darcy said steadily.

"I've not been," Grant argued, even though he knew she was probably right. She'd been by his side for all those years, so if anybody would know, it would be Darcy.

She shot him a look. Okay, she *did* know.

"I'll get over it," Grant said, taking a sip of his drink, setting it into the side console, reaching for his bag for the laptop he'd stowed there. He could get some work done, in the next two hours, at least.

"No," Darcy said and grabbed the bag and held it before he could use it as a deflection or a subject change. "No, you don't get to do this. I know you don't want to talk to me about it, but you *need* to."

"Why? What does talking about it change?" Grant demanded, feeling his temper spike unexpectedly. Why was she pushing this?

Darcy didn't let go of the bag, even as he tugged at it, and her brown eyes regarded him steadily. Sympathetically, even. And that stung, even worse, somehow, than his own self-pity.

"I've worked for you, for what, ten years? Eleven?" Darcy didn't let him answer the question, just kept going. "In that time, we've done a lot together. You've worked like you were on fire, like the world might burn down if you didn't, and it's paid off. But never, not once, in those eleven years, have I seen you do something impulsive. When you bought the Condors, that was crazy."

"A little," Grant admitted. It *had* been. At least there was no danger in admitting that.

"I didn't know why, why *this*, until Deacon showed up, and then it became really clear," Darcy continued. "And for the first time, you slowed down a little. Made a friend. Let yourself get distracted."

Grant didn't know whether he was supposed to be apologizing or begging forgiveness or—

Then Darcy kept talking, inexorably, like she was afraid if she stopped, he wouldn't keep listening. She wasn't entirely wrong. "And it was the best thing you've done in eleven years. Made you seem human, for the first time. It's *good* to have a life, Grant."

"It can't be with him," Grant said.

"Says who? Cheryl? The commissioner? You're a *billionaire*, Grant. You own an enormously successful business *and* a professional football team. You can do whatever you want, and if Deacon's what you want, then you should just tell the world to fuck off."

"It's not that easy, or that simple. If it was . . ."

If it was, what would he even do about it?

Sure, he'd imagined it so many times, but he'd never felt like he was in a position to *do* anything about it.

"It's exactly that simple. Did the NFL take Robert Kraft's team when he got in trouble for getting happy endings to his massages? No, they did not. Did the NFL ever say a goddamn word about Al Davis and all his weird shit? They ignored him, at worst, and at best, *celebrated* his idiosyncrasies. I'll sit through a hundred more shitty, passive-aggressive calls with Cheryl—a *thousand*—if it would mean you'd get what you want." Darcy shot him an unamused look. "But I think you're afraid of actually *getting* it. Business is easy—"

"Business is *not* easy," Grant interrupted.

But Darcy wasn't his best friend and his most trusted advisor for nothing. She never failed to give as good as she got.

"Business isn't easy, fine, but it works by rules. You learned the rules. Same as programming. You learned the rules of what was possible, and then you could break the rules, think out of the box. But you had to learn the rules first. And there are no rules, no guidelines, no safety net, with Deacon. He's a wild card, and you can't control him. You could get really hurt. There's no protection, no conservative path you can fall back to. You're *afraid*. Yeah, maybe this boss thing, it's a concern, but it shouldn't be enough to stop you from working your Grant magic and turning the situation around to your advantage. Maybe for the rest of this season, you're his boss. Maybe he continues working for the Condors, and you stay his boss. But you could work around that. I *know* you, and you've never taken no for an answer, not in your entire career. Why start now, with something you really care about?"

Grant couldn't answer that question.

No—that wasn't accurate. He *could*. There were a thousand reasons he couldn't take the risk.

But maybe she was right. Maybe all those reasons were really excuses. Maybe he was afraid.

Deacon had always been the one who got away.

Grant had stuck him in that category, had gotten comfortable with that situation.

Had used Deacon and his lingering crush as an excuse for why he couldn't date. For why he worked so much.

"I . . .I don't know," Grant answered.

Maybe he *was* afraid. But he didn't just worry about his own reputation, his own security. He worried about every single employee under him, all of whom depended on him. And Deacon. He worried about Deacon. He'd come here, to Charleston, and spent nearly a billion dollars, to make sure that nobody could ever say shit about Deacon Harris again.

And to give everyone the opportunity to do that?

To make snide, sly comments?

To insinuate he wasn't the player he was because he was *Deacon Harris*, but because he sucked Grant's dick?

He couldn't bear it. Not after all the work he'd done to guarantee otherwise.

"Exactly," Darcy said. She let go of the laptop bag. "Think about that, okay? For me, but mostly for yourself. 'Cause anyone who makes you feel this bad, they *matter*, and we don't get an unlimited number of those."

An unlimited number? Grant nearly laughed. There'd only been one, ever, who mattered the way that Deacon did.

"Noted," Grant said. Because if he told her the truth, that he'd only ever wanted Deacon in that achingly real way, she wouldn't let him just consider it. She'd intervene. Darcy's best attribute was that she fixed problems, but in this case, nobody could fix this except for Grant.

"You promise you'll really think about it?" she asked archly.

"I promise," Grant said. Because even though he didn't *want* to think about it any longer, there was no question that he would, anyway.

"Bro, you tryin' to set the single game tackle record?"

Deacon glanced up to see Nate standing there, in front of him.

On the field, Riley and the offense were about to head into the red zone. It had been a long drive too, but Deacon's breath was still caught in his chest.

He *had* been pushing. He knew it.

Jem wasn't here to call him on it. He'd seen both Beck and Micah shoot him a few concerned looks before exchanging a handful of their own, always in their own unspoken language. They couldn't know that even seeing them, locked up in their happy little bubble, made him even angrier.

Even sadder, too.

Up until now, Nate had steered clear, seemingly oblivious to why Deacon was trying to single-handedly annihilate the Pittsburgh offense, only excited that he was doing it. But now he was here, in front of Deacon and questioning him.

Deacon looked up tiredly. "Don't care about the record. Don't care about any record. Just care about the scoreboard," he said. It was true—and when he looked up at the scoreboard, it showed the Condors winning 24 to 7.

That wasn't even considering the touchdown Riley and Landry and Carter were attempting to score right now.

"Well, we're kicking ass." Nate flopped down next to Deacon. "You, specifically."

"You got in on the last sack," Deacon said.

He'd just been about to drill the Steelers' quarterback solo, after pushing through their offensive line like it was butter and he was a hot knife, when he'd spotted Nate coming from the other side, evading the left tackle with one of Jem's old moves, and they'd sacked him together.

"Yeah," Nate said grinning. "It's a good move."

"It isn't mine." Deacon couldn't even be mad because it wasn't like Jem would be angry he'd taught Nate his tricks—he'd only encourage the passing of the torch.

Nate and Micah and Beck, they would be his legacy, when Deacon retired.

What else would he have?

Not someone to come home to, that was for fucking sure.

He still couldn't believe Grant had told him, after kissing him back, the way he'd always imagined, the way he'd always *dreamed*, that they were only going to be friends.

Every time he thought about it, he was furious.

Furious at Grant, for lying to him. Furious at Grant, for lying to himself.

Furious at his own stupid naivety, for thinking it could be different.

Furious at fate, for setting the one man in his path that he couldn't have, when he'd never wanted anyone else.

After taking the snap, Deacon watched as Riley took off, sprinting the remaining fifteen yards, nearly untouched, to the end zone. Landry was right behind him as he crossed the line, and after he turned, he lifted his boyfriend up high, towards the lights, Riley laughing as he threw his head back in delight.

Deacon wasn't ever going to have *that*.

It wasn't that he didn't understand Grant's concerns. He did. Technically, Grant was his boss—though after this season was over, that was up for debate. If he stayed with the team and just worked as a consultant, for no salary, why did it matter if technically Grant was still his boss? But Grant had never let him suggest it. Had just unilaterally informed him that this thing between them wasn't happening.

Well, newsflash to Grant Green: it was *already* happening. They'd kissed twice. The first time because Grant had kissed *him*.

Grant telling him it wasn't happening didn't change anything because he was already invested—more than that, he was already head over fucking heels for the guy.

"You ready to go?" Nate asked as he stood.

"Yeah," Deacon said, hauling himself to his feet.

"Wait," Beck said, turning towards him. "I don't know if you're going back in, Deac."

"It's only 31 to 7, third quarter," Deacon argued. "Why wouldn't I be? It's not like it's a million to zero."

Micah shot him a look. *Micah Rose,* for God's sake.

When the kid had gotten here, he'd been a mess. A *recovering* mess, sure, but a mess nonetheless.

Yet he was the one giving Deacon that look—the equivalent of a stiff arm to the facemask; one that said he *would* make Deacon sit if he wouldn't do it himself.

"Let me talk to Coach Rufus," Deacon said, shouldering Micah and Beck out of the way.

Coach was standing apart, eyes glued to a tablet.

"Deac," he said, without even looking up.

"You can't bench me."

"We're up three scores," Coach said bluntly.

"And?"

"And you've done plenty, Harris."

"You playin' Nate and Micah and Beck? Eric?"

Coach finally looked up. "Yeah, I am. They need the practice. The snaps. They're still learning."

"But what am I? Washed-up? Done? Finished?"

Coach sighed. "You know that's not what I'm saying. I'm saying you did your time, today. Take a load off. Grab a headset."

Deacon shook his head emphatically. He couldn't not play for a quarter and a half. If he just sat there and thought…*no*. He couldn't. The only way he'd survived this week was by working his body and his mind as hard as possible, so there wasn't a moment of downtime, not even a minute of time to feel like shit, when he fell into bed.

But if he sat here, and just *sat*, he'd go down the rabbit hole.

It wouldn't matter if he had a headset. Wouldn't matter if he helped Nate and Beck and Micah, coached them through the remains of the game.

He'd still turn himself outside in, trying to contain his anger.

Trying to contain his sadness.

Because he and Grant weren't ever going to be *friends*. He knew that was impossible. They'd always been so much more than that—and so much less, too.

And now they were going to be nothing, because Deacon couldn't hang around him, be in Grant's life, and *not* fight for him. Not want him with a fierceness that was nearly impossible to deny.

If he couldn't do either of those things anymore, then what was the point?

"Deacon," Coach warned.

"Just a few more drives, Coach. Please." Normally, Deacon didn't beg. He hadn't even begged for Grant to listen, or to reconsider. Would it have made a difference if he had? Probably not. Grant had seemed conflicted, yet also so fucking certain. That spine of steel, refusing to bend, never mind break.

Coach though, he was a different story. He could probably see the fire in Deacon's eyes, could see how desperately he wanted to go back in.

"Fine, one more drive," Coach said, giving in, not exactly gracefully, because he was definitely rolling his eyes at Deacon's insistence, but Deacon didn't care. He'd gotten a reprieve. Not for the rest of the game, but *something*.

"Thanks, Coach," Deacon said, patting him on the shoulder. He grabbed his helmet from the bench and headed to the field.

"You're such a suck-up," Beck teased him as he entered the huddle. "What did you say to Coach to get him to put you in?"

"I asked, nicely," Deacon said.

Aware, as he was too often these days, of Nate's semi-worshipful expression as he leaned in next to him.

"You? Nice?" Micah chuckled.

"Yeah, not this week." Beck's words made sense, but not his knowing tone.

Nobody except the two of them—and Darcy—knew what had happened on Monday morning. And none of them were blabbing about it.

As he took his spot on the line, a sudden fear cropped up in Deacon's brain. What if everyone had figured that something was going on between them? Even for an unusually circumspect team that didn't typically share their private business outside the facility, gossip traveled.

The last thing Deacon wanted was for Grant's reputation to be compromised, even though he'd done everything he could to prevent it.

Almost everything, Deacon corrected.

He wouldn't have kissed him, that first time.

Even as Deacon took his position on the line, he discovered he couldn't regret it, even if that happened.

Switching his speculation off, Deacon scanned the formation the offense was beginning to get set into.

This quarterback wasn't the most mobile in the NFL—he was no Riley, that was for sure—but he wasn't a slouch either. He *could* run, if the defense let him, if *Deacon* let him.

One of Deacon's jobs was to make sure he couldn't.

Right now, from the offensive alignment, Deacon thought it might be happening. It would be an aggressive way to start off the drive—but then the Steelers were down three scores. There was no reason not to try something new. Based on the film he'd watched this week, long into every night, it looked similar to some of formations he'd seen the Steelers use for their run option package.

Deacon leaned back on his heels, considering.

Always, the defense needed to stop the play before it developed, but even better was when they could fool the offense into thinking they were going to do one thing and then do another.

This seemed like an ideal moment to try it. Especially if this was one of the last drives Deacon was going to get to play today. No matter what the score was, he wanted to make his mark.

He settled down into his stance, checking down the line to make sure the defense was properly lined up, and exchanged a nod with Nate, on the far side, when he was happy with what he saw.

The ref blew the whistle, then the quarterback called out the snap count. Deacon shifted his weight, getting ready to spring. A deep breath later, the center snapped the ball to the quarterback. He dropped back. One step. Then another. Deacon could feel his eyes on him, waiting to see what he'd do, so *he* could decide if he'd hand the ball off to the running back, or he'd take it himself.

Deacon darted to the center, leaning his whole body in, selling the charade as best he could, watching as the quarterback took off, tucking the ball under one arm.

It was only then that he set his cleat in the turf and pushed the other way, shoulder dipping low, almost to the ground, but he righted himself, with long practice and hard-won balance, and took off towards the quarterback, reaching his full speed after only a handful of strides.

A moment later it was all over, Deacon smothering him with his body behind the line of scrimmage, the tackle clean but decisive, making sure that the quarterback couldn't escape.

He heard the whistle and popped up, reaching out a hand to the guy he'd just tackled.

He liked to win, sure, but he wasn't going to be an asshole about it.

These guys were already losing by three scores. It would be shitty to rub it in, and Deacon tried hard not to be shitty, even when his entire self felt like it was inflamed with temper.

"Shit," the guy said, shaking his head. "That's some fucking move you got there, Harris."

"Thanks," Deacon said, grinning.

They went only two more plays before they had to punt.

It was hard to recover from a loss of yards on the first down, and they never had.

As Deacon jogged back to the bench, Nate caught up to him.

"Jesus, what a move," Nate said. "I didn't know what you were doing, right away, but the way you moved after, what a fucking work of art."

Deacon just shrugged. He was pretty sure Riley was wrong and there was a *lot* of harm in continuing to let Nate's hero worship continue. He needed to nip this in the bud, before Nate started getting even more grandiose ideas, like somehow that person Deacon wanted to come home to was going to be him, someday.

And he wasn't ever going to be.

Deacon would rather it be nobody than the wrong guy.

Anyone other than Grant.

He shed Nate by moving down the sideline after the linebacker had already headed towards the bench, choosing instead to stand by Beck.

At least he wouldn't gaze up at him with stars in his eyes—because those stars were reserved entirely for someone else.

"So I take it the fighting for him didn't go too well," Beck said quietly a few moments later.

"How do you know?" Deacon asked, even though he already knew the answer to that question.

Beck shot him a look. "Because you've been in a pissed-off mood, since. You didn't try to step in and fix everything, did you?"

"I, ah, no. Not really." At least not exactly. That hadn't been the problem, anyway. He hoped though, that Beck wouldn't ask what the problem *had* been. Because what else could he say other than, *the problem is me? I'm the problem. My whole existence is why Grant can't be with me.*

Somehow, that hurt even more, nearly a week later, than it had the first time he'd realized it.

At some point, he'd expected his anger would fade, and he wouldn't be so pissed off anymore. He'd just be hurt. And sad. He'd be sad, and full of regret.

"Then what happened?" Beck asked.

"It's just not . . .it doesn't matter what I want, or even what he wants. It's not in the cards, Beck."

Beck looked floored. "So you're just going to . . .let it go? Let *him* go?"

"It was a pipe dream, anyway." Grant Green had always been a pipe dream. But the problem with pipe dreams was that sometimes they burst, unexpectedly and with force.

Sometimes that wasn't anyone's fault. It just *was*.

"Micah and me, that was a pipe dream. And we made it happen, anyway. We made it real, and we made it to last," Beck argued.

"Oh, was that what you were thinking of when you took yourselves off to a wedding chapel in Vegas?" Deacon teased, because the teasing, the *focus* on something other than the train wreck of his own love life, was easier.

"We weren't really thinking, at all, actually," Beck admitted, which Deacon had already guessed. "We just knew we wanted to pick each other—we *needed* to pick each other. And when it was over, when we were sober and back home, it was easy to keep doing that. It might've been fast. It might've been impulsive, but it was still exactly what we wanted."

Deacon didn't want to hate Beck. He liked him, actually, a whole hell of a lot, and had from the moment he'd been drafted by the Condors last year. But it still stung, what he said. The happy ending he was going to get that Deacon couldn't see for himself.

"Look at you all earnest and fucking in love," Deacon said, roughly, nudging him in the side with an elbow. Trying to keep things light and joking, but probably failing.

The empathy in Beck's eyes burned.

Deacon swallowed hard.

This was the way it needed to be.

Maybe after this season was over, he'd go to Christmas Falls, like Jem, and lick his wounds, too.

Of course, with the halting, hesitant way Jem had talked about his old friend, back there in the small town he'd grown up in, maybe that wouldn't help much, either.

"Hey, look, another field goal," Beck said brightly. "You gonna get Coach to put you back in?"

Deacon glanced up at the scoreboard. It now read 34 to 7, with the third quarter nearly over.

"No," he said. "No, I'm good."

But even with a win under their belts, Deacon didn't think that was true at all.

CHAPTER 9

GRANT OFTEN STAYED AWAY from the locker room after the game.

It wasn't like he didn't have some inkling what a half-dressed Deacon Harris might look like, but while there was a part of him that *desperately* wanted to see it in the flesh, for himself, he didn't want it to be like this.

No, you want it to be just the two of you, alone. And you want to be the one pulling off his clothes.

He did.

He always had.

But Nicole told him in no uncertain terms that she wanted him to mingle in the locker room, post-game. "Either you do it, and make nice with the media, say all the platitudes you want," she said, "or else I'm going to put you up on the podium, later. We need you to be front and center, to continue to combat the Rex rumors."

Grant did not want to get up on the podium. He wasn't ever going to be a Jerry Jones, coaching the team from the owner's suite, or through his quotes to the media. So he relented, and agreed with Nicole's request to make himself available in the locker room after the game.

It was easier, too, after such a big win.

He mingled with the players and staff, slapping some on the back, offering congratulations and praise, and made sure to stay far away from where Deacon was holding court with several reporters surrounding him.

Except once, when he glanced over and Deacon was looking at him, too, and their gazes met.

It was like every other time, heat blooming inside him—heat and joy and what *had* to be love, because why else did it feel so painful when Deacon looked away?

"Mr. Green," a voice called from behind him, and he turned, surprised but pleased to see Marlene Griffiths, one of the reporters who often covered business for one of the biggest newspapers in the nation.

"Good to see you, Marlene," he said, shaking her outstretched hand. "And you know I've told you to call me Grant." She was older than him, by at least a half dozen years, and it was always awkward when she referred to him so formally.

"Grant, then," she said, smiling.

"Imagine seeing you here; this isn't your normal beat," Grant said. There was a tiny warning bell dinging in his head, persistently, but he told himself that the only reason she was here was because of the Rex story that seemed to linger, no matter how he and Nic tried to dispel it.

She kept telling him the more they downplayed, the quicker it would fade, but if Marlene was here, clearly trying to dig up some kind of quote—or even worse, some kind of dirt—then maybe it wasn't going anywhere anytime soon. He *liked* Marlene and his pleasure at seeing her was genuine, but he couldn't help but be afraid of what her appearance promised.

"No, it's not." Marlene lowered her voice. "I'm hearing some interesting talk."

"About me? Or about Rex?" Grant kept his smile plastered on his face. Didn't let his concern show. But he was undeniably concerned.

"Rex James is a problem, of course, but I heard you dealt with that fairly cleanly—volunteering to send your drives straight off to the commissioner's office. That was ballsy of you," she said.

"It wasn't, particularly. We don't have anything to hide." Grant kept the casual, unbothered facade up, but that alarm bell was dinging louder, now.

"Maybe not about Rex."

The alarm bell was clanging now, right in his ear.

"What are you trying to get at, Marlene?" he asked, still pleasantly.

"I got an email from a source. Forwarded email. Originally from one of your old college buddies." Marlene glanced over at Deacon, and the alarm was now at DEFCON five. "You bought this team for Deacon Harris? How long have you two been involved?"

"I—" Grant stopped abruptly. He needed to find Nicole. Extricate himself from this situation. He'd wondered if seeing Marlene pick her way through the locker room of half-naked guys was bad news, and it was, undeniably. He might not know what the fuck Marlene was talking about, but it was definitely nothing good.

Especially when he might not be aware of the email she was talking about, but the general gist of her theory was dead-on correct.

"I didn't know owners could get involved with players," Marlene continued.

"They can't. We shouldn't and I definitely haven't," Grant said, glancing around trying to find Nicole or Darcy or *someone*, trying to keep his eye movements subtle so Marlene wouldn't know. Wouldn't realize just how close she'd come to hitting the nail on the head.

Where the fuck had she gotten this information?

And where the fuck was Nic? And Darcy?

"That's not what it sounded like to me," Marlene said.

That was the thing about her. She was too much like him—probably why they liked each other in a friendlier manner than was usual for reporter and subject.

She was friendly and incredibly easy to talk to, to *confide in*, right up until she went in for the kill, aiming directly for the artery with her blade.

"I don't know what you're talking about," Grant said bluntly. He nearly added, *I get a lot of emails, doesn't mean they're all full of facts.* But he shut his mouth at the last moment, clamping it tight. Not wanting to give away a word more than he needed to.

He needed to get her out of here, before one of the other sports beat reporters got wind of what she was saying.

Marlene sighed, tucking a strand of dark brown hair liberally streaked with silver behind an ear. "I came here, directly, to talk to you, and I didn't go through your PR rep or dig around myself first, as a courtesy to you."

He knew exactly what she was implying. Grant should repay her own courtesy by loosening his lips and telling her *something*.

But he couldn't tell her anything, other than cluelessness, because the other alternative was even worse. It was the truth.

Yes, I bought this team, spent nearly a billion dollars doing it, so I could save a boy I liked.

He'd never be able to hold his head up in a board meeting again.

Nevermind at the next annual NFL owners meeting.

If he even made it that far, once the commissioner's office got wind of this.

"I'd tell you, Marlene, if I knew what the fuck you were talking about." It was time to lie through his teeth, and at least, Grant conceded, he'd learned to do it well, out of necessity.

"You know it's not going to be just me talking to you about this," Marlene warned.

"This source said he sent the email to other journalists?" God, this was a living nightmare. What the fuck was Grant going to do about it?

He finally caught a flash of red hair, Nicole walking towards them.

"I'm sorry I don't know you," Nicole said, inserting herself in the conversation gracefully but also forcefully.

She'd probably seen the panic written in Grant's eyes.

Which meant that there was no way Marlene hadn't seen it too.

"Marlene Griffiths. And you're Nicole Edwards. You run PR for the Condors."

Nicole pursed her lips. "You're well-informed," she said crisply.

"Extremely," Grant retorted under his breath.

He should be taking advantage of Nicole's presence to get out of here. But instead, he stayed rooted in place, sick to his stomach, and more desperate than he could ever remember being.

"I was just telling Grant here about an interesting email I received," Marlene said.

"From?" Nicole's voice was still pleasant, but her eyes had narrowed, and she did not look particularly happy.

"An anonymous source. Claims Grant here bought the team *for* Deacon Harris."

"Don't be ridiculous," Nicole said, not missing a beat. "You don't buy a billion dollar professional football team like you'd buy a dozen roses."

Marlene tilted her head, acknowledging the argument. "I'm just saying what *they* said. An old friend of Grant's here, from college days. And you know, I can't believe we aren't talking about this more, but you two went to the same college."

"Lots of people went to that college," Nicole said.

"We ran in *very* different circles," Grant said, which was not technically a lie. He hadn't said they didn't know each other. That they'd never met. But it *was* hard to imagine that a self-professed nerd already working on his graduate studies and one of the stars of the football team would've been personally acquainted.

"Right," Marlene said. He couldn't say for sure if Marlene had proof yet that they'd met. She often played things close to the vest. They'd probably gotten everything they could out of her, at this point.

"Good to meet you, Marlene," Nicole said and took Grant by the arm and steered him to the door.

If Marlene couldn't connect them, couldn't prove that they *had* known each other, then this was a nothing story. Because why would Grant have bought a team for someone he didn't even know?

But Grant had hardly cared about burying his tracks from way back then. If Marlene dug hard enough, she'd find out he was a tutor.

Might even find some people who'd seen them in the library together. They hadn't been hiding, because back then it hadn't mattered.

He wanted to believe that it didn't matter now, either.

But it was stupid to assume that nobody would care—especially not if the story blew up.

Everyone would care.

Nicole stayed silent until they got to the elevator. When they were finally alone and couldn't be overheard, she turned to him. "What was that about?" she asked.

"A nuclear bomb that might go off, or it might not," Grant said. "She told me she had an email—I'm assuming from the drives we sent to the commissioner's office. Supposedly it's from someone who knew me in college that's claiming I bought the Condors to get close to Deacon."

"That's insane," Nicole exclaimed.

Yep, it totally would be.

And he'd done it anyway.

Okay, not *only* for Deacon. He'd meant everything he'd said to him, in the spring, before the sale had gone final.

He'd seen what the Riptide and the Piranhas were doing, and it *had* seemed like a complete fucking waste to drive a team into the ground, with no thought to the players or the staff or the coaches.

He'd meant all of that.

But at the beginning—and at every point when he might've changed his mind or given up—it had been all about Deacon. Only Deacon.

Sure, he could've had Darcy get his number, again. Asked him on a date. But they'd never been *that* kind of friends. They hadn't even really been friends at all.

"Yes, it is," Grant said steadily. "And it's true."

Nic's jaw dropped. "And this journalist knows? This could be . . ." She trailed off, probably unsure just how much to scare him.

But Grant knew the score. Just didn't know how to run the play.

"Really, catastrophically bad, yes. I don't think she's connected us, back in college, yet. It's not a story if she can't prove we knew each other."

"Right," Nicole agreed, nodding. "But you think she will."

There was a reason he'd kept her on, even after buying the team. She'd done good work when the prior owners had given her nothing to work *with*.

She was smart and capable, but even she had limits, and if this story blew up, there was nothing they could do to make it look less terrible.

"She's tenacious and very good at her job," Grant said. "She'll find it, if there's proof to find."

Nicole let out a hard breath. "But we have time, then."

"Maybe. She said she wasn't the only one."

"Just the only journalist serious enough to do their homework first, before publishing." Nicole paused. "So we should brace for the worst, then. A lot of rumors and gossip—possibly followed by a factual confirmation of everything."

She'd switched from disbelief and panic straight to business.

Another reason he'd kept her.

"It's a possibility," Grant said, shoving his hands in his pockets.

And then, if this whole conversation weren't humiliating enough, Nicole asked, "I need to know, are you and Deacon involved?"

Of course she did. She couldn't do her job to the best of her ability if she didn't know the whole story.

Grant didn't know if it was more embarrassing that he needed to say no—or that he'd done all this, bought a whole fucking football team, and then done *nothing* about it.

"No, we're, uh . . .still friends. Just friends."

Nicole's expression turned sympathetic. "Nothing's happened?"

He heard what she wasn't saying out loud: *you bought a whole goddamn football team, valued at nearly a billion dollars, and you didn't even get a date?*

"Well, not *nothing* but it's not happening now."

Nicole raised an eyebrow. "Not nothing?"

"Please don't start," Grant said, with an eye roll.

"I'm just saying," Nicole said, "and forgive me if this is way overstepping my bounds, but everyone sees the way he looks at you. The way you look at him. Why isn't anything happening now?"

"Because it's inappropriate. We knew it was and it got out of hand, uh, once. Twice. And don't worry. Whatever happened, it was . . .it was minor." *It was life-changing, anyway, and I'm gonna be dreaming about it for the rest of my life.* "It was just a . . ." Grant swallowed hard. "It was just a kiss. Two kisses. And nobody will know. Nobody *does* know. Except uh, Darcy. She walked in on us, once."

"Ah." There was a wealth of meaning in that one word.

Grant wanted to sink through the elevator floor and die—and yet he knew this would be *nothing* compared to how it would feel if the whole world found out.

The elevator doors opened. "You should tell him," Nicole said as they exited.

"What?" Grant couldn't believe what she was suggesting.

"No, no, not *that*. Though I suppose if everyone finds out, it doesn't matter *what* you do then. We might even be able to spin it as like some super romantic *Romeo and Juliet* kind of shit. Star-crossed lovers, forbidden romance, all that jazz. No, but what I mean is that Deacon shouldn't find out about the email from ESPN or even someone else on the team. You should be the one to tell him."

"Seriously?" Grant was incredulous.

"I know, it's . . .uh . . .maybe embarrassing," Nicole said, both her face and her voice softening, as she turned to him. "But wouldn't it be better coming from you than from someone else?"

"You want me to tell Deacon Harris I bought this football team for him."

"It's either you or someone else," Nicole said.

"God," Grant said. Feeling vaguely nauseous again. "I didn't even *send* this email."

"But someone did who knew about your . . .uh . . .your *feelings* back then. I'm assuming that's who sent the email to you."

There'd only been a handful of people Grant had been friends with back then, and even fewer he'd confided in about his crush on Deacon.

"It was probably Dougie. Shit. It had to be Dougie." He hadn't even stopped to consider who the sender of the email could be, not until now. Proof that he wasn't thinking clearly.

He'd never been panicked enough to cloud his mind, but he was definitely there, right now.

"Who's Dougie?" Nicole asked.

"A friend I worked with in my graduate studies. He helped me a little with my project, that turned into the product I founded my company on. We pulled all-nighters in the programming lab, sometimes."

On one of those nights, he'd been tired and a little lovesick about Deacon, and after too many espresso shots, he'd mentioned it to Dougie, who'd clearly remembered it, all those years later. Long enough to send him an email that had probably been shunted deep into one of his personal folders. He'd never even seen it, because his email assistant had probably been sure it was spam.

"Would he talk to Marlene?"

"I guess, maybe. If she could find him. I tried to hire him, a year or so after starting InTech, but . . ." Grant shrugged. "He'd gotten a better offer. I didn't expect to ever hear from him again."

"And yet he sent you that email."

Nicole stopped in front of the door that took him to the private parking level—and the car waiting to take him and Darcy back to the airport. Speaking of Darcy, where was she?

"Yeah, he did," Grant said. "I sure wish he hadn't."

"Oh it's gonna be a mess for sure, but . . ." Nicole dropped her voice, and put a reassuring hand on Grant's shoulder. "But maybe, something good can come out of it. Talk to Deacon. He deserves to hear this from you, and only you."

"Hear what?" He looked over, and there was Darcy, looking a bit windblown and harried. Very unlike her normal put-together self. "Where did you go? You left *so* fast."

"I . . uh . . .something came up," Grant said.

"Well, tell me about it in the car," Darcy said, pushing the door open.

"Sorry," Grant said. "She interrupted you."

"I was just saying," Nicole said, "tell him, and whatever happens, we'll deal with it."

"You realize what you're saying, right?" Grant asked slowly. If he told Deacon the whole truth, if Deacon knew how he really felt, he would keep fighting for him. He wouldn't ever stop.

One kiss wouldn't ever be enough.

The thought screamed through him in a dizzying rush.

One kiss wouldn't ever be enough.

"I do," Nicole said with a nod. "But I got you, boss. Now go tell Darcy, because I'm sure she's going to want to know all the details."

She would—though at least she already knew the truth of why Grant had bought the Condors.

"Thanks," Grant said. "I'm sorry to—"

"No, don't even apologize," Nicole said firmly. "I got this. I got *you*."

Darcy sat back in her chair on the plane and blinked once and then twice.

Picked up her spritz and took a long drink. Polished off half the drink that Benjamin had brought her only a few minutes ago.

"Well, shit," she said.

"My thoughts exactly," Grant said. "Cheryl's gonna have a fucking field day with this."

"Is she?" Darcy asked. "Or did she *cause* this field day, only to reap the benefits of it?"

"Benefits?" Grant felt like he was still wading through all the panic in his brain, and nothing was as clear as it normally was.

"Potentially, you—and to an extent, the whole Condors organization—looks bad. She takes care of us."

Grant flopped back in his seat and considered this. "Does she want to get rid of us, though?"

Darcy raised an eyebrow.

"I mean," Grant continued, "I kinda get the vibe from Cheryl that she *enjoys* giving us shit. We know they weren't going to force us to sell the team, unless it was really ugly, which let's face it, would've only happened if what Rex said was true. And we know it wasn't. This is enough to make noise, but not enough to get rid of me. Of you. Just enough to make us look bad. To guarantee—"

"That she has to keep 'monitoring' us. To put us in our place," Darcy finished with a grimace. "Yes, I see it."

"We've got no proof, and in the end, it doesn't even matter if it's true. If it *is* Cheryl. We knew the commissioner's office was a sieve."

"But we didn't think we had anything to hide," Darcy argued. "Admittedly, we didn't go through everything with a fine-tooth comb. There wasn't time."

"I don't know even if we had, if it would've mattered. I've never gotten an email from Dougie, before. We met, in person, when I offered him that job, ages ago. The email index didn't even know to prioritize his email. I bet you it was buried in like personal spam, or something."

"Probably. And fucking Cheryl found it. *One more round to make sure,* my ass," Darcy grumbled.

"Hey, hey, it's okay. It's not my fault or your fault. It's not anyone's fault." Though it definitely was Cheryl's fault, a little. That email never would've seen the light of day without her interference.

"It's Dougie's fault," Darcy said, chuckling a little.

"Or Deacon's, for being so stupidly irresistible I bought a whole football team to get his attention."

Darcy shot him a sympathetic glance. "Have you thought any more about what you're going to do?"

He'd told her about Nicole's admonition that Deacon deserved to hear the truth from him.

"I'll text him." Grant had already pulled out his phone, but he didn't even know how to start the conversation. *I'm sorry you're finding out like this, but I'm clearly, obviously, crazy about you. So crazy I bought your football team, the way other guys might buy flowers or chocolates.*

"You can't text him this," Darcy said, eyes wide.

"I mean, text him to *meet up*." Grant took a sip of his drink. "Nicole is right. I can't let him find out about this from someone else. It's bad enough as it is."

"You don't think he's gonna be angry about it?" Darcy asked. "How could he be? You came charging in like a knight on a white horse to save him and everything he loves. How can he be pissed about that?"

"I don't know, he was pretty mad this week. Justifiably." And that stung. He'd fucked this whole thing up, and even coming clean wouldn't fix it all.

"Well, text him then. Set up your *date*," Darcy said, gesturing to his phone. "No time like the present."

Grant glanced down at the screen. He kept imagining seeing a red alert text from Nicole, letting him know the shit had hit the fan.

But so far, so good.

"Just gotta figure out how to phrase it," Grant said, fingers hesitating over the screen.

It took him ten attempts and one and a half gin and tonics to construct a suitably personal and apologetic and yet casual message.

Words were not his strong suit.

Especially when they were this important.

"There," Grant said, as he sent the text off.

Darcy looked up from the book she was reading.

"Congratulations," she said wryly, "and now you wait."

It *had* occurred to Grant that Deacon might not answer right away, but it still sucked to wait.

He settled in with his drink and his laptop and told himself it would all work out, in the end.

CHAPTER 10

Deacon was still fucking pissed.

In love, miserable, and fucking pissed.

Not necessarily in that order, either.

His phone dinged, and glancing at his screen, Deacon was surprised to see a second text from Grant.

No, it was his third, in fourteen hours.

Not that Deacon was counting or anything.

You totally are. You're hoarding them like you're a dragon and they're filled with gold.

But of course that didn't mean that he'd answered them, or anything. He didn't know *what* to say to Grant. Why did he even want to talk? When Deacon had wanted to talk a whole freaking week ago, Grant hadn't been interested. Been dismissive, even.

And *now* he wanted to talk? To say something new? Or just to rehash everything he'd already said?

Deacon didn't know, but he didn't know if he wanted to face that again—*could* face that again. He didn't need to spend the next week even more pissed off than he'd been the one before.

He'd gotten more texts, too. From Carter and also from Micah and Beck and Riley, inviting him to the Pirate's Booty for their weekly victory party. And he loved his friends and teammates, he *did*, but no matter how great they were, they weren't a substitute for his *best friend*.

He missed Jem so much he was practically a lost limb. But he couldn't call him, because Jem was *so* happy with Mr. Lumberjack, back in Christmas Falls, and if he even had an inkling how upset Deacon was, he'd show back up in Charleston.

Deacon couldn't handle that guilt on top of everything else.

He'd texted the group chat back, letting them know he wasn't up for going out tonight.

He wasn't up for much. Nobody wanted to be around him when he was like this, no matter if they kept claiming otherwise, but then Landry, who almost never participated in their group chat, had texted him separately.

Don't hide. Hiding isn't going to change anything, except make you feel worse, was all he'd said, and Deacon had wanted to scream. Punch a wall. Throw his phone to the bathroom floor.

But he didn't. Because fuck it, he was an *adult*.

Clearly Riley had told his boyfriend about what he'd seen—admittedly, not much, but likely enough to put two and two together and get the correct answer of four—because Landry knew more than he should.

He texted Landry back, because he didn't know how to leave well enough alone.

And watching y'all couple off is gonna make me feel better?

Landry didn't respond right away, but by the time Deacon was out of the shower, contemplating whether to put on sweatpants or jeans—to spend the evening at home, like he wanted, or go out to the

Pirate's Booty, the way his teammates wanted him to—he'd texted back.

No, I'm not gonna pretend that doesn't suck, Landry said, and Deacon had to give him full points for honesty, **but we love you, you're our brother, and you're hurting. Better to do it around us than alone.**

And goddamn it, he was right.

It was at least a *little* better to do it with people he cared about than by himself.

Besides, Landry texted again, less than thirty seconds later, **Riley says to tell you that Nate's coming, he invited him. And maybe he can lick your wounds?**

A third text showed up right underneath the second, before he could even figure out how to respond. **I don't know what Riley's talking about, cause that's not gonna help you. But maybe I'm wrong?**

Deacon chuckled darkly and pulled out the jeans. When he was dressed, he responded back to Landry. **You're not wrong. I'm not into him that way, but tell Riley I appreciate the effort.**

Landry texted back a few minutes later. **Tell him yourself, when you come to the Pirate's Booty tonight.**

Deacon sighed, and just sent a thumbs-up.

He'd *mostly* decided to go. He'd put on jeans, hadn't he?

But he was still hesitating.

All he really wanted to do was go back up the stairs, crawl into bed, and pull the covers over his head. Pretend this week hadn't happened.

Pretend Grant's taste wasn't still in his mouth.

It was funny, because that particular iteration of his pity party was what decided him. He knew what would happen if he let himself do that. If he gave in to this insidious desire to do *nothing*. To wallow.

No matter how much he loved Grant, he refused to lose himself if he couldn't have him.

He'd lived without him before, for twelve years. He could live without him again.

The Pirate's Booty was full and buzzing by the time Deacon showed up, the bright cheerful sounds of the Bee Gees filling the bar as he walked up to it.

Kieran shot him a look, wordlessly promising to be with him in a moment, and Deacon took a seat. He didn't feel like dancing—even though after a glance down the shiny hardwood surface, he guessed the rest of the team had already moved from the bar to the dance floor. If they wanted to see him so fucking bad, they could come visit him *here*, Deacon decided.

"Hey."

Deacon glanced over and saw Nate standing there. "You came," he added, with a bit of a lopsided grin. "Didn't think you would."

"Why not?" Deacon asked, not unkindly, but directly. Because Nate had seemed to be particularly oblivious to the undercurrents going on between him and Grant. But maybe he was just ignoring it.

Nate shot him a look. "You've been pissed off all week. Just didn't think you'd want to show."

"Fair," Deacon said.

Kieran appeared in front of them, then, setting two napkins on the bar. "Whatever you think I should have," Deacon said, hoping that he wouldn't pour him another gin and tonic, even though he'd actually liked the last one.

But he'd never be able to drink another one, not without the taste of Grant mingling right along with the gin.

"You too?" Kieran asked Nate, and he nodded.

"So why *did* you come, anyway?" Nate asked. Sounding particularly hopeful.

God, Deacon was going to have to let him down—and easily, so that they could stay friends and teammates—because letting him have hope was worse than telling him the truth. It would feel like Grant kissing him, and letting Deacon kiss him back, and then Grant brushing him off.

Deacon knew how that felt: like absolute shit.

"Because I wanted nothing more than to stay at home," Deacon said.

For a moment, Nate looked very confused, and then his expression settled into something like understanding. "Ah, I get it," he said. "'Cause it would be real easy to just keep staying at home."

"Exactly," Deacon said.

Kieran set a bottle of beer in front of Nate, and goddamnit, another one of those clear fizzy drinks in front of Deacon.

He knew if he took a sip, it would taste like evergreen and Grant.

Deacon met Kieran's eyes and the bartender just shrugged.

"I don't make the decisions," he said.

Deacon sighed.

"This is great," Nate enthused after taking a long drink of his beer. "What is it?"

"New brewery, up in the Toronto area," Kieran said. "Glad you like it."

"Do you wanna dance?" Nate asked after a moment of silence passed.

Deacon internally winced. Okay, so this was going to be the moment. "Nate," he said kindly, "I like you a lot, you're a great kid—"

"A kid," Nate repeated, a little bitterly.

"And I've really loved helping you, coaching you up a bit. But that's all it's going to be," Deacon finished.

Nate looked resigned, but not upset. "You're into Mr. G, aren't you?"

Ugh. Maybe it would be easier to get over this—eventually, anyway—if everyone didn't keep bringing it up. "Did someone tell you that?" Deacon asked.

"They didn't have to," Nate said. "It was obvious when he showed up here, last Friday. Your face . . .I don't know what I'd do to have you look at me like that, but *something*."

Deacon patted him on the shoulder. "You're gonna find someone and they're gonna be great for you, I promise. But I know you don't really want to get into it with me. I'm . . ." *A mess. A hot garbage fire mess, who's in love with someone who probably feels the same, but won't give into it, no matter how much I push him to do it.*

"Hot as hell? Charming and funny and a damn good football player?" Nate grinned.

"Unavailable," Deacon said instead.

"I get it. It was a long shot, but worth the try anyway."

If only the situation with Grant had turned out like that.

He'd told Deacon no, and yet it had felt like the shittiest *no* he'd ever heard. Worse than any other.

Nate took another drink of beer, and Deacon *nearly* reached for his own drink, if only to do something with his hands that wasn't awkwardly touching Nate again on the shoulder, but then at the last moment, he remembered that it was a gin and tonic.

And Grant drank gin and tonics.

"Oh my God," an excited voice exclaimed behind them. "You *did* come. And thank God you did."

"Carter," Deacon said reasonably, turning his body towards Carter as he and Ian joined them at the bar. "I *did* come. What's up?"

"Did you *see* this?" Carter waved his phone. "No, scratch that, you didn't. Because if you did, you wouldn't be here, you'd be at—"

"Carter," Ian interrupted before Carter could keep going.

"What?" Carter said, exchanging a mysterious but clearly meaningful glance with his boyfriend. "He needs to know. I might as well be the one to tell him. Someone else is going to do it in the next five minutes, if I don't. And I *want* to."

"Tell me what?" Deacon asked flatly. He had a feeling he wasn't going to like this. Anything that had Carter this excited was probably not going to be *good* news.

"Did you not see it?" Carter said. When Deacon shook his head, he turned to Ian. "Oh my God, he *didn't* know."

"Know what? And where would I be if I'd heard this mysterious, magical news?"

"You'd be at Mr. G's penthouse, of course. Getting down on your knees—"

"Carter," Ian admonished again.

"What? He'd be getting down on his knees to *thank* Mr. G for what he did for this team."

"Carter." It was Deacon's turn to warn the guy—except that unlike Ian, who seemed to want to shut Carter's mouth, he *needed* Carter to start fucking talking.

"Mr. G bought the Condors for you. There's proof and everything. He's crazy about you. He bought you a *football team. Your own football team.*"

"What? What are you talking about?" Deacon heard the dim roar of panic in his ears.

"There's some leaked email. From one of Mr. G's college buddies." Carter waved his phone. "He emailed him and said something like, *it's a hell of a lot better gesture than some flowers or a box of chocolates.* More expensive, too. There's . . .uh . . .some other stuff too."

Deacon curled his fingers around his glass. Lifted it to his lips. Drained it dry. And somehow his throat was still parched.

"What other stuff?"

"Oh, uh, um . . ." Carter hesitated then, and the bottom fell out of Deacon's stomach. What could be worse than this?

The *whole fucking world* knowing that Grant had feelings for him? And assuming they were already involved? Even worse.

Deacon knew how much Grant craved respect.

This email would make it so much harder to be taken seriously. But even worse, it would mean Grant would never come to him and want to be with him just because he had the same feelings as Deacon.

No, if something happened now, it was because everyone already fucking knew anyway.

"Sex stuff," Ian supplied, finally. "Uh, some pretty off-color comments about your friendship in college. And . . ."

"How much Grant wanted to get on his knees for *you*, back then." Carter had apparently recovered his composure now.

Deacon closed his eyes and wished this would all go away, a shimmering mirage that he was dreaming.

A *nightmare* that wouldn't let him out of its clutches.

But when he opened them again, Carter was still staring at him. Gin and lime and *Grant* were still sour on his tongue. And ABBA was still singing over the speakers about wanting a man after midnight.

He was still in this bar.

"Shit," Deacon said, scrubbing a hand over his face.

"You heard then?" Deacon looked over and Riley and Landry were standing there. Beck and Micah too. There was a range of emotions in their expressions: shock, definitely, and anger, and something else, something else that *really* grated.

Sympathy.

They all had an inkling of what this would mean—or what it *wouldn't* mean.

"Deac," Riley said, reaching out and tugging him off the stool and into a quick hug. "I'm sorry. You shouldn't have found out this way."

It hit Deacon like a fist to the face why Grant had texted him three times in the last twenty-four hours, all variations of a message that they needed to talk.

He knew. And he wanted to at least give you a heads-up, before the news broke.

Deacon didn't think it was possible to feel even shittier, but he did.

"Yeah," he agreed, swallowing hard as Riley let him go.

"Are you gonna go see him?" Carter asked.

"Carter," Riley warned.

"No, no, I wasn't meaning to get on his knees, for, um, either reason. I promise. Just to . . .I don't know, *talk* to him. Or that knee thing, if you want to. Nobody's gonna judge." Carter made a face. "Okay, *we* won't judge."

When even Carter realized just how hard the world was going to come down on the pair of them—but mostly on Grant, who was supposed to be high up on a pedestal, respected and solid—it was *bad*.

"No," Deacon said. He didn't want to see Grant right now. Didn't want to see the final, damning rejection on his face.

He'd already known they probably weren't going to happen—Grant had made that clear enough the last time they'd talked; the last time they'd *kissed*—but that didn't mean this didn't hurt like hell.

He waved at Kieran, but when the man turned around, he was already holding a shot glass full of amber liquid. He set it in front of Deacon.

"No gin?" Deacon asked before he could stop himself.

Kieran shook his head. "Rum," he said. "The strong stuff."

Deacon raised an eyebrow but didn't hesitate. He downed the shot in one gulp, feeling it burn all the way down.

"What *do* you want to do?" Landry asked, because of course he'd be the only one thoughtful enough to ask.

"Come on, let's dance," Deacon said, and there was another shot there, next to the first empty glass. Kieran tilted his head, grinning at him. He took it as quickly as the first.

When he headed towards the dance floor, he had all his friends and teammates with him, and for a few minutes, as one song slipped to the next, as he danced with Riley and Carter and even with the husbands, Deacon was relieved for one thing: he wasn't *thinking*.

Not right now. His thoughts were dimmed by the booze and the music and the way he forced himself to focus on exactly what he was doing with his body.

Deacon didn't know how much time had passed when Micah tapped him on the shoulder. "Come on," he said, "let's get a drink."

He didn't know why Micah had pulled him away but he had a bad feeling he was about to get husband #2's best take at romantic advice.

Considering how epically Micah had fucked things up with Beck—and then how epically he'd fixed them—Deacon wasn't sure if what he was about to hear was legit, but he also didn't want to discount Micah. He was a good guy. The *best* guy, who'd learned the exact value of himself, and the friendship and loyalty of the teammates around him.

This time they didn't bother with grabbing barstools, just leaned against the bar. Kieran brought them two more shots, and they clinked glasses before downing the rum.

"Damn," Micah said, "that's good."

"Yeah," Deacon said.

Between the booze and the dancing, his brain had almost stopped screaming.

Grant bought the Condors for you.

Grant bought the Condors for you.

Grant bought the Condors for you.

"I know I'm not much for advice," Micah said.

"No shit," Deacon said.

He and Micah weren't as close as he and Beck were—there wasn't anything wrong with the guy. Deacon liked him just fine, but he and Beck had known each other for a lot longer. He was still trying to get there with Micah. And admittedly, that process was accelerated because of how freaking *married* Beck and Micah were, but nothing changed overnight.

"You know," Micah said, apparently not deterred at all by Deacon's blunt retort, "I loved him, and I thought I couldn't have him."

"Yeah, but a lot of that was in your own head. This is . . .bigger than me. Bigger than him. Bigger than the whole team, now."

Micah nodded. "I can see how you'd feel that way. But in the end, all that mattered was what I decided to do about it."

"I *tried* that." The words burst out of Deacon in a rush, helped along by rum and frustration. "I fought for him. I *tried*. He shut me down. And now? Now, it doesn't fucking matter."

Micah put a hand on Deacon's arm. "Of course it fucking matters. Your feelings *matter*. You care about the guy? You want him? If he feels the same way, then you don't stop, you don't quit. It's like third down, right? Sure, we could always get them off the field on the next set of downs—or we could do it *right now*."

Deacon couldn't believe Micah was turning his own football advice—his damn good football advice—into an admonition about his love life.

Or maybe, he could.

Micah Rose was that old adage about still waters running deep, personified.

Deacon sighed. "I didn't want it to be like this."

"Trust me," Micah said, "I didn't want a lot of things either. But now, I wake up every day, and I know I'm fucking blessed. Maybe this wasn't how I expected to get here, maybe Charleston wasn't where I thought I'd play, maybe I didn't expect to be married at twenty-four, but I'm *happy*. In the end, it was worth it."

"If you tell me to make it worth it . . ." Deacon gestured towards Kieran to get another round, but his gaze slid right over the pair of them.

Was the bartender avoiding him? He wasn't drunk, not by a long shot, he just needed something else to take the edge off . . .because there was nothing he wanted more than to march out the door of this bar and go to Grant's penthouse and *make it all worth it.*

"Hey, you said it, not me," Micah said, raising his hands in faux innocence.

"And I dragged myself out here, to 'have a drink.'" Deacon rolled his eyes.

Micah laughed, as Deacon tried to catch Kieran's attention again, but again, he didn't look in Deacon's direction.

"Ugh," Deacon said.

"You know," Micah said conversationally, "we *do* have practice tomorrow."

"Yeah, yeah, I know it," Deacon grumbled.

But at the moment, he really didn't give a shit.

What he wanted was a drink, so he wouldn't march right out this door and straight to Grant.

He turned, jostling the guy next to him, trying to get Kieran's attention again.

The guy shot him a sour look. "Watch yourself," he retorted.

Usually nobody was interested in giving Deacon a hard time. He was a big guy and had a look that he knew promised he didn't fuck around. But this guy was clearly a hell of a lot drunker than Deacon. It was obvious from the way he wobbled and almost didn't right himself when Deacon accidentally nudged him.

"Sorry," Deacon said, not sounding very sorry at all.

"Wait a sec," the guy said, turning back to him with that glazed expression. "You're Harris. You're that fucker the owner guy *bought* a football team for."

God, how fast and far had this news traveled?

Deacon hadn't even known about it when he'd left his house, and now, it felt like everyone on the street had already heard the story.

"Guilty as charged," Deacon said dryly. "That's me."

The guy stared at him blearily. "You don't seem worth all that."

"Trust me, I'm not." If Deacon ever talked to Grant about this—which he would have to, wouldn't he?—that was going to be the very first question he asked.

What's so goddamn special about me?

Deacon could hardly be pissed off at some guy who was wondering the exact same thing he was.

But then, he didn't stop there.

"Now that owner guy, he's hot. You got him on his knees yet, 'cause I bet—"

He didn't get the rest of the sentence out.

One moment, he was upright and the next he wasn't and Deacon's fist was aching.

"Holy shit," Micah exclaimed and grabbed Deacon's other arm, trying to tug him back, but the guy's friend, now visible, straightened, rising and rising and, *goddamn,* still rising, pulling himself up to his full height.

At least three inches more than Deacon owned.

And he'd thought the *first guy* was big!

"Shit," Deacon agreed, taking a step back and then another.

"What the fuck," the guy's enormous friend spit out. "Whatdya do that for?"

"He insulted my boss," Deacon said.

The guy's brows scrunched together. "And?"

"And he deserved to stop talking." *He deserved to stop breathing, for saying that shit.*

Except that Deacon already knew people were saying it—and worse. This guy's only sin had been to do it first.

"I don't like it," the guy pronounced slowly. He reached down and yanked his friend up. "Apologize to Rick."

Micah was still trying to pull him back, but Deacon was stronger and more determined, and leaned forward. "No," he said.

Enormous Guy took a step closer. "You think you're a big, tough guy, don't you? 'Cause you're a football player. And 'cause the owner of your team wants your cock."

"No," Deacon said. Tried to get his breathing under control, but as he realized, *this is how it's gonna be, with everyone, every moment, from now on,* his temper lit like dry kindling. "You're gonna get his name out of your mouth, though."

The corner of Enormous Guy's mouth tilted upwards. He looked amused. Like Deacon couldn't possibly take him.

But the way Deacon was feeling right now, he could—and *would*—take on the whole fucking world.

"I don't think so," he said.

That was all the reason Deacon needed to launch himself at the guy.

He got in one good punch and then another, dodging the guy's right hook, fighting him and also fighting Micah, who kept trying to pull him out of the fray.

Things had just started to get interesting when a loud siren cut through the roar. But it took the lights suddenly flicking on to finally make Deacon pause, just for a second.

That was all it took for Enormous Guy to get one good lick in, right across his jaw.

"That's it," Kieran yelled over the noise. "That's fucking it. You wanna fight, you go outside."

Deacon felt a weird pulse of guilt. He'd fought in Kieran's bar, and not just fought—he'd decked that guy without even a single syllable of warning.

"Jesus, you don't fuck around," Micah breathed into his ear, his fingers tight in Deacon's collar as he pulled him backward. This time Deacon let him. "Mr. G's gonna kill you."

It seemed likely, even if Deacon told him that he was actually defending his honor.

Grant wasn't the kind of guy who wanted anyone to brawl on his behalf; he'd always fought his own battles.

Not today, he didn't.

"Probably," Deacon said, and was only vaguely aware of how loopily he was grinning at Micah.

"Jesus," Micah repeated again, shaking his head. "You're crazy."

"But you get it," Deacon said.

Micah had pulled him all the way to the other end of the bar. He looked at Deacon, and Deacon looked back—and yes, Micah *did* get it. If anyone said that shit about Beck, he'd have been the one throwing punches.

A wet towel plopped down behind him. Deacon glanced back and saw Kieran behind him, scowling.

"That's for this asshole," Kieran said to Micah. "Make sure he gets cleaned up. One of those guys' friends called the cops. You might want to clear out."

"No," Deacon said before Micah could suggest they do just that.

"Jesus," Micah repeated again, shaking his head. "More than crazy."

"I did it, didn't I? Might as well take responsibility," Deacon said ruefully.

He'd just finished wiping his face and wrapping the towel around the ice Kieran had dropped off, knowing he'd need to ice his jaw, when he saw the crowds part in front of them.

The cops, Deacon thought, but then the figure that stopped in front of him was very different and not in a familiar uniform.

Instead, he was in jeans and a Condors sweatshirt, wearing a frown that would make anyone worried.

But Deacon only felt a shot of pure, unadulterated love.

He'd come for him. Grant had come for him.

Of course he did. He saved you before, didn't he? Why wouldn't he come save your sorry ass again? He loves you, apparently, even if you don't really understand why.

Even if he's always fucking coming to your rescue.

"Grant," Deacon said, and the word came out of his mouth like Grant was an altar and he was worshipping in front of him.

Yep, Micah was right. He was crazy.

Crazy in love.

Grant didn't look away. His gaze was critical, but soft around the edges. Like he couldn't really be mad, even if he tried.

Deacon understood. He wanted so goddamn bad to be furious, still, but he couldn't find any of it. Not anymore.

How's he gonna keep pushing you away? The whole world already thinks you're fucking.

"Micah, can you take Deacon to my car? It's outside. The big black one. I'm going to talk to the police who just showed up. Luckily, they don't seem to want to charge anyone. Too much paperwork,

I guess." He kept looking right at Deacon, but he hadn't spoken to him yet.

Maybe he didn't trust himself to.

There was a weight in his gaze, so many unspoken declarations.

"Don't they need my statement or something?" Deacon asked, stumbling over his words.

"You mean, the statement about how you sucker punched some guy standing next to you at the bar? And then his friend punched *you*?" Grant shook his head, answering his own question. "No, I believe we'll get along pretty well without you."

"But—" Deacon began to argue, but Grant just shook his head, in that decisive and certain way of his, like Deacon was just one of the many idiotic peons who tried to argue with him, unsuccessfully.

Grant's expression pinned him.

Deacon wasn't stupid; he shut up.

"Micah," Grant repeated with the exaggerated patience of the very frustrated, "take him to the car."

"Guess we'd better go," Micah said, rushing over and tugging at Deacon's arm.

Deacon would've made some comment about how good he was at following orders, but he was following them, too, wasn't he?

"You're in for it," Micah muttered as the crowd parted in front of them and they made it to the door. "I don't know for what, yet, but you're in for it."

Deacon didn't know either. Would Grant ever talk to him again? Would he release him as punishment for the brawl—even though the Condors needed him to continue winning? Or would he press him into the black leather seat in the back of the town car and kiss him again and maybe even *more*?

They reached the town car, idling in front of the Pirate's Booty. Deacon pulled open the door and nearly climbed into the cavernous back, but then Micah hesitated, standing on the sidewalk. Clearly he had something else he wanted to say. So Deacon waited him out.

"He bought a football team for you. And you punched out two guys who might be related to Bigfoot. Don't you two think you've done enough proving that you belong together?" Micah asked, his question sounding rhetorical.

Deacon sure hoped it was, because he didn't have any kind of real answer.

He shrugged, and maybe it was a cop-out, but it was the best fucking thing he had, right now.

"That's what I thought," Micah said, sounding satisfied, and closed the door behind him.

CHAPTER 11

GRANT KEPT WAITING FOR his temper to die down.

It had begun simmering nearly twenty-four hours before, when Deacon had ignored his repeated texts. When he wouldn't even give Grant a chance to talk. To tell him the truth before he found out in the worst possible way.

It had flared even hotter a few hours ago when Nicole had called, saying the whole email had leaked. Deacon knew now, for better or worse, but Grant didn't feel any better about that. *I wanted to tell you myself, damnit.*

It went supernova when Carter had called him, in a panic, his stammered words announcing that Deacon was in a bar fight at the Pirate's Booty, and it was all, to quote Carter, *"because of you."*

He didn't need to ask Deacon why he'd attacked those two guys to know why he'd done it.

He knew.

He'd hoped that when the other guys, drunk as hell, didn't want to press charges and the cops had shrugged the whole thing off as a bar disagreement gone wrong, his temper would've calmed down. But it didn't. Probably because Grant was sure that only happened because of who he was and the team Deacon played for.

Grant was so tired of cleaning up these messes.

Grant stood in front of the car parked outside the Pirate's Booty, knowing Deacon was in the back seat, waiting for him, and he wished he was marginally less angry. But he wasn't.

He thought he might be even *angrier*.

What the fuck had Deacon been thinking? Going after those guys?

Did he think he could go after every single person who decided to weigh in on the truth of Grant's NFL ownership? And why would he, if he hadn't even been interested in hearing about it first from Grant's lips?

Because you pissed him off by rejecting him.

That one sounded remarkably like Darcy.

Grant sighed and opened the door.

It took his eyes a moment to adjust to the cavernous darkness.

Deacon was illuminated only by the subtle lighted trim on the opposite door, running down to the floor.

He was holding a rapidly melting bundle of ice against his jaw, and he didn't say anything.

Grant didn't say anything either.

Maybe they'd said it all—or *actually*, he'd never gotten that fucking chance.

Grant was so bitter about that.

Not that him informing Deacon about the email would've really changed anything.

It would still exist, out in the world.

Deacon, and everyone else, would still know Grant's truth: that he was hopelessly, more than a little pathetically, in love with him.

"I'm sorry," Deacon said softly, breaking the silence.

"About?" Grant's voice was clipped.

Yep, he was definitely still pissed.

Deacon opened his mouth to answer, but Grant beat him to it. "Are you sorry you ghosted me? Wouldn't answer my messages? Sorry that the whole world knows all my dirty secrets? Sorry that you punched that guy? Sorry you dragged me out of my place to deal with two men probably related to Andre the Giant, and a whole bunch of cops?"

Deacon snapped his mouth shut, then groaned a little.

Grant wasn't happy that he was in pain, but it *was* surprisingly satisfying.

That made two of them, then.

"I'm sorry for all that, okay?" Deacon finally said. "And sorry everyone has to know, when you didn't want that."

As usual, Deacon had missed the point.

If this had turned out differently, he never would've shut up about his feelings. If Deacon was *his*, he'd have trumpeted it from the tallest building. From the very top of the Condors stadium. He'd have taken out an advertisement on the jumbotron.

"That's not . . ." Grant sighed. "That's not it."

"It makes you look weak. Makes you look like I'm dragging you around by the dick," Deacon said gruffly, before Grant could elaborate on what it was exactly.

Maybe for the better, because Grant wasn't even sure how to begin describing it.

"You're not . . ." Grant said in a strangled voice. "Is that why you punched those guys?"

"They wouldn't stop insulting you. That's gonna be a thing, isn't it? It's exactly why you didn't want to do this." Deacon's dark brows drew together as he gestured in the space between them.

"Partly, yes," Grant said. "So Carter . . .Carter was not wrong, then."

"What did Carter say?"

Grant cleared his throat. It made sense to say it in his head. It was another to say it out loud, in the intimate darkness of the back of his car. The driver separation was up, and they were alone.

He hadn't felt it until this moment. He'd been too angry.

But without even noticing it, his temper had begun to seep away, slowly, and in its place was something else.

Something dangerous.

But is it dangerous if everyone already thinks it's happening?

If everyone already assumes you're together?

"Carter said you attacked those guys because of me. Uh, *for* me, specifically." And he'd been too full of righteous fury to think about the implications of that.

Too angry to realize just how goddamn hot it was.

Grant shifted in his seat, suddenly itchy and uncomfortable.

Horny. You're horny.

Okay. Fair. He was. Maybe if he just accepted it, acknowledged it was true, that would give those feelings less power over him.

But then, Deacon grinned, teeth flashing white in the dark interior of the car, and leaned in, and Grant's knees went weak. If he'd been standing, he'd have wobbled. Braced himself right against Deacon's big, strong body.

You'd have done a hell of a lot more with it than just use it as a prop.

"Yeah, I did," Deacon said.

"Oh. *Oh.*"

It wasn't like Grant didn't know their feelings were mutual. He knew. It was clear from the two kisses they'd shared they had a healthy dose of lust for each other.

"Yeah."

A trickle of moisture seeped out from under the towel pressed to Deacon's jaw. Grant reached out and swiped it up. Froze as he touched Deacon's skin, prickly with stubble.

He wanted to feel it all over his body.

"Just . . .uh . . .doing your part to defend the Condors name?" Grant said half-jokingly, trying to dispel the tension suddenly simmering between them.

"No," Deacon said bluntly. Shivering under Grant's touch.

Because he couldn't stop, once he'd swiped up the water. He was tracing all along Deacon's jawline now and couldn't have stopped even if there were a hundred people watching, a thousand.

"No?" Grant realized how hushed and intimate his voice sounded. How close he'd gotten, until his arm was pressed right up against Deacon's broad chest.

"No," Deacon said gruffly. "I didn't do it for the Condors. I did it for you. Because I love you, damnit."

Grant froze.

He wanted to shake his head. Argue. Something. But there was the truth of it, shining in Deacon's dark eyes. He genuinely believed it was true, that he loved Grant.

No wonder he hadn't wanted to talk to Grant after he'd blown him off, last week.

No wonder he'd lost his shit when those guys had started running their mouths.

"I thought it was just . . .uh . . ." Grant couldn't untangle his tongue from the words. Just the thought of them made his blood beat hot and his brain go hazy. "Uh . . .just sex."

"No," Deacon said. He looked darkly amused now. "Is it just sex for you?"

He could practically hear Deacon's unspoken question. *How could it just be sex if we weren't even having any?*

"No." That much was easy to say.

Deacon gave him a slow, leisurely perusal. As openly as he'd ever dared, his gaze tracing the curves of his body, which, to Grant, had never seemed particularly extraordinary, but from the way Deacon was looking, he might disagree.

"You gonna say anything else but *no*?"

"Do you want me to say yes?"

Heat flared in Deacon's dark eyes. "More than anything."

"Then . . ." Grant thought about saying something else. Justifying this decision, because even though they'd kissed twice before this, they couldn't do it a third time and walk it back. Not after Deacon had told him he loved him.

If he leaned in and kissed him now, this would be it.

What's stopping you? The whole world already thinks you're doing this.

That was what was stopping him, Grant realized. He didn't want Deacon, *who loved him*, to think he was only taking this step and bridging the gap between them because some old college friend had sent him a ridiculous email and then the whole world read it.

But Deacon took his hesitation another way. The *wrong* way. His eyes shuttered as Grant paused, on the knife's edge of giving in, just not sure how to take the leap while making it clear *why* he was doing it. He pulled back. Grant's hand dropped from his jaw to his chest.

"I get it," Deacon said, and he was turning away, his throat working.

He was . . .Grant realized, with shock, that he was . . .*emotional*. Close to tears?

Deacon had said it, of course. Had said the words, *I love you.*

But maybe Grant hadn't really, truly believed them, not until now. Not until he was faced with the evidence of what his rejection could do to Deacon.

"No, no, *no*," Grant said, suddenly ferocious. He grabbed Deacon's jaw again, ignoring Deacon's wince, and leaned in.

"You keep sayin' that word, and it doesn't exactly fill me with joy."

"I don't want you to think I'm gonna do this because of that stupid email. I want you to think I'm doing it 'cause . . ." And this was the crux of it, wasn't it? Grant wasn't sure whether he wanted to laugh or cry with relief. "Because I love you, too. And the more this goes on, the more I believe this isn't just us losing control or being stupid, but instead, the most fucking inevitable thing in the universe, you being with me."

"Is it?"

"Yes," Grant said and closed the final distance between them.

Their first kiss had been hesitant. Their second desperate.

This one was *ravenous*.

Deacon's arms went around his waist and as they devoured each other, he hauled him up and over, onto his lap, like he weighed absolutely nothing.

"God," Grant moaned as Deacon slid a confident hand right down his back, towards his ass, and hitched him even closer. Was that Deacon's cock pressed hard against him? It might be. That sent another shot of dizzying lust through him.

Deacon's head tipped back against the leather seat, and he was smiling in a way Grant had never seen before. He was happy. He was *happy*. Lighter, too, and more carefree than Grant could remember seeing him.

Except that wasn't true. He recognized this Deacon, from back in college. He remembered when Deacon would smile at him, just like this, over his statistics textbook.

"Yeah," Deacon agreed roughly. "We should . . .uh . . ."

But he didn't get any more words out, because Grant kissed him again, his tongue brushing against Deacon's as he forever wrecked the line separating them from each other.

It got intense fast, Grant groaning into Deacon's mouth as they kissed and kissed and lost track of all time.

He'd never thought he could have this—Deacon under him, moaning, hips shifting, trying not to thrust up against Grant, but losing that battle the deeper they got—but he'd imagined it so many times.

It had never felt like this in any of his fantasies.

"We should . . ." Deacon gasped for air, as they finally broke apart. "Go . . ."

"What, you don't want to have sex in the back of my car? Isn't that what all good billionaires do?" Grant teased, running his hands up and down Deacon's chest. It was so firm, the muscles taut underneath his fingertips. He couldn't wait to touch without this shirt in the way.

He couldn't wait to trace every muscle with his tongue.

"God, say that again," Deacon groaned.

"Sex?" Grant's tone was playful and he was rewarded with another fierce but quick kiss.

"I don't want to have sex *for the first time* with you in the back seat of your car," Deacon clarified. "Wanna spread you out on a bed. Take my time. Been wanting this too long to rush it, now."

The lust in Deacon's voice and the love in his eyes were nearly enough to undo Grant. To beg him to do it anyway. To take him *now*. To push them both and, finally, end this interminable waiting.

"But—"

"No," Deacon said firmly. "I'm not like any of those boys you've probably slept with before. I can control myself." He grinned wickedly. "Don't *want* to, but I can do it."

"Right, uh, yes," Grant said, swallowing hard. He'd never been so hot in his whole life. He was sweaty and damp under his collar, and it felt like all it would take was a couple of hard, relentless thrusts of Deacon's hips to send him right over the edge. Even then, Grant thought it might be the best orgasm of his life.

But Deacon was probably right.

They shouldn't do this here.

It was one thing to give in because it was *time* and it was another to do it recklessly and without a single care in the world.

Even if they *were* doing this now, Grant had every intention of keeping the truth of it under wraps, for now.

"Am I distracting you?" Deacon joked, looking like twenty years were dropping off his face, and Grant was drunk on the sight.

He nodded.

It almost felt like this had happened back then—even as he knew it hadn't.

It's even better.

They were the same people they'd been in college, but different too. Older. Having had experienced enough of life and love and loss to know just how much they both wanted this.

Having waited for it for all these years and rediscovered each other all over again . . .Grant felt breathless as Deacon's arms loosely encircled him. Not pushing him. But not letting him go, either.

Lots of people, especially after he'd become rich and successful, had wanted to pick Grant.

But never the man he'd always, secretly, desperately wanted.

Not until now.

He leaned over and enjoyed Deacon's sharp intake of breath as his mouth passed close by Deacon's. But instead he pressed a button on the control panel and tried to keep his voice level. "Richard? Can you take me back to my building, please?"

"Absolutely, sir," Richard said, and there was only barest hint of amusement in his tone.

Richard wasn't just his driver, though. He was also a friend. And he was most definitely aware that while Deacon had gotten into this car, he hadn't gotten out, yet.

"So this is the billionaire experience, huh?" Deacon asked.

Grant rolled his eyes. "It's convenient to have a driver. I conduct a lot of business in this car."

"And sex, too." Deacon's voice was gravelly. "Just not tonight."

It was too easy to lean in and catch Deacon's bottom lip between his teeth and tug, falling right back into the kiss.

Deacon could get used to traveling like this.

Not just quickly and easily in this long black car driven by someone else.

But going places with Grant in his lap and his mouth glued to Deacon's.

Of course, when the car stopped, then they had a problem.

By the time they made it to Grant's penthouse, they'd gotten hot and heavy again. It wasn't shocking, considering they both knew what was about to happen. When Grant pulled back from Deacon, his lips were red and wet and his bottom lip was swollen—probably because Deacon couldn't stop sucking on it.

Probably because of the way Grant made this deep, desperate sound in the back of his throat every time Deacon did it.

"We're going to have to get out of this car not looking like we were doing what we've been doing," Grant said, and to Deacon's disappointment, slid off his lap.

Deacon glanced down pointedly and Grant laughed, a hysterical little giggle that was absolutely fucking adorable.

"Believe me, I know," Grant said. "I've got a similar problem."

He sure did.

Deacon couldn't stop looking at the hard line of Grant's cock in his jeans as he tried to fix his hair, catastrophically messed up by Deacon's own hands.

"You're not even *trying*," Grant said as Deacon continued sitting there. Looking at Grant. He just couldn't stop, even if it wasn't diminishing his erection one bit.

Grant *loved* him. And they were actually, almost definitely, going to do this.

"No," Deacon agreed with a smile.

"Oh, fine, it's not like anybody's gonna see us," Grant said, giving in with a bashful grin. "It's late, and we're in the garage, anyway."

There was no point in trying, because Deacon knew ten minutes ago, Grant had told him he loved him. He'd *known*, of course. Been almost completely sure he wasn't feeling this way alone, but it sure felt different now, to realize Grant was no longer fighting it. There was that fact, and then also that in approximately ten minutes, he was going to have Grant naked in his own bed.

Nothing on earth could've made him soft.

He said as much to Grant, in a low voice, as they exited the car and he followed Grant towards a wall of elevators.

Grant steered him to the one on the far right. "You can't say shit like that," he retorted lightly.

"I thought you were enjoying it." Deacon wouldn't say he was *great* with his words. Not when it came to this. But with Grant, he'd sure as hell make the effort, because Grant was worth all of it—and so much fucking more.

Grant shot him a hot look as he hit the button and then typed in a code. The doors opened immediately, and they stepped inside.

There was only one button and a flat sensor panel. Grant dug a card out and pressed it against the panel, hitting the button after.

"Wait a second, is this your private elevator?" Deacon asked, awareness dawning on him thirty seconds too late, as the elevator started climbing.

"Yeah," Grant admitted. Looking slightly ashamed, like there was something wrong with him being brilliant and making lots of money off that brilliance.

"So, nobody else is gonna be in this elevator? We're not going to stop at any other floor?" Deacon asked, unable to hide his eagerness any longer.

"No," Grant said, shaking his head.

"You keep saying that word." He grinned. "Almost think you mean *yes*, now."

Grant gazed up at him. He looked as lovestruck as Deacon felt. "When it comes to you, yeah, I do."

What else was Deacon supposed to do then? It was impossible not to crowd him into one of the smooth stainless steel walls. The hiccupping gasp Grant made as he pressed his mouth to his neck and nibbled on the exposed tendon was intoxicating.

"I want you," Deacon murmured. "I *love* you."

"Gah, how do you do that?" Grant's laugh was high-pitched and a little hysterical. "It's only three words, but they make my knees mush."

Deacon grinned. "Long as they don't make any other parts of you mush."

The elevator dinged open. "Trust me, that's not gonna happen," Grant said, reaching down and taking his hand, squeezing it as he led Deacon into the dimly lit and incredibly spacious apartment.

Deacon was rich.

But he wasn't private-car-and-driver, penthouse-apartment-with-a-billion-dollar-view-of-the-city rich. Not rich, like had a priceless piece of art in the foyer, that Grant tugged him right by, like everyone had a Picasso on their wall.

He must've seen his backward glance though, because Grant said, "I was going to show you my bedroom, but if you want to stay here and look at the art, we could do that instead."

"No," Deacon said, and even though Grant looked solid, more filled-out than he had back in college, when he'd probably subsisted on black coffee and egg and cheese sandwiches from the little corner store at the edge of campus, it was easy enough to lean down and lift him.

Grant groaned and their mouths found each other again, his legs tucking behind Deacon. He stumbled forward, in the direction he hoped was the bedroom.

Grant's lips were intent on his, like he not only *could* lose himself in Deacon, he wanted to, more than anything else.

Deacon's knees hit something firm but soft, and he hoped to God it was a bed. When he set Grant down, chasing his mouth with his own for one last long kiss, he realized, that yes, it was.

Cushy and raft size, so much bigger than a man like Grant would need for just himself.

"Are we expecting company?" Deacon teased quietly, gesturing towards the bed.

"No, I, uh . . ." Grant flushed an even deeper red, his fingers tangling in the buttons of Deacon's shirt as he attempted to get it open.

Deacon raised an eyebrow.

"Fine," Grant grumbled. "I saw the bed the designer picked originally, and in a fit of optimism, told him it was too small. That someday I might want—"

"An NFL player in your bed?" Deacon grinned.

"How incredibly presumptuous of me," Grant said, pulling Deacon's shirt open the rest of the way, laying a palm on his bare chest.

Deacon shivered at the feel of them skin-to-skin for the first time.

"God," Grant said, his voice hushed as his fingertips drifted downwards, tracing intoxicating, teasing patterns on his skin. "I used to watch you, back then, during games. You'd lift your shirt up, flashing your abs, and it was ridiculous how much I wanted you. Though I didn't think you'd *ever* think of me this way."

"I *always* thought of you this way. Sat down across from you that first day and thought, *why'd I have to pick the hottest tutor on campus?*"

Grant laughed, his hands pausing on the waistband of Deacon's jeans. "You did not think that."

Deacon began to pant as Grant didn't go any further. Just stopped. He'd not begged anyone for anything in a very long time, but the *please* was right on the tip of his tongue.

"I did. I thought you were gorgeous," Deacon said, tipping his forehead to rest on Grant's. "And then I realized you were smart and funny and you gave a shit about me passing statistics."

"Spoiler alert: I thought if you passed, you might stay my friend. Might let me continue to ogle you shamelessly when you showed up for tutoring a few times a week."

"All you had to do was let me continue to shamelessly ogle *you*," Deacon teased.

"Should've done this ages ago."

"Years ago," Deacon agreed, and they were kissing again, fiercely, ferociously, like the intensity might make up for the fact that they hadn't.

Grant's touch drifted lower, and Deacon groaned into his mouth as his palm pressed against his hard dick.

Pleasure shot through him in a dizzying rush and he leaned into it, wanting more. Wanting so much, he wasn't sure what Grant gave him would ever be enough.

But he wasn't just going to stand here and take.

He'd intended to have Grant spread out in front of him, naked and needy, and Deacon wasn't going to be satisfied until that happened.

Gently, he pushed him back on the bed, Grant's green eyes going hot and smoky as Deacon shucked his own shirt the rest of the way off and reached for Grant's own, tugging it over his head.

"Shit," Deacon ground out. He'd never seen anything more gorgeous in his whole life as Grant wiggled out of his jeans, leaving him in only a pair of dark green boxer briefs, clinging to his slender but strong thighs and to his cock, straining against the fabric.

"Come 'ere." Grant beckoned, and it was the easiest decision he'd ever made to climb up on the bed, lips finding Grant's skin.

He tasted like fir and lemon—his soap, maybe, and something also undefinable, something that was just *Grant*. Sometimes, when Deacon was feeling really weak, he'd stand a little too close, just to *smell* him.

There'd been moments when Deacon had believed that was all he'd ever get from him.

But he was here, with him now. The taste of him on his tongue, the muscles under all that smooth skin twitching with desire. The view of him, sprawled against the bed, painted across his eyelids.

He was never going to get enough—which meant he was going to need to make it good enough for Grant that he never wanted to go anywhere else.

That he'd be content, and *happy* even, for Deacon to touch him forever.

His lips drifted lower, sliding along the dark brown hairs of Grant's happy trail, leading right to the waistband of his underwear.

"Oh, God, *please*," Grant begged. His hands found Deacon's hair and tangled in it, trying to push him closer to where his cock twitched against the cotton fabric, a spot of precome soaking through it.

Greedy, pushy Grant in bed was even hotter than Deacon could've imagined.

"Oh, baby," he teased, "I'm gonna give you everything you need."

"Yeah, yeah, oh God, *yeah*," Grant echoed.

Deacon swiped his tongue across that wet spot, groaning in the back of his throat at the taste of him, then tugged his boxer briefs down.

His cock bobbed out, so hard and flushed red, and Deacon had wanted to tease, to draw it out, to make Grant beg a little more, to make him wild and desperate, but once he got a sampling, his control splintered. He dove in, sliding just the head into his mouth, and sucking hard.

Grant groaned, and Deacon gave him more and more and more.

He was just as hard as Grant was, rocking against the bed helplessly, lost in the act of doing this, the pleasure echoing back through him like it was his own cock being sucked.

There was nothing he wanted more than for Grant to be just as overwhelmed as he was. His fingers, slick with saliva, traced his balls, and then pushed farther back, snubbing up against his hole, and Grant gasped, the noise loud in this silent room.

"*Please*," Grant begged again.

It was almost painful to pull off, to let Grant's cock out of his mouth, but the words spilled out anyway. "You want to come, filled with my fingers, your cock down my throat?"

A whole string of desperate gibberish spilled out of Grant's mouth.

God, how long had he imagined him like this?

And still the reality was nothing like those pathetic pale fantasies.

Deacon pressed a fingertip in, feeling the jolt of Grant's body as it tensed and then relaxed around the intrusion.

Grant didn't even need to keep moaning like that, like Deacon was giving him more pleasure than he'd ever imagined, because it was obvious just how much he wanted it. How much he *loved* it.

His cock twitched as another finger joined the first, Deacon hoping he'd found the right spot inside him.

He swiveled his hand, and Grant yelped, his cock blurting precome onto his tongue, and he knew he was close.

Come for me, Deacon thought intensely. Wishing his mouth wasn't full and he could say it, but he didn't need to, because only seconds later, Grant was clenching around him, emptying down his throat.

Deacon took his time taking Grant down, sucking him clean slowly and thoroughly, until Grant made a content noise.

When he glanced up, Grant was staring at him. His eyes glowing bright green, happy and satisfied.

"Good?" Deacon asked.

"Come 'ere," Grant insisted, and Deacon was helpless, a second time, to not do exactly what he said. He crawled up Grant's gorgeous body and kissed him.

Tried, very hard, not to hump his thigh, but it was really hard, because *God*, he was so goddamn horny, his own control hanging by a thread.

"It's alright," Grant said, when he broke the kiss, grinning wildly. "I got you."

He reached over and grabbed a bottle from the drawer in the table next to the bed.

There wasn't much blood left in Deacon's brain. "What are you doing?" he asked stupidly.

"Taking care of you," Grant said. And then there was even *less* blood in his brain because Grant was wetting his fingers with the lube and tucking them behind him.

"Jesus, what are you doing?"

Grant grinned. "Nothing to do with Jesus, I promise. Lie back. Come on. Yep, just like that," he said with an approving nod as Deacon collapsed onto the bed.

With his other hand, he made quick work of Deacon's jeans.

Still, it was pretty satisfying to see Grant's jaw drop.

"Have you been—*this whole time*?" he asked with a quiet gasp as Deacon's cock, as hard as he'd ever been in his life—screw you, mid-thirties, he felt like a goddamn teenager again—sprang out of his open jeans.

Deacon shrugged. "Maybe."

Grant's eyes went dark and hazy. Deacon wanted to make him look like that a hundred times. A thousand. "If I'd known you went *commando*, I'd have—"

"You'd have done what?" Deacon was genuinely curious.

"This," Grant said and pulled his jeans the rest of the way off, and before Deacon could figure out what exactly *this* was, it was happening.

Grant was straddling his lap, slicking up his cock with his lube-covered fingers. "I've been tested, recently," he said, teasing Deacon until his eyes nearly crossed with the pleasure of just his touch. "You?"

"No, I'm uh . . .I'm good," Deacon agreed.

There'd been nobody he wanted to do this with. Not for a long time.

Not that he'd been celibate, but it had been longer than anybody would probably imagine for him.

"I'm gonna uh...not..." Deacon ground out as Grant braced a hand on his chest, and began to grind down on his cock, both of them groaning as it slipped into Grant's hole.

"It's okay. I just want you to feel good. So feel good," Grant said in a hushed whisper and leaned forward, brushing his mouth against Deacon's.

Good was an understatement of the century.

Grant was tight and hot and kept doing this thing with his hips, making pleasure spike through him, splintering his control into too many pieces. He squeezed his eyes shut, overwhelmed.

But Grant's hand was on his cheek, cupping him. "Look at me," he said. "Don't look away."

Deacon wanted to shake his head, feeling the inevitable rush of his oncoming orgasm. Not wanting to surrender to it, because that would mean the first time, the very first time, would be over.

"Come on," Grant murmured in that coaxing way of his that always made Deacon want to follow, no matter what it was, no matter what it cost.

He planted his feet and thrust upwards as Grant fucked downward and *God*, it was even better. He felt like he was going to explode right out of his skin, and then Grant leaned in and kissed him one more time.

And that was all it took.

Deacon's orgasm didn't just happen, it overtook him.

When he finally emerged from it, legs still shaky from the intensity of it, Grant was still there, inches away, those glowing green eyes still happy.

"I . . .uh . . are you okay?" Deacon asked. He'd probably gotten a little wild there at the end. He'd lost himself, in a way that he normally didn't.

The last thing he wanted was to hurt Grant, who'd given him all that gorgeous pleasure selflessly.

"Never better," Grant said. He smiled, his lips tilting up. "I'm afraid we're about to make a mess."

"It was worth it," Deacon said.

Grant's head tilted bashfully. "Yeah?"

"You were really okay doing that, right after you came . . ." Deacon trailed off. Aware, now that he was really thinking about it, that it was the hottest thing in the world, that Grant had *still* wanted to fuck, even after his own orgasm.

"I like it, no matter what," Grant admitted. "And it's hard to do, with the life I lead. I don't trust many people. And I never wanted anyone the way I wanted you."

"Wanted?" Deacon asked, before he could stop himself.

"*Want*." Grant chuckled as he lifted himself, his biceps clenching and making something unfurl in Deacon's stomach. He didn't know how he could possibly still be hot for the guy, after what had just happened. But he was. It was undeniable.

And yeah, it *was* messy. But that there was an added benefit, Deacon decided as he got up and followed Grant to the bathroom, watched him as he flipped on the shower.

"Well, anytime you want me to fuck you, I'm not going to argue," Deacon said, leaning against the long countertop.

"No?" Grant tapped his fingers against the glass of the shower. "What about if I want you to get in with me?"

"That was a given," Deacon said.

Chapter 12

Grant had pulled a lot of all-nighters, but he'd never done it like this before.

His shower with Deacon had turned into a hot and lazy make-out session, his fingers buried into Deacon's water-slick hair, and then *that* had turned into a blow job, his mouth finally getting to taste Deacon's cock.

But before Grant could coax another orgasm out of him, he'd pulled out of Grant's mouth and leaned him over the bed and fucked him slow and insistent, leaving Grant panting and sobbing against the comforter.

By the time Deacon had finally wrung his second orgasm out of him, he'd been desperate and hysterical, thrusting his cock against the soft fabric.

Now they were clean again, tucked up in Grant's bed, Deacon's eyes sleepy and satisfied, Grant's own heart beating strong as Deacon slung an arm around him, tugging him flush against him.

Grant didn't even know what time it was.

Late, probably.

And he didn't give a shit.

Going to bed at a reasonable hour and not fucking twice in a few hours was overrated.

"Tomorrow's gonna be tough for you," Grant pointed out.

"I've gotten by on far less sleep," Deacon said. "What about you? You gonna be able to walk tomorrow?"

He sure hoped so. Deacon hadn't been rough exactly, but it had been a long time since he'd had more than his own fingers or his toy inside him, and Deacon was a *lot* bigger than that. "Guess we're gonna find out."

Deacon's fingers tightened against his shoulder. "I'm sorry if I was thoughtless that last time. I . . .I kinda lost my mind again. Even though I swore to myself that I wouldn't."

"Yeah?" Grant liked the sound of that. He wanted to break Deacon down to just the parts of him that belonged to *him*. Wanted to imprint himself in the spaces between. So Deacon could never even dream of living without him.

And you thought you could live without doing this, ever.

Okay, that had been a very stupid assumption on his part.

"I want you so much, you make me lose my mind." Deacon's voice was a deep rumble. Grant couldn't just hear it, he could *feel* it.

"I guess it was naive to imagine we wouldn't ever cross this line," Grant conceded. Because he felt the same. Out of control and unlike how he imagined the center of a hurricane felt, he was perfectly, insanely happy.

Like this was exactly where he was meant to be.

"I just wish it wasn't because of *Rex*, 'cause that's where they got the email, wasn't it? Because you gave your hard drives to the NFL."

"Yes," Grant said. There was no point in lying. Deacon was too smart to lie to, and Grant didn't even want to, anyway.

If they were doing this—and it was becoming increasingly clear there was no going back to before; no putting the milk back into the carton, now that it had spilled everywhere, all over Grant's bed—then they were *doing this*, in this one hundred and ten percent, no turning back now.

Deacon made a dissatisfied noise.

"What?" Grant asked.

He knew Deacon well, but he couldn't parse out this sound and what it meant.

"Just . . .I'm happy it's happened. Wish it had happened differently."

Grant sighed. "Me too. I wish we could tell everyone. I'd walk out with you onto the field next Sunday, to the fifty-yard line, and kiss you without a hint of shame."

"You'd do that?" Deacon's chuckle was a deep rumble against his arm.

"No, exactly. I wouldn't. I would *want* to, but I'm not going to. I'm responsible for too many people, their livelihoods, their families, their *lives*. I can't risk all of that, just because I want to tell the haters of the world to fuck off."

"I know you already said everyone knowing wasn't why, but you meant it, didn't you?"

Grant turned to him. "You told me you loved me. And I knew I loved you. Why shouldn't we have this? If we can keep it compartmentalized, keep it safe and secret and just between us when we're here? We were already a team in every way that mattered, outside, in the real world, why not make it real, solid, *unassailable*, when we're in this apartment?"

"We can't keep it a secret forever," Deacon said, and Grant hated how he was frowning. Was he saying this poorly? He probably was. He was smart, some people would even say he was brilliant, but he was so fucking shit at emotions. At deciphering his own. At expressing them to others.

"I'm not asking you for that."

"And I'm not asking for you to waltz out with me to the fifty-yard line and kiss me there," Deacon retorted softly. But there was heat there, in his voice.

"I'm probably fucking this up," Grant said.

"No, you're not. That—what we've been doing for hours—*sex*, that's easy. This is a lot harder. A lot shittier. I know you've got responsibilities. I don't want to ever get in the way of them."

"You don't. In fact, you make them easier to carry," Grant said seriously.

"Good."

"'Cause you take the weight, too. Not all of it. I wouldn't expect that. You're not the owner of this team. Or the CEO of InTech."

"God forbid," Deacon teased.

"But you make it easier for me to be Grant Green. And having this here?" Grant pressed a palm against Deacon's chest. "It makes it even easier. And it makes me lighter. It makes me *happy*."

"I get that you worry about everyone else. It's who you are, and you should do it. But your happiness matters, too."

"There's only a few people who feel that way," Grant said. Realizing, with a tight throat, that was true.

And also, that there was one more.

"Add someone else to the list," Deacon said, pressing a kiss to his shoulder. "I love you. Probably always have. Probably always will."

Grant's heart splintered in his chest. "You really mean that."

"Yeah. I do." Deacon sounded very sure.

But how could he be? What if he got tired of hiding? What if he got tired of Grant working twenty-hour days?

What if he got tired of Grant putting all his responsibilities ahead of him?

"I can see you thinking way too hard over there," Deacon said, a thread of amusement in his voice. "Don't, okay?"

Grant forced himself to relax. "Okay."

"Now," Deacon said, "it's my turn to tell you to come 'ere and relax. Close your eyes."

Grant did it. "What else?"

"Tell me you love me, too."

"Always," Grant said.

What was supposed to happen was they would get out of bed with Deacon's alarm.

That was *not* what happened.

As they'd fallen asleep, Deacon had made noise about needing to go home, grab a shower and a change of clothes before he headed into the Condors facility for a day of meetings and practice.

They *did* make it out of the bed, on time. Even though they'd only gotten a few hours of sleep, Grant still followed Deacon out of the warm, rumpled covers.

Grant didn't have to get up for another hour, but he did anyway. Was it because he felt especially rested? Or because he didn't want to lose sight of Deacon, after the most magical night of his life?

"How're you doing?" Deacon asked after they'd brushed their teeth and headed into the kitchen. It was way too fucking early. Grant needed *coffee*. You couldn't survive on sex alone. Even really, really great sex.

Deacon leaned against the counter as Grant worked the coffee machine.

He hadn't even bothered to throw any clothes on, and in the morning light, he was every statue Grant had looked at in museums in Florence and Rome.

"I'm good, just about ten quarts low on caffeine."

"No adverse effects?" Deacon leaned down and Grant sank into the warmth of Deacon's body behind him. He regretted even putting on his boxer briefs. He wanted to feel every inch of Deacon's skin against his own.

"None whatsoever, except a very fervent need to do it as soon as possible again," Grant joked lightly.

But then Deacon's mouth was on the curve of his neck, kissing and then nibbling down it. Suddenly, it seemed like *as soon as possible* might be *right now*.

He'd just turned around in Deacon's arms, reaching up to kiss him again, when a noise behind him made him pause.

"Oh my God. I'd say get a room but you *do* have a room." Darcy's voice echoed through the cavernous kitchen, and Grant felt Deacon freeze.

"I'm turning around," Darcy continued, sounding very amused, "and going back to the foyer. When I come back in five minutes, will everyone be clothed?"

"Yes," Grant said in a strangled voice.

He heard her footsteps clicking on the floor as she left the kitchen.

"Does she always just . . .let herself in?" Deacon asked under his breath as they hightailed it back to the bedroom. Grant found a pair of sweatpants in a drawer, glancing up as Deacon buttoned his shirt and pulled up his jeans.

"Uh yeah, I guess? It's . . ." Grant cleared his throat, suddenly embarrassed that for so long, until last night, there hadn't been *any* reason for Darcy to warn him. "It's been awhile since I had anyone over."

Deacon put a hand on his shoulder and to Grant's relief, he was smiling. "It's alright. I'm not particularly modest. I don't mind that she saw . . .uh . . ."

"Us nearly repeating last night?"

Deacon nodded. "Just disappointed that it didn't *actually* happen, again."

"It will. I have a crazy busy lineup of meetings today, but tomorrow night? I think I can clear my schedule after you're done with practice. We could uh . . .grab a late dinner."

"And then come back here?" Deacon's smile widened. "It's a date."

"Ah, yes, okay." Grant knew he should stop smiling back. Should get back out there and explain to Darcy that *yes*, in the future, knocking was going to be required.

Felt a happy little zing shoot up his spine at the thought.

"But you *are* going to talk to her . . . right?" Deacon asked.

"Oh, yes. *Yes*. Definitely."

Deacon's eyes dropped to his mouth. Grant knew he wanted to kiss him again, and he certainly wasn't alone. There was nothing Grant would've liked better than to tug Deacon back towards the bed, still warm from their bodies, and mess up the sheets even further.

Last night might've been started as a temporary insanity—a departure from the pressures and realities of their lives—but now they were continuing it into the harsh light of day.

Maybe even more insane, Grant thought, but worth it.

If he could really *have* this, without destroying his life—and the lives of everyone who depended on him—while preserving the Condors' and Deacon's reputation, too?

Wouldn't he do just about anything to have it all?

He would.

"I love you," Grant said, which was a much shorter, simpler way of saying, *I'd do just about anything to have it all: you* and *the rest, too.*

Deacon dropped a short, quick kiss on his upturned mouth. It was like they'd already been doing this for years. Like they'd said goodbye just this way a hundred times already, even though it was actually the first time.

"I love you too," he murmured. "I'd better go."

"You don't want to stay for coffee?" Grant asked. Because if he wasn't going to have sex as a wake-up mechanism, he *really* needed coffee.

"And have Darcy ogling me over her cappuccino? No, I'm good, thanks. I'm sure she's going to want to hear the full rundown, anyway, and it'll be easier for you to accurately judge my technique if you're not doing it in front of me." The corner of Deacon's mouth quirked upwards.

Like his technique hadn't been perfectly mind-blowing.

Grant rolled his eyes.

"I'll see you tomorrow then," Deacon said, looking delighted at Grant's response to that.

"Yes," Grant said. "I'll text you."

"Oh, I'm sure we'll be talking before tomorrow," Deacon said, as they headed out of the bedroom into the main living space.

"Yes," Grant said, trying very hard not to sound like an eager sixteen-year-old, making a phone date with his crush.

He might've just embraced it but Darcy was standing in the kitchen, eyes seemingly glued to her tablet as she drank her coffee. He wasn't necessarily *embarrassed* to do it in front of her, but it did mean the amount of shit she'd give him would be exponentially more.

After Deacon had said goodbye one more time, giving Darcy a brief wave, and the door had closed behind him, she turned to Grant, a knowing gleam in her eye.

"So," she said.

"So," Grant repeated, heading towards the coffee machine, setting it up for a double latte.

He pulled a mug down from the shelf and watched as the frother warmed the milk.

"You could've texted," Darcy said.

"I could've, but I was . . .uh . . .a bit busy," Grant admitted.

"Last thing I heard was you were heading to that bar to deal with that fight mess Carter messaged you about."

"Yes. I handled things at the Pirate's Booty," Grant said trying to keep a straight face as he said the name.

But Darcy was smiling. "Booty, huh? You becoming a buccaneer in this scenario? Or was that Deacon?"

Grant's espresso finally finished dripping into his mug and he poured the milk over. Took a long bracing sip. "I don't know if I'd characterize *either* of us in that manner," he said.

"Uh-huh." Darcy didn't sound convinced. And okay, maybe Deacon had definitely shivered his timbers last night. Twice, even.

"But yes, you can report back to Cheryl that the fight was a non-issue. Some drunk guys said some shit, Deacon took exception to it, but everyone saw reason once they sobered up."

"Or because you showed up looking all owner-y," Darcy said knowingly.

"Something like that," Grant said bashfully.

"You have to tell me how you got from smoothing over a fight to waking up with Deacon in your bed." She paused. "Bed? Or kitchen? Please tell me you were going to go at it in this kitchen. On the counter? On the *floor*?"

"In my bed," Grant said with an attempt at dignity.

"Ah, okay. So you did make it to the bed, then."

"We did." Grant took a long drink of coffee. Knowing he was already going to need another one, before they left. "So Cheryl called, huh?"

"She wants a meeting this morning. I fit her in between Frankfurt and Singapore," Darcy said. "I'm assuming also that we won't be sharing any other developments other than downplaying the Pirate's Booty fight and then an abject denial of this email situation?"

Grant finished his coffee. Because his day hadn't been busy enough—or shitty enough—without adding Cheryl to the mix. "You would be correct."

"Ah okay. So I did *not* arrive at your penthouse this morning to see you kissing Deacon Harris, then."

"It's my personal business. And when that email was sent—I certainly wasn't kissing Deacon Harris then. I can plausibly deny that, no lies required," Grant said.

Sure, okay, he hadn't really *thought* this through last night. Deacon had told him he loved him, and his thinking brain had just died, a little. But with two shots of espresso under his belt this morning and no Deacon currently in the vicinity, it was easier to think more clearly.

"Are you going to tell me how you ended up kissing Deacon? Again, I guess?" Darcy asked.

Grant headed back over to the coffee machine. Another double latte and a hot shower and he should be pretty much functional for this crazy long day, despite the three or four hours of sleep he'd gotten.

He'd done a lot more on a lot less.

And never for such a damn good reason.

Grant mentally debated. Darcy was his best friend. He knew he could trust her, completely. But was even including *one* more person in the magical love bubble they'd created enough to puncture it? To allow real life to come rushing in, way too fast?

But also . . .Darcy was his best friend.

"He told me he loved me," Grant said shyly, turning around and seeing Darcy's face light with joy.

"Oh, honey," she said and in a second she was across the kitchen, wrapping her arms around him. "I'm so happy for you."

"Yeah?" Grant's voice cracked. *He* was so happy for him. "Yeah."

"We're gonna make sure you can keep this, keep *him*," Darcy said in a no-nonsense voice as she pulled back. "Promise me you're not going to give him up, not when he makes you this happy. No matter what happens. How hard it gets."

Grant considered this for a moment. He knew Darcy and so he knew a promise made to her wasn't one either of them took lightly. He would have to *mean* whatever he said, or else she'd make his life a living hell afterwards.

"Yes, I promise," Grant said. Realized, that yes, he'd already made that vow to himself. He wouldn't have ever crossed the line with Deacon if he hadn't been very, *very* sure that this was it. This was the happiness he'd been searching for his whole goddamn life. Professionally, he'd done more than he'd ever dreamed. But he'd always been alone.

Not anymore.

"Good," Darcy said, nodding approvingly.

"Was Cheryl frothing at the mouth?" Grant said.

"She sure wasn't happy. In fact, she made a lot of disappointed noises."

"I'm sure she's *very* disappointed," Grant retorted.

"Don't let her get to you," Darcy said.

Grant chuckled darkly. "Oh, like she gets to you?"

Darcy rolled her eyes.

"I mean it," Grant said. "We'll get through this."

"Like we've gotten through all the rest?" Darcy threw up her hands in frustration. "I feel like every time we clean up a mess, there's only a second of quiet where we catch our breath and think, *oh, this is the last of it*, and then some other new crisis crops up, and you know what the craziest part is? It's often worse than the last one!"

Grant couldn't tell her that he hadn't had these exact same thoughts. Because he had. At the same time, he'd had at least *some* inkling what he was getting into.

Darcy hadn't had a clue—other than what he'd told her.

She'd never even watched a football game before he'd sat her down and said he was buying the Condors.

"Yeah, it's been a rough go. But think of it this way, Darcy. Some of the things that caused major friction between us and Cheryl? They were things that were genuinely *amazing*. The kind of things that were possible only because I bought this team. Like Micah and Beck? That was a really, really good thing, in the end. I can't even be mad about Rex, because his injury and what we found out about his gambling made it possible for me to bring Micah here. And he's fit in, with or without Beck, like he *belongs*."

Darcy sighed. "This is why you're so good at this. You see the human element when I can't."

"That's not true, you see it. You see it at InTech all the time. You're the one who pioneered a lot of our most popular employee programs. I think this football thing is just throwing you. You're not usually *so* close to the employee component."

"Maybe. Or maybe I just spend way less time ogling them in tight pants," Darcy said lightly.

"True," Grant said with a chuckle. "Okay, I'm gonna grab a quick shower, and then we can take off. Or do we need to take the first set of meetings here?"

"Here," Darcy said. "And then we'll have Richard take us to the Condors facility for the afternoon."

"How long do I have to brace myself before we get Cheryl?" Grant asked, finishing his coffee.

"A few hours." Darcy shot him a meaningful look as he rinsed out his mug and stuck it in the dishwasher. "Enough time to work on your poker face."

"She made it a video meeting, then?"

"Oh, was I not clear? She is *coming here*. She flew in this morning." Darcy looked mildly satisfied at his shock. Because yes, it was shock. Cheryl had never shown up in-person before.

"That's why we're going into the Condors today. We'll meet her there. Go put your best suit on, the one you had tailored in London. The one that makes you look every inch the billionaire."

"Ugh," Grant said and headed towards the shower.

"Cheryl," Grant said, shaking her hand briefly, keeping his face a smooth mask as he took a seat opposite her in the Condors' biggest conference room. He wanted to bend down, get her to lean in closer, and then scream at her.

Nicole was monitoring the media response to the email releasing, and it seemed everyone wanted a piece of the action.

The last update he'd gotten from her was some media outlets were hinting that they'd managed to track down Dougie, but even then Grant wasn't worried he'd talk, because Nicole had done her job and gotten to him first.

But still, despite the inevitable frustration that his personal business was splashed across every news and gossip site in the whole freaking world *and* he was face-to-face with Cheryl, currently wearing a smile he could only describe as *smug*, Grant was in a pretty damn good mood.

The reason for that wasn't very hard to figure out.

The reason was probably outside, on the practice field, and if Grant got up and wandered over to the windows as Darcy and Cheryl made viciously polite small talk, he would probably see him out there. Dark hair shining in the sun. He might even get a glimpse of some of that big, glorious body he'd gotten so lucky as to enjoy last night.

Darcy cleared her throat and sent a pointed glance in his direction. "Grant?" she asked, clearly repeating herself.

Whoops.

"Yes, sorry," Grant said, forcing his attention back to Cheryl.

Not who he wanted to be thinking about, that was for sure.

It was just like her, though, to create this mess, and then come here in person to chastise him about it.

Only years of dealing with hostile adversaries in boardrooms made it possible for him to offer her a bland smile.

Don't let them see you sweat. Ever.

Definitely don't let them see you bleed. Once there's blood in the water . . .

"I want to know what you're going to do to combat the rumors," Cheryl said.

"*You* want to know?" Grant enquired innocently.

He was one hundred percent sure she'd come here just to gloat. Maybe to dance on his grave a little.

But Grant Green never gave up without a fight—and now that he had someone he loved very much, someone he'd fight for tooth and nail—he wasn't going to roll over and play dead, no matter how much she hoped he would.

"The NFL, of course," Cheryl trilled. Tucked a strand of blonde hair behind her ear. "We're just very concerned. So many rumors. *Inappropriate* rumors."

"You're really concerned about rumors?"

"I'm assuming you *saw* the email," Cheryl said. Then laughed delicately. "Of course you did. It was sent to you, after all."

"And you'd have seen that I didn't reply to it."

"Not electronically, anyway."

"Mr. Green is too polite to say it, but we are *very* busy dealing with the fallout of this rumor, as well as all of his other *many* professional obligations," Darcy said. "Are you here to help? Or to just tell us how very *concerned* you are?"

"The commissioner wanted me to come here in person," Cheryl insisted. "So you understood just how very seriously we're taking these rumors."

"There's no evidence we've done anything wrong. I've opened up my business and let the NFL review all my correspondence," Grant said, "and the only thing that anyone found was an email sent *to* me, that I did not even reply to. I'm unsure why you aren't here offering your support to help us combat these malicious rumors."

"We're only concerned because of the truly inappropriate nature of the rumors," Cheryl said, making what he supposed was intended to be an apologetic expression, but nothing about her tone said she meant it.

"Are you asking me if it's true?" Grant said.

Because of course she was.

She'd probably found that email on his hard drive and been absolutely fucking delighted.

"Even the cursory digging we did proves you both attended the same college, during the same time period. Your attendance overlapped by two years. Are you trying to deny you didn't know Deacon Harris back then?"

"I did. And you know exactly how I knew him. I was his tutor. He was having trouble passing statistics. That was the extent of it then, and as for now, the *NFL themselves* asked Deacon to talk to me when I stepped forward to buy the team. As a final check, they wanted him to verify my intentions. He did. We've become partners, and friends, you could say, as we guide this team back into the light." Grant leaned forward. "Is that what you wanted to know?"

"I . . ." Cheryl stammered. Looked taken aback. Maybe she hadn't expected him to come clean about it.

Of course, he hadn't told the whole truth—but then, he hadn't lied, either.

"We have a few questions of our own," Grant said casually as he stood. Carefully divested himself of his flawlessly tailored navy jacket. He wandered over by the window. Caught sight, for a split second, of a big man with dark hair, who might be Deacon.

But he forced himself to turn away before he could really absorb the sight of him.

He couldn't afford to let himself get distracted.

Not when he was about to go in for the kill, and Grant wasn't convinced he could keep the joy of him buried deeply enough that Cheryl wouldn't catch even a glimpse of it.

"What questions?" Cheryl asked.

"How did the media get ahold of this email?" Grant pinned her with his gaze. "I certainly didn't allow any of my *personal data* to be released without my express approval."

"Leaks happen," Cheryl said with a wave.

"Oh, do they?" Darcy's voice was dangerous. "Funny how nothing else was leaked. Just this email."

"I could sue you," Grant said.

Cheryl's jaw dropped open. It *would* be ballsy to sue the organization that licensed the Condors and essentially *permitted* him to continue owning his nearly billion-dollar investment. It would be making an enemy of them, irrevocably, and the media would never stop hounding them, if he did it.

Which was why he had no intention of actually doing it.

But even the thought of it felt good.

Felt fucking brilliant, in fact.

Or maybe that was just the way Cheryl looked at even the threat of it.

"You wouldn't," she said.

"I don't know," Grant said dangerously, "I *might*. You took my personal information and released it to the media. It was completely uncalled for."

"*I* didn't," she spluttered.

"Right, no, of course not," Grant said smoothly. Even though everyone in this room knew it had been her.

"It was certainly frustrating that they got ahold of the one piece of potentially questionable information," Cheryl said. Still not sounding sympathetic.

"Certainly," Grant echoed. "Which is why I want to know, what are you doing to combat the . . .we'll say. . .*leakiness* . . .of your office."

"Combat?" she asked weakly.

"What are you going to do about it? Launch an investigation? Fire whoever was responsible? I certainly expect all those things to happen."

"I . . .we hadn't gotten that far," Cheryl admitted. Of course she hadn't even considered it, because she knew exactly who was responsible.

"Well, we certainly expect that as much of a hurry as you were in to get here and *remind us* of our professional obligations to the NFL, about how dangerous these rumors are, you'd be in just as much of a hurry to root out the corruption and untrustworthiness in your *own* office," Darcy said, going in for the kill with a delightfully pleasant smile on her face.

"I suppose," Cheryl said. She did not look particularly pleasant or in any way delighted.

Ten minutes later she was gone, and Grant leaned against the bank of windows, crossing his arms over his chest. "Well?" he asked, when Darcy came back to the room after showing Cheryl to her car, ready to take her back to the airport.

Darcy shrugged. "We made her sweat, that's for sure. You sent the message?"

"I did," Grant said. He might be the newest team owner but the other team owners sure wouldn't be pleased to hear about how much Cheryl's office resembled a sieve.

There was too much private, personal information that crossed through it to allow for that sort of continued behavior.

"I'm not sure she'll actually do anything," Darcy said.

"I'm actually counting on that," Grant said.

"You don't only want to make her pay, you want to professionally discredit her by proving she leaked the email and then didn't do anything about it," Darcy said. Grinned. "I love it when you go all killer instinct."

"You taught me," Grant said, because it was the truth. Of the two of them, Darcy was so much more vicious than he was. "And it's her own fault. She tried to make me look bad in front of the whole world. I don't think I should just let that go."

"Nicole still recommending *no comment*?" Darcy asked, taking a seat.

"Yes," Grant said. And even if she wasn't, he'd have insisted on it. Giving in to the rumors by addressing them was only giving them oxygen and room to grow.

And he had no intention of doing that.

"Going high is a tactic, for sure," Darcy agreed, stretching her arms above her head. They still had a long afternoon—and evening—of meetings ahead of them.

"You disagree, then, with *no comment*?" Grant was surprised because they almost always agreed on everything.

"I think you should be honest. Tell everyone the truth."

"Darcy, we *just* started . . ." God, what were they doing even? Besides being ridiculously, deeply in love? Dating? That felt too casual of a term. Grant couldn't wrap his head around the idea of calling Deacon his boyfriend.

He was so much more than that.

"And you've only wanted to date him for a hell of a long time," Darcy continued for him. "It's not like either of you are going anywhere, not now that you've finally got your shit straight."

"Maybe. Maybe not." Grant paced in front of the windows. "But wouldn't confirming it just give everyone more room to talk about it?"

"Honey, they're going to talk about it no matter what," Darcy said sympathetically. "If you don't tell them the truth, they're gonna speculate, until the story's bigger than it really is."

Grant raised an eyebrow.

"Okay, it's pretty damn big, anyway," Darcy conceded. "But the point is valid."

"I'll think about it," Grant said. "But for now, *no comment* is how we're proceeding."

"Alright," Darcy said.

"What's next?" Grant asked.

CHAPTER 13

"Here's the big man of the hour," Carter crowed as Deacon jogged onto the field for practice.

For a second, he wanted to demand what Carter knew—and then he realized that Carter was just talking about the fight at the Pirate's Booty, not everything that had happened with Grant after.

"It's no big deal," Deacon said. Like he got into bar fights all the time, even though honestly, he couldn't even remember the last one he'd participated in. He'd surely never *started* one.

Which reminded him—he'd better call Kieran today and make sure he was all squared away. Pay for any damages, though he hadn't seen any before Grant had shown up and demanded Micah take him to his car.

And well, after that, he hadn't been thinking of Kieran and the bar at all.

He'd stop by after practice. Make sure Kieran was taken care of and apologize in person.

"You punching some Neanderthal guy who wouldn't stop talking about Mr. G? I'm sorry, Deac, but that was pretty fucking epic," Beck chimed in when he walked over.

Ugh, was the whole team going to talk about this?

It seemed likely.

He still wasn't sure if he should tell any of them—even though they were his friends—what had happened after the fight. Not because they wouldn't be thrilled for him, because they would be. But because Grant was their boss. The owner of this team. Maybe Deacon saw him as a man. *Very* much a man, after last night. But they shouldn't, necessarily.

Grant might not want them to. And they hadn't had any time to discuss it yet, so until Grant gave him the go-ahead, he'd keep quiet.

"He was being unbelievably rude," Deacon said.

"We know," Beck said. "You were just doing what you had to do."

Beck *would* see it that way.

Hadn't he told him to fight for Grant, just a few weeks ago?

He probably hadn't meant it literally, but there he'd gone, taking it exactly that way.

"Don't try to minimize, make it less than the *super romantic, in your fucking face*, gesture that it is," Carter insisted, waving his arms around.

Deacon shook his head. What *did* Ian see in this guy? And even more than that, what did the long, *long* line of men and women see who'd visited his bed?

Deacon didn't get it.

The first—and the second, and the tenth—time Carter had hit on him, he'd had trouble not laughing.

That's 'cause there's only one man you wanted.

And now you've got him.

Deacon tried to school his expression into something less joyful and much sterner.

"Carter," he warned.

"I'm just saying," Carter argued. "It's romantic as fuck. I mean, not as romantic as a slow dance to Marky Mark, but it *is* romantic."

"Sorry to disappoint," Deacon said dryly.

"You really trying to say *nothing* happened after you took care of business that way? Micah told me he took you to Mr. G's car. That he *insisted* you be taken to it. Like he was gonna . . ." Beck paused and grinned. "Take good care of you, after."

"He just wanted to talk to me," Deacon said. Technically true.

"Disappointing. Talking. *Ugh*," Carter said.

"Don't tell me Ian doesn't want you to talk to him," Micah said, nudging Carter. "'Cause I know that he does. Ian's the kind of guy who likes the words, sometimes. Not just a healthy helping of dick."

"Maybe," Carter said, grinning.

"Practice," Deacon reminded them, as Riley and Landry emerged from the tunnel onto the practice field. "That's why we're here, okay? Not to gossip."

Beck trailed after Deacon as he headed over to the bench to grab one of his stretching bands. "You get it, right? They just wanna know if it finally happened," Beck said.

Deacon shot him a glare.

"What?" Beck said, throwing up his hands. "They do."

"And you're here in a completely innocent capacity, not interested at all in what happened last night."

"I wouldn't say I'm an uninterested party," Beck said. "But I know Jem's not here. And I know you haven't been telling him much."

"He text you that?"

"Yep," Beck said with a quick nod. "Complained about it, too."

"He's just…finally happy, I think? After everything. I don't want to derail that."

"I get it, but also, Jem's your person to talk to. So if you're not talking to him, who're you talking to?"

Deacon rolled his eyes as he stretched. "Don't tell me you're volunteering yourself."

Except that Beck would be a good person to talk to. He'd keep his mouth shut. Okay, he'd almost certainly tell Micah everything Deacon said, but he could trust the two of them would stay a closed circuit. They'd both learned the hard way how much it hurt when people shoved their noses into personal business.

"You know I am," Beck said quietly.

Deacon was silent for a long moment. *You already know what you're gonna do. You know it, so just do it.*

"Yeah," Deacon said shortly.

Beck didn't react and then, all of a sudden, looked floored. "What, *yeah*? Are you really saying what I think you are?"

"I said it, didn't I?" Deacon said.

"Wow, okay. Yes. You did." Beck still looked shocked.

"Were you expecting balloons and confetti and heart eyes or something?" Deacon wondered. Remembered, of course, because how could he forget, when Beck and Micah had come back from Vegas and everyone in a hundred-mile radius could tell they'd finally done something about all the tension surrounding them.

"I mean, we all sorta guessed. You were so smiley this morning, very un-Deacon-like. And then there's the fact you *punched* that guy for him. You might be big, but he was bigger."

"Thank you, Beckett, now you sound just like Carter."

"I've heard worse compliments," Beck observed. "*And* Micah said just how insistent Mr. G was that he take you to his car."

"You said that already. I was there, you know, right along with your better half."

"Right." Beck grinned. "So, how was it?"

Deacon tried to shoot him a look that was cold—frigid, even—but he was afraid it came out gooey and sentimental.

"Best night of my life," Deacon said.

Beck's smile was understanding. He patted Deacon on the shoulder. "Yeah, yeah, I get that."

Beck would.

Deacon hadn't even realized how much emotional baggage Beck had been carrying around when he'd come to Charleston as a rookie last year. How much the shit with Micah had messed him up, until Micah had arrived himself. Then when Beck and Micah had shown up married and happy, it was like meeting a whole new Beck.

"Nobody can know. I don't know if we're telling anyone—I would guess . . .*no*, cause he's still got the commissioner's office on his ass, and the email made all that worse."

"I'm a vault," Beck said.

"You and Micah, sure," Deacon teased. "A *shared* vault."

"You think I'd tell him about this, even if you asked me not to?" Beck looked upset—worried that *he* might be upset, Deacon realized.

"I think you're best friends and you're married and you tell each other everything. It's okay. I don't tell you things I don't expect him to hear eventually."

"Really?"

"Y'all are disgusting," Deacon said, meaning it, but also meaning *and I'm so happy you got the chance to be.*

"Takes one to know one," Beck retorted, but he was smiling now.

"Yep," Deacon said. The closest he was ever going to get to admitting to Beck that he was just as wildly, head-over-heels, soar-right-off-the-cliff-of-good-sense in love.

"Good." Beck's softened gaze made it clear he understood. "And I'm here, for whatever you need, man. You know that."

"I do, Beck, I do. And it means a lot," Deacon said and patted him on the shoulder again.

"Call Jem," Beck suggested.

Deacon rolled his eyes. "I don't need you to tell me to call my best friend," he said.

"Except, I kinda think you do."

"He met someone," Deacon said. "But it's early, and even though he's crazy about the guy, I think he might come back here, if he thought even for a second that we needed him."

"Ah." There was a wealth of meaning in Beck's single word.

"He's got a chance for a real life, you know? After this. He deserves it, don't you think?"

Beck's gaze was serious. "Yeah, 'course I think that. But I think you're the crazy one, Deac, if you don't think he can have that life and *still* give a shit about what's going on here."

Deacon didn't say anything, just watched as Beck jogged away, to join the rest of the secondary for their specialized warmup.

"What was that about?" Nate asked, as he walked up.

Deacon considered it for a moment.

"Beck telling me to get my head out of my ass," Deacon said, and Nate laughed.

"He'd really do that to *you*?" Nate wondered.

"He said it nicely. But yes." And he'd deserved it.

When Grant finally returned to his penthouse, it was nearly midnight.

He'd shed his tie in the car, and shrugged out of his jacket, dropping it on a chair in the living room as he collapsed onto the couch.

It had been an insanely long day. Probably not helped by the three or four hours of sleep he'd gotten last night.

Grant still wouldn't trade the night he'd shared with Deacon for anything, though.

Even if he didn't have this headache, exhaustion mingled with tension, that had persistently pounded behind his eyes for the last four or so hours.

His phone buzzed, and Grant groaned before digging it out of his pocket. He would've left it where it was, because he'd been working nonstop for nearly twenty hours at this point, and even if someone had an emergency, they could fucking wait. But he'd hoped, even though it was late, that it was Deacon.

It was.

Grant pressed answer, and even though he knew it was physically impossible, it felt like his headache receded just a little at Deacon's simple, "Hey."

"Hey," Grant echoed.

"Sorry, I know it's late," Deacon said. "But I was lying here in bed and couldn't stop thinking about you. And you did text me earlier, saying you were hoping you'd be home by midnight. Are you?"

"Yeah," Grant said. "Just got here."

"Good." Deacon was quiet for a moment. "How bad was it, today?"

"Not bad," Grant lied.

Deacon chuckled. "Don't lie to me."

"It wasn't anything I couldn't handle," Grant protested.

"Just 'cause you could handle it doesn't mean you can't give some of that to me. At least *tell* me about it."

"I set up Cheryl for a pretty shitty fall," Grant said.

"Does she deserve it?" Deacon's voice was rough and low, with tiredness. And yet he was on the phone with him. Grant felt warmer, more secure, less exhausted, just listening to him.

Maybe there *was* some benefit to sharing some of the burden.

"Yeah. Yeah, she does."

"Then you did what you had to do," Deacon said simply, like it was just that easy.

Probably for Deacon, it was.

But even though Grant knew he'd needed to take steps to combat Cheryl's influence and power, he hadn't *wanted* to. He hadn't enjoyed it the way Darcy did. He probably never would.

"Wish we could give some of that to Rex," Deacon continued, his voice growing harder.

It wasn't like Grant *wasn't* worried about Rex, but he was . . .well, inconsequential, when it came down to it.

"He's like an annoying symptom, and Cheryl is the sickness," Grant said. "But I get it. He betrayed you guys. You want retribution."

"I was kinda thinking though, the worst retribution for him would be to spout all this crazy shit that turns out to be wrong—and then nobody ever listens to him again," Deacon said thoughtfully.

"Yeah," Grant agreed. Closing his eyes, leaning his head back against the chair. "You seemed like you had a good practice today?"

"You watched?"

"I thought we established that I watch you and you *know* I watch you. You think that was going to change, once we . . .uh . . ." Grant hesitated. "Slept together?"

Except it had been so much more than sleeping together.

He knew it, and Deacon probably knew it too, but it was still hard to vocalize it.

Now that we've finally acknowledged that we're wildly in love? Now that we're going to be together, hopefully forever?

"I thought I felt your eyes on me, but yeah, knew you had a busy day. Wasn't sure if I was just imagining it," Deacon said.

"You weren't." After Cheryl had left, he'd wandered over to the bank of windows once, twice, probably at least five times. Enough times that Darcy had even said something.

"I'm looking forward to tomorrow night," Deacon said into the silence.

"Wish it was tonight," Grant said, chuckling low in his throat. Because yes, he was tired. Yes, he had this headache from hell. And he *still* wanted Deacon. Just hearing his voice, low and intent and intense, made him crave the man all over again.

"Why do you think I called?" Deacon said. Sounding frustrated, for the first time. "I thought I'd just collapse into bed and fall asleep, but somehow one night with you has conditioned me to want it—want *you*—every night."

Every night echoed in Grant's head, and it fit so nicely, so fucking perfectly, right next to his own thought of, *now we're going to be together, hopefully forever.*

"Maybe just because we *wanted* to for so long and didn't . . ."

"No," Deacon said.

"I'd suggest you could come here, but it's late, and we *do* need sleep, and I'm not sure we'd sleep if we ended up in the same bed," Grant said.

He wouldn't want to, that was for sure.

"Tomorrow night," Deacon said, soothingly. "But for now, this is enough."

Was it though? Grant could still feel the echo of his touch on his skin, lighting him up. He wouldn't be able to fall asleep as easily as he'd believed he would, either.

"I don't know about that."

"No?" Deacon's voice had gone even rougher. "Then how about this . . .you wearing one of those fancy suits of yours?"

Grant swallowed hard. "Yes. But no jacket. No tie."

"Too bad, because I like the ties," Deacon said.

"You do?" Grant had never imagined that ties could be a sexy accessory, but Deacon made them sound so different.

"We'll save that one for later. Unbutton your shirt. Slowly. One button at a time."

"Why?"

"Because even thinking about you naked makes me hard as a rock." Deacon's voice was hushed and intimate.

Shot a spear of fierce arousal right down his spine.

"Okay," Grant said. He'd never had phone sex before, but if Deacon wanted to, wanted to coax an orgasm out of him this way, paving the way to Grant sleeping like a baby after, then who was he to argue? He placed his phone on the arm of the chair, setting it on speaker.

With one hand, he began to thumb open the buttons on his shirt, thinking the whole time, every time his fingers accidentally brushed his skin, that it was Deacon doing it. Deacon's hands. Big and rough and so, so good.

"I'm—" Grant's voice cracked. "I'm done."

"Take your shirt off," Deacon said, so intense, like his entire focus had narrowed in on the one thing he wanted above all others.

Grant.

His cock was already throbbing in his pants, and he was so tempted to put a hand on it, to relieve some of the pressure, but he already knew he wouldn't.

Because Deacon hadn't told him to do it yet.

He only took off his shirt, discarding it on the floor.

"You being good for me?" Deacon asked.

"Yes." Grant barely even recognized his own voice, breathy and desperate.

"Good." Deacon sounded so smug and satisfied Grant's cock twitched with need.

"Touch yourself. Not your cock. Your chest. Your stomach. Your abs. Your nipples. Make it good. Like I'd make it good."

Grant groaned, unable to hold it in any longer. "You'd make it so good, Deac."

"I'd give you anything you wanted." He paused. "When *I* wanted it. You good with that?"

Was he good with that? Uh, *hell yes,* he was.

"Yeah," Grant said.

"Good, 'cause I'd treat you so good. You still touching yourself?"

He was—long, deliberate touches of his pecs, then his nipples, then his stomach. Feeling his ab muscles jump as he grew closer to what he wanted so desperately.

"Yes," Grant murmured. Took a chance. "Want more, though."

"You hard, baby? Your cock's so good. Tasted so good in my mouth, I'd want to suck it every day."

"You can't say shit like that," Grant panted. He was going to come in his pants, without even touching his cock. Just with Deacon's voice in his ear, all growly gruff filth, wrapped up in love.

"Oh, but I want to. I'm gonna say it all the goddamn time if it makes you lose your mind like this."

"Yeah. Please. *Please.*"

"You wanna come?"

God, did he ever.

"Put your hand on your cock. Don't squeeze. Just rest it there." Grant did as he said, and even through two layers of fabric—his pants and his boxer briefs—he could feel the pressure of it, the undeniable pleasure of it.

"You touching yourself too?" Grant had always prided himself on giving back as good as he got, and he realized this had been painfully one-sided.

"Yeah." Deacon's voice went even deeper. "Been doin' it for awhile, now. Thinkin' about touching you has got me so big and hard. All for you."

Grant moaned.

"But you're not gonna come just yet," Deacon continued. "Not just yet."

"It's not gonna take . . .much," Grant said in a strangled voice. Even the pressure of his hand might be enough, if Deacon kept talking like that. If he kept thinking of how amazing last night had been.

"That's okay, baby. I get it. It's hot, isn't it?"

Grant hadn't ever imagined being called *baby* would nearly make him come in his pants, but that was how deep he was.

All the way in, and he wasn't looking to ever climb out.

Grant made a noise he didn't even think Deacon could decipher as a word, but he must've agreed, because he hummed in unison.

"Unbuckle your belt. Unzip your pants. Take them off. All the way off," Deacon said, when Grant scoffed in disbelief.

But he did it anyway. Because that was where he was, at this point. Blindly willing to follow anything that might bring him the orgasm already building inside him.

"You good now?" Deacon asked.

"Yes," Grant said. The minute he'd taken to get undressed had pulled him back from the edge a little.

His cock was still red and twitching just against the air. If he touched himself, he was going to come all over his stomach.

But he waited for Deacon's instructions instead of just grabbing the pleasure.

"God, you're gorgeous," Deacon groaned. "Thinkin' about it, right now. You all spread out in front of me. Wanna make you come again and again."

"Just once would be good," Grant retorted.

"Touch your cock. Slowly. Gently. Not as much as you want to. And stick your other fingers into your mouth. Get them nice and wet for me."

Grant did it, groaning around them. Knowing what was coming.

"You sore?"

He had been, a little. But in the best kind of ways.

Not so sore he didn't want more. Didn't crave more.

He told Deacon that and was pleased to hear Deacon stumble over his next words. It felt so freaking good that it wasn't just him who was so affected.

"Just one finger, just a little. Just want you to feel it when you come. Want you to know what it felt like when you came around my cock so good last night."

Grant sobbed a little as he shifted down in the chair, twisting his body so he could do as Deacon requested.

The press of his finger, even wet with saliva, burned a little.

But it felt good too as he fisted his cock with his other hand and listened to Deacon's breathing change.

He was close.

And Grant was right there with him, balancing on the knife's edge.

"I'm so close," he forced out, twisting his finger deeper. Feeling his body clench around it.

"Me too," Deacon echoed. "You gonna come all over your chest? Wish I was there to lick it up after?"

That was all it took.

Grant exploded, pulse after pulse of come landing on his stomach and striping up his chest. The orgasms last night had been so intense, like they'd been practically wrung out of him.

But this was somehow even better—and they hadn't even been in the same room.

Dimly, he heard Deacon groan once, hard and intense, and his breathing went uneven as he came right along with him.

"Shit," Deacon muttered. "God, that was so hot. I almost wish tomorrow night we could do that again."

"We are gonna do it again. But together, next time," Grant promised. "I've cleared my evening. It's yours."

"You have no idea how much I love the sound of that," Deacon said softly.

Grant had an idea.

"I want you. I *love* you," Grant said, feeling soft and boneless as he came down from his orgasm. Not worrying so much about what he should and shouldn't say.

Deacon chuckled like he knew exactly what Grant was thinking. "Yeah? Me too."

"This is good, isn't it?"

"Well, I sure don't feel like it's bad," Deacon teased. "If it was, we might need to change things up. But I'd be okay with that."

"I mean . . .us together. Isn't it?" Grant wet his lips with his tongue, suddenly unsure even though he was sitting here in his living room, on a chair he'd probably never to be able to look at without getting hard again, with come drying on his stomach.

It sure as fuck seemed good.

But this wasn't just sex. Grant didn't want it to be.

He'd never have risked everything if that was all it was.

"It's all I've wanted."

Grant closed his eyes at the blunt honesty in Deacon's voice—and in his words.

"Me too," he agreed.

"I didn't tell anyone except one guy, a friend, what happened last night. And he asked me if it was good, and I told him . . ." Deacon cleared his throat. "I told him it was the best night of my life."

"Yeah?"

"The sex, yeah, but everything else, too."

Grant understood. Felt the same. "You think we can top it? Make a new *best night* tomorrow?"

"I'm planning on it," Deacon said. "Now go clean up and go to sleep, okay? I bet you're dead on your feet."

He was. But he still wanted to stay here, talking to Deacon. Just feeling his warm, deep voice wrap around him.

"A little," Grant admitted. Then corrected. "Okay, a lot. But I like talking to you."

"Could listen to you for hours, but you gotta get some rest, okay?" Deacon paused. "I love you, too."

Chapter 14

Deacon wasn't nervous exactly, but he still felt a frisson of anxiety wind up his spine as he entered the front door of Grant's building.

No basement garage drop-offs this time—Grant had texted him an hour ago and said he'd be half an hour late, so Deacon should just meet him at his place.

Deacon didn't normally feel unsure about anything, but as he approached the concierge desk, he had to wonder if Grant had informed them about his arrival.

"Oh, Mr. Harris," the concierge said, glancing up and giving him a friendly, welcoming smile. "Mr. Green said you'd be arriving and to show you to his private elevator."

"He did?" Deacon didn't know why it surprised him. It shouldn't have. Grant ran an entire tech empire, as well as the Condors. You couldn't do that without a healthy attention to detail.

"He certainly did. Welcome to the Palmetto, Mr. Harris. This way, please." The concierge waved his hand, gesturing towards a bank of elevators as he stepped out from behind the desk. "If it's alright to say, we're big fans here."

"Thanks," Deacon said.

"Not just of the Condors, but the way you handled yourself through it." The man's glance over at him was full of the kind of worshipful praise that always made him nervous. He never knew how to acknowledge it properly, or what to say in response.

"I only did the right thing," Deacon said gruffly.

"Well, there's many of us who appreciate someone who does," he said wryly. "And pleased too, of course, when Mr. Green bought the Condors. He knows what's right from what's wrong."

Ironically, they were probably doing something many people, including the NFL, would consider wrong. Deacon pushed the thought away as the concierge stepped around the regular elevator bank, and tucked back in the corner was an unmarked elevator, clearly Grant's.

"Yes, he's a good man." The *best* man. Deacon's heart clenched, glad someone besides him appreciated Grant as he *should* be appreciated.

"Here you are, Mr. Harris. If you need anything, anything at all, please let me know," the concierge said, gesturing at the elevator with one hand while the other pressed a black card against a discreet panel set into the wall.

The doors opened immediately. "Thanks," Deacon said shortly as he stepped in.

It was a short, smooth ride up to the penthouse, depositing him back in the foyer.

This time, with no Grant enticing him to the bedroom, Deacon took a second to look around.

There was the Picasso, of course, hung in the prime spot, the lighting making the bright colors glow.

The rest of the lights were dimmed as Deacon ventured farther into Grant's home.

Well, his home *here*. He had a number of other homes. A brownstone in New York. A lakeside house in Seattle. Another apartment in Palo Alto. He'd mentioned that his mother lived in Paris, in an apartment he'd bought there.

Deacon had plenty of money—more money than he could ever spend in his lifetime probably—but he couldn't even imagine what it was like to have so much you bought a Picasso and hung it in your Charleston penthouse like it was nothing.

There was no kitchen table, but two places had been set at the long kitchen island with expensive looking china and crystal, and there were a number of unlit candles scattered around the kitchen and living room.

Clearly someone had gone to some trouble to make the normally austere place look romantic, and Deacon's heart clenched again.

He settled himself down on one of the living room chairs, sighing at how comfortable it was. Usually these modern-looking pieces poked you in a hundred painful ways or were flat and hard as a board. But it was like the bed, like Grant had picked out furniture that was both aesthetically pleasing as well as comfortable for a big guy like Deacon.

How long has he wanted this?

He'd insisted that he hadn't bought the Condors *for* Deacon, the way that email had claimed, but the deeper they got into this, the more Deacon wondered how true that really was.

He pulled his phone out of his pocket, texted Grant that he'd made it here, and instead of waiting around for Grant to respond—after all, he was trying to finish up his work for the day—he considered what Beck had said to him at practice yesterday.

About Jem, and how he'd been distancing himself.

Should he call Jem? No—he wouldn't call. He'd text. A text was nice and casual, even if what he was saying wasn't.

For a long minute, he debated what to say. How to tell his best friend about what had happened, without making it seem like it was a big deal.

Okay, it *was* a big deal.

But Jem would make it a big deal, no matter what, so Deacon didn't need to bring the praise hands or heart-eyes emojis.

Hey, he started with.

Jem replied almost immediately. **Nothing from you for at least a week, and that's all I get? Hey?**

Shit, he had been ignoring Jem. Not on purpose. Well, okay, a *little* on purpose. Jem was trying to find a new life and wasn't particularly happy with it. Deacon could only imagine how tough that was. And how much tougher it would be with constant reminders of what he'd lost.

Deacon didn't blame Jem for going back to his hometown of Christmas Falls. He'd known his best friend was slowly losing his mind every moment he spent on the sidelines, not playing.

But maybe he'd put *too* much space between them. It had made sense to Deacon at the time, but now he felt a pulse of regret.

Sorry, he typed back. **Didn't mean to ghost you.**

Like you could, Jem responded. **You're not that good.**

Except that he was. Grant had said so. Deacon knew this was the perfect time, the perfect opening. He should tell Jem about Grant. He *wanted* to tell Jem about Grant.

But still, his fingers hesitated over the screen.

Maybe this news was too big to break over text.

Jem sent a second text. **You guys hanging in okay?**

We're fine. Deacon would've said the same even if they weren't fine. Would've said the same if the whole team was currently on fire. The quiet happiness he'd heard in Jem's voice when he'd told him about his old friend and new boyfriend, Murphy, had guaranteed that Deacon wasn't going to do or say anything that would make Jem feel like he needed to come back to Charleston right now.

Are you though? That email, Deac . . .

Ugh. Deacon felt another pulse of unwanted guilt.

It was a lot. Did it change anything?

No, he'd been wrong before. This was the perfect time.

I punched a guy in the Pirate's Booty who said I had Grant's dick on speed dial.

Deacon could only imagine Jem's scoff when he read that.

We're gonna skip over the whole 'punched a guy' for Grant and settle on the question of WHEN are you gonna have his dick on speed dial?

How do you know I don't already? Deacon replied after a nice long pause. Not because he didn't know what to say. But because it wouldn't hurt to make Jem sweat it out a little bit more.

DO YOU??????

Deacon barked out a laugh.

I wouldn't call it that, exactly. More like I'm sitting in his penthouse, only two dozen feet away from a genuine fucking Picasso, waiting for him to finish work so we can have dinner.

Once he'd started, he couldn't seem to stop. He just word vomited it all up right onto the screen.

So, what you're really saying is that Mr. G has YOUR dick on speed dial. And now he could hear Jem laughing, the sound echoing in his head.

Fair.

Deacon sent the second text before he could overthink it. **But it's not just the dick, though that's real nice, I can't lie. I'm in love with him. And crazy enough, he seems to feel the same way about me.**

A second later, his phone buzzed, but it wasn't with another call. It was Jem, calling.

When he picked up, Jem was still laughing. "You asshole," he said. "You were really going to tell me all that in a *text message*."

"Yeah," Deacon said, feeling surprisingly bashful.

"God, you're the worst," Jem said. "But I'm still damn happy for you, man. You two deserve it. But seriously, *crazy enough that he seems to feel the same way about me*? He bought a freaking football team for you. He spent nearly a *billion* dollars for you. Even for a guy with a freaking Picasso on his wall, that's a big deal."

"He didn't do that."

"Uh, I disagree—"

"He didn't even know about that email," Deacon interrupted.

But he knew the truth had nothing to do with the email. The email was only how the rest of the world had found out about Grant's feelings.

They'd existed, apparently long before it, and it didn't matter that Grant hadn't even responded to the email. Didn't even matter that he'd never seen it.

"I wasn't even talking about the email," Jem said softly.

Ugh, it sucked having a best friend who knew your own mind better than you knew it yourself. Sucked, and yet was also the greatest thing in the world.

"Right. Uh. Well. Yes. Maybe. A little for me."

"A *lot* for you," Jem insisted. "And that's okay, you know? You love to save people, too, Deac."

"Yeah." He did. Hadn't ever really thought about it in those terms, before, but he was always trying to help, wasn't he? And Grant did the same thing.

"You two are gonna always be trying to out-rescue each other. It's cute."

Deacon didn't know what to say to that. "It's still new," he said, trying to be cautious. Because Jem was already talking like they were going to be together for the long-term. Like they were already ride-or-die for each other.

He hoped it was true. He *wanted* it to be true.

But how could it be, if they hadn't even been on one single freaking date yet. *You've had sex three times though—if you're counting last night, and you sure as hell are.*

"Yeah, but is it though?" Jem retorted kindly. "You've been danc-ing around each other since the summer. And for a long time before that, if what you told me about college is true."

"You're really annoying, you know?" Deacon said.

Jem laughed. "AKA, *Jem, you're so fucking right.*"

"Sure," Deacon said, but the knowing tone of Jem's voice made it clear that they were on the same page. Warmth spread through him that his best friend not only knew now, but clearly approved.

"You'll have to come down here, after the season. Visit. I . . ." Jem's voice caught, and he cleared his throat. "I'm buying some land here, I think. Going to look next week at a few plots just outside of town."

"You're moving back to Christmas Falls." Deacon didn't know why he was surprised. After all, he'd known Jem was retiring. Knew Jem was dating Murphy, and since Jem didn't date all that often, frankly even less than Deacon had, he had to be fairly serious about this guy.

"Yeah, I think so. Splitting my time between there and here."

"It's a good move," Deacon said, even though some deep part of him ached with the inevitability of it.

There'd be more of these phone conversations and text exchanges and fewer quiet beers on a free night, in the future.

It wouldn't change the fundamental way he and Jem were friends, but it was going to be different going forward.

"I'm still gonna be around," Jem promised, but it didn't matter what he said, Deacon knew it wouldn't be the same.

But then, he couldn't even lay that change on Jem's doorstep, because it had been coming since Deacon had decided to retire.

"You'd better be," Deacon retorted fondly.

Against his ear, his phone dinged, and he glanced at it, saw it was a text from Grant. "Hey, I gotta go," he continued.

"Your boy calling for your dick?" Jem teased.

Deacon rolled his eyes but it felt good to hear Jem call Grant *his boy*, even though Grant was a hell of a lot more than just *his boy*.

Grant was the kind of guy who could contain multitudes. He could be a CEO and an NFL owner and a billionaire and a person who owned a Picasso and *also* Deacon's boy.

Deacon's *man*.

"Yeah," Deacon said.

"Have fun and wear protection," Jem said and before Deacon could argue, he'd hung up.

He glanced down at his phone and made a face at the text Grant had written.

Sorry, it read, **got delayed here again. Give me another hour.**

Deacon would give him a lot more than another hour. He'd give him every hour he owned, going forward.

Sure, he texted back. **Whatever you need.**

He tilted his head back after putting the phone on the armrest and closed his eyes. He'd just get a quick little nap in, be nice and refreshed for when Grant finished his work.

Grant walked into the darkened penthouse, worry settled deep in his stomach, a hard ball that wouldn't be dislodged no matter what kind of text Deacon had sent him.

He'd been understanding, telling Grant to take the time he'd needed.

But then he'd not responded when he'd texted twice after that.

Once to say this meeting was interminably boring, and he'd much rather be eating dinner—and *more*—with Deacon. The second to say he was on his way.

Part of Grant had worried, as the car had pulled up to the elevator in the basement garage, that when he arrived upstairs, the apartment would be empty.

But Deacon was still here.

Grant stopped in his tracks as he spotted him, sleeping and snoring gently in the big chair Grant had enjoyed himself in just last night.

He didn't startle or move. Didn't wake up at all, in fact, even though Grant had hardly been quiet while walking in.

For a long moment, he stared at the man he loved. His hair was pushed back from his face, a lock of it falling onto his forehead, smooth in sleep. Every line of his big body was relaxed, so unlike the watchful caution it felt like was Deacon's status quo.

He was so handsome and so perfect and so *Grant's*.

Not just because he was here, but because he'd waited, without a single complaint.

Whenever he'd tried to date before this, the men in his life had always gotten frustrated at the tiny tidbits of time Grant doled out to them—and he couldn't even blame them for that—or they ended up resenting how little of his heart was available to them.

But Deacon wasn't going to have that problem, because all those unavailable parts of Grant felt like they'd been held in waiting just for him.

Still, it wasn't going to be easy to be his partner. He was going to be late more than he was going to be on time, and Deacon would have to be okay sharing him with all the other people who depended on him.

With anyone else, Grant would've been worried that might be too much to ask for.

But he already knew, with a certainty that terrified him, that Deacon wouldn't get angry with him over it. Wouldn't eventually fade out of his life because it was hard.

That was the thing about Deacon: when shit got hard, he dug in and only fought harder.

That knowledge settled sweet and hot into Grant's chest, effortlessly unwinding the last of his anxiety. He was so grateful, so fucking *pleased*, it just made sense to show Deacon just how much his casual acceptance of Grant's life meant.

Before Deacon could wake—though it looked to Grant like that wasn't happening any time soon, frankly—he slipped off to the bathroom, took care of what he needed to, and less than ten minutes later, was back in the living room. Naked.

Kneeling at Deacon's feet, he gently put his hand on his knee then slid it up to his thigh.

Deacon twitched but didn't wake up, and Grant decided that was a green light. He reached up higher, carefully unbuttoning his shirt, hoping his fingers weren't too cold when they brushed Deacon's stomach.

Deacon groaned but still didn't waken, even when Grant lifted himself, resting his elbows on Deacon's knees and pressed his mouth against Deacon's skin.

He was so warm, and salty-sweet against Grant's tongue. It was easy to get lost in the feel of him, in the heady thought that he was *finally* getting to lick his abs the way he'd wanted to, all those years ago.

They might be a little less cut than they'd been in college, but they were just as beautiful to Grant. Maybe because back then he hadn't gotten to touch—and now he could, all he wanted to.

Deacon groaned a little at the back of his throat, and when Grant glanced up, lips coasting down Deacon's chest towards the waistband of his jeans, he realized the man was looking at him, eyes dark and intense.

"Sorry, I fell asleep," Deacon mumbled. "But not *that* sorry, if this is the way you're gonna wake me up."

"Yeah?" Grant was surprised to hear how gravelly and rough his own voice sounded.

Deacon's hand cupped his cheek. "I was having a really fucking great dream, and then I wake up and find out it's not even a dream."

His throat tightened with emotion and he tilted his head up, meeting Deacon's mouth as he leaned down.

It would be so easy to get lost in his kiss. To just keep kissing until his neck cramped. But he'd had other plans, and he intended to see them through.

Grant broke the kiss and kept up his meandering pace down towards Deacon's dick, clearly hard, even in the loose denim of his jeans.

"Oh, God, yeah," Deacon groaned, and his fingers tangled in Grant's hair as he unbuttoned and unzipped his jeans, tugging them off. Taking in the gorgeous view of Deacon's powerful, thick thighs, and his big dick, pressing against the fabric of his boxer briefs.

Grant glanced up, meeting Deacon's stare. "Underwear tonight?"

Deacon grinned, one corner of his lips tilting up in amusement. "Maybe I thought you'd make me squirm and wait til after dinner for relief. So I thought, better be prepared. Luckily for me, you couldn't wait either."

"You know, I was sitting right here, in this chair, last night," Grant murmured as Deacon traced his face with his fingertips.

Watched as Deacon's eyes darkened even more. "Really?"

"Right here," Grant said, patting the cushion. "And all I thought about today, all day, through every single meeting when my mind wandered even for a second, was getting you in this chair and doing exactly this."

He leaned down and was rewarded with another deep groan of Deacon's as he pulled his underwear down. His cock bobbed out, finally free of its underwear prison, and Grant licked a stripe up the underside.

He'd gotten a brief taste of Deacon's cock the other night, but it hadn't been nearly enough. Settling down between Deacon's legs, he let it slip between his lips, curling his tongue around the head and sucking hard.

If losing himself in the feel of Deacon's skin and the muscles shifting underneath it was easy, it was nothing compared to how simple it was to just give himself over to this. To the motion of dip and retreat, to the slide of Deacon's cock in and out of his mouth, taking it as deep as he dared—which still didn't feel deep enough.

He wanted more, he wanted it *all*. But Deacon was big, and Grant was out of practice.

Of course, it wasn't like Deacon wasn't enjoying himself. A litany of moans and nonsense words of approval kept falling out of his mouth, and then his thighs tensing and relaxing as he tried to hold back.

He let Deacon's cock slip out of his mouth. "Someday," he said, voice rough with desire, "you're gonna fuck my mouth."

"Jesus, you can't say shit like that, not when I'm so close," Deacon said, panting. A faint sheen of sweat covered his face, his temples damp with it, and Grant realized just how horny *he* was. How hot this had made him. How seeing Deacon like this, totally at his mercy, made him just about as hard as he'd ever been in his life.

"Are you?"

"Close?" Deacon shot him a hot look. "Baby, if you did any better, I'd have already come down your throat."

Grant swallowed hard, like what Deacon had predicted had already come to pass.

He had other plans, so he couldn't fulfill that particular desire—but he could fulfill another one.

He stood, his knees wobbling, and Deacon looked surprised as he settled down on his lap. His cock brushed against Deacon's abs, and it took every ounce of willpower he possessed to not just mindlessly rub against this man's skin. To stop this test of control and just give himself up to the pleasure.

But he wanted more. He *always* wanted more.

Deacon's mouth dropped open in surprise as he positioned his cock under his hole, rubbing the head back and forth a handful of times, making them both groan.

"Did you—" Deacon stopped and then swore as Grant's body dropped down an inch and then two, slowly enveloping him.

He'd done the bare minimum of prep, as quickly as he could, before Deacon could wake up and Grant would lose the element of surprise, but if they went slow, it would be fine.

"Yeah," Grant said, trying to breathe through the stretch.

"God, that's the hottest thing ever," Deacon said, and his fingers dug into the arms of the chair, his forearms flexing. Trying, Grant imagined, to control the urge to just thrust. To just *take*.

Grant wanted that, too. Wanted to sit on Deacon's lap and let him send him right over the edge, but he needed a minute first.

"Did you sit here in this chair last night and think about doing this?" Deacon murmured, leaning forward, lips brushing Grant's ear. "Just like this?"

"Yes," Grant said, groaning. He gave another experimental thrust down, and finally his thighs connected to Deacon's, every inch of his cock inside him now.

"Goddamn it," Deacon ground out. "You gotta, I'm gonna—"

"I got you," Grant said and moved a little. Lost himself to the way it felt, so tight, but so right.

"Come on, baby, fuck me good," Deacon said. Then kissed him.

It felt like the most natural thing Grant had ever experienced to sink into the feel of Deacon's mouth on his, Deacon's cock inside him, moving easily in and out now. His cock kept bumping up against Deacon's abs, smearing them with precome, and Grant found the edge so much quicker than he'd imagined he might.

One of Deacon's hands had gone to his neck, holding him down, holding him in place, and the other to his hip, gripping him. One second it was gentle and sweet. And then the next they were racing to the finish line in a sweaty, frantic explosion of movement, their bodies crashing together.

Grant moaned into Deacon's mouth as he exploded, painting their skin with stripes of come, and Deacon bellowed a second later, shaking beneath him.

Grant collapsed onto Deacon's chest, knees giving out entirely.

"Fuck," Deacon exhaled in a sharp breath.

"That was . . ." Grant's lips found Deacon's neck. The skin there was damp with sweat and felt so freaking perfect against his mouth.

Deacon's arm wound its way around him, and Grant only had a moment to register his coiled strength before he was lifting him and standing, cock still buried inside him, and he walked them right into the bathroom, setting Grant onto the counter, slipping out of him.

A second later, before Grant could even find something to clean himself with, Deacon appeared with a handful of tissues.

"Thanks," Grant said bashfully. Fantasies always felt really hot in your own mind, before confronted by the realities—and the inherent messiness of sex.

"It's the least I could do," Deacon admitted. "The *very* least. Especially when I think you blew my mind right out my ears. I'm not sure I'm ever going to be the same after that."

Grant could agree with him on that point. He'd believed that the other night had been some of the best he'd ever had—but tonight, they'd left merely *good* sex far behind them.

He got the worst of the mess cleaned up and glanced over at the shower. "I'm actually going to hop in real quick," he said, gesturing towards it. "You wanna heat up dinner?"

Deacon raised an eyebrow. "You seem very certain of my capabilities."

Grant patted him on the cheek as he hopped down from the counter. Flipped the water on in the shower. "I promise—I think you're very capable of heating up food in the microwave. The chef left instructions on top of the containers, and they're all in the fridge."

"I got it," Deacon said.

Grant took a fast shower, but even though he'd been quick about it, by the time he re-entered the living area of his apartment, Deacon had re-dressed—not entirely, his jeans weren't completely fastened, and his shirt flapped open, giving Grant a few tantalizing glimpses of his stomach and abs—and not only had the food heating, but he'd found a lighter and had lit all the candles Grant had asked to be scattered throughout the place.

"Hey," Grant said, leaning against the counter. "See? Told you that you were capable."

"The only thing I'm missing are a dozen red roses," Deacon said, coming over and pressing a kiss against his mouth.

Would he ever get used to the fact that they could do this now? That Deacon wanted him, as much as Grant wanted him back? Or the undeniable love in Deacon's eyes as he bent down?

Probably not.

But then, the best way to kill something dead was to take it for granted.

"Darcy did suggest some rose petals scattered on the bed, but I told her we'd do just fine there without them," Grant said.

"And here we didn't even make it to the bed," Deacon teased. He trailed fingertips down Grant's t-shirt he'd thrown on, along with his favorite pair of gray sweatpants. "Though I'm all for making another effort later."

"Later," Grant agreed. He still felt like his brain was partially blown out from how intense his orgasm had been. But even despite that, his blood heated up again at the thought of coming together like that again.

"Dinner first," Deacon said, waving towards the two place settings at the island. "Sit down. Let me bring it to you when it's done."

"You want wine?" Grant asked, making a detour to one of the glassed-in fridges built under the island. Tugged out a bottle of New Zealand Sauvignon Blanc he favored. He was pretty sure Darcy had specified they'd be having roast chicken, and he could smell the rich, succulent scent of it in the air as it heated.

"Sure, I'll take a glass."

Grant gestured towards one of the cabinets, and Deacon grabbed glasses and he poured them each a good measure.

They'd shared meals before. Always casual and unplanned, though, like they'd both realized, subconsciously, that if it was more, if it was purposeful, it would be too intimate.

And this *was* intimate, undeniably.

But it also felt so comfortable, like they'd performed this dance together a hundred times already. They sat next to each other companionably, candles flickering around them, knees bumping together, as they ate.

"This is good," Deacon said, taking a sip of his wine. "What is it?"

"Sauvignon Blanc from New Zealand. Little vineyard I visited during one of my trips down there and I invested in later."

"Do you always just . . .do that?" Deacon wondered.

Grant stabbed a roasted carrot with his fork, popped it in his mouth, chewed and swallowed. "What do you mean?"

"Always save people who need it."

"Ah, I don't know about that." But he did know about it. They both did it, that much was very clear to Grant.

"Yes, you do," Deacon said, glancing over at him as he cut his chicken.

"Well, everyone likes it when you give them money," Grant said, trying to play it off as it was just that simple.

"But you don't just give them money, did you? Don't tell me you just gave this winery money and then moved on. That's not like you."

Grant sighed. He loved it when Deacon really saw him, but he also wasn't used to it—especially when it wasn't Darcy doing it. He was out of practice having a real kind of relationship, where you actually shared things.

With Deacon, he already knew him so well, them growing closer over the last six months, that there was no hope of pretending otherwise.

"Yeah, I did give them some help," Grant admitted. "Some marketing advice. Sent their labels to my marketing department, who offered some suggestions to help bump up their visual interest."

"Then you *do* just do that, then," Deacon teased, nudging Grant's foot with his own socked one.

"I guess I do." Grant didn't know why he felt ashamed of it. Why he didn't want to admit it.

"You're more than your bank account, you know," Deacon said matter-of-factly, like he wasn't routinely reduced to the number of zeros he possessed.

"Thanks."

"I mean, you should *act* like it. And also realize how much you do. Lots of billionaires don't work as hard as you do."

"And lots of them do."

"But they're working hard trying to squeeze the last dime out of everyone. That's not you. That's never been you. You have all these programs for the InTech employees." Grant couldn't help but be surprised that *one*, Deacon knew about his InTech work, and *two*, that Deacon would care. "And then there's everything you did for the Condors. You could've just bought the team and fixed the worst of the problems and called it good. But you didn't."

"I like fixing problems. But not just surface-level stuff. That's easy. No challenge there. It feels good to have rooted out the worst of the shit here. To offer InTech employees the best of me with the hopes they give the best of themselves back."

"Then why isn't the NFL grateful every fucking day for everything you've done?" Deacon wondered.

Grant made a face. Shoved his chicken around his plate. "Good question. I mean, I'm not exactly some kind of savior, I'm not doing anything special. I'm only doing what's right, what *everyone* should be doing, that they're not doing—"

"No," Deacon interrupted him. "No. You're not just doing what everyone else should be doing or might be doing, if they were better people. It's more than that. *You're* more than that."

He couldn't help it; he stared at Deacon. "You really think that?"

"Uh, *yeah*," Deacon said. "You think I'm routinely in the habit of seducing my bosses? Even when I knew them from when I was younger and stupider and had crushes I didn't know what to do with? Yeah, sure when you showed up in March, wanting to buy the Condors, I thought, huh, what a nice coincidence for me. Maybe I'll finally put these thoughts about you that wouldn't ever leave me alone out of my head. But then I got to *know* you, know how you are, how you act, how you treat people with respect and expect respect in return. How you don't just flounce around like God's greatest gift to the economy, and it was so easy to love you. Even when I thought I couldn't have you. And then I find out about this winery, and how you helped them. You help *everyone*, and it's so . . .so . . ."

As Deacon trailed off, Grant set his fork down. Slowly. Deliberately. His heart swelling in his chest.

There was only one person in his life who'd ever really, truly seen him. And he loved her like a sister. His platonic wife, he'd always called Darcy.

But this was more, this was someone he *loved*, who really saw him.

Saw all of him, and not only didn't resent him for it, but loved him *because* of it.

"Deac," he said quietly, "kiss me."

And Deacon leaned over and did exactly that.

Chapter 15

"I think the cameras spent half the game panning to you," Nicole said as they exited the owner's suite after the game against the Raiders.

"Did they?" Grant wanted to pretend ignorance, because how could he tell when a camera, a hundred feet away, was turning his direction?

But of course they had.

Probably every single time Deacon had made a play.

Probably every single time Deacon was on the *field*.

Even though the Condors had won today, and in fact had led for almost all four quarters, Grant had spent most of the game frustrated and annoyed.

Nicole had been reluctant to tell him what social media was saying or what the media coverage looked like, but since it was her job to monitor those things, he'd insisted she keep him informed.

Would he feel any different if it had happened and he just hadn't known about it? Grant didn't know. But he wasn't the kind of man, or the kind of CEO, who thought it was okay to just stick his head in the sand.

"You know they did," Nicole said. She'd been trying to make light of it, but they both knew that the only reason everyone had been so wild to talk about Grant was the email, and the rumors.

Everyone was looking for even the slightest hint on his face that he was in love with Deacon. Or even just fucking him. Either one. Grant wasn't sure they even cared which it was, only that it was salacious and juicy and they could fill up a hell of a lot of on-air hours talking about it.

"It's fine, they were just all *very* excited about the possibility that you're not just a brilliant robot but a man with actual emotions. It'll pass," Darcy soothed as they entered the elevator that would take them to the ground floor with the VIP garage and also the locker room. They were headed to the former, not the latter. There was no way Nicole was going to allow him anywhere near the locker room, not after the email.

Darcy was trying to put a positive spin on it, and Nicole was trying to make light of it. With the two of them, Grant didn't even need a diagram to tell him how bad it was.

The elevator dinged open on the ground floor, and the moment the doors opened, Grant flinched.

There was a literal *wall* of sound and motion and people in front of them. All holding cameras. All shouting questions, all a variation on the same theme: *was he involved with Deacon Harris?*

Nic stuck a hand out, both keeping the elevator doors from closing again and also attempting to quiet the media rabble. "Enough!" she shouted over the noise. "Let's let Mr. Green pass, please."

Nobody moved.

He *had* security, of course, but he'd never needed security to keep him safe at his own goddamn stadium. In fact, he rarely needed them at all. He looked unassuming, and lots of people didn't even recognize him on sight—which was something Grant had very much enjoyed, up until this moment.

He exchanged glances with Nicole. There was no way, even if he called them now, that even the general building security would arrive in time. And if they did magically transport down here, their appearance would only add to the frenzy.

The last thing they needed was a whole round of media stories about the mob scene involving the new Condors' owner.

He held up his own hand and wasn't surprised that the noise quieted somewhat. Everyone thought he was going to say something, and nobody wanted to miss it.

More fool them.

He plunged into the chaos, hand clasped firmly in Darcy's as he pulled her, Nicole leading the way through the mass, towards the door.

They followed him all the way to the car, yelling questions, some of them even dragging out some really ugly comments, no doubt in an attempt to get a reaction out of him. But it was surprisingly easy to keep the stone-cold expression plastered across his face. Easy to stay angry.

Richard was there, holding the door, and they all slid into the back seat, and he shut it behind them.

"Shit," Nicole said.

He wasn't angry at her, necessarily, but she was the head of Condors' PR and if there was a rabid mob of reporters in his stadium, she should've known about it.

"What the hell was that?" he asked. Still angry, but trying to rein in his temper.

"Not what I expected, that was for sure," Nicole said wryly. "I knew we issued more press credentials for the game. But I thought they were all just going to crane their necks up at your suite windows, try to get a reaction out of you. Maybe hope I'd lose my mind and put you up at the podium after the game to make a statement. But I didn't think they'd do *that*."

"They were at that level, because of the locker room," Darcy guessed. Often, after games, Nicole would give access to the locker room to certain press, so they could interview any players who hadn't gone up to the podium.

"Yes," Nicole said. "I don't usually put a restriction on the locker room visitors, because it's never an issue."

"You'll do it now," Grant said, and Nicole nodded, grimly.

"Next home game, we'll station security at the elevator, and I'll make a list of reporters who I know won't do . . .any of that." She made a face of distaste. "I didn't even recognize most of them."

"I'm not sure they normally cover the sports beat," Darcy said gently. She glanced over at Grant, and he knew what she was thinking.

What she'd suggested the other day: that he come entirely clean, giving nobody any room for continued speculation.

But he and Deacon had been on exactly one date.

Deacon had slept in his bed for only three nights.

Maybe Grant knew that he wanted him in it for every night after this, but that was a lot to ask of anyone.

They didn't even know how to be a couple yet. Going public about being a couple now was moving way too fast.

"We continue with no comment," Nicole said. "But I am going to put out a statement that the sudden and rife speculation on our owner's private life is intrusive and unwelcome."

They all knew that wouldn't do a goddamn thing to calm anything down, but Grant was glad she was trying something.

"That's a start," Grant said.

She turned to him, and he didn't envy her the job she'd be doing for the next few weeks. "I'm sorry about that. Truly sorry. I had no idea, and that's inexcusable, I know, but I never imagined—"

"None of us did," Grant said gruffly. He'd waltzed down to the elevator without a worry in the world, only annoyed at all the social media chatter over the game coverage—half of the viewers had seemingly only tuned in to see if Grant was wearing a Deacon Harris jersey and the other half were annoyed they were showing him at all—but he'd never expected this either.

"I'm still sorry," Nicole said. "And if you want to take action—"

"No," Grant interrupted her. "*No*. You're going to handle it."

"Yes, I am," Nicole said flatly. They dropped her off around the corner, where she'd parked for the game, and in the car, he and Darcy headed back to his penthouse.

Grant's phone buzzed. He pulled it out of his pocket, glancing at the screen. Not surprised in the least at who it was and what he'd said. **What the fuck**, Deacon texted. **Apparently there was a**

whole mob of photographers outside the locker room, waiting for you?

Grant sighed.

Darcy glanced over at him. "Deacon worried?"

"How did you guess?" Grant asked.

"Because you both are weirdly obsessed with protecting everyone—and when you don't, *saving* them."

Grant made a face.

"He's not saving me. Or protecting me. Just make sure he doesn't punch any of those guys like he did those two at the bar."

"He won't," Darcy said, shooting him a look. "You know he won't."

It was a little hairy, but we got out okay, Grant replied.

We're going to the Pirate's Booty, Deacon texted back. **I'd invite you, but I can only imagine what kind of sensation that would cause.**

Grant felt a pulse of regret. What if nobody had ever gotten ahold of that stupid email? What if they'd figured out their relationship in private, without the whole world trying to peer in? What if they'd controlled the rollout?

Then maybe, he could've gone to the Pirate's Booty with Deacon, and nobody would've blinked twice at his appearance.

But that was not how it had happened.

Before the email, he'd been too tied up with the idea that he was not only preserving Deacon's legacy with the Condors by keeping his hands off him, but making sure that he didn't do anything personally to damage any of his businesses—or the people who worked for those businesses.

Now he could see that had been a major misstep. If he'd been proactive, instead of defensive and worried . . .well, it was too late for that now.

Now, everything was a mess.

An exposed, public mess.

It's okay, I've got work. That was true. He was sure he could work every hour for the rest of his life and not get through all of it. But at the same time, he'd had something that *wasn't* just work in his life for the last week, and that had been . . .well, different and nice.

Really, really nice.

Don't work too hard.

Grant slid his phone into his pocket, and when he looked up, Darcy was looking at him.

"Do you want to talk about it?" she asked.

"I'm sorry, I thought we had the sort of relationship where you *knew* I didn't want to talk about it, and you talked about it anyway, because you decided I needed to."

Darcy raised an eyebrow.

"Sorry. That was bitchy. I'm just . . ." God, what was he even? Grant scrubbed a hand over his face. "I'm not used to fucking up like this."

"And you're used to nobody giving a shit what you do, or who you do it with."

"Yes. That. Exactly." Before he'd bought the Condors, he could walk down the street and nobody would look twice at him.

He'd known purchasing an NFL team would come with an increased profile, but he hadn't ever imagined it would be like this.

Of course, without the email and the wrinkle of his and Deacon's feelings, it wouldn't have been like this.

"This is the new norm," Darcy said. "You know what I think. You can't run from it. You can't hide from it. You just have to embrace it."

"We *just* started dating, Darce. How can I go to him and say, *hey, let's go public and tell the whole world we're in love?*"

"I don't know. I just think you do it, and say I think this is going to help. You don't think Deacon wouldn't walk across hot coals for you, if you asked? Even if you *didn't* ask?"

Grant sighed. "I don't think I'd need to ask, and he'd already be saying yes. That's the problem."

"I don't know, it kinda feels like the solution to me," Darcy said reasonably. "He loves you enough to do it. Isn't that exactly the point?"

"No," Grant said miserably.

"Then explain it to me." Darcy leaned forward.

"I don't want to take advantage. I don't want to force him into something he isn't ready for, that *we're* not ready for, just because he loves me. That would be taking his feelings and . . .using them." Grant made a face. "Then there's the fact that we've been on exactly *one* date. Would you want to crow about a relationship to the world before you've ever established that relationship?"

Darcy's expression turned sympathetic. "I know. But you know what, too? You *can* lean on people, sometimes."

"I lean on you, plenty," Grant argued. Though he knew she was right and that Deacon would agree with her, a hundred percent.

But the problem was that Grant was pretty sure he was *also* right.

What was the solution then? Something in the middle?

Or continuing to say *no comment* and hoping that the furor would die down, eventually?

Would it take the rest of the season? Would it spill over into the offseason?

Would they start the *next* season, even though Deacon would be retired, with speculation still rampant that something inappropriate had happened?

"Yes, you do, but only because I force you to do it."

"And I pay you for the privilege," Grant said.

She nodded. "That too. But think about it. Really think about it, okay? Because I'm not thinking Nicole's statement is going to do anything and I don't think this speculation is going to go anywhere. People are fascinated by this. It's never happened before—an owner and a player. And if your friend from college does indeed do an interview . . ."

"You know he's not going to. We took care of that."

Darcy waved a hand. "But money talks. He might fold, even though he knows you'd probably sue the shit out of him. Still, you know how people go wild for a good love story. Give them one. Give them all the cheese and the sappy reunion."

Grant frowned. "It wasn't a sappy reunion."

"That's what *you* think," Darcy said. "I saw you two together at the very beginning. It was a sappy reunion, even if you two were too blind to notice."

"I'm not going to create some *narrative*, Darcy. This is my freaking life. My life and Deacon's life."

"I know," Darcy said apologetically. "But if you don't write it, someone's gonna write it for you, and I don't know if you'd like not having control over the result. Or what the result *is*."

Grant thought about it after Darcy left.

Thought about it as he sat on the couch and pondered grabbing his laptop and actually doing the work he'd told Deacon he'd intended to do. Even considered putting on some sort of mindless TV. Take his mind off the suggestion Darcy had made that kept circling his brain like an overactive toddler hopped up on too much sugar.

Of course, what he *did* end up doing was turning the TV on but not scrolling to something mindless. Instead, his fingers navigated him to ESPN.

Sunday Morning Football was doing their wrap-up for the day, Neal Fisher talking about the Toronto Thunder's big win against the New York Giants, and flashing right there, across the bottom of the screen was the headline, endlessly scrolling, *Grant Green refuses to talk to media post-Condors win.*

Grant made a face, but then he'd asked for this, hadn't he, by turning this particular channel on?

He was deeply absorbed in what Neal and Drew Brees—the newest addition to the panel—were debating over, when he heard a noise at the front door.

Glancing over, he was both surprised and not very surprised at all to see Deacon walking into his house.

"Sorry, the concierge said I could just come up, and then I didn't know . . ." Deacon trailed off. Like he'd worried he'd be intruding. Like he'd *actually* worried that showing up unannounced would piss Grant off.

"No, no," Grant said hurriedly, muting the TV and standing up. Deacon leaned in and gave him a quick kiss. Too quick, if Grant had anything to say about it.

But Deacon was already looking behind him, at the TV. It might be silent, but it was still speaking volumes, because there was Deacon's face, right next to Grant's.

"What are they saying?" Deacon asked, sounding very calm.

Too calm.

"Nothing new, because there isn't anything new to say," Grant said hurriedly. Even though that hadn't exactly stopped anyone from speculating. Even on this supposedly "serious" sports broadcast.

Neal Fisher *had* said that he felt like Grant had proven so far that he was a man of honor and a quality owner and that he wouldn't do anything inappropriate, so maybe his private life *should* stay private.

But then Brees had started to play devil's advocate—and that was all Grant had watched before Deacon appeared.

"I thought you were going to the bar tonight, with the guys," Grant said.

"I did. I stopped by." Deacon hesitated. Gave him another kiss. Longer, slower, this time. Sweeter, too. "But it wasn't where I really wanted to be."

"Oh." Grant was undeniably pleased, leaning into Deacon's bigger body. "What did you want to do?" he asked. "I could order in—"

But Deacon didn't let him get another word out. Just kissed him, fiercely and possessively, and Grant could only sink into it, because it was all *he* wanted, too.

Much later, when his breath had finally slowed and they'd cleaned up, cuddling back into bed like they'd done this a hundred times, not only a handful, Deacon took in Grant, his sharp green eyes now soft and lazy, and said, "Carter called me out, right before I left."

"Hmmm?" Grant stretched, and even though he'd just been satisfied, a flicker of want pulsed through him.

Before the last few weeks, he'd have sworn that Grant wasn't a distraction. And he wasn't, still—not exactly, anyway. But it was something more, too. A fire burning under his skin that only Grant could quench.

He could focus on something else, but it was still there, all the time, and he was always aware of it.

Part of him was always desperate to reach for what he wanted.

"Carter told me I was whipped," Deacon said. Not even angry about it. He'd willingly admit to being owned by the way a single touch of Grant's quieted that wanting.

He didn't know how he'd lived without it all these months.

All these years.

"Well, he'd know these days." Grant's voice was wry.

"He would."

"I wasn't ever expecting that my wild child wide receiver would settle down, happily. Especially not with the guy we hired to straighten him out."

"You gotta give Ian credit, he *did* it," Deacon said, chuckling dryly.

"He sure did."

Deacon hesitated. "You know, I gotta tell you the truth. Yeah, I wanted to see you, but I didn't just leave the Pirate's Booty 'cause of that."

"What happened?" Grant sounded more alert now. Almost worried. Deacon regretted bringing it up, but he'd needed to know.

"Nothing major. Nothing like last time. Just . . .I got so fucking tired of people asking me what was going on. Strangers. People I didn't even know. Thinking they could stick their noses into our business."

Grant settled down against him, his palm flat against Deacon's chest.

"Darcy says it's because they're surprised—and happy, I guess—to learn I'm not just a machine with a brain, but a man. They'd never seen me that way before, and that's why they're so interested."

"A machine with a brain, huh?" That was weird to Deacon, because he'd *always* seen Grant as a man. Even from the first moment, when he'd sat across from him in the old musty library on campus, hoping that he wouldn't fail statistics.

"You disagree?"

"No. But I also think this is pretty big news. People like to hear about a romantic story."

He could feel Grant grinning against him. "That what we are, a romantic story?" Grant wondered.

"Well, we're definitely not a sad one."

"Not even after all this?"

Deacon couldn't really believe Grant was suggesting it. But then, he supposed he could. They both had a lot to risk—Grant more than Deacon. There was a reason they'd stayed away from each other.

"You think the NFL's gonna punish you somehow?" Deacon asked. His fingers tightened around Grant's shoulders, digging into his skin. *Don't tell me I'm gonna lose this. I can't lose this.*

"No, no. I mean, I don't know, not for sure, but they rarely hold owners accountable for their fuckups. I'll probably be fine. I'm sure I'll just be under the oversight of Cheryl the bitch for quite a bit longer. I can handle that. It's annoying, but not the end of the world. I meant, you're not going to get cold feet and freak out at all this attention?"

Deacon couldn't believe it. But he could, all the same.

Of course it was a lot. Of course he didn't enjoy turning on ESPN and seeing a whole panel of old guys speculating about his sex life. Of course he could leave the pushy, drunk people who hadn't wanted to leave him alone with his teammates tonight. Of course he *hated* it when Grant got that worried crease between his dark brows, when his green eyes looked haunted and concerned. When he got hounded by the media. When people made nasty assumptions about him. That just because he liked cock meant he was somehow less of a man. Less of a genius.

That made Deacon want to fight the world.

But it didn't make him want to leave Grant.

It made him want to take his hand and never let it go.

"No," Deacon said. Because he could have said all that. But he didn't know if it was too soon—or too much. There was a reason he didn't do relationships. Everyone always thought he was tough all the way through.

Grant never had, though.

Maybe that was why Deacon had never forgotten him.

Not because his statistics tutor and hopeless college crush had become rich and powerful, but because Grant had always been special.

"No," Deacon continued, haltingly. "No, not even close. I . . .yeah, it makes me angry and frustrated, sometimes. Mostly because of the shit people say that couldn't be further from the truth. Judgments about you and me, and about you. I don't give a shit what people think about me, but I do care about what they think and they fucking *say* about you. But none of that crap makes me want to leave you. I . . ." Deacon hesitated. "If you want me to leave, at any point in the future, you're gonna have to say so. Because I won't. I don't ever want to."

"Even if—"

"No," Deacon said.

"Just *no*?" Grant turned in his arms and pinned him with a look.

"I love you," Deacon said. Because surely that explained everything better than he could. Words, after all, had never been his strong suit.

Grant, who clearly between board meetings and inventing so many brilliant technologies he'd become a billionaire had found time to spend time in the gym, pressed Deacon's body down with unexpected force and pushed himself up, on top of him, dropping his head down low.

"I love you, too," he murmured, eyes intent on Deacon's. "And I'm not going anywhere. And I sure as hell don't want *you* going anywhere."

"Good." Deacon's hands slid up Grant's sides. Marveling in the way just touching him—Grant touching him in return—quieted everything inside.

Made him happy.

Happier than he could ever remember being.

No matter what, then, they were going to have each other. And each other's backs.

CHAPTER 16

DEACON KNEW SOMETHING HAD happened from the ripple of noise that went through the practice field.

He lifted his head up from where he and Nate were facing off against each other, working on the linebacker's spin move.

"What is it?" Nate asked.

"I don't know, but something," Deacon said.

Practice didn't start for another half an hour, but he'd agreed to help Nate, even texting Jem to send him some advice for the guy. Jem had done more than that. He'd watched film of Nate's last few games and had sent extensive pointers, even going as far as to record a video—or have Murphy record a video—of him showing exactly how to do his famous spin move, broken down into a dozen slower parts.

Deacon knew it was exactly what he feared when Riley broke off from the main group gathered on the sideline and began to head towards him.

"Hey," Riley said, shading his eyes from the late afternoon sun. "You got a minute?"

"Yeah," Deacon said. Hating that he sounded like the world was *this fucking close* to ending. He was supposed to be happy. He *was* happy.

But it still felt like every day he was waiting for the bubble to burst. He and Grant repaired it, each and every time, because what else could they do? But that didn't mean it didn't suck.

Didn't mean that every time the arrow came at them, Deacon wasn't incredibly pissed off.

Pissed off and more than a little confused because Riley kept glancing over at Nate. Not him, who the world currently couldn't shut up about, but *Nate*.

Then Riley looked over at him, worrying his bottom lip, and Deacon's concern skyrocketed.

"What is it?" he asked flatly.

Riley looked over at Nate again. "I know you're the defensive captain, and it's your job to deal with players on your side of the ball."

Deacon knew whatever was coming he was not going to like. Not one fucking bit.

"But you're the quarterback. You lead this team," Deacon said. Riley had gotten that from the moment he'd arrived, even as a last-minute signing. He'd stood up and *led*.

Most of the time, Deacon assumed that it came pretty easily and naturally to him, because he'd seen his older brother do it so effortlessly. But there were some days, some moments, when it really fucking sucked to be the one everyone looked to.

Deacon had a feeling this was one of those times.

"Yeah, I do." Riley turned to Nate. Who was cringing now, like he knew what was coming, and that was even worse, as far as Deacon was concerned. "Were you even going to say anything? After you were so eager to run your mouth?"

Nate shrank under Riley's tough—but still kind—gaze. "I guess I didn't know it was such a big deal. I was defending Deac, after all."

"What did he say?" Deacon said, forcing himself to stay calm, directing his question to Riley, not Nate.

The guy was a rookie. Jem would tell him Nate was very young and as a result, still very stupid. Jem would remind him of how young and stupid they'd been at one time. How there hadn't been enough help to go around, to be any *less* stupid.

But still, the last guy Deacon had expected to run his mouth to the media was Nate.

"They just kept saying shit, and asking questions, like they *knew*, and I have to tell you, Deac, I didn't like the tone they took. Or the way they were talkin' about you or about Mr. G. So I just told them that your relationship was none of their fucking business."

Deacon groaned softly and Riley shot him a knowing look.

"Next time," Riley said firmly, "you tell them *no comment*. Repeat it with me, Nate. *No comment*."

Nate looked ashamed, now. "No comment," he said miserably. Then he turned to Deacon. "Deac, man, I am so sorry. I didn't even realize, I didn't even *know*—"

"I know," Deacon said, before guilt could tug him any harder. "I know you didn't mean to confirm everything, but you kinda did."

Riley eyed him but didn't say a word. Let him handle it.

"I just—"

"I get it. They're fucking vultures, right? They just push and push and push . . ."

"Yeah. I didn't even realize it was a thing until it was out of my mouth, and then I thought, well, maybe it *won't* be a thing."

So young, Deacon thought, and so stupid.

This was the biggest sports story on the planet right now. The reporter Nate had talked to probably thought he'd just won the fucking lottery.

"Next time, if you're even a little bit worried it might be a thing, go to Riley. Come to me. Talk to us. We'll figure out if it's a big deal."

It probably wouldn't have mattered if he and Grant had known about this ahead of time. It still would've been the brief flame the story needed to *really* catch fire.

"Yeah, yeah, I can do that," Nate said, nodding in understanding. "I got this. God, I just feel like shit. After all you've done to help me, Deac."

"It's alright," Deacon said, patting him on the shoulder. "Go take a moment. Get yourself together before practice."

Nate trotted off and Riley looked at him. Didn't say a word. But he probably didn't *need* to. Didn't need to say that he was *also* a rookie.

"You got a brother who was already a superstar when you showed up here," Deacon said. "You knew the ropes, already."

"It's gonna make things a hell of a lot tougher for you and Mr. G," Riley said.

Yes, it probably would. But things would've been tough already.

What was one rookie player's offhand confirmation, anyway?

Everyone already believed it was happening.

Deacon told himself it was going to be fine, that this wouldn't affect them strongly.

But from the moment practice began, it was clear it—or *something*—was on everyone's mind.

Landry fumbled a pass he'd have caught ninety-nine times out of a hundred. He shrugged it off, like it was just the hundredth time, but he saw Riley's lips compress and Deacon hated the surge of guilt he felt that he was fucking up everyone else.

Jem would tell him he was allowed to want things. That he was even allowed to *have* them. But Jem would also tell him that the team came first, *always*.

Nate was clearly miserable too, and way off his game. Nevermind learning Jem's spin move, he was unable to do more than fruitlessly and pointlessly push back against the offensive line.

Not that it changed much. Riley missed open receivers. Carter dropped another one of his passes. Everyone felt distracted and off, and by the time practice ended, Deacon was finding it hard to believe that just this morning he'd been so fucking happy.

That he'd been naive enough to think they could weather this shitstorm without it impacting anyone else.

"Hey, it's gonna be okay," Landry said, stopping by where Deacon was sitting on the sideline, sucking down Gatorade.

He'd made himself run sprints, at the end of practice, until he could barely move. Had straight up lied to himself that this wasn't punishment.

But it felt like punishment.

Grant knew the moment Darcy walked into his office, her mouth a tense, flat line, that something was wrong.

"What now?" he asked, as he finished typing an email. After re-reading it quickly, he hit send and then looked over at her.

She'd not taken a seat, the way she normally did, just stood in front of his desk. "One of the rookies gave a quote about you and Deacon to a reporter."

Not ideal. But they could deal with it.

"Initially, of course, the headline was just about as bad as it could get. Just about as bad as they could *make* it," Darcy continued. "But if you read the article, the full exchange was in there. I do think, in his own rookie stupidity, the kid was trying to defend you and Deacon."

"Of course he was." Grant wouldn't tolerate anyone on his team whose first thought—or second or third or thousandth—was to go sell out their team by blabbing to the media.

Didn't mean the kid hadn't created a firestorm, anyway.

"Are we still going with *no comment*?" Darcy asked. He heard everything she wasn't saying. Everything she'd already said.

"Yes," Grant said.

He had no intention of catering to the media. No intention of stooping to their rumor-mongering, gossip-first level.

"Alright," Darcy said. She didn't seem happy. Well, that made two of them. Grant hadn't wanted his private business splashed all over the front page of every website in the whole fucking world. "And Coach K called up. He wants to see you, if you have a minute."

"Do you know what about?" he asked.

Darcy shook her head. "Just said he wanted a minute, if you had it free."

Even without details, Grant had a good idea what he wanted to talk about. It didn't take a rocket scientist—or a billionaire—to figure it out.

"Practice is over then?" He'd resolutely forced himself to stay at his desk. Not to wander over to the windows and look down. See what Deacon was up to.

He'd sworn to himself that *one*, they could compartmentalize this, and that *two*, it wouldn't affect the team.

But if reporters were hounding his players over their relationship, *two* was barely holding up.

As for *one*, the fact that he'd had to resolutely force himself into his desk chair at least half a dozen times, when he'd kept rising out of sheer instinct, said it all.

How had this happened?

Grant didn't know the answer to that. But he *did* know that it wouldn't have mattered if they'd still kept their hands to themselves. Even if they weren't doing the things the world kept speculating they were, behind closed doors, everyone would still assume they were.

"Been over for an hour," Darcy said. "There was more in the article. Some speculation about Deacon leaving a players get-together at that bar early. A very blurry picture of a truck that could've been Deacon's, or another thousand in this town, pulling up at your building half an hour later."

"We need more security," Grant said, turning to his computer again, beginning to draft another email to the company he contracted with to not only keep him safe but his private business *private*.

Of course that was kind of a fool's errand, these days.

"Grant," Darcy said, and he looked up in surprise, because she'd come around the back of the desk and was right there. "You can't fight this like you normally would. You can't outsmart it or buy it into submission."

"I wasn't—"

"Yes, you were," Darcy interrupted, gesturing at his screen, where there was the barely started email to his security contact. "You can't stop people from taking pictures of Deacon's truck."

"You said it yourself, it could've been one of a thousand in downtown Charleston."

"And it wasn't, was it?" Darcy looked resolute. Hard-edged, in a way she almost never did. Only when she was going in for the jugular.

Before she'd only done it with their opponents and their enemies.

Never with him.

"What does it matter?" Grant said, throwing up his arms, but not in defeat. "Okay, yes, he came over last night. Do you need me to draw you and the rest of the fucking world a diagram of what we did after? Is that what you want?"

"It's not about that and you know it," Darcy retorted. "You knew when you began this that it was probably only going to end one way. It was why you told me, that time in the plane, why you couldn't just wait to do this, until later. Until after Deacon was retired. It was always going to be a sensation. It was always going to blow back on both of you. You *knew* that. It was why you said you could never get involved with him."

"What are you saying, then?"

Grant hated fighting with Darcy, and he knew she felt the same, so the fact she was willing to go toe-to-toe with him on this meant a hell of a lot.

"I'm saying, *think* about it. You give them a taste of what they want, maybe it'll be intense for a little bit, but then it'll fade away. Another story will crop up. They always do."

"I don't want to be the story," Grant said bitterly.

But he *did* want Deacon. Desperately. Fiercely. With every molecule in his body. With every single bit of his heart.

"Then you're gonna have to figure out how to deflect, and I'm telling you right now, this is not doing it. This is not the way."

"I'll think about it," Grant said.

If he was convinced she was right, he'd have given in immediately, called Deacon and then Nicole and done the interview tomorrow.

But what did it matter if they gave the world what they wanted if it destroyed him and Deacon in the process? They were too new to weather this, no matter what Deacon believed. No matter what Grant wanted to believe.

This was like standing in the middle of a hurricane and claiming you had a generator, so it was all going to be good.

"Good," Darcy said and skirted back around the desk. "I'll go grab Coach K."

When Jonathan Kelley walked in, Grant's heartbeat had not quite returned to normal. He was still frustrated that Darcy wouldn't stop pushing. Still mad and pissed off that the whole world wouldn't quit it either.

"Mr. Green," Jonathan said, settling down on the chair in front of Grant's desk. The one Darcy had refused to sit in. Yeah, that was going to fucking sting for awhile.

"I've told you to call me Grant more times than I can even remember," Grant reminded him.

Jonathan cracked a smile. He looked a little older, a lot more worn than when Grant had hired him earlier this year. "Right then, Grant."

"I'm not going to pretend either of us are stupid, and I don't know why you're here," Grant said, leaning forward and putting his elbows on the desk.

"Good," Jonathan said with a nod. "You see practice today?"

"No," Grant said, and he didn't even have to lie. He'd forced himself to stay away, after all.

But no doubt, much later, when he and Deac talked, he'd hear about it.

Not that Deacon was much of a talker, but even the few words he'd say would be enough for Grant to parse what had happened.

"Everything okay?" Grant asked when Jonathan didn't continue.

"We're distracted. We're distracted, at the worst time, when we should be zeroing on what really matters: a playoff spot."

"I know," Grant said. Forced himself not to apologize.

"We're going to take care of Nate. I'll talk to the rest of the team, too." Jonathan sighed. "I just don't want this to undo everything we've been building."

"And," Grant guessed, "you're here to ask me if all of this is worth it."

The other man settled back into his chair. His light blue eyes were keen. Maybe as keen as Grant's. He'd liked the coach from the very beginning, even though he hadn't been his first choice. "No, I'm not. You're not a stupid man. You've been everything this team needed. Everything it didn't get last year—or for too many years before that. What I *am* asking is how the fuck did you let everyone find out about it? It's not so hard to carry on something under everyone's nose, without them finding out."

Grant was not often surprised. He was shocked now.

"From personal experience?" he asked, his eyebrows creeping upwards.

Jonathan nodded succinctly. "Who I was dating wasn't—*isn't*—anyone's business." *Including yours,* was his unspoken addition.

Grant could hardly argue with that, not when he'd been lamenting the loss of his own privacy.

"There was a leak in the commissioner's office. A leak I'm working on plugging." A leak he was working on *eliminating*. But getting his plan to come together was taking time. He had about a third of the other owners on board but he needed a bit more pull, considering he was their newest member. Then he would still have to take everything he'd learned, all his proof, to the commissioner himself.

"If it wasn't for that," Grant continued, "nobody would know a thing about this. In fact, I'm not sure anything *would've* happened worth reporting."

It was the coach's turn to look shocked. "You're saying before this, you weren't—"

"Yes, that's exactly what I'm saying," Grant said firmly.

"Guess I don't need to give you the shovel talk then," Jonathan said, in a darkly amused voice. "You wanted the best for him."

"It's all I've tried to do." He wouldn't tell Jonathan just how painfully accurate that leaked email had been. That would only make him look ridiculous. Like a grown man with a crush he couldn't let go of, long after he should've.

Accurate, a voice that sounded suspiciously like Darcy's echoed in his mind.

"Alright, I'm sorry, I've misjudged you."

"Doesn't matter," Grant said ruthlessly. "Your judgment doesn't change a damn thing. Doesn't change the media that's hounding your players. Or camped out outside the locker room. Or focusing on me instead of what matters: the game we're playing."

"What are you gonna do about it?" Jonathan didn't say *you can't change what other people are doing*, but he didn't have to. By now, Grant was painfully familiar with that.

"Working on it." Grant paused. "What are *you* gonna do?"

He liked Jonathan Kelley—he *did*. Up until now, he'd been convinced that Deacon had been right, and hiring him had been the correct call. But now . . .if he couldn't get a hold of this team—if he didn't have the experience or the force of will to do it—then, he wasn't going to be the right coach going forward.

Because one thing was always guaranteed in an NFL season—there were going to be distractions and messes and garbage fires, and Grant needed someone who could handle himself *and* the team around him.

Jonathan chuckled darkly. "You know, before I took this job, someone told me you were the scariest motherfucker he'd ever met. I didn't believe him. After all—"

"I don't exactly look it," Grant said, actually smiling now. Maybe this *was* the right guy for the job.

"No," Jonathan agreed. "No, you do not. I saw it a little, earlier this year, the way you ruthlessly trimmed out the rot. But I didn't really see it, not completely, until just now."

Grant got it. The coach had come here, to his office, to read Grant the riot act about the distractions he'd created for his team, for getting involved with one of his players, and Grant had neatly turned it back on him.

It was how he'd won boardrooms for years. Won *or* worn them down until they just didn't want to fight any longer.

But he didn't want that for Jonathan. They needed to be on the same page, here.

"You know how Bruce Banner likes to say, *you wouldn't like me when I'm angry*? That's me. You don't want to see me when I've been backed into a corner. I don't like it, and I'm gonna fight like hell, underhanded and every other way I can think of, to get out of the trap."

That was why he hadn't dismissed Darcy's suggestion outright. It was unexpected, and he *liked* unexpected.

But one thing was holding him back, for better or worse. Because he was terrified it would mean the end of this thing he shared with Deacon, and he could risk a lot, offer to sacrifice even more, but he wasn't willing to put that on the chopping block. Even if it didn't ruin it, the chance was too great, the pain too immediate whenever he thought of it.

He'd met too many men in business who'd shoved their personal lives and feelings to the side, ruthlessly ignored everything they felt in order to climb to the top. To a man, they'd ended up rich, and always too bitter to actually enjoy the spoils of their victories.

Grant wasn't going to be yet another one in that long line.

He refused to accept less than *everything*, and maybe it was ego talking, but if anyone could grab it all, it was going to be him.

"I believe you, and I wouldn't ever bet against you," Jonathan said. He stood. "I'll talk to the team."

"Do you want me to do it?" It was another test, even though Grant believed the coach was smart enough to see through it.

And he did, shaking his head. "No, I've got it," he said.

After his conversation with his coach, Grant's mood improved marginally. He *could* do this. He had the best staff. He had a sharp brain. He could defeat this.

But then Nicole walked in an hour later, and if Darcy's face had telegraphed her news, Nic's expression screamed it.

"What now?" Grant tried to keep his voice calm and level but it had an undeniably testy edge.

"Rex wasn't getting enough attention with his gambling accusations, so he's switched gears." Nicole collapsed onto the chair in front of his desk. She looked as tired as he suddenly felt.

How could he win when the vultures kept swooping out of every shadow, salivating over what they kept assuming was the Condors' carcass?

"Let me guess," Grant said sarcastically, "my personal life is his new target."

"He claimed you preyed on him and several others, even though they weren't queer."

"He used a worse word, didn't he," Grant said heavily.

Nicole nodded.

"Shit."

"By this point, he's hardly credible, so we can contain this," Nicole claimed. And he had no doubt that she could. Rex had already blown his load with the gambling shit and then had been proven wrong. Not many people would believe any of this. It was just more fucking *noise*, when they were already in danger of being drowned out by it all.

"Sure, we can. But how am I gonna keep Deacon from killing him?" Grant said with a heavy sigh. Because that was really the problem. And if Deacon said or did a single fucking thing, that was all Rex would need to bleat about it forever.

"That's your problem, not mine," Nicole said.

She didn't have to say he'd *have* to handle it, because they both knew what would happen if Grant couldn't convince Deacon to stay out of it.

They didn't need everything to go from merely dire to catastrophic.

"I've got it."

"I *am* going to release a statement making it very clear he's lying out his ass," Nicole said. "We can't *no comment* this."

No, they couldn't. Not when Rex was essentially accusing him of sexual harassment.

"But," Nicole added, "you know what would help? If we added a little about your love story with Deacon. Make it clear that you're not just some horny maniac who can't keep your hands off your players, but that it's different with Deacon. That Deacon's *special*."

"Darcy talked to you, didn't she?"

"Yes, but she didn't have to," Nicole said. "It's the right move. The sooner everyone realizes you're not just scratching a fucking itch together, the sooner this is containable."

"No," Grant said inexorably. *Not yet. Don't make me do this yet.*

"Grant—" Nicole argued.

"No," he repeated firmly. "If our strategy changes, you'll be the first to know."

She looked annoyed. "I don't have to tell you that a love story looks better than a story about a sexual predator. I don't think it would fix everything, but it would sure make it less terrible," she said.

"Talk to him," she reminded him, standing up.

"Despite the rampant and insane speculation about us, we *do* actually exchange words and not just fluids when we get together," Grant muttered.

Nicole laughed. "I never doubted it. It's the rest of the world I'd like to convince."

"Noted," Grant said, and a moment later, she walked out, leaving him alone with a whole brain full of unpleasant thoughts and so many questions he didn't have answers to.

He sent a text to Darcy, and when he got the reply, he closed up his laptop, shoved it in his bag, and after sending another message to his driver, headed to the garage.

He'd just started contemplating the keypad next to the door of Deacon's truck, wondering what four digits Deacon might find memorable enough, when he heard footsteps behind him and turned.

Deacon's hair was still damp and his gray t-shirt clung to his pecs and his biceps, and *okay*, there was definitely a part of Grant that wanted to exchange bodily fluids with him.

But he hadn't come down here for that—even if it ended up being a pleasant supplement.

"Hey," he said.

"A surprise?" Deacon asked, shooting him a look as he unlocked the truck, but didn't get in, just threw his bag into the back. "What's the occasion?"

"We need to talk," Grant said.

There was no way he hadn't heard about Nate—or about Rex, too—so it was foolish to assume he could break the news gently and easily. But that didn't mean they could get away without discussing it. At the very least, he could encourage Deacon not to tear Rex apart.

"Yeah, I was going to text you," Deacon said.

But he hadn't.

And a frisson of unease skittered down Grant's spine. What if, in trying to preserve this, he'd lost it already and just didn't know it? Deacon's gaze was still warm on him, but what if *his* version of talking was actually a breakup?

Grant ruthlessly shoved aside the part of his brain that piped up that if he had, it would make everything a hell of a lot easier.

He didn't *want* easy; he wanted Deacon.

"But you didn't," Grant said.

"No," Deacon agreed, ducking his head. "Come on, get in. Let's grab some dinner."

"You haven't eaten yet?" Grant said, opening the door and sliding into the truck.

Deacon shook his head. "Worked out after practice. Probably too hard. But . . ." He trailed off, not needing to explain why he had.

Nate and then, so much worse, *Rex.*

"Dinner it is. You got a place in mind?"

"Yeah," Deacon said shortly, but then didn't turn the car on. Instead, he looked over at Grant. "You here to make sure I don't kill him? Or because you wanted to see me?"

"Yes," Grant said. Because they were both true.

Deacon sighed. "I'm not that stupid. Even if I *wanted* to, even if I wanted to find him and make him take it all back, it would only make it all worse. It wouldn't exonerate you, in the end."

"No," Grant agreed.

"I hate . . .I *hate* that this gave him the opening to make everyone think that maybe you'd do this with someone else. Maybe we shouldn't have—"

"No." Grant interrupted, repeated himself, but stronger this time.

Deacon looked surprised. "I'm not saying *never*. I'm saying . . .cool it for a few weeks. A few months."

It was only what Darcy had told him once. That when Deacon retired, whenever the season ended for the Condors, there was nothing stopping them from starting a relationship then.

Grant had never been as convinced as her that nobody would care, even if Deacon was retired—and for so long, he'd never wanted to do a single fucking thing to tarnish Deacon's reputation, not when he'd worked so hard to preserve it, or to jeopardize any of the employees who trusted him to make the right moves.

In the end, he hadn't been able to help it. Selfishly, he'd dismissed the space between them and crossed the line himself.

"No," Grant said for the third time.

Deacon shook his head and chuckled under his breath. "How're we gonna solve this, then?"

"I don't know," Grant said, as Deacon started the truck and headed out of the garage.

Grant nearly brought up what Darcy—and now Nicole—kept suggesting. But he wasn't ready to take that risk, and he knew if he said it, even if he even breathed a word about it, Deacon would be willing to do it.

In any other scenario, Grant would've been thrilled at the thought Deacon would be willing to do anything he asked, if he thought it would help him in any way. They were the same, that way.

He'd bought a fucking football team—he'd spent nearly a *billion dollars*—when Deacon was in trouble.

Would Deacon be willing to get in front of any number of reporters and tell every single one of them that he loved Grant?

It wasn't even a fucking question. Which was the whole problem. Deacon would save him—right until they went off the cliff, together.

Relationships rarely survived the intense scrutiny, the invasive questions, and the media digging into every aspect of the participants' personal lives. How could a relationship only a week or so old hope to survive it?

To Grant's surprise, Deacon didn't stay in town, but drove them out of town and then drove and drove until he pulled up at a shack, all the way out towards the ocean, tucked out on an inlet.

"What's this place?" Grant asked, stretching. They'd been mostly quiet on the drive.

"Shrimp shack. Best one in the county," Deacon said, glancing over at him. "You okay with this?"

Grant rolled his eyes. "Don't tell me you're asking if I'm okay with paper napkins and eating with my hands and the fact that this place looks like it's been around for at least fifty years."

"No, no, of course not. Just . . .it's *real* rustic," Deacon said. "Carter suggested it, though, so it comes highly recommend, at least. He lives out this way."

"Carter lives all the way out here?" Not much surprised Grant but that astonished him.

"I know, right?" Deacon said, grinning as they walked up to the shack and he held the door open for Grant. No doubt even if someone out here recognized them, Grant had a feeling they wouldn't give two shits.

"Carter sure has unexpected depths," Grant said.

The hostess—if that was even her job, other than smacking her gum and lazily waving them towards an empty table—brought menus after they'd sat. They were laminated in plastic and consisted of one thing—shrimp—with a variety of choices of sides.

"The seafood's the best thing about living out here," Grant said, leaning back.

Deacon looked amused. "The best thing, huh?"

"Okay, second best."

"I was kinda gunning for occupying the top five," Deacon confessed, leaning forward across the pitted and scarred wooden table. "What do I gotta do to get there? Go down on you right now, in the middle of this place?"

Grant choked on the beer the waitress had just brought them. It was only available in bottles here, which was probably safer, all around.

"Or," Deacon added with a lopsided grin, "how 'bout I just say I love you?"

"You could start with those, and how about you tell me too what happened in practice? Coach K seemed a bit shaken up."

Deacon groaned. "Just everyone pissed off by Nate runnin' his mouth. That was all."

"If you're gonna tell me sometimes practice goes bad, and it's fine, you can save it."

"Yeah, you know that happens," Deacon said. But his back hunched over, muscles suddenly tense, and Grant regretted saying anything. Especially when Deacon had been so charming and flirtatious since they'd arrived here.

But they couldn't just ignore this, sweep it under the rug like it didn't exist.

"Sure, it happens," Grant said lightly. "So you don't want to talk about it?"

Deacon shot him a look. "Not really. I'm still pissed as hell at Nate, and he deserved it. It wasn't his place to say that shit."

"Except it wasn't shit. He was trying, in his completely misguided way, to defend you. And me. I'm only disappointed he didn't really listen to what Nicole said about *no comment.*"

"Yeah, yeah, and then of course I felt guilty 'cause I was angry. Now Rex? I don't feel guilty about being angry about that. I wish he'd just go away." Deacon sighed. Took a long drink of his beer. "Doesn't seem like that's gonna happen, though."

"Oh, I wouldn't be surprised if this is his last shot at attention," Grant said. "He was wrong before. If he's wrong twice—and despite his chatter, there's *no* evidence he can possibly produce to prove anything he's claimed—then he'll go away. Nobody will even be willing to listen a third time. And then there's Cheryl."

"You think Rex will finally shut up? God, I hope so." Deacon let out a sigh. "And I thought you said you were taking care of Cheryl."

To Grant's surprise—they *were* practically in the bayou backwater of South Carolina—he reached out and took Grant's hand and squeezed it, but didn't let it go, either.

Held on to it, calloused thumb caressing the sensitive skin on Grant's palm.

"I *am*, it's just . . .it's not as simple as it sounds. She's been in her job a long time."

"Just hate it when he talks about you. The way *everyone* talks about you," Deacon said.

"I don't particularly enjoy it, either. But when it gets us out here, away from everything else, well, I don't hate *that.*"

"I kept meaning to take you here, thought you'd like to get away from the chatter, and I'm only sorry it took me so long."

"Don't you dare apologize for that," Grant ordered him, but couldn't help his smile.

"I won't. Or for how much I love you," Deacon said.

CHAPTER 17

"AND WE'RE GONNA TAKE this week of practice," Coach K announced, continuing his pre-game speech, "and we're gonna tell it to go fuck itself. Okay? I don't care how shit it felt all week, I know you're capable of more. I know you're capable of moving the ball. Capable of defending the ball. You've shown it to me, in every game we've played this season. Even the games we've lost."

"Yeah!" Carter yelled, and for a split second Deacon considered telling him to pipe down, to let Coach talk, but the mumbles around him grew louder after Carter's outburst, and he realized that maybe it was a good thing.

Good that not just their coach believed in them, but that *they* believed in them.

"We're gonna fly," Landry called out, and the noise became deafening, Coach K smiling as the team took over for him.

Maybe, Deacon thought as he gathered himself from the bench in front of his locker, it would be enough to turn things around.

For them to leave behind the worst week of practice he could remember the team having all year. Even the week Nelson Perez had blown out his knee and they'd had to practice with the backup hadn't been this bad. Even the week after Jem had been injured, they'd managed.

But this week they hadn't managed to do anything right, and instead of playing an easy game at home, they'd had to head up the coast to Baltimore, to play the Ravens in their own stadium.

That was never going to be an easy task.

But it was even harder now.

Five minutes later, they jogged onto the field to a whole chorus of boos, and after the anthem, out of the corner of his eye, Deacon watched as Micah and Beck did their special pre-game routine.

He and Jem hadn't had anything that official. But still, before every kickoff, they'd found each other and said, "good game," like they could manifest it, no matter what happened.

Deacon hadn't really missed hearing it until today.

But right now, he wished he could turn to his right, and Jem would be standing there, a calm expression on his face—not worried, not overthinking—just accepting, just readying himself for the job to come. Not just knowing, but believing, deep down, that they were capable of handling their own business.

"Hey," a voice to the right said, and Deacon started, glancing to the side, but of course it wasn't Jem.

It was Nate.

He hadn't necessarily been *avoiding* him. He couldn't. Not really. After all, he was the defensive captain. Nate was his responsibility.

But he had given him as wide of a berth as he could, not giving him the kind of personalized attention he had been during previous weeks.

Deacon was sure Nate had felt his absence and had understood why.

But of course that wasn't going to help anything—or *change* anything, either.

"Hey," Deacon said, acknowledging him with a nod.

"I just wanted to say, again, that I'm sorry," Nate said. "I certainly didn't mean to make things worse."

"I know," Deacon said.

"Good." Nate looked relieved, and Deacon felt another pulse of guilt.

He was supposed to be leading this defense, and he *had*, but he could acknowledge to himself that he'd only done the bare minimum this week. Instead, he'd been thinking about Grant—and how to permanently erase that frown line between his eyebrows.

Deacon dragged his attention back to Nate and to the sideline.

"Hey, really, it's alright," Deacon said and clapped him on the shoulder. Let his hand linger there, making it clear it wasn't just an obligation, but a meaningful gesture. An olive branch.

"You ready to kick some ass today?" Nate asked, the relief clear in his eyes.

Deacon nodded, and they both smiled.

It was the last time Deacon smiled.

From the moment the offense took the field, the players jogging out behind Riley, it seemed like they were off-balance.

Some of Riley's throws were too high. He didn't have enough time to make others. He took a bad sack. There was a penalty. Then on the fourth drive of the first half, he rolled out to the right and instead of tossing a five-yard pass to Landry and getting some of the distance to the next down, he threw downfield to Carter, and the wind picked up the ball, and it floated right to a Ravens' safety, who took it all the way back to the opposing end zone.

Scoring another goddamned touchdown.

"Shit," Deacon muttered. This was the *last* thing they needed right now. He was still short of breath from the last Ravens' drive, where they'd managed to score a field goal.

In fact, because the offense couldn't seem to find a rhythm and move the ball, the Condors' defense, which usually could hold their heads high, was struggling. It was just too much time, too many drives, and not enough rest in between.

Eventually, they'd find a way through, and they had.

In fact, even before that pick-six, the Ravens had been up thirteen to zero. But now the score was twenty to zero, and from Riley's face when he marched over to the sideline, Deacon didn't think anything was going to get better.

"Shit," Riley exclaimed.

"Hey, hey, you're okay," Landry said, catching up to him. "We can get it back together. Score this drive, and then it's only a two score game after that."

Deacon sure hoped they'd get it together, because he needed more time to gather his poor, exhausted defense together so they could make another stand.

"How you doing?" he asked, approaching Beck and Micah after Riley and Landry and the offense went back on the field after the kickoff.

"Could be better," Beck said wryly.

Micah nodded.

"We gotta stop the run," Deacon said. "Did you hear Coach Rufus talk about you moving up, Beck?"

"You want me to?" Beck said.

"I've got Flowers," Micah said, referring to the Ravens' dynamite receiver, and how before this point, Beck had been giving him a much-needed assist in the coverage.

"I know you do," Beck said, turning to him. "But I want to—"

"You heard Deac," Micah said, putting a hand on his shoulder. "We have to stop the run. You can do that. I got this."

Beck wouldn't ever be stupid enough to question Micah's confidence—or his capabilities—in the middle of a game. Or probably *after* a game, even. Not if he didn't want to spend a few nights on the couch.

But Deacon had known Beckett for almost two years at this point, and he knew he wasn't convinced. Not necessarily because he didn't believe Micah could stop Flowers, the Ravens' deep threat receiver, but because the game, already going badly, could go so much worse if Flowers got a step ahead of Micah or took a slightly better angle.

It would only take the tiniest, most miniscule mistake for things to get ugly.

Okay, Deacon conceded, uglier than they already were.

"We on the same page?" Deacon questioned, meeting every one of his players' eyes. He didn't have to say, *it's on us now,* because they all understood.

If they had a hope of winning this game, they had to keep the score close enough that the offense could close the gap.

"Same page," Micah said, and Beck nodded next to him.

With how the offense hadn't been moving the ball, Deacon had expected they'd get the kickoff, and the defense would be back out there almost immediately. He'd been prepared for it.

But instead, Deacon watched as Riley dug down and found a new well of determination to drink from. There was a reason Grant had been one hundred percent sure Riley Flynn was their guy, and it was right here, in this gritty performance as he practically put the whole Condors offense on his back and dragged them down the field. Anytime his receivers were covered—which felt like it happened nearly every down—Riley took off himself, carrying the ball and taking the beating that resulted.

Slowly but surely, they worked their way down the field until Riley rolled out and tossed a gorgeous little arc of a pass to Carter, who'd broken free of his defender, and he brought it down for a touchdown.

It wasn't enough—not nearly enough—but not only did it give the defense a bit of a lift as they headed out onto the field, it had given them the break they sorely needed.

Deacon nearly ran into Riley as he picked his helmet up, readying to hit the field again. He had at least half a dozen green turf stains smeared across his jersey and sweat shone on his brow, but he was smiling grimly. "Great drive," Deacon said, grabbing his gloved hand and pulling him into a quick embrace. "You got it done."

"Better if I hadn't started it by throwing that interception," Riley said self-deprecatingly.

"No, you got this," Deacon said.

Riley nodded and his eyes were glowing with that determination that shone so brightly from inside him. A lamp that nobody could ever extinguish.

Deacon couldn't believe he hadn't seen that light when Grant had, but he was just glad he had.

The Ravens hadn't gotten the memo, though, and they didn't line up to run the ball like Deacon had expected.

Surely they were wanting to run clock now, being up two scores, but instead, the Ravens went hard, and of course, the first play, they tried to throw deep to Flowers.

The only way to prevent the pass was to hope Micah could defend it—or for their core defensive unit to get to the quarterback.

Deacon was pushing against the center, trying to get to Jackson, so he couldn't actually throw the pass, and in his periphery, he could see Nate struggling against the left tackle's block.

Jackson backpedaled another few steps and then pulled his arm back, letting the ball fly.

Deacon's eyes tracked it across the sky, a bullet straight towards where Flowers and Micah were jostling each other forty yards downfield.

There was a yell trapped in Deacon's throat as Micah marched right up to the line of an illegal play and, before Flowers could haul in the ball, crossed right over it.

Goddamnit.

Deacon wasn't even surprised when the yellow flag flew.

"Shit," he heard Micah yell, throwing his hands in the air, even though he knew he'd crossed the line.

He'd been playing corner for long enough to know when he'd be called for defensive pass interference, and that had been a textbook move.

Of course, he'd *had* to take the risk. If he hadn't, there was a very good chance Flowers would've caught the ball, and then they'd be deep in Ravens territory and headed towards scoring yet again.

"Hey, hey," Beck called out to him as he jogged over towards his husband. "It's all good. It's fine. You did what you needed to do."

Micah made a face, clearly visible even under the darkened visor of his helmet.

"You did what you had to do," Deacon told him, repeating what Beck had told him. He patted him on the shoulder. "We weren't expecting a deep pass there."

"Yeah, they think they can put us away, drag the corpse behind the shed," Nate muttered.

"Well, maybe. But we're not going to make it fucking easy for them," Deacon announced as his defense huddled up around him. "They want it? They're going to work their asses off for it."

At least, Deacon thought, as the game finally ended, they had.

They'd only scored two more field goals in the whole game, but it hadn't been enough, because the Condors offense, even with Riley's superhuman effort, just hadn't gelled. It was definitely a situation of too little, too late, but the platitudes Coach K spouted didn't make him feel any better.

Not when they'd come here, thinking they could clinch a playoff berth, and all they'd done was shit the bed.

They'd been outpaced and outplayed.

This was the bar, and they'd fallen way short of it.

The worst of it was that Deacon was sure it wasn't just their skill or their effort. You could only drown out the distractions for so long before they overwhelmed you.

Were the Condors overwhelmed?

He didn't know—but he was afraid of the answer.

Maybe that was why when his phone dinged, on the plane ride home, he glanced at the screen and then stuck it back in his pocket.

He didn't want to talk to Grant right now.

He wasn't angry with him. He didn't *blame* him. But Deacon couldn't help but hold himself responsible.

He'd wanted this, and he'd made it happen, refused to take Grant's *no* for an answer. Pushed, because that's what he'd always done when there was something he craved. He was such a stubborn, selfish asshole.

But before he could descend into his sulk, his phone dinged again.

God, of course, Grant wouldn't give up.

He pulled his phone out again, but this time when he looked at the screen, it wasn't a text from Grant.

It was from Jem.

Tough loss, he'd written.

Probably knowing that anything else would be lost on Deacon right now.

Yeah, Deacon texted back. Didn't say, *if you'd been with us we might've pulled that out,* because he wasn't stupid enough to believe Jem would've been the difference.

The Condors had shown up disorganized and distracted, and the Ravens had been an arrow, piercing their armor before they'd even realized they were under siege.

But Jem knew him well enough to understand how much worse that was.

This game had been winnable, if they'd been focused. If they'd had a solid week of practice under their belts.

You okay? Jem asked.

Was he okay? No, he was not okay. He was . . .guilty. Guilty as hell.

He wanted to get up in the front of this plane, in front of all the players and the coaches and the staff and apologize for not being able to keep his dick in his pants.

Wanted to apologize for falling for the last person he should've picked.

But it was already done. He couldn't go back in time and stop it.

Just the same as they couldn't redo this week of practice and replay this game. They could only move forward.

No, Deacon texted back. **But I'm trying to be.**

It's not your fault, Jem immediately responded, before Deacon could even glance away from his phone screen. **Don't you dare decide it's your fault.**

You know me too well.

Deacon was considering sending something else, maybe even asking his best friend how the hell he was supposed to *not* blame himself, when a body dropped down into the empty seat next to him.

Unsurprisingly, the rest of the team had sensed his terrible mood post-game and given him a wide berth, but this person—*Riley*, Deacon realized, glancing over—hadn't gotten the memo.

Or maybe he had.

"Talking to Jem?" Riley asked innocently.

"Did you tell him to text me?" Deacon heard how gruff his question was.

He didn't need this team to coddle him. Not when he'd so epically let them down.

"Nope, but it wasn't too hard to guess. You didn't have that sappy look in your eye that you normally do when you're talking to or about Mr. G, so Jem was an easy choice."

"Ugh," Deacon said. Not sure if he was happy or worried that he looked *sappy*. But then that couldn't come as too much of a surprise. He *felt* sappy about Grant.

Still. Even. Despite everything.

"Don't worry, it's cute," Riley said, cracking a smile.

Deacon wanted to argue and say it wasn't, that it *couldn't* be, but wasn't it adorable when Grant blushed? When his cheeks flushed bright red and he stared at Deacon like he couldn't quite believe he was real?

"So, Jem tell you not to blame yourself?" Riley asked, not letting Deacon relax for even a moment.

"Yes," Deacon said cautiously.

"And you don't believe him, right?" Riley said.

Deacon didn't know what this was—but he did know that instead of Riley coming up to him and comforting *him*, he should be the one apologizing. Yet, here Riley was anyway, with not even a hint of blame in his expression as he gazed at Deacon.

"I don't know what to believe."

"Yes, you do," Riley said firmly. "If you're going to say you let us down, sure, maybe, yes, it *was* a distraction this week. Nate went around the whole week moping, and you looked like a thundercloud half the time and loopy the rest, and we couldn't move the ball if our lives depended on it. But it's not just you. You two were crazy about each other before you did anything about it. And that email would've come out regardless, with all the noise it inevitably generated. Shit happens. We have to be able to move past it if we want to be better. If we want to be the team *I* know we can be."

"And we didn't do that." It wasn't really a question, but a statement. It felt weird, not taking full responsibility. Deacon didn't think he liked it.

"No," Riley said. "We let the storm consume us, instead of us fighting the storm. And that's on us. If we're free to be together, like Landry and me, and Beck and Micah, then we can't blame *your* relationship for derailing us. That's not fair."

"Life's not fair," Deacon pointed out dryly.

"No, but neither is you taking all the blame. Which you were doing."

"I—"

"No," Riley said firmly. "*No.*"

"It's just that I . . ." Deacon swallowed hard. "I always want, I always *need* . . ."

Did he really have to voice it?

Probably not.

But Riley did anyway, putting a reassuring hand on his arm. "You want to save everyone. You want to be the knight in shining armor for the whole goddamn team. And you can't be. Not always. Especially not when it's on all of us."

"Right." Deacon had thought he'd sound more hesitant. Not quite convinced. But his voice said it all. He thought . . .well, he'd be damned, but he thought maybe Riley was onto something.

"Just thought you should know," Riley said, dimples showing as he grinned at him.

"Thanks," Deacon said.

And when Riley left, going back to his own seat, a few minutes later, he reached for his phone and he sent two texts.

One to Jem, which said. **Gonna be okay, I think. Thanks for the pep talk.**

And another one to Grant. **Tough loss, but we're gonna be okay. Love you, and see you tonight.**

Chapter 18

"Oh, Deacon, I'm so glad I caught you," Darcy said as he turned around, hearing the rapid fire sound of heels against the pavement as he walked to his truck after practice a few days after the Ravens loss.

"Yeah, what's up?" Deacon asked.

Practice had been better the last two days. There hadn't been any other new explosive rumors, at least, and the team seemed to be working through their adversity. Coach K had taken them back to basics, and it was helping to focus on doing things they already knew how to do—but doing them even better.

"Grant forgot this," she said, gesturing with a small tablet in her hand. "And he'll want it, tonight. I was going to courier it over, but if you're going to his place . . ." Darcy trailed off, a knowing look in her eye.

Okay, everyone knew how they were spending their evenings lately—even though Grant had installed a bunch more security around his building and the blurry photographs had at least gone down—and who they were spending them with. *That* shouldn't come as a big surprise.

But it was still hard for Deacon to look Darcy in the eye—Grant's employee and his closest friend—when all he'd been thinking about for the last hour was stripping Grant down, pressing him against the nearest vertical surface, and getting his mouth on him.

"I am," Deacon said.

"Great." Darcy's expression was full of amused relief. "I was hoping so."

He took the tablet from her hand. "This is all he needs?"

She grinned. "Not everything, apparently."

"Ah, uh . . ." Deacon stammered.

"Don't worry, I'm on your side, too," Darcy said, patting him on the arm. "You're good for him. Remember that. Even if he tries to deny it. And *especially* if he keeps pretending that there isn't a solution to all these problems, sitting right there, waiting to be deployed."

"A solution?" Deacon didn't know what she was talking about, but it was pretty goddamn easy to focus on *that* word when all they'd been doing for weeks was trying to find a way for the whole world to stop giving a shit about their relationship.

"Don't tell me he didn't tell you," Darcy said.

"Didn't tell me what?"

Darcy sighed. "Nicole and I think if you two went more public, gave a short interview, confirmed some things, that the speculation might die down. The media might find something else to latch on to, then."

"You really think that's true?" Deacon couldn't believe it. Less than a week ago, when Rex had started claiming Grant had made "advances" towards him, they'd had this very conversation. Deacon, hoping for a solution, and Grant claiming he wasn't sure what the right way forward was.

Had there been an option this whole goddamn time and Grant hadn't wanted to do it—hadn't even wanted to *tell* Deacon it was a possibility?

Sure, maybe it wouldn't fix everything, but they would be *doing* something, instead of just being sitting ducks.

Deacon didn't get pissed very often—or very easily, but temper was flaring inside him now. Maybe he wasn't as smart as Grant was, but he wasn't stupid either, and if there was a way out of this mess, he'd at least deserved to hear about it.

"We both do," Darcy said. "He didn't tell you."

"No," Deacon said shortly.

"Well, it's complicated," Darcy hedged. "It wouldn't fix everything, necessarily. And obviously, there'd be a lot more intense scrutiny at first. But the hope is, with confirmation, and less *room* for speculation, it would die down, eventually."

Deacon didn't care how complicated it was. Didn't even care if it didn't work right away. If all he had to do was stand in front of a few reporters, hold Grant's hand, and say a few things about how he was his sun and his moon and his sky and had been for a hell of a long time? Not that hard. Deacon did harder things, every single goddamn day.

"I don't know that it's all that complicated," Deacon said, frowning.

Maybe Grant thought because he was a football player and not that into *talking* about his feelings, that he wouldn't do it. That he wouldn't even consider it.

But that was crazy. Deacon had told Grant he loved him *first*. He'd been the one to speak up when they'd been mired in that horrible, painful *should we or shouldn't we* mess.

He'd grabbed it by the throat and said what needed to be said.

Why the fuck wouldn't Grant believe that he'd do it again?

"You'll figure it out together." Darcy patted him reassuringly. "You two have got this."

But did they?

How could they have a hope in hell of navigating this situation if they weren't honest with each other?

Deacon drove to Grant's building, this time painfully aware of every flash that he saw. There were photographers camping out on the sidewalk, despite all the security Grant had hired, and he nearly considered flipping them off as he drove into the garage, but Grant already had enough headaches.

But not so many he couldn't share Darcy's idea with you.

"Mr. Harris," the concierge greeted him as he walked in and headed towards Grant's private elevator.

"Told you to call me Deacon," he teased as he typed in the code.

"Sorry about the photographers, but they're technically off our property," he said apologetically.

Deacon glanced over at him. "It's fine," he said.

"Mr. Green is pretty upset about it," the concierge said.

He *would* be. But then, if he was so freaking upset, Deacon thought as the elevator doors opened, then why hadn't he done something about it?

Something like Darcy had suggested.

He'd considered *not* bringing it up right away. Maybe letting the knowledge simmer inside him for a bit, and maybe he'd find a reason why Grant hadn't told him. Or, at the very least, he'd be slightly less pissed by the time the subject came up.

But the moment he walked in, Grant glanced over at him, wearing those black-framed, sexy-as-hell-and-yet-undeniably-nerdy glasses, and said, "What's wrong?"

Deacon sighed. Set his bag down on a barstool. Leaned over and brushed a kiss across Grant's mouth.

Maybe he was pissed, still, but he'd have to be dead not to want to kiss his guy.

Grant didn't lean into the kiss though. He pulled back, that crease between his eyebrows returning. "Seriously, what is it?"

"Why does it have to be anything?"

Grant shot him a look. "I know you. I know how you look. You look pissed. Did something happen, again?"

"No, not . . ." Deacon took a deep breath. Passed Grant the tablet from his bag. "Darcy stopped me on my way out, said you'd forgotten this."

"Okay . . .still not sure what the deal is."

"She also mentioned a plan of attack she and Nicole were trying to convince you of. A plan you didn't tell me about at all."

"Oh, is that it?" Grant set his glasses down on the counter and rubbed his eyes. He looked tired. Exhausted, really.

Deacon had known how hard he worked before they'd gotten involved, when they'd only been friends, but now he was intimately familiar with the sheer number of balls he was constantly keeping in the air. Just how indispensable he was to two huge organizations.

Maybe he shouldn't have brought it up—but he wasn't going to lie. Not when he'd discovered how it felt when Grant had lied to him by omission.

"That's it?" Deacon asked. "Darcy—and *Nicole*, who freaking sets the Condors' public relations strategy—had an idea, a *plan, even,* to get us out of this mess, and you didn't even suggest it to me. I had to find out about it from Darcy."

Grant's eyes widened. And okay, yes, he sounded really pissed.

"You're angry . . .with *me*," Grant said, with surprise.

"Not angry." Deacon clenched his fists. Though he kind of was, wasn't he? "Didn't you trust me? I would've done it. I'd *still* do it."

Grant put a hand on his arm. "Of course I trust you."

"Then why the hell didn't you ask me what I thought?" Deacon shed his touch and began to pace through the kitchen.

"Because of what you just said. You would've done it. You'd still do it. And God only knows if it would work, and God only knows if it be too much pressure for us to handle, in the end."

"And what, you're the only one who can take one for the team, is that it?" Deacon challenged.

"No, no. That's not it." Grant laughed but didn't sound very amused. "I . . .that wasn't why at all."

"Then what the heck was it?"

"Because you said you'd do it! Just as easy as that!" Grant exclaimed. Ran a hand through his hair. "You'd do it, without even blinking or hesitating. And then what happens afterwards?"

"I don't know. We live our fucking life?"

Grant looked pained. So pained that Deacon nearly wanted to take it back. But he'd lied before, and he still wasn't making any fucking sense. Deacon might not have had a lot of partners—definitely not any partners he'd wanted for the long haul—but he knew enough to know if they weren't honest with each other, all this was pointless.

"Yeah, and for how long?"

Deacon stared at Grant. "You think—"

"That we'd break under the pressure? Maybe. That going public would change everything? No question."

"Maybe it wouldn't change it for the worse. Maybe it would do what Darcy said—take the pressure off."

"Not at first, no. And there's no guarantee it would help, and then we'd be . . .fucking exposed. To the whole world. I never wanted it to be this way. Not my personal life. And definitely not my personal life if it ever involved you."

As well as Grant knew *him*, that went both ways. And Deacon could see the panic and the fear written plainly across Grant's face. He'd believed going public might finish them off.

But Deacon wasn't that easy to kill. Not even that easy to budge, when it came to it.

It occurred to Deacon, staring at the man he loved, that maybe he knew him well, maybe Grant *thought* he knew him well, but he didn't understand this. Not the way he needed to.

"Grant." Deacon skirted around the kitchen island and tugged him off the barstool and into his arms. Grant went, but every muscle in his body was tense, and he didn't even relax once Deacon pulled him close.

"Yeah," Deacon murmured into his ear, "sure, if we give an interview, or whatever, it'll change things. That's inevitable. But I'm not going anywhere. I told you before—if you don't want me any-more, you're gonna have to tell me to leave."

Grant pulled back a fraction, but he was still frowning. "You think I would? You think I'd tell you to leave?"

"I hope not. I believe you wouldn't." It was hard not to squirm under Grant's intense green gaze. It flayed Deacon deep, right down to his marrow. Laying all his truths bare.

"But you're still afraid," Deacon stated.

"It's hard as hell *not* to be. Not when this matters so much to me." Grant paused. "I'm sorry I didn't tell you. I was afraid. I *am* afraid. We just finally got together. I don't want to risk that or lose that. Media exposure is hard enough on established relationships, and we've barely begun to figure out how this works between us. And Darcy and Nicole's plan isn't a guaran-tee. It would mean a lot *more* attention, at least initially. We'd be betting that it would die off naturally, on its own, after. And again, there's the NFL. They wouldn't be very happy about it if we got up together and held hands and said, yes, we're together."

"Isn't it worth the risk? We're . . ." Deacon swallowed hard. "The team's distracted. We did that."

"How'd I guess you'd be blaming yourself?" Grant sounded darkly amused. "But you can't."

"That's what Jem said. And Riley." And Coach Kelley, when he'd cornered Deacon yesterday, after practice.

He'd made sure Deacon understood that, before he'd let him go.

But the feelings had lingered anyway, despite everyone telling him that the loss hadn't been his fault.

"They're smart. They know what the hell they're talking about. And I'm telling you, too. It's not our fault. But I get it—it's hard not to internalize the blame."

"But you're not ready for Darcy's plan." Deacon didn't need Grant to say it to understand that he wasn't.

Grant shrugged. "I don't think so," he said. "Let's see what happens next week. It's Christmas Day, at home. That's a distraction. Maybe things will die down. I think we can use some of that motivation and push to put last week's loss in Baltimore behind us. And the last thing I want is to rush into this without considering all the angles."

"God, is it Christmas already?" Deacon said with a little bit of a groan. He should have realized. Everywhere he went he couldn't stop hearing Mariah Carey singing about what she wanted for Christmas, and then there were the luxurious holiday decor all over the lobby of Grant's building.

Even the street Deacon's townhouse was on was festooned with plenty of lights.

But he hadn't really put two and two together. He'd been too busy—and too distracted—by the Condors' push for the playoffs and then by Grant himself.

"Yep. What do you want?" Grant asked.

Of course he would be thinking about gifts right now.

Deacon rolled his eyes and leaned down. Stopped a fraction of an inch away from Grant's mouth. "I thought I'd made that clear," he murmured.

Grant kissed him, and it was a blessing and a relief to fall back into this familiar pattern. To know, with Grant's mouth moving confidently and surely against his own, that they loved and wanted each other. That they had each other's backs, no matter what.

That nothing the world said about them, that no matter what they announced—or didn't announce—to the world, would change a goddamn thing.

"Hey, hey," Deacon said as Grant tried to tug him towards the bedroom. "Where you goin'?"

"Bedroom," Grant panted into his mouth.

And yeah, it had gotten hot and heavy fast, like it always did with them.

All of Deacon's self-control evaporated pretty much the moment he touched Grant—or in this case, the moment today he'd started *thinking* about touching Grant.

"No, here," Deacon said and pushed Grant up against the kitchen island as he went to his knees.

Grant was still wearing one of those flawlessly cut and tailored suits, this one a dark green with a tiny white and gray stripe, and the pants hugged every slim, gorgeous line of his legs.

Deacon just sat there, rocking back on his heels, as he admired the view. Especially admired the hard line of Grant's cock as it pressed against the zipper.

"Yeah?" Grant said breathlessly, one of his hands gripping the edge of the counter and the other tangling in Deacon's still damp hair. "You gonna get on with it, or just sit there and look?"

"I don't know, the view's pretty goddamn amazing," Deacon said, his tone going dark and rough, guttural almost, as he reached up and unbuttoned Grant's pants, letting them slide down after he'd taken care of the zipper.

"How's that one?" Grant teased.

Deacon leaned in and enjoyed the way Grant's cock twitched at just the feel of his warm breath through the cotton of his briefs.

"Even better," Deacon said.

Grant almost stopped him.

Almost told him, *get up and let's go to the bedroom.*

Almost apologized, again.

He hoped the lingering guilt that Deacon had caught him and confronted him in a lie of omission might be permanently extinguished if he did.

But then Deacon shuffled a few inches closer and tugged down his briefs, one of those big calloused hands closing around his thigh, holding him in place, and the other curling around his cock, and the pleasure whited out his mind.

Maybe what he needed to banish the guilt wasn't another apology but just this.

Deacon and him, together. The way they were meant to be.

"I know you want it," Deacon said.

"I know you want to give it to me," Grant teased back, straining against Deacon's hold. He didn't have a hope or a prayer of touching Deacon's physical strength and also yet, Grant knew he held every card, every bit of power. The instant Deacon didn't think he was as into this as he was, he'd stop.

There was nothing surer—nothing *truer*—than Deacon's heart.

He'd said it, Grant realized. *If you don't want me anymore, you're going to have to be the one to tell me to go.*

It had been easy enough to think it, to accept it, to take it as a given, but it was another to *believe.*

Glancing down, watching as Deacon's tongue flicked out, his expression morphing from sweet and playful to worshipful, Grant thought for the first time that he might actually believe it.

Funny thing about guilt—it went hand in hand with fear—and it felt as though every pulse of bone-melting pleasure that surged through him as Deacon's tongue trailed up his length, curled around the head, banished both of them.

Deacon's hand holding his hip dipped lower, to his ass, cupping it, kneading it, and then slipped in between his cheeks, pressing against his hole, and Grant groaned.

"Yeah, baby, I know what you like," Deacon said, between long, leisurely sucks. It felt like he was barely breaking a sweat, but he was still demolishing Grant one bit at a time, reducing him to a writhing mass of pleasure and overwhelming need.

"I'm gonna suck your cock, just like this, and you're gonna come on my face, and then we're gonna go in the bedroom, like you wanted, and I'm gonna fuck you until you can't even *dream* about being afraid anymore."

Grant choked out a groan. "Yes. That. Please."

Deacon took him deeper, like he too could barely wait for what he'd just described, and then Grant was tensing up as Deacon's thumb pressed inside him, and it was all over.

He exploded, right as Deacon pulled off, and stripes of come fell across his face, bits of white settling into the dark scruff on his cheeks.

"That," Grant panted, "should not be as hot as it is."

"Yeah?" Deacon asked casually as he used Grant's briefs to wipe off.

And God, if that wasn't even fucking hotter.

The matter-of-fact way he just used Grant—used whatever of Grant's he needed. It made him desperate and horny, all over again.

Yeah, he wouldn't get hard again right away.

But even though he knew eventually Deacon was going to bury his cock in his ass and send him to heaven, again, it wasn't going to happen anytime soon.

No, he'd have his chance to recover.

Deacon wouldn't be rushed.

Though, Grant thought as they stumbled into the bedroom, Deacon landing on the edge of the bed, maybe *he* could push them a little.

He grabbed the lube and squirted some on his fingers as Deacon shed his sweatpants. And God bless post-practice habits, because it felt like Deacon never came here after his shower wearing underwear.

His cock bobbed out hard and dripping.

Grant's mouth watered, and he could barely wait until Deacon's feet were free of his sweatpants to lean forward and let his dick slip into his wide, waiting mouth.

"God, yeah, you are so goddamn hot like that," Deacon groaned and his fingers tangled in Grant's hair. Not pushing him, exactly, but guiding him. And it was so easy to give himself up to it—the stretch of his mouth around Deacon's cock and the stretch of his fingers as they pushed inside of himself. He squirmed at the slightly uncomfortable burn and then sank into the pleasure of it, loving just how right it felt. At how right it was going to feel in a minute, when Deacon finally slid into him.

Deacon must've been just about as impatient as Grant was to experience it because it felt like no time at all had passed and Deacon was hauling him up, onto the bed, one of his big fingers joining Grant's own, making him moan.

Grant flipped over, and Deacon was on him in a second, caging him in, kissing him with so much desire he felt dizzy with it.

Deacon's cock pushed at his hole and then slid inside, and they both moaned. The muscles of Deacon's arms flexed and shook a little as he tried to go slowly.

But Grant didn't want caution; he wanted to be overwhelmed. He wanted to dive right into the fire and get burned.

"Please, Deac," Grant begged. "Harder."

It was beautiful watching as Deacon's control broke.

He started fucking him in long, hard strokes, Grant's cock already hard again, rubbing between their bodies, right up against Deacon's abs.

Grant couldn't quite get a hand on himself as Deacon fucked him into the mattress, but it turned out it didn't matter. He didn't need it. He could come, just like this, with the friction of Deacon's skin, Deacon's mouth on his, Deacon's cock rubbing so perfectly inside him it lit him up until he was falling off the edge.

A second later, Deacon came with a deep groan, and they fell to the mattress still intertwined together, not letting go even for a second.

"Love you," Deacon mumbled into Grant's shoulder.

Grant's fingers spasmed as they gripped Deacon's biceps. "Love you, too," he murmured.

Pulling back, Deacon looked at him for a long moment. Didn't say anything. Just looked.

Grant recognized that look. It was the look that so many girls and boys at school had said turned them inside out. That they'd have done anything to have directed their way. But it was different, too. Softer. More intimate. Like Grant was seeing deeper, all the way down to Deacon's soul.

"You understand that's true." Deacon's statement wasn't a question.

"Yes," Grant said.

He did, now.

Just as surely as Deacon had always owned his heart, he had the same hooks right back into Deacon's.

He'd wanted it for so long, and hadn't quite believed it could be true, but there it was, unmistakable.

"We'll see what happens after the Christmas game," Grant said softly. He didn't want to make this even *more* about him—about them—but he would, if push came to shove.

If he thought that it would save this team.

"You know I'm with you, every step of the way, no matter what it is," Deacon promised, his lips lingering on Grant's cheek.

And maybe Grant had hoped it was true, but now Grant knew it, in a way he hadn't before.

CHAPTER 19

"Merry fucking Christmas to us," Carter groused as he flopped down on the bench in front of his locker.

"You okay, Carter?" Deacon asked.

The game against the Bills hadn't been a blowout, not like last week's against the Ravens. No—they'd been in it until the last second. In fact, Deacon had been sure they had the win in the bag when with a minute and a half left, Riley had driven the offense down the field and had scored what everyone believed was the winning touchdown, a beautiful little slant to Landry.

But then, Josh Allen had done Josh Allen things, extending a play when Nate had been sure he had him wrapped up in a sack, way behind the line of scrimmage.

He'd thrown a long, deep pass to Stefon Diggs, who'd been, as far as Deacon and Micah and Beck had believed, covered.

He and Micah had grappled with the ball—and nobody on earth could blame Micah for losing it at the last second. The refs had reviewed the play for what felt like an eternity, and Deacon had been sure that the play was going to go their way and they'd call it an incompletion.

But they hadn't.

That had given the Bills the ball at the twenty-five yard line, and they'd only had to send their kicker to make a fairly easy field goal.

With five seconds on the clock, they'd done just that, and suddenly the Condors weren't on the brink of being a lock for the playoffs, they were barely hanging on to their wild card spot, in serious danger of losing it with only two games remaining on the schedule.

"I'm bummed, but I'm okay," Carter said, shoving a hand through his hair. "God, that was shitty. But maybe you should be asking Riley over there if *he's* okay."

Riley had thrown his helmet on the sideline after the field goal had been good.

"I'm fine," Riley said, but there was an edge of testiness in his tone. Deacon recognized it, because he felt it too.

It was the fucking worst to lose.

Especially like that.

Deacon turned around the other direction, making sure Micah hadn't descended into self-recrimination and self-doubt—and no, he looked pissed, Beck with an arm around him, as they sat in front of their lockers, but he didn't look devastated.

To a point, anger was the most productive emotion when it came to this moment.

Guys could take it too far, like Carter did sometimes, but being fighting mad was always an improvement over giving up and feeling defeated.

"Hey, guys," Deacon said, raising his voice. "You know, we've got two more games. We've still got a real chance to make the playoffs. Take this feeling. This feeling right here, where you're pissed and you're annoyed and you want to fight the world—take it and use it.

We can win these next two games, and hold on to our playoff spot. There's nothing stopping us, except us."

"Except Josh Allen," a voice in the back of the room said morosely.

"Josh Allen didn't beat us. *We* beat us," Deacon re-affirmed firmly. "Take this and bring it to practice this week. 'Cause I don't know about y'all, but I'm not going down this easy. I'm not going down without fighting for every goddamn inch."

"Damn straight," Landry said, raising his voice too, and giving Deacon a high-five. "We're gonna fight."

"Every step of the way." Riley's smile came a little easier now.

But after Deacon showered and changed, when he stepped out of the locker room, Grant was leaning against the wall, and he was *not* smiling. Security was greatly improved from a few weeks back, when he'd gotten mobbed, and that was good, but Grant's expression was not.

"Hey," Grant said, brows drawn together.

"Hey," Deacon said.

He knew what Grant was going to say before he said it.

There was a chance he could change his mind; after all, they hadn't lost today because they'd been distracted. They'd lost because of a technicality, really, and they'd fought for every point they'd scored—and against the Bills for every point *they'd* scored.

But the problem was Deacon didn't really *want* to talk him out of it.

"Rough loss," Grant said, still frowning.

"Yeah," Deacon agreed. They hadn't discussed what they were doing after the game, but it just made sense to follow him as Grant pushed off from the wall and headed towards the door that led to the VIP garage under the stadium.

"You want dinner?" Grant asked, as the car pulled up.

"Sure."

"I've got a good place in mind. But it's—" Grant paused.

Deacon didn't need it spelled out for him, or for Grant to explain exactly what he was really asking.

"Whatever you want is always fine by me," Deacon said gently and put a hand on Grant's shoulder, squeezing it, then trailed his fingertips down his arm, to his hand.

He gave Grant time to move. After all, there were plenty of people in the garage—staff and a few coaches, and even players, heading towards their cars. But Grant didn't move, even though his hand trembled a little as Deacon gripped it.

Grant's smile was grateful and full of love. "You did say that," he said lightly.

"Yeah, maybe you finally believe it now."

"I always *wanted* to," Grant admitted.

The car pulled up, and Richard got out.

Deacon gave him credit for not looking surprised in the least to see him, or for batting an eyelash at the way they were holding hands.

"Mr. Harris," he said, "can I take your bag?"

Deacon hesitated for a second—he was definitely not the "Mr. Harris" and the "let me get your bag for you" type—but Grant was, or Grant was *now*, and if he wanted to be with Grant, then he was going to have to get used to living this way.

"Sure," Deacon said, handing the bag to the driver. He was glad that a few years back Jem had forced him to get rid of his nasty old duffel bag and invest in something nice. It had cost a fortune, but Jem had argued that he was worth it—and also a multi-millionaire now, so he needed to look the part.

Well, he needed to look the part more than ever now.

Speaking of that . . .Deacon glanced down at his jeans. He'd just thrown a pair on and one of his favorite long-sleeved t-shirts. Was he dressed nicely enough? Grant was in another one of his suits, but he'd pulled his tie off, leaving the collar of his rust colored button-up open at the neck.

"Am I dressed alright for where you wanted to go?"

Grant smiled at him. "You're fine, but honestly, they aren't going to turn us away."

"Yeah, but I don't want to . . ." Deacon cleared his throat, unused to feeling this way. Not sure if he liked it or not. He was always sure and confident. And if someone didn't like him or something about him, they could fuck off. But not now. Not when he was with Grant and their opinion also reflected on him. "I don't want to create trouble for you."

"You couldn't possibly," Grant said, as they climbed into the back seat of the car, Richard shutting the door behind them.

"Actually, I've created a hell of a lot of trouble," Deacon said wryly.

"*We* have, more like," Grant agreed. He leaned back against the seat. "You know what I'm going to say, don't you?"

"You think it's time to go public," Deacon said.

"I must be losing my touch." Grant scrubbed a hand across his jaw.

"Just to me." Deacon squeezed his hand. "And I'm not just any-body."

"I think I'd already decided, before Josh Allen threw that pass," Grant said, with a reluctant sigh. "It's the right thing to do. And I'm not ashamed. Terrified, maybe, but not ashamed. If you're still up for it, then yes, I think we should do it. It's the right thing to do."

"Well, hold onto me, 'cause I'm gonna make sure we get through this. Alive *and* together." Deacon knew he couldn't make guarantees, but he could make promises.

And he was promising that he wasn't going to leave. Wasn't going to flinch, even if things got ugly. Okay, *uglier*.

"You're kind of a badass, you know?" Grant said lightly, but there was a certainty glowing in his green eyes that Deacon loved to see.

"I'd say I'm your knight in shining armor, but I'm not good or noble, like Jem."

"No, no, you're not. But I like you just the way you are. I'm not wildly in love with Jem." Grant paused, as Deacon's thumb pressed insistently into his palm. "How is he, by the way?"

"Happy. In love. Learning he doesn't want to leave that town he grew up in again." Deacon sighed. "And you know, I'm happy for him. But also it kinda sucks."

"That he's happy and in love?"

"That he's got his place. I still don't know what I'm doing next year."

"I'm assuming various people in the Condors organization have made you offers," Grant said.

Deacon nodded. Coach Rufus, in particular, really wanted to hire him to coach the defensive ends. He was practically doing it now.

And it would mean he'd not have to leave *and* that he would be somewhat removed from Grant's direct authority.

He didn't give a shit about that, but he assumed the NFL would.

"Well, how's this for an offer," Grant continued. "Work for me."

Deacon knew he should be used to the twisty, clever way Grant's mind worked by now—and he thought he had gotten a handle on it, at least—but this was the last offer he'd expected Grant to make. He'd assumed Grant would want that separation, too—or at least require it, if he wanted to stay with the Condors organization.

But apparently not.

"Guess I'm not losing my touch after all." Grant grinned.

"Work for you? But—"

"I know. Seems like the worst kind of idea. Maybe it is. I know I told you that you were a great coach, earlier this season. You are. But I also think you're the best judge of talent and skill I've seen. I'm okay, but you're better. More than that, you can look at a guy, talk to him, and *know* if he'll be suited to the NFL. Not everyone with talent and skill is, but *you* can tell."

"You want me to be a scout."

"*My* scout."

Deacon couldn't help but love the proprietary way Grant said it. The look he gave him that was practically a caress.

Maybe some other man might be embarrassed or ashamed of being Grant's man.

Not Deacon.

Grant Green was hot as hell. A respected, successful businessman. And brilliant, with a mind that never quit. He could have anybody he wanted, and who he wanted was Deacon.

So if he wanted to brand Deacon with his initials, Deacon would gladly kneel at his feet.

"What would that mean?" Deacon asked. Not because the answer would determine his own, but because he was curious.

"You'd work with me and obviously with the rest of the scouting department, to help me fill this team with the kind of guys we want."

Deacon knew he wasn't just talking about talent or skill—though that was obviously part of it. "So kind of what I helped you do, during the off-season."

"Yes," Grant said with a nod.

"You were right about Riley," Deacon pointed out. Maybe it was a bad idea to counter a job offer with evidence he wasn't as good as Grant wanted him to be. But he *had* been wrong about Riley, and Grant had been dead-on.

"There's no guarantees in this business. Or in *any* business," Grant said. "It was a hunch and it paid off. You told me Rex was bad news, last summer, and I didn't listen to you, then. Maybe if I had, we wouldn't be in this position."

"Yeah, and maybe I wouldn't be doing this," Deacon retorted and leaned over, kissing him. It was a lot of different kinds of kisses, all in one.

It was a *thank you*. It was an *I love you*. It was an *I'd do anything in my power to help you.*

When Deacon pulled back, Grant's breath was short and choppy. For a moment, he almost gave into the nearly irresistible desire to say *fuck dinner, and let's go home.*

But Grant had let Deacon take him to the shrimp shack last week.

It was time to let him do the same.

Besides, this would be as good of a time as any to talk about what this was going to look like. Him being Grant's scout. And them talking to the public about their relationship.

The car came to a stop, and the driver called over the intercom that they had arrived.

"You still want to go to dinner?" Grant asked, biting his lower lip and nearly destroying all of Deacon's good intentions.

But he held firm.

"Yeah, I do."

"Alright then," Grant said, and the door opened.

When they emerged from the car, into the night air, Deacon recognized where they were immediately. Maybe he should've been surprised, but he wasn't, really.

Grant had brought him to a restaurant that even Deacon had heard of—an impressive feat in and of itself. A place owned by one of the city's most popular up-and-coming chefs, where reservations were highly sought after. In fact, Carter had complained the other day that he'd tried to get Ian and him in, and they'd just laughed.

It was also a place where you went to be seen.

They would not be keeping things under cover here.

Grant glanced over at him. "This okay?" he asked casually—even though they both knew what he was asking.

"You said you'd decided," Deacon said quietly.

"Yes, but I hadn't been sure if we'd have dinner here, or somewhere else." Grant shifted his weight from one foot to the other. "I thought the game would end and I'd still be conflicted, but then Darcy asked me if I still wanted the reservation or she'd take it—and

I knew I wanted it. Wanted *this*." He reached for Deacon's hand this time and gripped it hard.

"I was already decided. Ages ago." *Years ago*, Deacon didn't add, but he probably didn't have to, because he was almost sure Grant knew he'd been his, forever.

"Yeah?" Grant flushed, and maybe he didn't.

Deacon used his free hand to open the door for Grant and then let it rest on his back right above the waist as they walked up to the hostess stand.

He'd wanted to do this forever, and now that Grant was telling him he could, he wasn't going to waste a second of it.

"Oh, Mr. Green," the hostess said, clearly delighted by his appearance. "And Mr. Harris! You played great today, sir. So sorry about the loss."

"Hey, it happens," Deacon said. "Sometimes Josh Allen is gonna Josh Allen. And other times, we're gonna stop him." He shrugged. "I feel good about our chances regardless."

"Me too. You should be very proud of the team, Mr. Green," she said, smiling.

"Oh, I am," Grant said, exchanging an intimate glance with Deacon.

"I'll show you to your table, now," she said, walking them to a small table tucked away in a dark-ish corner. But it wasn't that big of a restaurant. And as they walked there, Deacon could feel every eye in the place on them.

Maybe Grant hadn't been as recognizable before this latest round of rumors, but he had been playing in Charleston since he was drafted, and he *was*. And then of course, there was the very minor fact that they were here, together, holding hands, after all the gossip about their relationship . . .

"Your waiter will be with you in a second," the hostess said brightly as they sat. "Enjoy your meal."

"You're still sure this is okay?" Grant asked after she left and Deacon had picked up his menu.

Deacon chuckled and shook his head. "If you'd leaned over the table in the library, way back in college, and kissed me, I'd have dragged you into my lap. I don't care who sees us. Or what they say."

Grant flushed again. "Really? Way back then?"

"Oh come on, you knew I had a huge crush on you."

"No, no, I did not," Grant said, laughing. "Besides, I'm not sure that Grant would've had an idea what to do with the great Deacon Harris."

"Whatever you're doing now." Deacon pulled out his wallet. Why hadn't he shown Grant this ages ago? He didn't know. But he should see it now.

He opened it and slid it across the table. Carefully tucked in the plastic-covered slot usually reserved for IDs was the Post-it note Grant had stuck to his check, all those years ago.

Grant looked down, glanced up, and then did it twice more.

"You really *kept* it? That stupid Post-it I couldn't . . ." Grant cleared his throat. "I didn't know what to say. Only that I should say something. I should have said more, but I was afraid that if I did, I'd say *everything*."

At first, of course, he'd been so fucking pissed at that short, impersonal email that Grant had sent him. Then, the check, with its Post-it note. It hadn't been much, but as the years had gone by,

Deacon had realized—and hoped—that maybe the sheer coldness of the message had been covering up for something else.

It wasn't until they'd met again that Deacon had truly begun to know just how much Grant *hadn't* said.

"I think you did just fine," Deacon pointed out. "If you'd said more back then, who knows what would've happened. Maybe I'd have kidnapped you and tied you to my bed."

"Really?" Grant took that somehow creepy suggestion and grinned. Because of course he did. If Deacon hadn't been so completely sure this was the man for him, that smile would've done it. "I was so sure you were gonna guess *you* were the reason I didn't want to leave school."

"I didn't." In fact, he was kind of glad he hadn't. Because if he had, maybe he *might* have gone to extremes to keep Grant around, and that, ultimately, would have set them both on the wrong path.

Grant toyed with the corner of his menu. "So . . .are we going to talk about this, during . . .well, whatever we end up doing? An interview would be the easiest, least painful way to go . . ."

"We can do an interview." Deacon didn't really enjoy talking to the media, but this was different—and he couldn't imagine Darcy, Nicole, and Grant not controlling every aspect of whatever they ended up doing.

"And do you want to . . .talk about *this*, our past?" Grant asked, gesturing to the wallet as he pushed it back towards Deacon.

"Some of it, yeah." Deacon didn't know where the line was. He had a feeling he wouldn't know the line until someone crossed it.

Grant pulled his phone out of his pocket. "An interview, then. We'll pre-approve questions and subjects. But two things I know

I want to address . . ." He took a deep breath. "Rex's accusations, obviously. And the other is the rumor that I bought the Condors for you."

"What?" Deacon asked in faux outrage. "You didn't?"

Grant made a face. An adorably cute scrunched-up nose kind of face. Deacon was charmed. "I was going to say *yes*, partly, I did buy it for you. Because I knew you. I knew what kind of man you were."

"I might've changed. Been a long time since we'd seen each other."

"Unlikely, since you're not exactly the flighty type," Grant said, shooting him a hot look.

"Nope." Deacon grinned.

"And you know why else I bought the team—and I have talked about it, a bit, right after the sale went final, but I want to address it personally. In context to the other rumors."

"And you think that's going to lead into talking about when we met."

"It seems the obvious transition," Grant said.

"Alright."

"I'll send these notes to Nicole. Let her arrange it. She'll find someone she trusts. Though . . ." Grant pondered this. "I kinda want to go a different direction."

"What do you mean?" Deacon felt like he *should* ask, not just give Grant his blanket approval—even though that was exactly what he wanted to do.

"There's a reporter, who actually tipped me off right before the email leaked—she'd gotten a copy of it. She's covered me a lot, on the business side of things."

The waiter appeared then. Took their orders and promised to bring Grant's wine and Deacon's beer quickly, along with the appetizers they'd ordered.

"You don't want to give this to a sports reporter?" Deacon asked after he'd left.

"Aren't they the ones who've sensationalized this whole goddamn thing?" Grant questioned, and Deacon couldn't disagree.

"They're gonna be pissed. Not just them, but the NFL too."

"Oh, I'm planning on it." And there was that man again, the man Deacon adored. That brilliant, twisty mind in the gorgeous package. No wonder Deacon had been unable to resist him, then or now.

"I thought you were tired of dealing with your NFL contact. I forget her name . . ."

"Cheryl," Grant said, making a face. "I'm still working on that problem. I think I've got it mostly sorted out. I'm sure she'll hit the roof when we do this interview and it comes out."

Deacon couldn't help but feel a spike of worry. "Are you sure you want to do it, even if they . . . hate it?" He didn't want to compromise the man he loved, even if the man he loved was ready to compromise himself.

"They can hate it all they want to. We haven't done anything *wrong*. We haven't made anyone look bad. The interview will clear that up."

Deacon was not convinced.

"If Cheryl does come charging at me, this time I'll be ready for her. And she'll regret doing it."

It was hard not to be confident when Grant was clearly so sure of himself.

"You're not going to tell me what you have planned, are you?"

"Let's just say," Grant pointed out softly, but with a fierce look in his green eyes, "that the other owners don't really like it that her office is a sieve. With every piece of info she leaks to the press—and I know it's her, and am this close to proving it, too—I win one more over to my side. Does the commissioner run the NFL? Sure, he does. But we owners have plenty of power, too. And he's not going to want to override the majority of us."

"That's what you're doing then," Deacon said, mostly in awe. Grant was attempting to outmaneuver the commissioner of the NFL.

"Just trying to remove someone from their job who has an axe to grind," Grant said, shrugging. Like it was no big deal.

It was a very big deal.

And Deacon believed that, if anyone could do it, it would be Grant.

"I would do this even if I didn't have almost all my pieces in place to remove her," Grant added. "I think it's the right thing to do. I think we're strong enough to weather this. I know I love you enough to fight, and fight hard. And I believe, completely, you're on the same page. I don't want to hide anymore."

"I don't either," Deacon agreed. "And honestly, I don't care who does the interview. If you think this reporter friend of yours is the right call, then that's the direction we'll go."

"I just think Marlene would at least treat it semi-seriously, with our history. She wouldn't sensationalize it more."

"You're brilliant. You know what you're doing. Just don't micro-manage Nicole," Deacon teased. "Let her do her job."

Grant finished typing on his phone and then slid it back into his pocket. "I intend to. She can figure it out."

"When will we do it?" Now that the plans were in motion, Deacon realized he was more ready than ever to just get it over with. Hoping, of course, that it would actually work.

"Couple of days. As soon as Nicole can arrange it. Soon as possible, as far as I'm concerned." Grant let out a heavy breath. "I don't want to be responsible for another loss."

"You weren't responsible for this one," Deacon said.

Grant didn't look convinced, so Deacon kept going. "We were dialed in. Focused. Not like last week. It was a different thing, entirely."

"Same result."

"Sure, yeah, but you can't put this one on you. Just like I told Micah in the locker room after the game—and Riley, too. Football is a game of inches. We just came up an inch short, today."

Grant frowned. "You seem remarkably calm about it."

"What, you thought you'd have to talk me off a cliff?"

"No, not exactly. Just . . .sure you'd be pissed."

"Oh," Deacon said. "I'm pissed. But I'm not bringing the fight to you. I'm bringing the fight to practice. And to our last two games. We win those? We're right in the thick of it."

The waiter arrived with their drinks, and Deacon picked up his beer. "And even if we don't make the playoffs," he said, tipping his bottle lightly against Grant's wine glass, "I think we had a hell of a run. More than anyone else could've predicted, anyway. No matter what happens, this year hasn't been a failure."

Grant's gaze was warm on his. "Best year of my life."

It had been full of highs and lows. It felt like they'd been on a near-constant rollercoaster ride since Grant had bought the team, but Deacon realized that he wouldn't trade it for anything, either.

CHAPTER 20

"It's a damn good article," Jem said, his voice echoing over the truck's speakers as Deacon pulled out of his townhouse's garage.

"The reporter seemed pretty reasonable, all things considered," Deacon said. They'd only done the interview a few days ago, but he knew both Grant and Nicole had wanted to get it out into the world as soon as possible—and Marlene, the reporter Grant knew, had seemed equally as eager.

Probably because she knew what a sensation it would cause.

"You mean, all things considered AKA Grant made sure that nobody asked a question he wasn't prepared to answer."

Deacon chuckled. "Something like that, yeah."

"Were photographers camped out in your flower beds again this morning?"

"Yes. Fuckers." Deacon knew how grumpy he sounded. "I called Grant's security company and they promised to send someone to roust them out, but God only knows what they'll get in the interim. I pulled all the blinds in the house, so they couldn't take pictures of the inside—"

"What the hell are they even going to get from your empty house?" Jem sounded mystified.

"God only knows. Grant worried the interview might make more waves at first, but the hope is now that it's all in the open, eventually the speculation will calm down."

"Well, all they gotta do is see the inside of your house to know you've got nothing to hide and there's nothing for them to even write about." Jem laughed. "I *know* the inside of your place, Deac, and it's like you barely even live there. Even during season."

It was true.

Maybe why Grant had yet to see it. It was just easier—and definitely more secure—to spend the evenings and the nights at Grant's penthouse.

Not that Grant's penthouse was really all that personal either. But it still looked like he *lived* in it. Multi-million dollar art and all.

"So, how do *you* feel about it?" Jem asked, when Deacon didn't take his bait.

How did he feel about the interview?

"I feel . . .okay. It's fine. Just . . .a lot." Deacon didn't know what else to say. Was it a hell of a lot more than he'd ever wanted out there, in public, before? It was. But then he'd never felt about anyone before the way he felt about Grant.

He'd been willing enough to sit down with Marlene, the journalist Grant had handpicked, and cautiously reveal his feelings to the public. To talk about how they'd known each other in college, how Grant had been his statistics tutor, and yes, they'd liked each other back then, but how the "timing had been wrong," Grant had added with a quick grin in Deacon's direction.

Marlene's gaze hadn't missed a thing.

She'd seen the smile.

No doubt she'd seen every glance they'd sent each other.

The way Deacon had clenched down a little on Grant's fingers when he'd mentioned, even briefly, the mess that they'd been forced to clean up when the team had changed hands.

"Did you read it?" Jem asked.

"Of course I read it," Deacon retorted. He hadn't really wanted to, but Grant had forwarded it to him and asked him specifically to make sure there wasn't anything in it he didn't want in the public eye.

Some of Marlene's phrases had been rocketing around his brain since he'd scanned it.

Meant to be.

Two men who both tend to fight for everyone else, fighting for each other.

Same wavelength.

All those things were probably true. But reading the article, Deacon had been struck by exactly what had worried Grant about doing this.

Suddenly their relationship wasn't just their own. It was everyone's, packaged for their easy consumption. Deacon hadn't considered what it would be like to read about it from someone else's point of view.

Marlene had taken it easy on them and had been kind and undeniably supportive, even, but Deacon still found it really freaking weird.

"You don't sound particularly happy about it," Jem said gently.

"I'm not . . .unhappy about it. It's just an adjustment."

"Yeah. No kidding. You barely dated before this. Nevermind dated someone like Grant. Or talked about your feelings to a journalist who works for the *New York Times*. I was kinda expecting you to go running and screaming from all of this."

"Thank you," Deacon said dryly. "I'm not going anywhere."

"Yeah, I realized that, too. Look, it's a lot of people with their noses in your business—which you hate; you can't even tell me you don't, because I *know* you hate it, Deac—but you fight for the shit you really want. And you've always wanted him—"

"Jem," Deacon interrupted warningly.

"Don't even bother saying you didn't," Jem said.

"Okay, fine. I wanted him."

"And you got him." Jem's tone had gone impudent. "So why would you let him go if things got tough? In fact, things getting tough only probably made you cling to him harder."

"You're the worst."

"You love me," Jem teased.

Deacon rolled his eyes even though Jem couldn't see it.

"Did you find an architect yet?" Deacon asked.

"Not yet. None of them are willing to let me to backseat architect them, and that's what I'm holding out for. Lots of input into the design," Jem said. "And don't try to change the subject."

"I wasn't," Deacon claimed, even though that was not exactly true.

These days it was easy enough to divert Jem's attention, just by bringing up the house he was building in his hometown of Christmas Falls.

Or Murphy, Jem's oldest friend and his new boyfriend.

But if Deacon went in that direction, Jem *wouldn't* stop, and that was another kind of problem. He didn't have an unlimited amount of time before he got to the practice facility and there was something he wanted to discuss with his best friend.

"You were, and it's okay. I know it doesn't sit easy on you, all this public attention."

"The idea is it'll eventually *kill* all this public attention," Deacon grumbled.

"I don't know, you two are awfully cute. I wouldn't be surprised if you keep going viral."

"Speaking of cute, are you and Murphy willing to leave your love nest? I thought I should meet this guy of yours, and you should be here for the last game." *My last game.*

"You're playing the Piranhas, yeah?" Jem asked. "But you're in Miami for it."

"Yep." Deacon didn't need to go into detail about why it was such an important game. Not only were the Piranhas a division rival, but they'd lost to them earlier this year. *And* it was seeming more and more likely that if the Condors wanted that playoff spot, they'd need to win that game.

Really, they'd need to win the next *two* games. But the hard one was going to be the Piranhas, no question.

"I'll ask Murph, but I can't imagine he wouldn't want to come. He wants to meet you, too, you know," Jem said.

"Well, the feeling's mutual."

"I know, even though you didn't say it." Jem sounded pleased. "You're both important to me. The last thing I want is for y'all to not know each other."

"Talk to him. But I'll get you tickets, to one of the suites, yeah? Unless you want to be on the sideline."

Jem sighed.

Deacon knew what he really wanted was to be on the field. It was where Deacon wanted him, too. But they both knew it wasn't going to happen.

It was time to accept it.

"No, I think it'd be harder . . ."

"Think about it," Deacon said firmly. "You don't have to decide right now."

"Alright. But count us in for the game, at least. I want to be there, and I know he'll want to meet you. I've talked about you enough."

"Good things, I hope," Deacon said.

Jem laughed. "Wouldn't you like to know?"

Deacon was nearly changed for practice when Carter swanned into the locker room, a wild grin on his face that did not bode well.

Deacon gave him a glance and then a second glance. And yep, he was carrying a bunch of printed-off pages.

He braced himself, because he knew exactly what was coming.

"And," Carter said, raising his voice to be heard over the low rumbling of chatter in the locker room, "watching the two of them sit together, holding hands like they're each other's lifeline, I'm surprised to learn this relationship they're in is a fairly new development."

"Carter," Riley warned, but he was smiling, and next to him, Landry was openly laughing.

"I asked them, bluntly, if they felt this way about each other for so long, why they didn't do anything about it." Carter lowered the pages and skewered Deacon with a look. "I'll tell Marlene Jeffries," he continued in his own voice, clearly not reading the profile any longer, "we *tried* to make both of you do something about it."

Deacon waved. "No, no, it's alright. Roast away. I don't mind."

"It's all out of love," Riley said loyally, putting a hand on his shoulder. "We love both of you."

"Yeah, honestly, we're real happy for you guys," Beck said.

The corner of Carter's mouth quirked up. "I'm a little disappointed she didn't manage to get out of you two when you *actually* got together."

"Don't tell me you still don't know," Deacon said. He glanced over at Micah and Beck, who had both managed to keep their mouths shut.

"No, we do *not* know," Carter said emphatically, disappointment radiating out from him.

"You gonna tell him, Micah?" Deacon asked, glancing over at the man, who was sitting quietly next to Beck.

"It was the night you punched that guy," Micah said. "Mr. G told me to take you to his car. Was insistent on it, in fact."

"You said you only talked," Carter argued.

"Oh, we talked," Deacon said.

"And more?" Carter added hopefully.

Deacon raised an eyebrow.

Riley nodded. "That's enough, Carter," he said. But Carter was smiling now and looking very pleased with himself.

"Yes!" he said, punching the air with a fist. "That means I win the pot."

"*What*," Deacon said, before anyone else could respond.

"I think Riley bet on after the season. Landry was right after the last game. Beck—remind me when you said? I can't remember," Carter said, pulling out his phone, the printed interview pages forgotten and fluttering to the floor.

"You bet on us getting together," Deacon stated bluntly, standing up and striding over to where Carter was very absorbed in whatever was on his phone's screen. Deacon plucked it out of his hands before Carter could react.

And yep, sure enough, there it was.

A list—practically of the *entire fucking team,* quite a few staff members, and even *Darcy*—Grant was going to shit a brick when he saw this—of everyone who'd bet on them.

"Fuck," Deacon muttered.

"Hey, it was all in good fun," Beck said.

Carter looked worried. No, he looked *terrified.*

Good.

Deacon tossed him the phone, which he caught, easily, because this was Carter and he was one of the best people in the world at catching things.

"Are you gonna—" Carter stopped short, right in the middle of his question.

No doubt Riley was behind him, gesturing frantically for him to shut the fuck up.

"It's cool," Deacon said. "You won the pot?"

Carter nodded.

"I'd better see that you donate it to charity," Deacon said firmly.

"Oh, definitely," Carter said, nodding emphatically. "Or maybe after we win next week, you can bring Mr. G to the Pirate's Booty, and I'll buy both of you a drink."

It wasn't like Deacon hadn't considered it. After all, Grant had gone to the Pirate's Booty once, at Carter's invitation.

But Carter exhorting him to come was not the same as Grant coming *with* Deacon.

Technically, they *could* now. Everyone—except the handful with their heads currently buried in the sand—knew they were together now.

"We gotta win first," Deacon reminded him. "We're not taking anything for granted. Not this week. Not the next two weeks. 'Cause I'm assuming you wanna be on the field during Wild Card Weekend and not chilling on the couch trying to get in Ian's pants."

Carter rolled his eyes, but Deacon could see the way his jaw tightened with determination. Carter might talk a lot of shit—a *lot* of shit—but he was as competitive as any of them. Maybe even more.

"Yeah, you got it for me this week, Maxwell?" Riley challenged.

"Oh, I got it for you, Flynn," Carter said, and the fierceness in his face melted away, revealing his goofiest smile.

Landry smacked him. "Stop flirting with my boyfriend," he teased.

"Tell him to stop being so hot, and I will," Carter retorted.

"Maybe I'll tell *Ian*," Landry said.

"You're assuming Ian wasn't the one to point just how delectable our quarterback is. He's taken, not blind."

"Ugh," Landry said. "You two are kinda the worst."

"You mean the *best*," Carter said with a leer. "The most terrible twosome."

Deacon sighed and picked up his helmet. "Carter, at least *try* to remember Ian was brought here to . . ." He couldn't find the best way to describe it.

Control wasn't it.

Monitor wasn't it, either.

"Oh, don't worry." Carter's eyes were twinkling now, his face softened into undeniable affection. "I remember exactly why he was hired. And how fantastic a job he does, every single day."

"Ew. How many times do we have to tell you we don't want to know about your sex life," Beck retorted. "Deac—stop him. Please. Before all our ears start to bleed."

"Better him than me," Deacon said, laughing shortly.

"Don't worry," Riley said, patting him on the shoulder, "if you ever did decide to share, we'd all be *plenty* interested."

"Yeah, you two are *fire* together. So much hotness," Carter echoed. He leaned down. Picked up the pages he'd dropped earlier. "Speaking of hotness—"

"Ugh. Forget I said anything," Deacon interrupted.

"Yeah, respect your elders," Micah said, smacking Carter upside the head.

When Deacon headed out towards the tunnel, leading to the practice field, he wasn't surprised to see Riley and Beck join him.

"You know he means well, right?" Riley asked as they emerged onto the field.

"Yeah, he might be kind of an asshole sometimes, but he's doing it because he's happy for you guys, genuinely. We *all* are," Beck said.

"I assumed you would be," Deacon said dryly.

"Huh," Beck said, glancing over at Riley. "I kinda thought he'd be freaked out—but he's like all calm and shit."

"That's 'cause he's in love," Riley said.

"Guys—" But Deacon didn't get any more words out.

"It's alright, we get it. You don't want to talk about it. But if you *did*," Beck said, "we're here. We're *all* here, for you."

"Maybe not Carter," Riley joked.

"Not if you want to give a rundown in the middle of the locker room," Beck said. Though they all knew Carter could run his mouth, Deacon knew the man could also keep a secret. After all, he'd known Deacon was retiring after the end of this season long before the rest of the team, and he'd never said a word.

Every time he even thought about how few times he'd jog out here like this, as a player, on the way to practice, it made his heart hurt.

But he knew it was the right decision, no matter how much it stung. Deacon had played in the NFL for twelve years now—longer than most players had—and knew what it took to do this job, and that no matter how much he wished otherwise, he didn't have it any longer.

With only two games left, though, he was increasingly aware of how many *lasts* he was about to have—and all he truly wanted was to enjoy the time he had left, with this team. With these guys.

He put his arm around Riley's shoulders. "What I want is to put this losing streak shit behind us. And make the playoffs in my last year. We gonna make that happen?"

"You bet your ass we will," Riley said, and if Carter's determination had been obvious, Riley's was blazing like a fire in his light blue eyes.

"Yeah, we're gonna send you out the *right* way," Beck promised.

And Deacon believed, looking at both of them, that it might really happen.

That *they* could make it happen.

"She's on the phone, isn't she?" Grant asked Darcy, lifting his head from his laptop as she walked in, a grim expression on her face.

There were only a handful of people who could make Darcy look like that.

Cheryl was currently topping the list.

He'd feel sorry for her, but then it was difficult to find sympathy for someone who'd attempted to destroy him.

She might think she'd actually accomplished her goal, but the keyword was: *attempted*.

"Better than that," Darcy said. "She's *here*."

Grant was not often surprised. And he was sure Cheryl had hoped showing up at the Condors facility the morning the interview came out would not only be an unexpected move, but also aggressive and inconvenient for Grant.

But Cheryl didn't know a lot of things—though, Grant thought she was *about* to be a hell of a lot better informed.

"Huh," Grant said, grinning as he leaned back in his chair and Darcy smiled right back.

"You want me to bring her in? Here? Or the conference room?"

"Show her into the conference room. Even she must realize we're not always immediately at her beck and call, so let her cool her heels for half an hour or so. I'll gather the rest of what I need, make the final call to the commissioner, and I'll let you know before I go in."

"I'm gonna want to be there to see her face," Darcy said.

"Believe me, I know, and you'll be there because you deserve it," Grant said. Darcy had done a lot of the hard work setting all this up—much of the logistics and coordination was thanks to her. Even though he'd set her on this path to begin with, she'd dug in with relish, enjoying the opportunity to get back at someone who'd seemingly taken every chance they could to stab all of them—Grant, Darcy, Deacon, and really the whole goddamn team—in the back.

And not because she seemed to hold a particular grudge against Grant. No. Once he'd started touching base with the other team owners, he'd figured out it was more about the power than anything personal. She *liked* having something hanging over his head, over *all* their heads—and when he'd pushed back and tried to eliminate the sword she'd kept insisting existed, she'd snapped and leaked that email to the press.

He was sure it was supposed to be a reminder of who was really in charge.

But instead of Grant being cowed, he'd fought back, and now Cheryl was going to discover just how much she really did not want to piss him off.

Darcy shot him a grateful smile. "Thanks. She just . . .ugh, if you even know how smug she looked when she showed up today."

"I can only imagine," Grant said. Already thinking about how satisfying it was going to feel to wipe that look off her face.

"Then she said something about how that email must've been true, after all, even after all your denials, if you're out giving interviews about your relationship." Darcy huffed out a breath. "I want to say she was implying you lied to her, but it was more than an implication. It was an accusation. I really wanted to punch her in the face, to be honest."

"You're going to get to do one better," Grant promised.

"Right. *Right*."

"Just remember that," Grant said.

"I will." Darcy paused, beginning to turn, but then she cocked her head. "And Grant?"

"Yeah?" Grant glanced up, mind already whirling through all the things he needed to do before he confronted Cheryl. He'd hoped that she'd email and demand they set a conference call to discuss the interview—he'd known she'd be pissed and make noise about it—but he hadn't expected her to show up. And *today*.

"It's a great article. Great interview."

Grant smiled. "You said that already, when you read it two days ago. You vetted every line of it, didn't you?"

Darcy and Nicole had gone through the whole thing. And honestly, they'd brought him barely any changes. Grant's gut feeling about Marlene had proven to be right. She'd been the perfect choice. Tough on them, but not digging for sensationalistic gossip, either.

Even the two lines they'd been unsure about, he'd told Darcy and Nic to leave in, because if the whole thing felt too curated and kindhearted, then it would lose its impact.

"We did, but I just still wanted to say it. And that I'm proud of you. I know it wasn't easy to take this path, but you did it anyway."

"I'm not one for hiding."

"But not one for sharing your feelings with the masses, either," Darcy pointed out wryly. "And you did that, anyway."

Grant set his elbows on the desk. "You were right. But then you usually are."

He'd been considering several different ways to show Darcy just how much he appreciated her—and the one he was leaning towards . . .well, she wouldn't expect it. And she'd probably turn it down, at least initially. But he'd fight her on it, because she was too smart to keep waiting on him and doing his bidding. She deserved to have a whole fleet of PAs catering to her every whim.

And, extra bonus, it would free him up to focus more on the product development side of InTech—and also on the Condors, which had become so much more than a passion project and a way to save Deacon from the demons determined to swallow him whole.

Grant had discovered he actually loved owning the team, and not just because of the man who played on it.

"Thank you for that," Darcy said with a dimpled smile. "Any other times you want to tell me I'm right, feel free."

"I intend to," Grant said. Little did *she* know, too.

"Just let me know when you're ready. I'll be in my office," Darcy said, turning to walk out.

Thirty-six minutes later when the two of them walked into the conference room together, Grant had difficulty reining in his *own* smug expression when Cheryl looked up, frowning.

"I don't expect to be kept waiting here like an employee," Cheryl complained.

"You showed up without an appointment," Darcy said, her tone still cordial but her smile baring her teeth as they took seats across from her.

"You had to expect that we'd be concerned about this article," Cheryl pointed out, sliding the printed pages across the smooth wood surface of the table.

"Concerned means you contact us and ask to have a call," Grant said firmly. "Not just show up at our facility and demand to be seen."

Cheryl leaned back in her chair and sniffed. "I suppose if we were *less* concerned that you'd lied to us about your involvement with Deacon Harris, a call would have sufficed."

"Cut the shit," Darcy broke in. "You're not 'concerned' or anything else. You came here to act like we're in the mud, but we're not."

"You're not?"

"We're not," Grant said. "Remember that investigation I asked you to perform to discover the culprit leaking my private emails to the press?"

Cheryl barely blinked. He'd give her credit for that, at least. Even with the teeth of the trap about to close around her, she still seemed unconcerned.

"I ask you to remember," Grant continued, "because it didn't seem to me like there was actually *any* investigation happening at all. Every time Darcy inquired about one, you brushed her off. Said you'd taken care of it. But when I asked if anyone had been let go from the commissioner's office, from *your* office, I was told that nobody had."

"We didn't find anything."

"You didn't find anything because you didn't bother looking," Grant said inexorably.

"That's not true," Cheryl complained. "And I didn't come here to be abused like this. You're the one who should be under investigation. For lying to our office about being involved with Deacon Harris."

"When I told you I wasn't involved with Deacon Harris, I *wasn't* involved with Deacon Harris. If you'd read the article, you'd see our relationship is a new development."

Cheryl tossed her hair. "I read the article. But you could easily lie. You lied before, when you said you didn't know what the email was talking about."

"I don't think you want to get started on who's lying," Grant said softly, dangerously, leaning forward. "You never investigated the leak, because you already knew who it was. It was you, Cheryl. You found that email on my hard drive and then *you* shopped that email around, to various media outlets."

Grant was gratified to see her go a little gray in the face. "You have no proof of that, and it's just slanderous to go around telling lies about me," she insisted.

"You know what business Mr. Green is in, Cheryl?" Darcy asked smoothly.

She shrugged. "Something to do with technology."

"Security, Cheryl, *security*. And do you know whose program is installed on your computer?"

Cheryl went white then. "You can't spy on me! That's illegal!"

"According to InTech's terms of service, no, it's not. And not with the software agreement that the NFL signed. Also, *they* own that computer, not you. So for extra verisimilitude, we received additional permission from them and from the commissioner himself. To investigate, of course. The case you wouldn't touch. With just cause, we can track IP addresses. Where emails came from. We know who sent the supposedly anonymous email that went out to the media. Incidentally, all *your* media contacts, Cheryl, which would be pretty damning on its own. But that wasn't all we discovered. We have proof *you* sent those emails. We have the email address you sent them from. And we can link it to you."

"This is all a terrible coincidence," she spluttered. "I did no such thing."

"Yes, Cheryl, you did," Darcy said. He could see how much she was enjoying this, and so he went on.

"I was sufficiently concerned with the results of this investigation that I talked to some other people about them," Grant said, ruthlessly clamping down on any sympathy he might feel, because Cheryl's face had now gone from gray to white to bright brick red. He clicked the remote in his pocket and the screen on the other side of the conference room lit up. Six different boxes meant six different NFL owners. He didn't need to identify the names on the call. She could see all of them, listed right there in black and white. Not everyone was available, but at the last minute, Grant had put together a decent enough group of other owners, all equally concerned that the commissioner's office was sending private information to the media, without their permission.

"These other owners and I are very concerned," Grant said, feeling no remorse about using the same term she'd overused when it came to every single thing that cropped up during his Condors ownership. She'd brought all of this on herself. By overstepping, for one, and also for leaking that email.

She'd made it a crusade, where one didn't need to exist.

"Very concerned, Cheryl," Rudy Gonzalez, the owner of the Piranhas, echoed Grant. "It's very worrisome that you'd leak any information about an owner or his team to the media."

"I didn't . . .I *wouldn't*," she spluttered, lying out of her ass.

Because he knew she did. He had the proof. All he'd have to do was press send and the report would go public. The commissioner had given him permission—but he hoped he wouldn't have to do it.

"When we had that internal disagreement between the coaching staff and our player personnel VP, somehow *that* leaked to the media," Marisa Lyon, the daughter of the Riptide owner, chimed in. "Everyone here at the Riptide claimed they knew nothing about it getting out. But it did, anyway. I realized when Grant came to us that *you* knew."

"Too many leaks," Rudy agreed. "No more."

"I don't know what you expect me to do," Cheryl practically shouted.

"I think your path forward is very clear," Grant said. "Resign. Today."

"You want me to *resign*?"

"Resign or be fired. Your choice," Darcy said, and now her smile was undeniably vicious as she leaned forward. "And if this report we have happens to make it to the media . . .don't be surprised. Maybe we'll even use that email address you were so convinced was anonymous."

"To anyone else, it might've been," Grant said modestly.

"Good thing you're so good with computers, Grant, or we wouldn't have ever known who the culprit was," Marisa said, chuckling.

"Fine. *Fine.* I'll resign." Cheryl stood, shooting each and every one of them a look that promised retribution, but it was too late for that. She was tied up. She couldn't exact any revenge on them, not without her deeds becoming common knowledge. And she couldn't risk that—or she'd be risking all her credibility going forward.

Grant had even talked to the NFL commissioner himself, before any of this had gone down and made sure he was fully on board with whatever punishment he deemed appropriate. The commissioner had also reassured Grant that as long as Deacon retired at the end of this season, the NFL considered the matter of "inappropriate behavior" fully closed.

This would end, and it would end right now.

"Today, Cheryl," Grant said, his voice still pleasant.

"*Today*," she echoed, glaring at him.

"Excellent. Well, thank you for coming by, then," Grant said, watching with satisfaction as she stomped out, clearly furious.

"And that," Darcy said, after Grant had thanked all the owners for showing up for him, and they'd signed off, "was one of the most satisfying things we've ever done."

"Teamwork for the win," Grant said, grinning.

"Why do you think she did that?" Darcy asked, frowning. "Not to us. I know why she'd have it out for us—well, for *you*, anyway."

"I think she just liked the power of it," Grant said, shrugging. "But we'll never know for sure."

"I do know one thing for sure." Darcy grinned. "We'll never have to deal with her again."

CHAPTER 21

"You know what we need to do today," Deacon said, raising his voice as he watched the defense circle around him. He'd done this for so many games, so many seasons.

It was unbelievable to consider that next year, he'd be watching from a suite, or from the sideline.

But for now, he would immerse himself in every moment, knowing that there were only a finite number left.

"Fly!" Beck cried out. "We're gonna fucking fly!"

"Damn straight," Deacon yelled back.

"How many more games?" Micah asked, his expression as hard as Deacon had ever seen it. While he hadn't necessarily internalized the blame for the touchdown that had lost them last week's game, Deacon knew it weighed on him—and also that he was approaching this game as a chance to destroy any lingering doubts about what kind of corner he was.

"Two," Beck said. He leaned in, tapped the facemask of his helmet with his husband's, and with the intensity in both of their faces, Deacon wouldn't ever bet against them.

He wouldn't bet against *any* of them.

Not today.

"We got this, but you gotta believe. If we don't believe in ourselves, it's already over. Is it over?"

"No," Beck repeated. "*Hell* no. It's just beginning."

As they lined up for the national anthem, Deacon knew part of why he was willing to retire, why he knew it was the right decision for him, was that the leadership of this defense was well in hand.

Would Beck and Micah and Nate step into his place without faltering?

No. But then Deacon hadn't either. He'd stumbled plenty, but he also knew them, and knew they wouldn't ever let a few missteps keep them down for long.

These guys—this whole fucking team—was made to fly.

"You good?" Riley asked, walking up to him before the game started.

"Never been better," Deacon said. "You?"

Riley nodded. He had that same fierce determination in his eyes that Deacon had seen earlier that week, in practice. "I'm ready," he said.

Which was different than good, and in Deacon's humble opinion, even better than good.

It had been three days since the interview had come out, and while yes, the interest level in his relationship with Grant had reached a fever pitch, Deacon could already see it making a difference.

The team had relaxed—maybe it was leaning into that pressure of needing to win one, and most likely, both of their remaining two games, but Deacon had a feeling that wasn't all of it. They weren't worried any longer that there was some big super-important secret the media kept trying to get out of them.

Darcy had been right; going public had calmed everyone down, and they could focus exclusively on the next two games on their schedule.

Deacon could feel it on the sideline, in the lines of everyone's bodies as they prepped for kickoff.

This team was ready—and from the first drive, it was clear they weren't going to go down without a fight.

Deacon didn't always know what the offensive game plan was, but when Riley came out throwing, it was clear it was an aggressive one.

Riley's first pass was a thirty-five yard arc of beauty, right into Carter's hands—and that wasn't all either. He kept throwing, holding it once and running for a much-needed third down, until they got to the red zone, and then the defense, Deacon recognized, was gearing up for yet another pass.

But Riley handed off the ball to Darius, who dodged between two offensive line blocks to catapult right into the end zone.

"Come on, let's get this shit done," Deacon said to Nate as they gathered their helmets.

The Packers were never slouches, even when they weren't playing at Lambeau, but this was the first year of a new quarterback, after Aaron Rodgers had been traded. Jordan Love didn't quite have his feet under him and as he got set, Deacon could sense blood in the water.

No doubt he'd been hearing all week about the Condors' intense pass rush, and Deacon intended to make it not just a fear, but a reality.

Deacon leaned down, gloved fingers digging into the turf, met the eyes of the offensive lineman across from him, and took a deep breath and then another, waiting for the center to snap the ball.

The moment he did, he launched himself, grappling with the lineman as he attempted to block Deacon. But Deacon had been making mincemeat out of these guys for a long fucking time, and he pushed him to the side, using his sheer strength to break the block, and took off, sprinting around the corner to hit the quarterback, but Nate had already come around the other side, and a moment before Deacon got there, he took Love right down.

"Hell yes," Deacon bellowed, holding out a hand for Nate, helping him up after the whistle blew and giving him a quick embrace.

Nate's face was shining. He'd come along so well, after Jem had gone down with his injury. With how satisfying coaching Nate had been, for a bit Deacon had been sure that maybe he wanted to be a coach.

But ever since Grant had suggested that he should be a scout—his own *personal* scout, in fact—helping impact the direction the Condors took tomorrow and for every year going forward . . .well, he couldn't lie, that sounded better than coaching ever had.

Of course, it was risky too, because what if working together added pressure to the relationship he shared with Grant?

But even that worry had fallen apart, because hadn't they worked together all year? Hadn't he been integral in Grant's buying and rebuilding the team? And all that closeness had only made them stronger and more in love than ever.

Deacon wanted to talk to Jem about it—in person, *not* on the phone—when he came to Miami for the final Piranhas game.

Nate's sack on the first play of the Packers' drive not only set the tone for the defense, but it energized everyone.

Three plays later, the Packers punted.

It was the first time during the game, but it wouldn't be the last.

They got two first downs only in the first half, and with the Condors offense scoring another touchdown and a field goal, right before halftime, the Condors went into the locker room leading seventeen to zero.

"Great game so far," Riley said, clapping Deacon on the back as he sat down on the bench.

"You're the one tearing it up," Deacon said.

Riley raised an eyebrow. "I don't think Love's gotten a chance to drop back without seeing you or Nate or even *Beck* in his vision. That's impressive. He's gonna have freaking nightmares about you guys."

"That's the idea," Beck said.

"You're making it so fucking easy on me," Micah complained as he joined them. "I'm shadowing these guys downfield, but they've not got a chance to even catch a ball. Love's not even got a freaking chance to *throw* the ball."

"You're welcome," Beck said, patting him on the back, grinning.

"Ugh," Micah said. "Make me work for it, at least."

"Oh, honey, I'm gonna," Beck teased.

Deacon made a face, because *ugh*, Beck and Micah's sex life, but deep down, he was both amused and pleased.

How could he be anything else when it finally felt like the Condors had their shit together again?

"And here I thought I was the king of oversharing," Carter teased.

Micah shot him an unimpressed look. "You fucking are," he said.

Carter grinned. "Guilty as charged. You guys see that fucking dart Riley threw me on that last drive? What a gorgeous ball. It was pure pleasure to catch it."

"Yeah, and then you got tackled right after," Beck said, elbowing him in the side. "So how good was it really?"

It had been really fucking good, actually.

Riley had put the ball where only Carter could grab it, and Carter had done one of those insanely acrobatic toe-touches on the very edge of the sideline before tumbling out of bounds. That move had stopped the clock, giving the Condors enough time to get their field goal unit onto the field.

"It was a thing of beauty," Deacon said.

"Here's a man who knows his shit," Carter insisted.

"Hey," Nate said, sliding next to Deacon as Carter and Beck's argument continued.

"What's up?" Deacon asked, shoving his sweat-slicked hair back.

"I was thinking—that running back, he's got kinda a loose hold on the ball. I've almost caught him a couple of times. I bet that you could punch it out, if you went for it. You're insanely fucking strong, Deac. If anyone can do it, it's gonna be you."

"Going for the ball instead of going for the tackle is always a risk," Deacon cautioned. He'd seen too many defenders play that game and lose. He also hated how Nate's comment—even though he hadn't been here last year—sounded far too similar to how the old coaches had wanted the Condors to play.

As dirty as fucking possible.

"Yeah, but we're up three scores," Nate pointed out.

Deacon gave him a hard look.

"Just saying," Nate said, putting his hands up in surrender.

"I'll think about it," Deacon said slowly. Still unsure how he felt about it. He knew that lots of teams coached punching the ball out. But after what had happened last year, with how dirty the coaches had wanted them to play, he still felt unsure about it. "If the situation presents itself . . ."

"Right." Nate grinned.

"Thanks for the tip, though, I don't know if I'd noticed that." And he should have, Deacon knew. If he needed more evidence that he was a step slower and less sharp than was the ideal, here it was.

Would it kill him to not play next year? A little, yeah. But it would kill him more to suit up and not be at the height of his skill and power.

To watch those slowly disintegrate until he was no longer the force he'd once been.

That would be the equivalent of torture, and then ultimately, death.

Deacon couldn't—and *wouldn't*—put himself into that position.

"Hey, if you hadn't taught me that spin move, I'd never have gotten to Love on that first play," Nate said loyally.

"Yeah, you asshole. Robbed me of a sack," Deacon teased, putting a hand on Nate's shoulder and rubbing it. "But you're playing so solid, man. Proud of you."

Nate beamed.

"But let's not take the foot off the gas," Deacon said.

"I got you," Nate said.

And he did.

In the next two quarters, Nate got another sack—and a half a sack, which he shared with Deacon.

The Condors offense continued to roll, racking up another touchdown and a field goal, and even though the Packers did eventually put a touchdown drive together, it was only because, as Micah claimed after, on the sideline, he was "so fucking bored in the backfield, you don't even know."

In reality, they'd all been playing back, just trying to prevent the deep pass.

That meant the Packers had been forced to take short gains all the way down the field, which sucked up a ton of game time, and by the time they did finally get in the end zone, almost the whole fourth quarter was gone. All Riley and the offense had to do was go out, get two first downs, and then take a knee.

"Told ya," Beck said, grinning, as they embraced on the sideline. "One more to go, old man."

"Who you callin' old?" Micah demanded with a teasing glint in his eye. "That old man still runs circles around you."

Deacon had been concerned about bringing Rose here, but it was both reassuring and heartwarming that, in the end, he'd been wrong about that too. He'd been trying to protect Beck, but now, he'd lay his ego and his pride and his life on the line for both of them.

They were *both* his guys. And it felt damn good to know that went both ways.

"Aw, Rose, I knew you were a sweetheart under all that bluster," Deacon said as they walked into the tunnel towards the locker room.

"You know he'd better be," Beck said, glancing over at his husband.

"Honey, for you, *anything*." Micah's tone was full of amusement, but his eyes, as Deacon looked over at him, were dead serious.

This, more than anything, this love and loyalty these guys felt for one another, was enough for Deacon to know they'd be okay next year, and for so many years to come. Of course, he wasn't planning on leaving them completely—they'd probably see more of him than they *wanted* to.

But no matter what fell out with him and Grant and job he'd offered him, Deacon had hoped they would be okay, but now he *knew* they would be okay.

He'd finished showering and had slipped on a pair of boxer briefs and was just about to find his jeans when Carter started cat-calling, loudly.

"Ugh," Deacon muttered.

"I'm almost sad Carter Maxwell never hit on me," Nate said mournfully, next to him.

"No, you're not," Deacon said.

A second later, he realized why Carter had made that noise in the first place. Moving through the crowd in the locker room, doling out smiles and high-fives and hugs, was Grant.

He'd felt the echo of this feeling when he'd watched Beck and Micah earlier.

But now it was here, full force, pressing into his chest, and the feeling was so enormous, so all-encompassing, Deacon could barely take a breath as Grant came to a stop in front of him.

They had not discussed how to handle themselves in front of teammates or staff. Deacon had assumed they would be taking an understated, *less is more* approach.

He'd also assumed he'd be taking any and all pointers from Grant and working within whatever parameters he established.

Grant raised his hand, but instead of keeping it to a friendly "good job" pat, he laid it on Deacon's bare shoulder and then squeezed, letting his gaze leisurely peruse all of Deacon's nakedness currently on display.

Nobody looking at the heat in Grant's eyes, or the way Deacon was trying to keep his pulse—and his dick—under control, would think they were platonic.

"Great game," Grant said, and did he sound breathless?

Deacon thought he did.

"Yeah," Deacon said.

Grant's fingertips dug into his skin, and Deacon felt branded, *owned*, and before this man, that was something he wouldn't have wanted at all, ever. But instead, he relished the feeling of it. The way Grant looked at him—and the way he looked back.

Grant's suit today was maroon, with a pale pink shirt, no tie, and he'd opened a few buttons. He looked delectable, and Deacon wanted to eat him alive.

"Hey, Deac, are you going to the victory party tonight?" Riley asked as he approached.

It was clear he hadn't seen Grant at first, not until he stopped short.

"Oh, hi Mr. G, didn't see you there," Riley said awkwardly.

"*Everyone* saw him there, Riley," Nate hissed next to him.

"Uh, yeah, so . . .Pirate's Booty?" Riley asked again, flashing him an apologetic smile. Clearly he hadn't meant to interrupt what was quickly becoming a moment. A Moment, even, in capital letters.

Of course, Deacon wasn't sure Grant had meant it to be A Moment either—but maybe it was better for the team to see them like this. Even though they'd talked about their feelings and their relationship in the interview, they'd very scrupulously held the line in public and in front of the team.

But then, it'd become A Moment anyway.

Maybe Grant had intended it; maybe, in the end, he couldn't help it.

Either way, Deacon wanted to feel all of that cool, firm touch everywhere.

"Um, not sure what my . . ." Grant tilted his head imperceptibly as Deacon stumbled. "What . . .uh . . .*our* plans are."

Okay, he could do that too. They could touch. They could have plans together. Everyone knew they did, anyway. They'd admitted to it. It was stupid to think they couldn't be open and freer here, now. Deacon didn't know why he hadn't believed they would be.

"You asking me what I think?" Grant asked softly.

Okay, if Grant could lay down the gauntlet, then Deacon could definitely pick it up.

"You want to go to the Pirate's Booty for the victory party . . ." Deacon paused, hoping that everyone was listening. "With me?"

"Yes," Grant said, nodding. His hand slipped from Deacon's chest. Deacon nearly grabbed it back. "I'll meet you outside."

When Grant moved on, finally, Nate let out a screech-gasp. "Oh my God," he exclaimed. "You two are . . .geez, I think I might be combusting just from the looks you give each other."

"Thanks," Deacon said dryly.

Grant waited outside the locker room, resting his back against one of the drab walls.

What had gotten into him?

Before going into the locker room, he'd decided it was okay to blur the line a little—after all, the team *knew* what was going on, now—but he'd lectured himself firmly about staying professional. These were still Deacon's teammates.

But when he'd gotten to Deacon, and *oh God,* he'd been mostly naked, treating him the same way he'd treated every other player in that locker room had seemed all kinds of wrong.

Darcy was always telling him he spent far too long looking before leaping, so he'd just done exactly what he'd wanted, and from the undeniable heat in Deacon's gaze, he hadn't hated it at all. In fact, he'd leaned into Grant's touch, like he couldn't get enough.

As for the victory party . . .he'd definitely had no intention of attending another of those again. That was Deacon's scene. *His* teammates celebrating. But when he'd asked, there'd only been one question echoing through Grant's brain.

Why did we do that interview if it means we're still hiding all the goddamn time?

He'd attended a victory party, once before, at Carter's invitation, but he and Deacon were together now. Everyone on planet earth knew they were together. Why *shouldn't* they attend it together?

"Done overthinking?"

Grant glanced over and Darcy was standing there, grinning.

"I wasn't—"

"Yeah, you were. And it's okay. But I'm glad you got out of your own head, for once."

"You heard," Grant guessed.

"And saw," Darcy said with a nod, her eyes gleaming with amusement. "Good for you. What's the point of having such a hot, successful football player for a boyfriend if you don't show him off, once in awhile?"

"Darcy," Grant chided, but he was smiling.

"And you're not looking too shabby yourself. Happy and in love is a good look on you. A *great* look on you."

"Speaking of that . . ." Grant hadn't intended to bring up the promotion now, but he had a feeling she'd say no a bunch of times before she finally said yes, so he might as well prime her for the idea of it. Let her start stewing over it, properly. "I've decided that I'm going to transition out of the InTech CEO role."

Darcy shot him a look. "You keep saying that."

"Yeah, the problem was I couldn't trust any of those people the board kept suggesting. But I've fixed that. I've found the right person. You're going to do it."

She gaped at him. "What? Are you kidding? I'm not qualified—"

"You're literally the *most* qualified," Grant interrupted her.

"I sincerely doubt that." Darcy tossed her hair. "Did you get drunk on all the testosterone in there or something?"

"Now, back then, *I* wasn't qualified. But I learned. You're better off than I was when I got started. And the way you keep saying I can't do this forever, you're right. I want to focus more on product development, and yes, on *this* team."

"And now that you actually have a life you want to live, you'd like to stop working eighteen-hour days," Darcy said. As usual, cutting right to the heart of the matter—which was why she was going to make such a kick ass CEO.

Grant nodded, and she sighed.

"I'll think about it," she said.

"Think about what?" Deacon was standing there, wearing jeans and a short-sleeved button-up in a silky nearly transparent dark navy fabric. He looked insanely hot, and Grant nearly whimpered.

"My new job," Darcy said, patting him on the arm. "Great work out there today, Deac."

"Thanks," Deacon said. He turned to Grant. "You ready to go?"

He nodded.

"Have fun," Darcy said with a sly smile. "Enjoy not thinking about *anything*."

Grant shot her a look as she walked away, but it turned out she was right. It was nearly impossible to think about anything at all when Deacon leaned down, put his hand on the small of his back and led him to the door that went to the VIP parking garage, where his car was waiting.

"What was that about?" Deacon asked as he waved Richard off, opening the car door for Grant himself.

As if the man hadn't already reduced him to mush.

"What was what about?" Grant asked as he slid into the car and Deacon followed him.

He pressed the intercom button and let Richard know they'd be going to the Pirate's Booty instead of his place.

"You and Darcy. You looked intense. And she looked unsure, which isn't something I associate with her."

"Oh. Well. I offered her my job," Grant said.

Unlike Darcy, Deacon did not look surprised. "Well, you couldn't do it forever?" he said. "And she seems very good at what she does."

"She's as good as me, if not better at the day-to-day employee management and operations. She's got a fantastic head for business, and she should take what I'm offering. Will she? I hope so. But we'll see."

"And what about you?" Deacon settled back against the leather seat and flashed a smile that shorted Grant's brain out. He wanted to climb him like a freaking tree.

He nearly told Richard to forget about the Pirate's Booty entirely and take them to his penthouse, so they could be alone.

"What about . . ." Grant trailed off as Deacon reached over and took his hand, tugging his body closer as the car started to move.

"You seem very distracted today," Deacon teased. "What will you *do* if Darcy takes your job?"

Grant rolled his eyes. Deacon knew exactly what he was doing to him. Like he really *needed* to be seduced by this point. "I can't imagine why. And what will I do? Work more on product development. Manage this football team."

Deacon's thumb was swiping across his hand in leisurely, intoxicating touches. "And that's what you want? Not what you feel you *should* do?"

"You of all people know that's not always an easy distinction to make," Grant said, swallowing hard. Deacon's fingers had tucked their way under the cuff of his suit jacket, flicking open his cuff links and finding bare skin at his wrist, stroking there.

"Make it anyway," Deacon said.

"Yeah," Grant finally said. "Yeah, I want to do that. I want to have a life, again. I've spent the last ten years working every single waking moment. I don't have to do that anymore. I don't even *want* to do that anymore. Not when . . ."

Deacon grinned. "Now that you've got me."

"Exactly."

It was hard to think when Deacon was touching him so intently, even though the trip to the Pirate's Booty was hardly long enough for either of them to cash in on the promises he was making. Still, Grant was hardly a quitter.

"You like the sound of that?" Grant asked. He already knew the answer, but it wasn't ever going to get old to hear it.

The look in Deacon's dark eyes was intense. "Yes," he said.

Deacon's fingers closed around his wrist, and Grant wasn't sure if he pulled him, or he leaned over, but a moment later, they were kissing.

"God," Deacon ground out as his hands gripped Grant's waist.

Grant could feel the power of him, and it was the most intoxicating feeling to know all of that was *his*.

He'd told himself they wouldn't get carried away—after all, the bar wasn't *that* far away—but when Deacon touched him with all that leashed strength, he lost his mind.

He lost it tonight.

He was about a thirty seconds of intense kissing away from suggesting that Deacon lay him down on this seat and do whatever he wanted to him when the car pulled up and Richard beeped across the intercom, letting know they were here.

"Shit," Grant said, scrambling away from Deacon's warm body, trying to right his clothes, and fix his hair.

"Here, let me help you," Deacon said. Clearly unconcerned if he looked mussed, like Grant hadn't been able to get enough of him, even on the short car ride over.

And that's true, isn't it?

Grant froze, fingers trying to rearrange his hair back into his normal style. Then he lowered them. "No," he said firmly. "I'm good."

He shrugged out of his suit jacket, unbuttoned another button of his shirt at the neck, and shot the other cuff link through, tucking both of them into his pocket, before rolling up his shirt sleeves.

"Hot," Deacon said, his voice sounding darkly amused.

"It's a bar, not a board meeting," Grant said. He was going to have to find other clothes than suits and the old, ratty sweatpants he liked to wear around his place late at night. Especially if he was really serious about having this real life—a real life with Deacon.

Deacon wore t-shirts and jeans. Casual clothes. Went to places like the shrimp shack, without worrying about his image.

"We're good," Grant informed Richard, after pushing the intercom.

After Grant's nod, Deacon opened the door and after sliding out of the car, held it open for Grant.

The Pirate's Booty was as unassuming as it had been the first time Grant had visited. The second time, too, when Deacon had gotten into that fight that changed everything between them forever.

"You're sure about this?" Deacon asked as they headed towards the door.

"Why wouldn't I be?" Grant wondered, even though he knew perfectly well why he was asking. This wasn't just a casual run-in. They were arriving together, in enough disarray that nobody was going to be wondering what they'd done on the ride over. And then there was Deacon's hand, resting firmly on the small of his back, warm through the fabric of his shirt, as they walked into the bar.

A quick perusal of the inside by the long bar told Grant that a *lot* of the team had come out tonight. No, the win today was not a guarantee of their playoff berth—but if they did win again, they'd be locked in.

"Just checking," Deacon said. "You want a drink? Gin and tonic, right?"

"Doesn't the bartender decide that?" Grant asked.

"True, true," Deacon said with a smile. "Come on, then. I see Carter. Let's get his teasing out of the way first."

To an extent, Grant expected the smiles and the jokes, especially from Carter.

He was not expecting when Carter turned and saw them, Ian tucked under one arm, his red hair shining under the dim bar lighting, for the guy to smile wide—but instead of making a joke, or teasing them about being together, he just gave them a look of complete and total understanding.

"Hey, Carter," Deacon said. "Ian."

"Hey, guys. It's great to see you here. Especially you, Mr. G," Ian said, smiling too.

"I think you can call me Grant, especially since we're very much off the clock," Grant said.

"Nice to see you," the bartender said—Grant was pretty sure his name was Kieran—as he approached their group. "I'm honored you'd stop by, especially after the last time, Mr. Green."

"Grant," he repeated, giving the guy a smile and extending his hand across the bar. "Please. Call me Grant."

"Kieran. What can I get you?" the guy said, shaking his hand briskly.

"I thought you had some kind of magic superpower when it comes to drink choices," Grant said.

Kieran regarded him for a minute, his gray eyes narrowing in on Grant's face. "You sure?"

Grant nodded.

"Me too," Deacon said.

"Well, that makes it easy then, because you guys are drinking the same thing," Kieran said, getting out two glasses, but to Grant's surprise, he didn't spoon ice in. Instead, he turned towards the row of taps lined up on the back counter and pulled a beer and then a second beer.

"I didn't know you drank beer, Mr. G," Carter said.

"I don't usually." He had in college. Cheap drafts, usually the cheapest drafts on the menu. After starting InTech, he'd graduated to well gin, and then when he'd made some real money and no longer worried about what drinks cost, his favorite kind of gin.

Kieran set the beers on the bar.

"Last time, didn't you both get gin and tonics?" Carter asked.

"Yep," Deacon nodded, shooting Grant a knowing look. "I appreciate y'all at least *mostly* letting us work this out on our own. You kept the interference to a minimum."

"Mostly," Grant said, and Carter laughed.

"Fair," Carter admitted. "But we *tried*."

"And in your case, sweetheart, that's pretty damn impressive. If you even knew how much he *wanted* to interfere," Ian teased.

"Oh, we knew," Deacon said, chuckling under his breath.

"I'm just happy we're all, you know . . .*happy*," Carter said, and he was practically glowing with it. Happiness and love and friendship.

"I won't say all this coupling up made my life easy—" Grant said. The opposite, in fact. There'd been weeks—maybe even *months*—where he'd lamented about why his players had to be so ridiculously interested in each other.

"Gave him a fair number of headaches, in fact," Deacon inserted.

Grant turned to him, grinning. "Yeah, maybe. But if I could choose a situation where it didn't happen, I'd still prefer it this way. And not just because of us."

He hadn't worried about how this would go, but it still felt so right, for Deacon's hand to settle possessively around his hip. To feel Deacon's warmth at his back.

This is going to be how it is all *the time.*

"Aw, they're so cute," Beck said putting a hand over his heart as he and Micah approached, Riley and Landry in tow.

"It's our turn," Deacon said.

"Cheers," Grant said, and clinked their glasses together.

"You wanna dance?" Deacon asked.

Grant hadn't let himself overthink after the game, and now didn't let himself overthink, either.

"Yes," he said.

"God, I've wanted to do this since we left the stadium," Grant groaned as Deacon pinned him to the door just inside his townhouse and kissed his neck.

Deacon lifted his head. "Me too," he said, his dark eyes gloriously intense and intent on Grant. Like nothing could move him from this moment.

"But it was fun to go out too, with your guys. Not as Mr. G, but as *me*," Grant murmured.

"I know you were worried the publicity of being together would make things tougher," Deacon said. "Do you still think that's true?"

"Yes. No. Maybe." Grant sighed. "It was really fun tonight. This was the good side of it. Do I still worry that the public pressure will get to be too much? Yeah. Of course I do. But it's easier to dismiss that voice, now."

"I hope so. 'Cause I love you—and I'm not going anywhere. Not without you."

Grant believed him now. Had *always* believed him, but it had been easy to lose that certainty in the face of all the worry.

But they'd worked through that, and they were past it now. Tonight had proven it.

"I love you, too." Grant paused. Leaned in farther. Felt Deacon's erection against his own. But he didn't need that kind of proof. He'd never doubt Deacon's desire, not when he was looking at him like that. "Take me to bed."

Would he ever get used to Deacon leaning down and just picking him up? Using all that strength to carry him up the stairs, barely even breathing hard as he deposited Grant on the edge of his bed?

No. No, he absolutely fucking would not get used to—or tired of—that situation.

Deacon leaned down and was about to kiss him again, fingers working on Grant's remaining buttons. All great things, which he really did want, but also . . .

"Hey, wait—" Grant said, reaching out a hand and just enjoying the feel of Deacon's strong chest underneath his fingertips.

"What is it?" Deacon rocked back on his heels.

"I've just . . .never seen your bedroom before." Grant looked around, surprised that it looked so basic. Blue comforter. Pale beige walls. The furniture was dark wood, with plain lines. While the simplicity of it all reminded him of Deacon, nothing about it felt particularly personal, either.

"And you wanted to?" Deacon's voice was wry.

"Wanted to for some time now," Grant admitted.

"Wanted you here for some time now," Deacon said and leaned down again.

This time Grant didn't stop him, just sank into his kiss.

Deacon's mouth was hot and insistent on his, but while the man might be insanely powerful, with muscles that made Grant whimper, he'd never once felt like Deacon would overpower him.

And maybe this was evidence of the trust between them, but he wanted it now.

He wanted to be overwhelmed until he didn't know anything other than Deacon.

His tongue stroked Deacon's, Deacon groaning into his mouth as Grant's palm pressed against the erection in his jeans.

"What do you want?" Grant asked, his mouth slipping from Deacon's, down to the intoxicating plane between his ear and his collarbone. Nibbling there until Deacon's fingers dug into the bare skin at his waist.

"You." Deacon's voice was breathless. "Only you."

Grant wiggled back on the bed, Deacon following like he was helpless to do anything else. "Take me," he said. "Fuck me. Own me. *Love* me."

"Anything and everything," Deacon said, and he crawled over Grant and his kiss, which had been hot before, was incendiary now, burning Grant from the inside out.

It blew the rest of Grant's mind at how completely Deacon took over. Like he'd just been holding back, waiting for the minute Grant asked for it, his hands working Grant's pants off and then his underwear. Each brush of those big calloused fingers made him harder, until he was panting and straining against Deacon's hold.

"I got you," Deacon murmured, and he disappeared for a second but was back before Grant could think about moving.

He leaned down, the first brush of his lips against Grant's cock making him moan. Before Grant caught his breath and adjusted to the pleasure shooting through him, there was a single wet brush of a fingertip between his legs, against his hole.

Grant squirmed.

"Yeah, yeah, you're gonna take everything I give you, baby," Deacon crooned.

Then, dipping his head low, he began to suck Grant's cock in earnest, slipping it between his lips and driving Grant crazy with the teasing brushes of his fingers.

Finally, he slid just a fingertip in, and Grant had to squeeze his eyes shut, the visual of how fucking gorgeous Deacon was, like this, given over to his pleasure, sending him right to the edge.

He didn't want to be there yet. He wanted to enjoy this. Wanted Deacon to slide his cock in and take him apart from the inside out.

"Not yet," Deacon murmured.

Had anyone ever been so in-tune with what he wanted—what he *needed*? Grant didn't think so. Every lick, every brush and thrust of his fingers unwound him a little bit. But each time it felt like he got close, too close to losing it, he didn't stop entirely, but pulled back just enough.

Enough to drive Grant wild.

By the time Deacon was three fingers deep, thrusting lazily and with intent, Grant was sobbing into the pillow, thrashing his head as Deacon wrung out more and more pleasure from him than he thought he could possibly take.

But it wasn't only Grant at the edge of his control—when Deacon finally slipped his fingers out and shed his jeans, gripping Grant's thighs with a power that left grooves in his skin, Deacon's fingers were shaking and his breath was coming in long, drawn-out gusts.

"God, I want you. I *love* you. Seeing you like this . . ." Deacon said unsteadily and then pushed inside.

Grant cried out, and it was so easy to lose himself to the easy thrusts of Deacon's body. The way he took him over, turned him inside out, made him cry with how goddamn amazing it felt.

He knew the moment Deacon lost it, too, because his thrusts went deeper, harder, and it only took a brush of his hand over his cock for him to clench down and fall into his orgasm.

Deacon followed half a second later, groaning loudly as he ground into Grant's body.

A few minutes later, Deacon settled back into bed after he disposed of the cloth he'd brought to clean both of them.

Grant flopped over his chest, unable to help the slow smile that overtook his face.

"That was . . ." Grant sighed, happily.

"Yeah." Deacon's voice was gruff but full of affection.

Grant could have easily fallen asleep like this, but he could feel a tiny bit of tension in the man underneath him. So he waited. There was something Deacon wanted to say, but it was no use rushing it out of him.

"You know," he finally said, "you're not the only one who likes that."

That was not what Grant had expected him to say.

They hadn't ever discussed it—but then why would they, when clearly Grant loved being fucked so much, especially when the man doing the fucking was Deacon?

"Really?" Grant didn't mean to sound so surprised, but he did.

Deacon chuckled, a low rumble underneath him. "I don't usually do it during the season. I worry, probably more than is necessary, about it affecting my performance on the field. But yeah. If there's someone I trust, I do. And I trust you."

"That means we've both got something to look forward to, when the season ends."

"You'd be interested in doing that?" Deacon sounded unsure.

"Hey, just 'cause I like it a hell of a lot when you put your dick in me, I wouldn't be averse to the other way around. Could be fun to have you at my mercy."

Deacon shuddered a little, like he was already imagining it.

"Well, then, we've got that. And . . ." Deacon paused, and Grant twisted his neck, craning it until he could look Deacon right in the eyes. "And the rest of our lives, too."

Grant didn't think Deacon had ever lied to him.

But a different kind—a brand-new kind—of belief settled inside Grant at his words.

"Yes," Grant said. "No matter what happens with the last game, we'll have that. Forever."

"Forever," Deacon echoed.

CHAPTER 22

One more game.

Deacon walked onto the field. This might be the last time he did this, before a game.

It had been a bittersweet week, knowing that every practice he went to, every drill they ran, every time he looked over and saw Nate on the other side, in the spot that he'd made his own after Jem's injury, each teasing remark Micah and Beck tossed back and forth, might be the last.

It was sad. But it was also something more, too. Not happy, not quite yet, but Deacon had carried what he'd said to Grant with him all week. *We'll have the rest of our lives. We'll have forever.*

This was just the end of *this* chapter. Not the end of everything.

"Hey," a voice called out, and Deacon turned, because he'd recognize that voice anywhere.

Maybe Nate had made that spot on Deacon's other side his own, overcoming the intense pressure of replacing Jeremiah Knight in the lineup—and in Deacon's trust—but nobody could ever occupy that spot the way Jem had.

And now Jem was here. Not to play, but *here*. Because Deacon had known he wouldn't miss it.

"Hey," Deacon said, greeting his best friend with a big embrace. Jem didn't let go right away, just held on.

"Hey, big guy," he murmured. "You doing okay?"

"Yeah," Deacon said, and to his surprise, yeah, he was.

The same way Jem had figured out how to go on after football, he would, too. And there was so much life left.

So much happiness and love and *possibility*.

"Good," Jem said and then turned to the man next to him—because yes, there was a guy next to him, clad in a t-shirt with a plaid shirt thrown over, sleeves rolled up to the elbows, with a thick beard and kind eyes.

"Murphy, this is Deacon. My best friend."

"Good to meet you, Murphy," Deacon said reaching out to shake his hand. But Murphy just smiled, those eyes twinkling, and pulled him into a twin of the hug he'd just shared with Jem.

"Feeling's mutual," Murphy said, letting him go.

He'd seen pictures of Jem's guy, of course, because the two of them seemed inseparable these days, but pictures didn't do the size of him justice. Deacon felt like *he* was craning his neck, and he rarely ever had to do that with *anyone*.

"I figured I'd either find you here, sobbing into the turf, or calm and resigned."

"I'm calm," Deacon said. "But not resigned." He wanted more games—not another season of games, maybe, but he didn't want this one to end. He wanted to go to the playoffs with his guys and prove everyone wrong who'd said the Condors were done and finished.

"Sounds like the Deacon I've always known," Jem said with a nod of approval.

"You gonna watch from the sideline?" Deacon asked, and he already knew Jem's answer before he shook his head.

He didn't know if next season, when he was scouting for Grant, he'd walk the sideline again. The ache of it might be a little too sharp to bear.

"Nope," Jem said. "But we'll be up in Grant's suite, rooting for y'all."

"Grant, huh?" Deacon teased.

Jem just shrugged. "He's your boyfriend now, not the owner of my team any longer. Should get used to it. Thinking of him as a man, not just my super rich untouchable boss."

"I never thought of him that way," Deacon said.

"And that, Deac, has always been your problem." Jem grinned.

"Maybe his solution too," Murphy added quietly.

All it would ever have taken for Deacon to like Jem's boyfriend was that his best friend was happy. His standards were fairly easy that way. But now he liked Murphy even more than that, because just from hearing about his relationship with Grant secondhand, he'd come to the right conclusion.

"Yeah, I think so, too," Deacon said, nodding.

"We'll let you get your pre-game routine in," Jem said. "I just wanted to come down. Say hi. Introduce you to Murphy."

"I'm sure Carter's putting together some kind of party when we get back to Charleston. You two should come back. Stay for that."

"Win or lose?" Murphy asked, eyebrows shooting up.

"Yeah," Deacon said firmly. "Win or lose."

"Then we should," Murphy said. "This is still your team, Jem. Still your brothers."

And Deacon knew then that Murphy was the absolute right guy for Jem.

No question about it.

Jem seemed to know it too, but he wasn't surprised by it, either. He'd already known it, apparently. "Yep," he agreed, smiling.

After Jem and Murphy left to find their suite, Deacon had twenty minutes of quiet, just him and the turf. Slowly the other players began to trickle onto the field for warmups.

Deacon could see the Piranhas on the other side of the field. Could see Sebastian Howard and Wade Lewis laughing together. Paxton Kelly warming up along with his quarterbacks coach and boyfriend, Davis Abernathy.

Davis, whom Deacon had missed when he'd been replaced at the Condors and had turned up as a coach for the Piranhas instead. Deacon had fought so hard against that particular injustice, but in the end, it hadn't made any difference. They'd still treated Davis like shit and brought in Tom Taylor, that human garbage can, to replace him, anyway.

Scott Callaway, the defensive coordinator for the Piranhas, was on the sideline, shading his eyes as he took in the Condors side of the field. Asa Dawson, his husband and the head coach for the Piranhas, was nowhere to be seen.

From everything they'd heard, the Piranhas would be playing most of their starters, hoping to lock up the number one seed in the AFC. The Condors, on the other hand, needed this win to secure their own playoff spot.

It would've been easier, Deacon knew, if the Piranhas had been secure in their own playoff berth and not trying for a better seed, and they'd sat half the starters.

But they hadn't.

Deacon decided he was glad about that.

If they won this game, it would be because they fought hard and came out on top.

"How're you doing?" Beck asked as he approached, Micah trailing a dozen feet back.

"Why does everyone keep asking me that?" Deacon rolled into another stretch.

Beck gave him a knowing look. "You know why."

"Yeah, 'cause this could be my last game. I know. I get it."

"There's a way we could get into the playoffs even if we lose," Beck pointed out.

Deacon knew that was true. But if they lost this game in Miami, making the playoffs was a statistical improbability. They really needed to win.

Plus, Deacon—and he knew, the rest of the team—wanted to win not just because of the playoff implications, but because it would mean something if they could go down to Miami and beat this team that had only lost a handful of games this year. That was practically everyone's unanimous pick to win the Super Bowl.

Deacon would've wanted to win this game even if it hadn't meant anything else.

"Doesn't matter," Deacon said firmly. And he knew from the way Beck looked back that he understood.

"How's Micah holding up?" he asked.

It wasn't ever going to be easy for Micah to play his old team twice a year. Especially when he was still close with those guys.

"He's solid," Beck said, but the hesitation before his words made it clear—it was going to bother him. But if Beck said he was solid, then he was solid. Beck wouldn't lie to him, even about Micah.

"His first time back in Miami, yeah?" Deacon asked.

Beck nodded.

And yep, it was definitely going to be hard that first time.

Hopefully, Micah still continued to play lights out, like he had all year, since he'd come to Charleston. Deacon hoped the pressure wouldn't get to him, but he also wouldn't blame Micah if it did.

Micah had become more than a player to him—a way to solidify the backfield and a means to that end—he'd become his good friend Beck's husband, and then his *own* good friend, too.

"I know you'll handle it, and support him," Deacon said, "but if you need a hand, I'm here for you two. You know that, right?"

"We know it," Beck said with a grave nod.

He'd taught Beckett to be a professional football player from the moment he'd set foot in Charleston for the first time. He'd trained him to not be so stupidly stubborn; to ask for help if he needed it. He and Jem both had done that. Hoped that maybe rookies' transition today would be better than their own years before.

"Hey, man, feeling good?" Deacon asked as Micah approached. He'd been waylaid on his way to see Deacon and Beck by Scott Callaway, who'd embraced him fully for several long moments.

"Yeah, it's actually good to be back here." Micah smiled. "And I'm ready to kick their asses, too, if you were worried about that."

"I wasn't," Deacon reassured him.

"We've got this."

"You've covering Nicholson, yeah?" Deacon asked, and Micah nodded. "You got lots of practice doing that, I'd imagine."

"And he'll still keep me on my toes," Micah said. But his eyes were gleaming with excitement and anticipation, like he actually couldn't wait to go head-to-head with one of the NFL's most exciting young receivers.

"I know a lot of Wade's moves, too," Beck chimed in, referring to Tristan's boyfriend and the leading tight end for the Piranhas. "He thinks he doesn't have tells, but he has tells."

"Aw," Micah said.

"Don't tell me you're feelin' sorry for Wade now," Beck teased.

"Hell no. I'm looking forward to comparing notes, after this game." It was clear from the smiles and the looks they exchanged it would be a friendly sort of competition—but one that was going to end one way: with them both winning.

Probably in bed.

But Deacon definitely didn't want to know *anything* about that.

"You guys see Jem?" Deacon asked.

"Yeah, and that boyfriend of his," Beck said. "He seems great. And *huge*. I thought you were big, Deac."

"He does something artsy, yeah?" Micah asked.

"He carves *gnomes*," Beck retorted. "Can you believe?"

"That guy? Seriously? Built like a freight truck?"

Beck nodded earnestly.

"I like him," Deacon announced. Because the husbands could get going down a path and any rational conversation was gone. It was like the two of them vibrated on this whole other frequency, and nobody else could hope to understand, nevermind intervene.

"Oh, we like him, too," Beck reassured. "Just . . .why is that guy not tackling for a living? Or moonlighting as Captain America?"

"The Hulk." Micah frowned. "No, *Thor*. The guy looks like Thor."

"Don't be ridiculous," Beck exclaimed. "That's *Landry*. You know that."

"Two people we know can be Thor," Micah argued.

Deacon started laughing, because it was impossible to help it, not anymore.

"You alright?" Beck asked, turning to Deacon.

"Yeah, yeah, I'm good, just . . ." Deacon broke off into more laughter. "You two. I'm gonna miss this. So I'm just . . .enjoying it while I can."

"Don't worry," Micah said with an impudent grin, "I fully intend to argue with my husband in front of you, plenty of times, after this."

"Why does that not surprise me?" Deacon said with a last chuckle.

"Doesn't surprise me." Beck was grinning.

"Where's Mr. G?" Micah asked. "Thought I might see him down here."

"Nah, he wouldn't come down here."

"He wouldn't . . .then why is he—"

But Micah smacked a hand over his husband's mouth. "Enough of that," he said. "Come on, West. If you have a dream of matching me for defended passes today, you'd better get warmed up."

They wandered off, and Deacon was still guffawing a bit as he finished up his own stretches.

Stood up and then understood exactly what Beck had been trying to say.

Grant was standing there, awkwardly, with hands shoved in his pockets.

"Lookin' good," he said.

Deacon didn't want him to think he was unhappy he was here—sure, it was not normal for a team owner to come down to the field before a game, to mingle with his players, but then nothing about their situation was precisely *normal*.

"I know I said I wouldn't be coming down here, but I made it all the way to the suite—and I just . . ." Grant shrugged helplessly. "I couldn't stop thinking about what this is."

"Don't say it's my last game. Not you, too," Deacon warned. "I've had a whole parade of people walking by me trying to put a good face on. I've made my peace with it, but I'm certainly not going to go down today, not without a fight."

Grant took a few steps closer. Put a hand on his shoulder pad and tilted his head up towards Deacon's. "You wouldn't be the man I love if you did. I just came down to wish you good luck."

"You did that, last night. Twice, in fact." Deacon grinned, remembering how good it had been between them. How good the sex always was between them.

"Well, this is more of a G-rated good luck," Grant said.

"How about stretching it to PG?"

Grant raised an eyebrow. "What did you have in mind?"

"Would the NFL lose their fucking minds if you kissed me?"

"I think that ship has already sailed. But honestly, I don't really care what they think anymore."

"Not after you removed the pebble that was stuck in your shoe," Deacon drawled. Grant had told him all about how he'd resolved the Cheryl situation, and he'd listened, enthralled and impressed at how goddamn brilliant his lover was.

"Yep," Grant said. And then, before either of them could overthink it, he leaned in. Brushed a quick kiss across Deacon's mouth. Before he pulled back, he murmured, "Good luck," and then he was gone.

"Goddamn. Here I thought I did the most to piss the NFL off," a man drawled.

Deacon turned and Coach Dawson was standing there, smirking.

"Coach," Deacon said, nodding respectfully because Asa Dawson wasn't just one of the most successful collegiate coaches of all time, he'd already begun to make his mark in the pros.

"Sorry to hear you're hanging up your cleats," Coach said.

"It's time," Deacon said. Because while he respected the hell out of Coach Dawson, he wasn't interested in going into a long list of reasons why he knew he was done.

"Understood. If you ever want a job . . ." Coach grinned. "Just come see me."

Deacon's jaw dropped. "You're serious."

"Serious as a heart attack. You'd make a fine coach. Or an even better scout."

Deacon laughed then. "You aren't the only one who thinks that."

"I figured I wouldn't be. You're sticking with the Condors, then? I guess I can't be surprised." Coach smiled. "Keepin' it in the family, and all."

He'd been ninety-nine percent sure he'd be taking Grant's job offer before this moment, but Coach Dawson paying him the ultimate compliment of thinking he was good, too, convinced him.

Deacon hadn't really believed Grant was offering him the job because he loved him. Still, there'd been that little niggling voice in the back of his mind, but now he wouldn't wonder. He'd *know* that while Grant's love and affection and loyalty to him were all unconditional, they weren't why Grant wanted to hire him.

"Yeah I am. But thanks. That means a lot."

Coach eyed him. "Worried you were just getting hired for your pretty face, Harris?"

"Not really, but it's nice to hear that I'm not, anyway," Deacon said with a bark of laughter.

"Tell your Grant that any of us with half a brain molecule knew he'd never stoop to gambling or foolin' around with that asshole, Rex."

"I don't think many people believed him," Deacon said. In fact, Rex had already seemingly crawled back into the hole he'd come from. Continuing to make implausible and baseless accusations was a surefire way to get anyone who mattered to ignore him.

For a moment, there, Deacon had wanted to take his revenge on Rex, Cheryl-style. But when he'd mentioned it to Grant, he'd just shaken his head. "He's paying the worst price he could imagine right now, which is being insignificant and unimportant. Out of the conversation," he'd said.

And Deacon realized now that was true.

Rex wouldn't hate anything as much as he'd hate just plain being ignored. Of course, Grant had also added that if Rex *did* stick his head up again and make more trouble, he would have no trouble—and would *enjoy*—taking his ass down once and for all. The guy was already out of the NFL due to the gambling, but now he was entirely irrelevant.

"They didn't, but it was sure bullshit he was allowed to spout that crap," Coach said reaching out and taking Deacon's hand, shaking it firmly. "Good luck today, and if you ever need that job, call me up."

"Don't think I will, but appreciate the offer," Deacon said.

"Shit," Riley said flopping down on the bench. They'd had to settle for another field goal—only just keeping up with the Piranhas—instead of the touchdown Deacon knew he'd wanted to put them on top, with only a few minutes remaining in the game.

"You gotta watch out for Howard," Beck pointed out, and Riley made a face.

He'd warned him before. In fact, he'd warned Riley several times this week alone that Howard could jump a route as easy as breathing. And he'd done that once already today, neatly picking off one of Riley's passes to Landry.

Then, nearly again, on the last drive. But this time, he'd at least only batted down one of the most important third downs of the game, when Riley had thrown to Carter, trying to convert and take the Condors deeper into the red zone.

But instead, they'd settled for a field goal—and right now, the score was tied, with the Piranhas getting the ball, after the Condors kicked off.

"Hey, we got this," Nate told him. He glanced over at Deacon. "Yeah, boss? We got this, right?"

Deacon took a deep breath. Holding back the Piranhas' offense was like trying to hold back the tide, but if they didn't, then the game would be over, and they wouldn't leave Miami with a win like they'd wanted.

"We got this," Deacon said firmly. Raised his voice so everyone could hear. So everyone could believe.

"One more drive," he continued, as the defense gathered around him on the sideline. "You've got one more drive in you. If you do, then we get another game. And then maybe another one. At the very least, we can prove to everyone who told us that we were shit that we're not shit."

"Hell no, we're not," Beck echoed him.

"And we're gonna prove it," Micah chimed in. His face had gone hard, behind his face mask, and Deacon didn't know the kind of toll this game was taking on him—but he was holding up his side of the backfield. Tristan had been held to only a few catches, and even those had been highly contested.

Some media pundits had claimed this would be a high-scoring game, but Deacon had known better. He'd known both the Condors and the Piranhas would be fighting for every inch of turf.

It made sense to him that the game would come down to the final drive.

This was it.

The Piranhas were less invested than they were—even though Deacon could tell they wanted to win—because no matter what, they were headed to the playoffs. But the Condors were not only playing for that playoff spot, but for pride.

To redeem themselves, finally, in the eyes of the world.

As he jogged onto the field, he saw Coach Dawson on the other sideline, chin raised, eyes serious, and Scott Callaway, his husband and the Piranhas' defensive coordinator, standing next to him.

Maybe another coach would have benched his star players—players he'd *need* to be healthy for the playoff run they'd be making after this—but the fact they were all taking the field meant something.

Deacon could feel Coach's respect for their team and how far they'd come.

"We doing this?" Nate asked, and Deacon nodded, bumping helmets as they got set on the line.

Not surprisingly, the Piranhas were leaning on their new running back—a rookie they'd just drafted to replace Kenyon Ellis, who'd retired at the end of the last season. If the Piranhas wanted to run clock, it was a great move.

But Deacon had warned his guys they were going to run, and even though the Piranhas' offensive line was excellent, it was tough to run when that was exactly what the defense was expecting.

"Third down and long," Beck reminded him, breath coming in short pants as he returned to the line.

"Watch out for Wade. Pax likes to throw short to him—they're just gonna want to get the first down. Burn clock and hit a field goal with the time expiring," Deacon reminded him.

Beck nodded. "I got him."

"They might be crazy enough to go deep. I'm not going to give Nicholson much lead on me," Micah promised.

"See that you don't," Deacon said. "And Nate?"

"Yeah, Deac?"

"Let's sack the quarterback."

Nate nodded.

Paxton Kelly had been elusive the whole game, but Deacon didn't believe in giving up, even when they'd been unsuccessful so many times. Eventually their pressure would get to him, even if he was so good at evading the pocket collapsing around him.

"Three minutes left," Deacon noted.

He wasn't saying it but he knew they all understood that if they wanted to win this game, they needed to get the ball back.

Only a few more first downs, and none of this would matter. The Piranhas would kick the field goal and win the game.

Deacon got set, the rest of the defense fanning out behind and next to him, and the ref blew the whistle.

The play unfolded as he'd expected—Pax dropped back, ball in his hands, and Deacon pushed hard, legs churning on the turf, hitting the tackle with all the speed he could find in his body and pushed the guy back. He was still blocking him, because he was one of the best tackles Deacon had ever gone up against, but he was slowly, inexorably being pushed back by Deacon's force.

Just a little more, Deacon thought as he dug down hard into his reserves.

All those years of conditioning and weights. It felt, in some ways, like they were leading to this moment, to give him that little extra bit of push to make this play.

But before he could push the tackle the last few steps back into the pocket, colliding with his quarterback, Pax threw the ball.

Deacon's eyes followed it, and he swore under his breath as Beck and Wade both went up for it.

And Wade came down with it, hitting the turf hard as he held on to it.

The Piranhas had needed eight yards for a first down, and that had been eight yards and a fucking inch.

"Shit, shit, I'm so sorry," Beck exhaled hard as he hit the huddle.

"It's all right," Deacon said. But they all knew their task had gotten impossibly harder. "I'm not expecting them to throw again."

"Is that new running back vulnerable?" Micah wondered. "I don't really know him."

Made sense, because Micah had only spent a few games with the Piranhas this season before he'd been traded to the Condors. He'd be a lot more familiar with the Piranhas' old running back, Kenyon, who'd retired after last season.

"We can go after the ball," Beck said.

"We should go after the ball," Nate agreed. "Punch it out."

Deacon hesitated.

He remembered, all too well, how the last game between the Piranhas and the Condors had gone when they'd played a season before. The old defensive coordinator, desperate to win, had encouraged everyone to play dirty.

Punching out the ball was allowed, of course, and often even encouraged. But after last year, it made Deacon squirm, even though he knew that was one of their only options left to actually stop the Piranhas.

"It's kosher," Beck said under his breath as the huddle broke up. "You know it. It's not like before."

"Still feels like before," Deacon said shortly.

"Deac—we're clean. We've played a fucking clean game. You know that. You brought us back. You and Mr. G. You *have* to believe that." Beck's voice was earnest, his eyes wide and pleading.

Deacon tested out the feeling. Did he believe Beck? He sure as hell wanted to. But Beck was right, he needed to believe it for himself.

"I . . .I do." He *did* believe it, he realized. Beck was right. They'd played a clean season. And even if any of them managed to grab the ball from the Piranhas' running back, it wouldn't change anything. They wouldn't fight dirty to get it, they weren't built like that anymore.

Now, they were built clean and shiny and new.

He'd done that. He and Grant, both.

That, more than anything else, Deacon knew, meant that it was time to go.

"Good," Beck said, patting him on the shoulder. "Now let's go finish this."

Sure enough on first down, Pax handed the ball off. Second down, too. Nate and Deacon and the rest of the defensive line stopped him pretty easily. Kept him from getting close to getting the first.

Then third down, it was the Piranhas' running back again.

Deacon had studied how he was holding the ball—and he thought it was possible. Especially because on a third down, he would push for as many yards as he could get, hoping to get the Piranhas closer to the first. Closer to their end zone. Dylan, the Piranhas' kicker, was seriously good, but he wasn't *that* good.

He braced himself and making one more superhuman push, at the whistle, went after the guy. Went after the *ball*.

Nate held him up, stopping him in place, and their eyes met over the guy's head.

Do it, Nate's gaze said.

And Deacon did it, went for the ball. Pried it out of the guy's hands, until it bounced and landed practically in Beck's lap.

Beck had come up, to help on the run defense, and he scooped the ball up, and Deacon watched with wonder as he ran down the sideline, Micah joining him at one point, throwing a block against Wade Lewis, that meant that Beck could go the whole way, all the way to the Condors' end zone.

"Holy shit," Nate exclaimed, as they joined the celebration in the end zone. "Holy fucking shit! We did it!"

But Deacon couldn't speak.

So many times people had asked him this week if he was okay.

He'd been okay every single one of those times.

He wasn't okay now.

Swallowing hard, he looked around at the guys celebrating around him and thought, *yes, we did this. And we're gonna keep on doing it. Long after I'm not on the field anymore, this legacy Grant and I created, it's not going anywhere. Not anymore.*

There were still thirty seconds left on the clock, but it didn't matter. They were up eight points.

Pax came out again, and there was that same respect in his eyes as he took a knee.

"Great game," Pax said, as he stood up, clapping him on the back. "Great fucking career, man."

"Thanks. You guys are gonna kill it in the playoffs," Deacon said. He was still having trouble speaking. But he made the effort, because he respected the hell out of the Piranhas' quarterback, and he knew the feeling was mutual, now.

"I see you didn't need the luck."

He turned around, and Grant was standing there, looking so much less awkward now.

We needed this win. We needed to believe that we were more than what they said, and this was the proof we were looking for.

"I needed it," Deacon said, and he didn't hesitate. Just pulled Grant into his arms, game sweat and all. Felt Grant embrace him back, just as fiercely. "I'm always gonna need it from you."

"And," Grant said softly, into his ear for only him to hear, "I'm always going to say it."

EPILOGUE

Grant leaned in and straightened Deacon's tie.

"You look great," he said, still fussing with the rust and red striped fabric.

It was easier than looking in Deacon's eyes and seeing the emotion so close to the surface.

Would he cry today?

Would they *both* cry today?

It seemed very likely.

"If I do, it's only 'cause of you," Deacon said, voice gruff and low.

And okay, sue him. He'd gifted Deacon a fully tailored suit for this occasion—and he wore it well, the dark gray material draped flawlessly over his broad shoulders.

Deacon had played his last game a month prior, and though he'd already been decided, Grant had encouraged him to wait and give himself some time to really be sure retirement was what he wanted.

But it had become very clear it was, and that Deacon was ready, too, to move on and start his new job as a scout.

Grant had asked him if he wanted to do an official retirement ceremony at the Condors' facility, or if he just wanted to record a message for Nicole to post on social media.

He'd assumed that Deacon would vote for the latter, but to his surprise, Deacon had insisted that he wanted the full ceremony, with introduction, and the media present, too.

"I have things I want to say," he'd said.

Grant understood.

Because he also had things to say—and he knew there were others who would want to say a few words in honor of Deacon.

Of course, Deacon didn't know about that.

He only thought he'd be giving his speech, and then Grant would be getting up and giving a few remarks of his own.

The audience was filling up—there were a lot of media representatives here, of course, but also a lot of players had come as well. Carter was there, with Ian next to him. Micah and Beck, Jem sitting with them. Riley and Landry had flown in, looking tanned and rested.

Spencer Evans, from the Riptide, had shown up, unexpectedly, along with his husband, power agent Alec Mitchell.

A number of NFL coaches had also asked to attend. Jonathan Kelley, of course. And then Grant had been a little bit shocked when Asa Dawson, Scott Callaway, and Rudy Gonzalez had reached out. But they were here, taking up most of one of the middle rows, along with Beau Dawson and his boyfriend, safety Sebastian Howard.

But even more than that, sitting next to Sebastian was Davis Abernathy, the first time he'd set foot back in the Condors' facility since he'd been unceremoniously booted out.

When Asa Dawson had reached out, Grant had made it clear that Davis was always welcome—after all, he'd played with Deacon for many years—but that he'd also understood if it was too much to ask for him to come back.

But there Davis was, sitting in a dark suit next to Pax Kelly, their heads close and their hands clasped together tightly. Deacon had gone over to him when he'd appeared, given him a long hug, and that had probably been the first moment today when Grant hadn't been sure he'd make it out of this room without bawling like a baby.

It was a large group, and they'd all come, going out of their way during the offseason, to pay tribute to the man Deacon was. The man Grant loved.

Nicole approached. "Are you two ready to go? Deacon?"

Deacon swallowed hard. "Yeah, I'm ready."

"And Mr. G, you wanted to go first."

"I felt like it was appropriate I introduce you," Grant said, patting Deacon on the chest when he shot him a look full of disbelief.

"But I told you, I wanted you to go *second,*" Deacon said.

"Yes, and only because you were afraid you were going to cry. I promise. I will keep the tear-inducing comments to a minimum. You can take care of those all on your own."

Deacon sighed. "Fine. But if I need a moment after you introduce me . . ."

"You'll have whatever time you need," Nicole promised him.

"You ready for this?" Grant asked when she left, heading towards the podium at the front of the room.

"I'm not sure I'll *ever* be ready to get up and try to say all this without losing it," Deacon said honestly. "But all these people came for me. To hear me. You're here, too. I think I can make a genuine effort, at least."

Grant pressed a quick kiss to his cheek. "That's all that's required."

"Good luck," Deacon said wryly.

"Shouldn't I be saying that to *you*?" Grant teased.

Deacon shot him one last knowing look, and then Nicole was walking up to the podium.

"Thank you all for coming today. First up, the Charleston Condors' owner Grant Green wishes to make a few comments about this important day."

Grant walked up to the podium, trying to keep his breaths even and composed.

If he lost it now, he'd never make it through.

"Funny," Grant said into the microphone after he'd set his notes on the podium. "Nicole said it was an important day, and it is, undeniably. But I think Deacon and I shared a much more important day, many months back."

He took another deep breath. Composed himself.

"As many of you are aware," he continued, "Deacon and I met in college. Deacon hired me to be his tutor. But after college, I started InTech, and we lost touch. The second time we met was at Mr. Gonzalez's estate in Miami, when I had put forward a bid to buy the Condors. Deacon was there as a representative of a coalition of players on the team who wanted things to improve. I didn't know it at the time, but I would get to know those gentlemen not just as faceless complaints, but as players on my team and then as friends. Beckett West. Jeremiah Knight. Carter Maxwell. They were just names to me then, in a way that Deacon wasn't. In a way he'd never been. But that evening we met, it struck me, even more than it had in college, just how much this man cared about those guys. They were *his* guys, and he'd come, volunteered really, to make sure that they'd be taken care of going forward. But not for him—because he'd already decided he was done, and retiring. Obviously I convinced him to change his mind. I told him I wanted to give him the legacy he deserved. To buff it to a bright shine. They weren't just words I was saying; I meant them. It was one of the reasons I'd bought this team. There were others, of course, but he was at the center of all of them. But back then, the thing I did not know, the thing I could not possibly know or understand, as I was still getting to know Deacon again as a fully grown man, was that he didn't need me to polish his halo." Grant paused. Swallowed hard.

"I promised him," he added, the audience chuckling, "that I would keep the tear-inducing comments to a minimum, but I will say this and only this. Deacon never needed me to save him. By coming to meet me, by demanding the very best that I could bring to the table, and because he never, ever stopped fighting for what was right, he proved that if he'd retired that day, or any day after, he would still be the incredible man and the incredible football player that he is. Ladies and gentleman, Deacon Harris."

Grant stepped back from the podium and only had a moment to compose himself before Deacon was enveloping him in a huge hug.

"You asshole," Deacon murmured in a choked, broken voice. His fingertips dug into Grant's sides and he didn't let go. "You *promised.*"

Grant tried to surreptitiously wipe his eyes. "And here I left out all the ways you make me a better owner, a better partner, and a better human being."

"God," Deacon groaned.

"Save that for later, baby," Grant teased, and that was the thing that did it. Deacon pulled back, letting him go but not letting him go far. His dark eyes were shining with tears, but he was smiling.

"Asshole," Deacon repeated.

"*Your* asshole," Grant reminded him and then took a step back. Let Deacon have the spotlight entirely to himself—because he deserved it.

Because all these people were here not for Grant, but for *Deacon*.

"Thank you for coming today," Deacon said, leaning into the microphone. He sounded a bit stilted. Nervous. And of course he was. "I'm incredibly honored that you'd travel here to Charleston during your off-season to help me celebrate this day. And yes, we are celebrating." Grant could see Deacon pinning everyone in the audience with that intense dark-eyed stare of his.

The one that back in college had made everyone flock to him, hoping for just a little of that special Deacon Harris magic.

Nothing had changed, not significantly, unless you counted the fact that Grant was the only one getting Deacon's magic these days.

"I know these are always the speeches where the retiring player cries, and everyone cries along with him," Deacon continued. "I'm not saying that *won't* happen, but I came here today intending to make this a celebration, not a funeral. This isn't the end. It's a beginning. I'll probably be around more than anyone else is thinking I will, and not just because of who owns this team." He shot a sly glance back at Grant.

"But while yes, this is the end, officially, of my time as a *player* for the Charleston Condors, there's nothing that can take those years I spent playing away. Nothing can take away that I'll be a Condor for life, and that the men I played with, that I laughed with and cried with and bled with, will be my family, now, and for the rest of my life."

Deacon's hands gripped the podium. Grant could see his knuckles turning white, but he kept it together. Kept talking.

"And while yes, this is the end of the road for me as a player, it's not the end of my life. Instead, it feels like the beginning."

When Deacon glanced back now, there was an undeniable love in his eyes as he looked straight at Grant. "This year has been one of the most special of my time in the NFL. We changed a hell of a lot of minds. We turned this team around. We became something I—and all of us—could be proud of. But more than that, I fell in love, and I discovered that there's something more important than what's on the scoreboard at the end of a game. That a muddy field doesn't define me. It's created me. Changed me. But it doesn't own me. It's just part of who I am, a part I'm forever grateful for, because of who it brought to me. My teammates, who more than ever before, are like my family, because we went through those trenches together. Nothing will ever change that. Especially not whatever paper I sign today. But because today's for me, there's one last thing I need y'all to do for me. One last thing as my brothers-in-arms, as my family."

Deacon paused and then gestured to Grant.

He didn't want to go up there, because this was *Deacon's* time, but if Deacon wanted him there, with him, who was he to say no?

This was the man he loved, and he'd follow him anywhere. Lead him wherever they needed to go.

"Ready?" Deacon asked, and the audience nodded. "Alright. Fly, Condors . . ."

And the resounding "Fly!" that echoed through the audience was enough to bring tears to Grant's eyes.

Deacon's too, as he reached out and gripped Grant's hand hard enough to hurt.

"Thank you," Deacon said, leaning in and kissing him briefly.

"For what?" Grant asked stupidly. In the end, what had he really done? He'd meant it. Deacon had saved himself. In fact, Grant wasn't sure a man like Deacon Harris had *ever* needed saving.

"For everything," Deacon said firmly. Solemnly. "But most of all, for loving me, just as I am, and for giving me this."

He spread his arms out, like a Condor, and also like a blessing, and the applause was deafening.

"Maybe," Grant said, leaning in so Deacon could hear him over the noise of the crowd. "But I didn't save you. Maybe what we did was save each other."

Deacon smiled then, through the tears. "You've never been more right."

At Micah and Beck's summer wedding reception, there's more than one surprise in store. Read the bonus scene here.

In 2025, there will be another football series from me – but for now, I'm really enjoying writing some other sports! To preorder my new MM baseball standalone, *Hot Streak*, click here.

INTERESTED IN READING MORE OF
BETH'S BOOKS?

CHECK OUT A FULL LIST OF TILES
BY SCANNING THE QR CODE
OR VISITING HER WEBSITE

WWW.BETHBOLDEN.COM/BOOKLIST

WANT TO FOLLOW BETH?

MAKE SURE YOU NEVER
MISS A RELEASE?

SCAN THE QR CODE BELOW
OR VISIT HER WEBSITE
FOR A SOCIAL MEDIA LIST,
NEWSLETTER SIGNUP,
AND SO MUCH MORE!

WWW.BETHBOLDEN.COM/ABOUT